Praise for W. Dale Cramer's earlier novels:

Levi's Will

"[A] beautiful and original story. . . . This is an accomplished work."
—*Booklist* (starred)
Named Best Christian Novel of the Year (2005) by *Booklist*

"Cramer's third novel (after *Sutter's Cross* and *Bad Ground*) expands on his unique talent for creating complex, fallen heroes and examining the complicated relationships between fathers and sons. . . . Highly recommended for all collections. . . ."
—*Library Journal* (starred)

"Will's long wrestling match with his father's will echoes into his relationship with his own sons. The generations, in Cramer's vivid phrase, grate against each other . . . If Cramer's work is anything to go by, at least part of the Christian book industry has finally figured out that a novel is not a theological argument. . . ."
—*Christianity Today*

". . . powerfully portrays the relationships between fathers and their children, the bitterness of rejection and the redeeming power of friendship, faith and forgiveness."
—*Publishers Weekly*

Bad Ground

"Cramer has a delicious way with a pen, whether he's crafting a lush Southern backdrop or offering glimpses of [his characters'] interior lives. . . . With its notes of hope, humor and redemption, this delightful book exemplifies what good Christian fiction should aspire to."
—*Publishers Weekly* (starred)
Selected by *Publishers Weekly* as one of the "Best Books of 2004."

"Cramer's second novel offers a refreshingly inventive perspective with its portrait of the dangerous world of hard-rock mining and the men who do it for a living. The spiritual message is clearly about the healing power of forgiveness, but the well-developed characters never fall into the cookie-cutter stereotype of being 'too perfect' as so often happens in Christian fiction. Both male and female readers will identify with Aiden Prine's physical and spiritual struggles. Highly recommended for its excellent storytelling and believable characters."

—*Library Journal* (starred)

Library Journal listed Bad Ground in the Top 5 of "Best Genre Fiction 2004," Christian Fiction category.

"Skillful storytelling, beautifully described settings, and original, fully realized characters set this novel of faith by W. Dale Cramer apart from typical coming-of-age stories. . . . This novel confirms Cramer as one of the brightest new voices in faith fiction."

—*Christianity Today*

"*Bad Ground* proves that *Sutter's Cross* [Cramer's debut novel] wasn't just beginner's luck. Cramer has an uncanny command of dialogue that can put a smile on your lips as easily as a tear in your eye. With a truckload of danger, a few traces of romance, and a heart that reflects God's own, *Bad Ground* should appeal to fiction lovers. Highly recommended."

—*CBA Marketplace*

"Cramer's detailed, enthusiastic portrait of rough men following the dangerous trade of hard-rock mining is original, and in the end, the novel is almost a hymn to working men."

—*Booklist* (starred)

SUMMER
of
LIGHT

A NOVEL

W. Dale Cramer

BETHANY HOUSE PUBLISHERS

Minneapolis, Minnesota

Summer of Light
Copyright © 2007
W. Dale Cramer

Cover photography by Steve Gardner, Pixel Works Studios, Inc.
Cover design by studiogearbox.com

Published by Bethany House Publishers
11400 Hampshire Avenue South
Bloomington, Minnesota 55438

Bethany House Publishers is a division of
Baker Publishing Group, Grand Rapids, Michigan.

Printed in the United States of America

ISBN-13:   978-0-7642-2996-1
ISBN-10:   0-7642-2996-6

Library of Congress Cataloging-in-Publication Data

Cramer, W. Dale.
    Summer of light / W. Dale Cramer.
        p. cm.
    ISBN-13: 978-0-7642-2996-1 (pbk.)
    ISBN-10: 0-7642-2996-6 (pbk.)
    1. Fathers—Fiction. 2. Child rearing—Fiction. 3. Domestic fiction. I. Title.
    PS3603.R37S86 2007
    813'.6—dc22   2006037949

For Ty and Dusty. My boys.

Books by W. Dale Cramer

Sutter's Cross

Bad Ground

Levi's Will

Summer of Light

SUMMER
of
LIGHT

1

The trouble with Dylan.

MICK Brannigan's daddy only gave him one piece of advice when he was growing up, but he gave it to him on a number of occasions.

He said, "Son, you need to sit down and shut up."

Mick's father was quiet most of the time—in the same way that a rattlesnake is quiet most of the time—but the genetic pendulum swung the other way a generation later, and Mick didn't inherit his father's taciturn nature. Constantly surprised and delighted by the things he heard himself say, he was often baffled by other people's failure to see the humor in it. The great turning points in Mick's life almost always hinged on things he wished he hadn't said, and yet it still came as a surprise to him when something he said got him dragged off the top of a twelve-story building and cost him his job.

It certainly wasn't his idea to stay home with the kids.

Layne's church friends, the homeschool crowd, were always pontificating on how the parenting of children was the highest calling and the noblest sacrifice. Mick didn't buy it for a minute. Those people seemed to live in a world that was very different from the one he lived and worked in every day, though he did manage, at least, to keep his father's advice and hold his tongue whenever Layne's church friends pontificated. But he never wanted to be a stay-at-home dad. He loved his job, and he'd sooner have sawed off his left arm than give up being an ironworker to stay home with three kids. In the end he didn't have a choice. He was forced into it by what seemed like a bizarre string of accidents, though after the dust settled even Mick understood that a string of accidents can only go on so long and can only be so bizarre before reason rules out chance. At some point, the sheer weight of the odds begins to argue for design.

It started innocently enough. The daycare center called Layne at work and asked her to stop by. Layne always dropped off Dylan in the morning and Mick picked him up in the afternoon, but whenever there was a problem the daycare people didn't mention it to Mick, no doubt because he showed up every day with rust stains on his hands and battle-scarred work boots on his feet, ragged jeans, hair mashed down in a sweaty ring by a long day under a hard hat. Mick never had much to say to them. He could understand why the ladies at A Small World daycare would rather talk to the polite, smiling, nicely dressed mother who dropped Dylan off every morning than the nasty ironworker who picked him up in the afternoon.

The first few times Layne sat facing him in the living

room with a yellow note in her hand and that look of deep concern on her face, Mick told her flatly that she and Dylan's teachers were overreacting, that Dylan was perfectly normal. Lots of kids preferred to play alone. Lots of kids refused to eat lunch. Lots of kids, particularly four-year-olds, fell on their faces whenever they tried to jump rope.

But then came the weird stuff.

A normal kid might gripe about his shirt irritating him, but he wouldn't strip down to his tightie-whities in public and leave a trail of clothes all over the playground.

"Itchy," Dylan explained. He had a normal vocabulary for his age but never used more words than necessary because he had trouble getting them right. He lisped a little, and his Gs came out like Ds. He was a gifted mimic and could imitate virtually any kind of noise with uncanny accuracy, yet he couldn't make words come out right.

For the most part Mick managed to calm Layne's fears until the evening she blocked his view of *Monday Night Football* and read him the latest note from Dylan's teacher.

"He does *what?*" He picked up the remote and muted the game.

"He licks her ankle." One of her eyebrows went up—a bad sign—and she sat there straightening out the crumpled note against her knee, staring at it. "He does it a lot lately, and she finds it . . . disconcerting."

"Which one?"

"Which *ankle?* What possible difference—"

"I meant which teacher," Mick said.

"Oh. Mrs. Fensdemacher. Why?"

He shuddered. "Well, if it was Miss Gabriel I could sort

of understand it, but Mrs. Fensdemacher . . . ugh."

"He's four, Mick. Grow up."

Two days later she took a day off and carried Dylan to the pediatrician, who asked a few questions and referred him to a child psychologist, who asked more questions and referred him to an occupational therapist, who asked still more questions and then put Dylan through a whole battery of tests. She put lead weights on his arms and legs to see how it made him feel, then laid him in the floor and put a weighted blanket on top of him. She had him dancing, hopping, marching, and literally jumping through hoops. None of the doctors was ready to commit to a diagnosis, though they all felt there was reason for concern. They scheduled more appointments.

But the day Dylan put Ryan Carden up against the wall and it took three grown women to keep him from strangling the larger boy, the call from A Small World was approaching hysteria. It would be their last warning.

"Boy needs discipline," Mick said. It was after supper. He was drying a plate while Layne washed. Dylan was in the tub and the other two were off doing homework. "You and those old ladies at the daycare center are too soft, that's all. My old man would've killed me . . . if he'd been there."

Layne let that one slide. She knew Mick didn't want to be like his father.

"Seriously, Mick, what are we going to do? The daycare people are trying to be sympathetic, but they see him as a threat now. The very next incident—no matter how minor—he'll get expelled, and then what do we do?"

"Find another daycare." He said this absently, sliding a plate into the cabinet.

"And then what? Wait for it to happen again? Mick, there's a problem here that we can't ignore. We have another appointment with the therapist tomorrow."

"Right. Doctors have to make their BMW payments."

"You're not *listening*," she said, and the fist holding the wet rag splashed down into the dishwater. He'd pushed her a little too far. "I've researched this pretty thoroughly, if you're interested, and what the doctors aren't saying yet is three words—*sensory integration dysfunction*. They don't want to put it on his record because once it's there it stays there, but that's what they're thinking. It's a serious problem, Mick."

"So you think just because he nutted up on Ryan Carden, Dylan's got this sensory whattayacallit disease? Listen, if that Carden kid is anything like his dad, I can understand it. I've thought about throttling his old man a time or two my ownself." He poked the towel down into a glass.

"It's not a disease, Mick, it's a developmental disorder. It's just that Dylan's brain doesn't get the messages from his senses exactly right. It's like his volume knobs are out of whack—some are turned way down low and some are up too high. He licked Mrs. Fensdemacher's ankle because he likes the texture of pantyhose on his tongue, that's all. But this stuff has got him so disoriented he just doesn't understand that he can't go around licking people's ankles. Then one day, when he feels like his feet won't touch the ground and everybody around him is speaking Chinese, he gets frustrated and takes it out on Ryan."

Mick blinked, lowered the towel. This was serious. "So. Is it permanent? I mean, is he like stuck with this thing for life?"

She shook her head, dropped a handful of silverware in the rack. "No. There are all kinds of different ways it can affect a kid, and all sorts of other stuff it can be mixed up with, like autism or ADD, but no. Sensory integration dysfunction by itself is usually just a matter of time and therapy." She went on at some length, describing Dylan's problem with a bag of words he'd never heard before— words like *proprioception* and *dyspraxia*. He knew she wasn't trying to show him up; it was just her way of making him see that she knew exactly what she was talking about. Layne was a paralegal. She did research for a living.

"If we work with him," she said, finally, "we can help him catch up with his senses, maybe in six months or a year. If we don't do something now it could affect him into his twenties—all the way through school."

But she stopped too abruptly and left her words hanging. There was something else—he could see it in her face.

"What?" he finally asked.

She bit her lip and squinted. "It's just that it's going to take a lot of work. One on one. He needs to be at home, in a safe, uncomplicated social setting for a while. And he's going to need therapy. He'll have to see a therapist once a week and he'll have to have special exercises at home every day."

"Sounds expensive," he said.

"Well, I think insurance will cover most of it, but that's not the point."

There was a sadness in her eyes, and he suddenly realized there was no way she could deal with Dylan's problems while working a full-time job. Layne had put her career on hold for five years while she was having babies, and when she finally got ready to go to work it took her six months to land a job with the right law firm. She loved her work, and she made good money. Most of all she felt incredibly lucky to have landed where she did. She felt it was a once-in-a-lifetime break, and she would never get it again. All at once it hit him just how cruel it would be for her to have to give up her job now, just when things were going so well. She needed his support.

"I see," he said. When she placed a bowl upside down in the rack he laid his hand on top of hers. "You want to know if it's okay for you to quit your job."

"Nnnnno," she said, with a sideways chuckle that scared him a little. "I want to know if it's okay for you to quit yours."

He froze for a second, staring at her, his eyes slightly wider.

"Um, my job? Quit my job? *Mine?*"

A nod.

"Ah, no. Never gonna happen." He picked up three plates at once and shoved them into the cabinet with a decisive clatter. Case closed.

She smiled, too sweetly. "But Mick, dearest"—*dearest* was her patience word—"someone has to do it. You can see that, can't you? It's the only way."

"All right, then do it. Knock yourself out. I can pay the bills while you're not working. I've done it before."

For a while she said nothing, standing there looking at him with a little smile that made his palms sweat.

"Layne," Mick said, and he heard the faint cry in his own voice, "you *know* why. I have to bring home a paycheck. I *can't* not make a living."

She knew. Over the years he'd told her plenty of times how his father had left them high and dry, and what they had to do to make ends meet. He wouldn't—*couldn't*—put himself in that position. Layne didn't say anything for a while, just stood there scrubbing a pot with a Brillo pad. She seemed so calm. Finally she took a deep breath and drove a spike through the dialog.

"Well," she said, "I'll pray about it. We'll see."

That was the worst. Layne had an irritating way of trumping an argument by saying she'd pray about it. He knew better than to bring it up in front of her church friends but it always seemed kind of bogus to him. As if the God of the universe would pick out a man's tie for him. Layne prayed about everything, which was fine if it made her feel better, but when she ran it out there as a closing argument it almost felt like she was using religion as a lever to get what she wanted. Appealing to a higher court.

"Yeah," he muttered. "We'll see."

2

What the day will bring.

THE NEXT day started off with the usual insanity, hitting the snooze button one too many times and then flying out of bed in full panic mode—from zero to sixty in one bleary-eyed glance at the clock, shouting three kids up and into their clothes, shoving cereal at them, digging socks out of the dryer, hurling orders for teeth to be brushed and hair to be combed, slinging book bags into the back seat of Layne's Ford Explorer. Mick threw on yesterday's jeans, grabbed his coffee in a travel cup, nuked a quart of water to boiling for his lunchbox thermos and ran out the back door at the height of the yelling. He had to be at work an hour earlier than Layne, so the kids were mostly her problem in the morning. Madness. It was all madness, but it was *their* madness and they figured it was no worse than anybody else's.

"At least ours is a two-parent home," Layne always said,

"and marginally functional, despite appearances."

By the time Mick merged into the river of traffic the whole argument from the night before had come back to sit on his head. He liked his life. He liked things the way they were, and he couldn't quite fathom how a kid licking his teacher's ankle added up to a full-grown man, an iron-worker, quitting his job.

At the time, he was working the high steel on a new sixty-story office building in downtown Atlanta. It was one of those retro designs with wedding-cake layers like the Empire State Building, except the outside was going to be all glass and no concrete. They had just poured the twelfth-floor slab and Mick's crew was erecting the steel skeleton for the next phase. He'd been an ironworker for fifteen years, ever since high school. He never went to college and never regretted it for a minute. He loved the high steel. There was just something about working every day in a place where sane people were afraid to go. A man came alive.

That morning he went straight to the top. The weather had turned bitter cold for November and the wind up high cut right through him, but Mick still didn't want to be any-place else. He could have dropped in at the office trailer and stayed warm until the whistle blew, but he didn't care anything about hanging around a bunch of ambitious young jocks fresh out of Industrial Management, arguing about college football and learning to leave paper trails.

There was freedom up there where nobody could reach him. He liked being out in the weather all day, and he liked the feel of steel in his hands. He liked looking back at the end of a hard day and being able to actually see what he had accomplished. He liked everything about the job except for the pressure brought on by a bunch of bureaucrats who could cite code sections from memory but didn't know a spud wrench from a turnip. Truth is, those boys didn't care whether the job got done or not, so long as they could prove it wasn't their fault.

That particular morning Mick needed to be alone. He had tied himself in a knot thinking about doctor bills and therapy and somebody needing to stay home with Dylan. Whatever his flaws, Mick had never been indecisive—he'd rather go ahead and make a decision even if it was wrong, but this time he couldn't see a way. For the first time in his life he just couldn't see a way. He didn't have an answer. Dylan was *his kid*, his flesh and blood, his responsibility. Layne was undeniably right about somebody needing to stay home for a while, and when he got right down to it, he could see that it didn't make sense for her to quit her job because they'd replace her and the position would be gone for good. Mick, on the other hand, could quit for a while and get another job easily.

But staying home while his wife worked was completely unacceptable. Out of the question. His old man had left when Mick was in middle school—disappeared, no forwarding address—and never sent home a dime after that. They made it through, his brothers and mother and him, but it was tough. Layne knew that. She knew about the sweltering summer nights without electricity, and the times when they ate mac and cheese for a week. She knew Mick needed to bring home a paycheck. He *needed* it, because there was always the possibility that someday his old man would show up, or he'd run into him on the street, and

Mick wanted to be able to punch him right in his hook nose with a clean conscience. He did not want, *ever*, to be that man.

So when he got to the job that morning before dawn, Mick went straight to the top and climbed up a beam—just hooked his feet into the sides and shinnied up into the dark and the wind. He knew from long experience that nothing would clear a man's head like hanging his toes off a twelve-inch I-beam at the top of the world in a cold dawn. The wind was gusty, so he slung his lanyard around a vertical beam, snapped it onto the D-ring of his safety belt and stood there snug in his Carhartts, soaking up the whole round earth. The sun hadn't peeked over the horizon yet, but the middle distance was striped with clouds like fish bones, and their bottoms were all lit up with a hundred different pinks and oranges and purples. When he turned the other way the same sky broke itself into pieces on the glass fronts of the towers downtown. Like a million other times when he'd been at the top of the world and seen things nobody else ever saw, he wished he had a camera with him.

At times like that he could forget where he was. He forgot the cold, the job, the honking of cars, the exhaust fumes riding on the wind. He forgot himself. He was just a bump on a steel skeleton, a nameless point that the light passed through on its way from the dawn to the city.

He hated not knowing what to do. It hurt. Standing on the dark end of the sky that morning Mick was as alone as a man could get, and he fell to wondering, like most men do sooner or later, whether there really was any point to life. A purpose, a design. Back and forth to work every day, head down, working, working, and for what? To pay for a truck so he could drive to work? To pay for his kids' education so they could get a good job, so they could pay for their kids' education? But that wasn't all of it—it was way bigger than that. It felt like all the life-questions he'd ever owned came together all at once and rolled themselves into a ball too big to hold. Something welled up and burst out of him then, like a surprised bird. He didn't know what it was. Layne might have called it a prayer, but to Mick it felt more like a sigh or a scream, a big fat burning question that words couldn't touch.

Then the sun cracked the edge of the sky, the whistle blew, and Mick unhooked himself and slid down the steel to the twelfth-floor slab so he could get his crew lined out for the day. He felt kind of heavy and disappointed, and he supposed it was because he never got an answer. He didn't know exactly what he expected to happen, but he *had* expected something. Maybe not voices from the clouds, but something.

By noon the wind died and the sun warmed the concrete, so the whole crew came down out of the steel to eat lunch on the slab. All that new concrete glared white like a desert, and it felt nice and warm after they had been up in the wind all morning. Sitting on a wire reel, Mick peeled the paper from the top of a foam cup of ramen noodles and poured hot water into it from his thermos. After fifteen winters working outside, Mick knew how to pack a lunch: a steel thermos of boiling water and a whole bunch of instant stuff. One little cooler could haul instant coffee, hot chocolate, oatmeal, grits, all kinds of soup, ramen noodles, and hot cider—all at the same time and light as a feather.

An apprentice they called Pudd'n plopped down beside Mick with his brown paper sack—a ham sandwich and some potato chips. Danny Baez and an electrician named Spence sat down and spread out their lunch on another spool right there with them.

Mick and Danny had worked together for years. Sometimes Danny ran the crew and Mick worked for him, but on this job it was the other way around. It didn't matter, really—neither of them ever pulled rank. Danny wore a beat-up old hard hat with decals all over it from places he'd been, and like all the ironworkers in the high steel he carried a pointed spud wrench in a wire hanger on his hip. Mick would never forget the first time he ever worked with Danny. They were stringing steel cable for the suspension roof on the Georgia Dome back in '92. It was Mick's first cable job, and Danny was the one who showed him around when he signed on. Whenever he passed a radial cable up in the rigging, Danny would take out his spud wrench, give the cable a good whack, and it would give off a high-pitched *choop* sound like one of those guns in *Star Wars*. When Mick asked him what he was doing he said he was listening.

"Everything's got a pitch," Danny said. "They got machines for checking tension on these cables, but I don't trust machines. I've seen 'em break, seen 'em lie, seen 'em get out of calibration. I trust my ear. When I was a kid we had a sailboat, and when she was dead on and humming right down the middle of the wind she'd sing—steady as a rock, and always the same note. Everything does that, one way or another. Everything's got a pitch. You just gotta learn how to hear it."

Danny definitely knew what he was doing, and he was a bit of an amateur philosopher, too. That was all right with Mick, because Mick was no ordinary redneck. He'd always considered himself an enlightened and open-minded redneck, and he understood that there was nothing wrong with a man having deep thoughts as long as he kept them to himself.

When they sat down to lunch that day, nobody said anything until Danny bit into his sandwich and made a face. "Salami again. Every day for ten years, the same thing. Nothing but salami, mayo and lettuce. *Man* I'm sick of this."

It was a trap. Mick had heard it a million times, but Pudd'n took the bait.

"Why don't you tell your wife to fix you something else?" Pudd'n asked. He was really green.

Danny looked at him like he was crazy. "My wife don't get up," he said. "I make my *own* lunch."

They hadn't been there ten minutes when the big crane boom started moving—the same crane they'd been using to hoist I-beams into place. Just beyond the parapet wall the thick steel cable crawled slowly upward, and they could tell by the way it was shaking that it was bringing up something heavy.

Danny cussed, spat, and said, "Don't that operator have a watch? We're tryin' to eat lunch here."

They were sitting in toward the middle of the building, where the steel structure rose out of the concrete, but an old man in a hard hat stood out by the edge, leaning over the parapet wall and looking down at whatever was coming up on the crane cable.

"What is it?" Mick yelled.

The old guy turned around and shouted back, "A beam. A big one."

Danny threw his sandwich down and heaved himself to his feet, shaking his head. "I'll take care of it," he said, then hollered at the old guy out at the edge, "Flag him up here and I'll catch the tag line! We'll rest it on the deck until lunch is over."

Danny just assumed the old guy at the rail worked there and knew the hand signals. Everybody up top knew how to flag the crane operator, but that old man just gave Danny a look. Until he pulled his "hands" out of his jacket pockets none of them realized it was the homeless guy known as the Man With No Hands. All he had was hooks where his hands should have been. Danny rolled his eyes and trotted over there to flag the load himself. Mick put his lunch down and moved to a clear spot so he could grab the tag line when Danny boomed it over to him, and guide the base of the beam down onto the concrete.

Leaning over the wall, Danny signaled the operator with his thumbs, guiding the beam up over the slab. Those main support beams were monsters. They didn't look like it from a distance but they were thick as a phone booth and heavier than a pickup truck. Once the base of the beam cleared the parapet wall Danny's signals changed, the crane boom pivoted, and the beam swung over toward Mick. He caught hold of the twenty-foot rope hanging from the bottom to steady it, to stop the beam from swinging while the crane eased it down onto the concrete near where they'd been sitting. As soon as the base touched down Danny had the operator drop just enough slack in the cable so the top tilted a little, then he dogged it off.

Glaring down at the crane operator, Danny put his fists together and made like he was breaking a twig, then flung his hands up over his head. The message was clear—"Take a break, fool! It's lunchtime!" Then he stomped back over to his wire reel to finish his lunch.

The Man With No Hands put his hooks back in his jacket pockets and stayed out there at the edge with his back to the ironworkers.

Now, everybody on the job knew *about* the Man With No Hands, but nobody actually knew him. They knew he was homeless, which meant that he lived at Overpass Plantation, which was the name they had assigned to the cluster of makeshift boxes and tents thrown up under a couple of bridges close to the job. There must have been two hundred homeless people living there at the time, and a kind of uneasy truce existed between them and the construction workers.

The bums from Overpass Plantation cruised the job all the time, and they were almost invisible because the first thing they would do is steal a hard hat. It was simple; put a hard hat on the average homeless man and he looked just like a construction worker. There were always a few bums wandering around on the job looking for tools they could pawn. They considered it their job, and they were good at it. Conscientious. Mick could remember one guy who walked around for a year carrying a length of half-inch pipe on his shoulder. It was a great disguise. The yellow hard hat and that piece of pipe labeled him as an electrician, so nobody paid any attention to him—he just dropped right off the radar screen.

They'd walk around on the job like they were going someplace, and if they saw a portable band saw or a big drill laying around unattended they'd gather it up, wind the cord around it and walk casually away with it on their shoulder, as if it belonged to them. And yet they had a kind of code. They'd steal power tools in a minute, but they never touched a man's hand tools. Bums wouldn't ordinarily steal from a workingman. Workingmen had to pay for their hand tools out of their own pockets, but the company bought the power tools, which meant they were deductible. And insured. Besides, if a guy was homeless, jobless, and didn't mind doing jail time, there wasn't much a company could do to him even if they caught him. A mad pipefitter could do plenty.

But the Man With No Hands was different. He had a reputation. It was more a matter of rumor than fact, but rumors will sometimes grow into legends when mere facts won't. First, the Man With No Hands had never been known to steal anything. He never took his hooks out of his pockets if he could help it, most likely because his hooks marked him—as soon as he took his hooks out of his pockets everybody knew who he was, and that he didn't belong there. But the main thing, the thing that started the whispered rumors, was what had happened to a fitter named Joey Montrose.

Joey was down on his luck. He had just come back to work after a long layoff, his wife had been real sick, and he was about to lose his truck. He was on his way to the laydown yard one morning, walking past a sump pit covered by a piece of plywood, when he heard a voice calling for help. He moved the plywood and found the Man With No

Hands down in the pit. Sometime in the night while nobody was around, the old man had passed through and stepped on the loose plywood, which dumped him into the sump pit and then flipped over, covering the hole. It wasn't that deep, and he wasn't hurt, but he couldn't pull himself out with those hooks. Joey climbed down into the hole and shoved the old man out, then gave him a five and told him to go get some breakfast.

"God will bless you," the old man said, and several of Joey's buddies heard him say it. They remembered it later, maybe because of the way he said it. Not "God bless you" but "God *will* bless you." Still, they all would have forgotten about it anyway within a day or two, except that on his way home that afternoon Joey bought a lottery ticket that paid him a hundred and twenty-three thousand dollars. From then on the Man With No Hands was a legend. Most of the construction workers had endured enough bosses to know that a man who can bless you can also curse you. Whether they would admit it or not, most of them were afraid of the Man With No Hands. But not Mick—he'd never been the superstitious kind.

Sitting there eating lunch and staring at that old man's back, Mick kept thinking about the way he pulled his hooks out of his pockets when Danny yelled at him. One of them had snagged on the edge of his pocket, just for a second, and he had to shake it loose so he could hold it up and show Danny. Mick started to feel sorry for him, which was a new thing. He'd always figured a man's life was a lot like his dog or his computer—it did what he trained it to do. If a guy was living under a bridge, then he must have made all the right moves to get himself there. But when the

Man With No Hands shook his hook loose to show Danny who he was, Mick saw a little piece of humiliation flash across his face and it started him wondering what the old man was doing on top of the building, and why he bothered to climb twelve flights of stairs. It finally dawned on him that in the middle of the day that open slab on top of the twelfth floor was the sunniest place in the world—the warmest place to be. It had been a long night and he was wearing a light jacket. The old man was just cold.

Mick looked at all the surplus in his lunchbox. He called out to the old man, who turned around and looked.

"You want a bowl of soup?" Mick yelled.

He nodded, then headed in Mick's direction. While he was waiting, Mick opened a Styrofoam cup of soup and poured hot water into it.

"You'll have to wait a minute for the noodles to soften up," he said, handing over the cup.

"Thank you." He pinched the lip of it with his hook and stood there holding it, leaning his face into the steam. He was pretty good with those hooks. They were the double kind, with wires and pulleys so he could grip stuff with them.

Mick handed him a plastic spoon. "You can sit on the gangbox if you want," he said. The old man was just standing there. He could have sat down on one of the reels with the crew, but it was easy to see why he might not want to. He didn't have the right. Didn't belong. He scooted himself onto the top of the gangbox, where nobody else was sitting, and hunched over his soup.

He could have used a shave, but apart from that the old man didn't seem too bad off. He was maybe fifty-five or sixty. His clothes were about as good as Mick's, and he didn't look crazy. Mick had always figured anybody who lived under a bridge had to be a few degrees out of plumb, but this guy didn't look it. It might have been better if he *had* come across just a tad wacko because Mick would have known how to deal with that. Half the people he worked with were a tad wacko. But apart from the hooks this guy looked almost normal. He seemed reasonably intelligent and didn't talk much—a combination that made a lot of people nervous. When the men finally figured out it was okay to ignore him the same way they did each other some- times, they relaxed a little and forgot about him.

"It ain't fair," Danny said, unwrapping another salami sandwich.

"You still fussing about the girl?" Mick asked. Danny had been snippy all morning because the company hired a girl and put her in his crew. At the moment she was down at the roach coach.

"She can't carry her own weight," Danny said, tearing into the sandwich. "She just ain't big enough. Worse than that, she ain't half bad looking, so the single guys are already competing with each other, trying to do her job for her. She bats her eyes and they take up her slack."

"I hate when that happens," Spence the electrician said. "Couple months ago I had to run a rack of four-inch pipe across the ceiling of the mechanical room and they sent a girl to help me."

"What did you do?"

"Nothing. I put a stick of four-inch on the floor at the foot of the ladders and did nothing. After a while the fore- man came around yelling at us to get after it, so I picked up my end and waited. You should have seen it. I mean, a ten-foot piece of four-inch weighs a hundred and ten pounds, right? It was a scream—him standing there watching, and she couldn't even pick up her end of the pipe, let alone go up the ladder with it."

"Did he tramp her out?"

"Nah, they just moved her to the trim crew, putting on switches and receptacles so she wouldn't have to do any heavy lifting. They couldn't fire her."

"Right," Danny sneered.

"What's wrong with letting her put on switches and receptacles?" Pudd'n asked. "Somebody's gotta do it."

"Yeah, somebody does," Mick told him, "but when you give the light work to a girl, some *old* guy gets laid off because he can't handle four-inch pipe anymore. Some guy that's been doing his share of heavy lifting for thirty years, and now he's got a bad back, blown knees or a skippy heart, but he still needs to feed his family. He's paid his dues, but he gets laid off anyway because the light duty goes to some twenty-year-old girl."

"Right," Danny said, without the sarcasm. They thought a lot alike, Danny and Mick.

"I've never seen a woman who could carry her own weight on the job," Mick said.

Maybe it was his imagination, but he could have sworn the Man With No Hands kind of paused when he said that. He was bringing the cup of ramen noodles up to his face, one hook holding the lip and the other supporting the bottom. When he heard what Mick said he froze, just for a second, and the corners of his eyes smiled.

Then he looked straight at Mick with that little twinkle

in his eye and asked, "Does your wife work?"

"Yeah, but that's different. She's got an office job." This made Mick a little nervous. He hadn't mentioned a wife, and like a lot of ironworkers Mick didn't wear any rings because they tended to get smashed or ripped off, taking fingers with them.

The Man With No Hands nodded and went back to eating, but he kept that grin on his face and it grated on Mick. After the first couple thousand times he got tired of people assuming he was an idiot just because he wore a hard hat, and there was something not quite right about getting a lesson in political correctness from a guy who lived under a bridge.

There was tension in the air for a minute or two, but then Spence the electrician got things back to normal when he started chirping about the Democrats, about who they might put up for a candidate next time around. There was nothing Mick liked better than a good political argument during lunch. He didn't particularly care which side he took, either, and Spence was just too easy. Mick couldn't resist launching into a Neal Boortz diatribe about how nobody with any self-respect would ever vote for a bunch of unprincipled socialists.

Danny was used to it. He enjoyed Mick's rants as much as Mick did, so he stirred the pot a little. "Aw, come on, Mick. We all know a workingman voting for a Republican is like a chicken voting for Colonel Sanders," he said.

It was an old standard. He might as well have put it on a tee.

Mick rolled his eyes. "Oh, please. You really think you need the government to lay out your clothes in the morning and tell you when you can go to the bathroom?"

"No," Spence the electrician said, "but I don't need the company to do it, neither. I just want a little security, that's all." He was almost whining. This was going to be fun.

Mick snorted. "You make your own security, Spence. A man's only security is in his own two hands."

He had forgotten about his guest, sitting there listening, but when Mick said that the Man With No Hands sort of smiled and looked down at his hooks. He turned them over and examined both sides of them very slowly, and Mick felt his ears turning red. A hard silence fell over the crew and they tried not to stare.

He finally looked up—not at Mick, but off into space.

"If that's true, that a man's security is in his own hands, then all is lost," he said. "All that remains is despair."

Mick couldn't make sense of it, and he was pretty sure the others couldn't, either. They didn't know this man, and they were already a little uneasy around him. When he dropped a nugget like that it sent everybody's wackometer spinning into the red zone. If he had been one of the crew somebody would have come back with a smart remark and they'd have moved on, but the Man With No Hands was strange to them, so they just sat there until Mick couldn't take it anymore.

"Look, I didn't mean—"

The old man waved a hook, shook his head.

"I was speaking figuratively," Mick said. "All I meant was, a man's got to control his own circumstances, that's all. A man has got to pull up his bootlaces and get to work. He can't wait for somebody to take care of him, he's got to control his own destiny, decide his *own* future. A man's got to be the captain of his own ship."

The Man With No Hands laughed then, just a little chuckle.

"The mind of a man plans his way, but the Lord directs his steps," he said. "You don't know what the *day* will bring."

Somehow, the argument had gone from politics to religion. Dangerous territory. And there was something in that little laugh of his that Mick didn't like. It made him nervous, the way he had said "the *day*," but it was the way he laughed when he said it that made Mick mad. He was fine with an argument, but condescension was another thing altogether. Danny and Pudd'n and Spence the electrician were looking at Mick, waiting to see what he would say. There were rules, boundaries. Religion was one of the few things they never argued about at lunch, but the old man had started it, and Mick wasn't about to back down now.

"Whatever the day brings," Mick told him, "I'll handle it. I always have. If *God*," he said, putting maybe a little too much weight on the word, "has ever planned my day, he sure didn't tell *me* about it."

"Maybe you never asked."

They all looked at Mick, waiting.

"Maybe I never needed to. If there is a God, I figure he's probably too busy running the universe to be my secretary. If there is a God, I've never heard the first peep out of him."

It didn't come out right, as usual, and Mick ended up sounding like some kind of heathen, which he wasn't. He was born and raised in the South and grew up going to church like everybody else, but he had figured out a long time ago that most of what went on there was a dog and pony show. He knew plenty of Jesus Commandos, and mostly he tried to stay away from them. He didn't hate them or anything, he just found them tiresome. Mick believed in God, sort of. At least he didn't *not* believe.

He held the old man's stare because everybody was watching him, but the Man With No Hands didn't answer that last volley. He just went back to eating his soup. If what had just happened was a skirmish then Mick figured he won it, but he wasn't sure if what he felt next was triumph or pity. It was kind of delicate, the way the old man held that plastic spoon in his hook. Watching him eat, Mick was pretty sure Pudd'n couldn't have done any better with both hands.

After a while the Man With No Hands said, out of the blue, "That's the wrong beam." He didn't even look up from his soup when he said it.

Danny stopped chewing and frowned at him for a second, then tilted his head back and looked up at the I-beam. The bottom of it rested on the concrete a few yards to his left, and the top of it leaned against the taut crane cable like the Tower of Pisa. When he turned back around, Danny had a really funny look on his face.

"How'd you figure that out?" he asked.

The Man With No Hands shrugged, blowing on his spoon. "It's shorter," he said.

Mick hadn't even noticed it himself. It was downright bizarre for an outsider to spot something like that.

"You mean he's right?" Pudd'n asked.

Danny nodded. "Yeah. This one goes up on the next level. It's a few feet shorter than the ones we're using now.

I didn't catch it, and I do this for a living." He frowned at the old man. "How'd *you* spot it?"

"I saw them pick it up from the yard," the Man With No Hands answered. "They got it out of a different pile. Looking at the piles from up here it's easy to see the difference."

"I'll go down and straighten it out," Mick said. "Soon as I'm done eating."

Danny wolfed down what was left of his sandwich and stood up. "Nah, I'll go. I'm already done, and I want to tear a chunk off of that operator anyway." He walked off dusting his hands, his cheeks puffed out with the last of his sandwich.

Mick felt a little awkward, sitting there alone with Pudd'n, Spence the electrician, and the Man With No Hands. Nobody talked, and the silence was strained. Mick already knew there was no point in trying to carry on a conversation with Pudd'n about anything outside of dirt bikes or girls, and Spence the electrician was still sulking over his politics. When the Man With No Hands finished his soup he put the empty Styrofoam cup down and stared off into space.

"Obliged for the soup," he said after a while. He still wasn't looking at Mick. "What I owe you?"

"Nothing." Mick was pretty sure the old guy didn't have any money anyway; he was just being polite. He shifted his weight, leaning back on his palms. The quiet tension drove him nuts, so Mick made a move to patch things up.

"Name's Mick," he said, but didn't offer to shake hands. It would have been awkward, with the hooks and all.

The Man With No Hands crossed his legs and linked his hooks around his knee. "Most people just call me Preacher," he said, staring off across the city skyline.

"So. You a preacher?" No way a real preacher lived at Overpass Plantation.

The old man shrugged, didn't say anything.

"I just wondered if you were a real preacher or if it's just a nickname," Mick said. That didn't come out right, either, so Mick tried to explain. "You know, because in the trades, when we call a guy 'Preacher' it usually means he's some kind of religious fanatic, a guy that likes to beat you over the head with his Bible." He gave it up, figuring he better stop apologizing before a fight broke out.

"Nickname, I guess. It's just a word," the old man finally answered.

"I didn't mean anything by it," Mick said. "Some of those guys just rub me the wrong way, that's all. If they can get away with it they'll spend all day pestering somebody with their religion—*on the clock*, while the company's paying them to work. I guess they missed the part about *Thou shalt not steal*. Anyway, most of the 'Preachers' I've known on the job were know-it-alls and judgmental prigs."

The Man With No Hands laughed out loud then, and looked him right in the eye. "Yes. I'll try to remember not to be judgmental."

Spence the electrician cackled, slapped his knee, pointed.

Mick sucked a tooth, raised an eyebrow. The old man was starting to get on his nerves again.

The zigzag shadow of the crane boom laid right across the Man With No Hands. When the shadow moved a foot or two the big beam twisted a little and the heavy steel base ground against the concrete making a deep groaning noise Mick could feel in the seat of his pants. Pudd'n had finished his lunch and was leaning on his elbows with his head thrown back taking the sun. He glanced around to see where the noise came from, then rapped against Mick's leg with his fist and pointed with his eyes over to the ladder from the level below. A white hat was coming up the ladder.

"Squint," Pudd'n said.

The guy they called Squint was the worst of the safety police, a chinless little twerp with no sense of humor and a deep conviction that his engineering degree made him somehow better than men who worked for a living. Everybody called him Squint because he blinked and squinted all the time like his glasses hurt his eyes. He was standing there in that expensive sheepskin coat he always wore, looking around for somebody to bust.

The ironworkers picked up their hard hats and put them on, very casually. The Man With No Hands didn't have to because he hadn't taken his off, but he eased his hooks into his pockets.

Squint's shiny white hard hat rotated, scanning the slab. There was a cluster of carpenters and some laborers down on the other end, but Mick and his crew were closer, so eventually Squint's radar locked on and he headed toward them. He stopped next to Spence the electrician and just stood there with his arms crossed, looking up at the I-beam standing on the deck beside them.

"Whose beam is that?" he asked. He was looking at Spence, ignoring Mick.

"Belongs to the ironworkers," Spence said. "I ain't touchin' it."

Squint and Mick knew each other. They'd had words before. Mick figured he had to be making some kind of subtle point by ignoring him. Squint knew who the beam belonged to.

"No offense, Squint, but I can probably handle things up here," Mick said.

Squint stared directly at him for the first time. His jaw flexed, and Mick knew he'd scored a direct hit. Nobody called him Squint to his face.

"There's supposed to be somebody manning that tag line," he said.

"What tag line?" Mick smiled sweetly, a sign of intense hatred.

"The tag line attached to the bottom of that beam. That rope right there. Anytime a suspended load is within reach of the ground and/or a working surface, a workman *will* be assigned as necessary to control the load by means of a proper tag line. *At all times*."

Squint took a little spiral notebook out of his sheepskin coat, propped it on his knee and started to write something. The price of attitude was about to go up.

"Danny's gone down to talk to the crane operator," Mick said. "I'll get him to hold that rope for you as soon as he gets back."

Squint's glasses looked up and he squinted, wrinkling his lip. "And if there's an accident in the meantime, who's going to take *responsibility* for it?"

It was the latest buzzword. The brass had just had a job-wide safety meeting where they brought in some expert in a suit who made a pretty speech, made everybody play some silly little game to illustrate his point, and left them with a new slogan—"Safety Is Everybody's Responsibility." Word around the job was, they paid him ten thousand dollars for it.

"All right, I'll take care of it, but I'd kinda like to finish my lunch." Mick was already finished eating, but his box was still open and he was still off the clock, so it was a perfectly acceptable lie.

Squint's eyebrows peaked and he said, "Would you like to finish the *day*?"

The squint-eyed little twerp was pulling rank, and there was nothing Mick could do about it. It seemed really silly because the beam clearly wasn't going anywhere, but where safety was concerned Squint was judge, jury and executioner. Mick knew better than to argue with the officious little geek, so he shoved himself to his feet, went over and snatched up the tag line, looped it through the D-ring on his safety belt and jerked a good tight bow-line knot in it. Then he sat back down on the wire reel, crossed his arms and glared.

"Happy now?"

Squint scribbled something else, then put away his notebook and walked off shaking his head.

After he was gone Spence the electrician said, "Man, you and him don't get along too good, do you?"

Mick shook his head. "Knew he was trouble the first time I laid eyes on him. I mean, look at him." Squint was heading for the little group of carpenters on the other end of the slab. "He's got a crease in his jeans. Mark it down,

Spence—as long as you live, never trust a man who makes his wife iron his work jeans."

The Man With No Hands had been very quiet while Squint was there, but now he looked up, puzzled. "Why?"

"Because he takes himself way too serious, is why. That's just plain arrogant."

The old man touched a hook to the brim of his hard hat, pushing it back on his head. That little grin was on his face again. "Well. Sounds like you've got it all figured out."

Now he was *really* getting on Mick's nerves.

"I been down a few dirt roads," Mick said. "Probably not as many as you, though, Preacher."

The Man With No Hands dropped his head down, smiling at his lap like he was remembering something. "Well," he said, "It doesn't matter how many roads you go down, you won't find wisdom there anyway. It's always at the beginning. Wisdom is in the heart of a child."

"Ooooo-kay," Mick said. He might have even rolled his eyes a little. His wackometer tipped over into the red and he made a mental note to stay away from the Man With No Hands. His watch said lunchtime was over, and for once he was glad. When Mick got up, the Man With No Hands stood up, too.

"Thanks again for the soup," he said. "You sure I can't give you anything for it?"

"Nah." Mick had lost several minor skirmishes and a major battle in the last ten minutes. He was feeling a little cranky, which probably explains why he fired a parting shot before the Man With No Hands got out of hearing. It didn't come out right. He meant it to be clever, but it just wasn't. Looking back on it later, after he'd had ample time to rethink it, he was pretty sure that what came out of his mouth next was the single dumbest thing he'd ever said.

"Unless maybe you can find a way to impart some of that childlike wisdom."

The old man had turned away, heading back out toward the wall at the edge of the building, but he stopped and turned around. He looked back at Mick with that same half-grin, only his eyes narrowed a little and his head tilted. Turning away, he shrugged. Raising a hook in a casual wave, he said something Mick couldn't hear very well.

It sounded like "Whatever you say."

Mick stood there watching the Man With No Hands walk across the slab, and there was something wrong about it. Something *bad* wrong. Mick couldn't figure out what it was at first, because he was so focused on the Man. The old man had nearly made it to the parapet wall when Mick figured out, all at once, that it was the shadow. The Man With No Hands had walked across fifty feet of concrete, and the zigzag shadow of the crane boom had stayed right on him the whole way. When Mick finally put it together it went through him like an electric shock.

The crane boom was swinging away.

Mick saw the whole thing all at once. He could picture Danny getting mad while he went down twelve flights of stairs, and then biting a chunk off of the crane operator when he got there. He could picture the crane operator chomping his cigar and jamming levers, that big diesel growling and the boom swinging.

The shadow followed the Man With No Hands because the boom was swinging away. In a second it would be followed by the massive steel beam shackled to the end of the cable.

A second after that the beam would be followed by the idiot tethered to the bottom of it with a twenty-foot tag line.

Mick grabbed for the knot, but even before his hands found it he felt the deep groaning of tons of steel twisting on the concrete. And then silence, as that monster beam lifted off and swung gracefully away.

Once, when he was a kid, while waterskiing up at Lake Lanier, Mick's crazy uncle decided to pull him off from the dock. Mick sat on the edge of the timbers while the boat got about a thirty-foot running start, then the rope went tight and snatched him clean out of his bathing suit.

This was a lot like that, only Mick was tumbling and bouncing across concrete instead of water, which is probably how he sprained his knee. Then he slammed into the parapet wall, which is *definitely* where he broke his nose and lost his two front teeth. A half-second later the rope caught up again, snatched him like a rag doll over the wall and flung him cartwheeling out into space.

A strange thing happened then, while he was swinging upside down twelve stories in the air. The last thing Mick remembered seeing before he passed out was the Man With No Hands—just a face above the parapet wall, watching. He was smiling. Like he knew something.

3

To be a man.

WHEN Layne skidded into the hospital room all out of breath Mick knew he was going to have to whitewash the story for her. The truth would have killed her graveyard dead. Layne had never been afraid of anything much, except that she had a perfect horror of heights. And she feared more for other people than she did for herself, like the time they went to Lookout Mountain and her knees buckled whenever one of the kids got near the railing. Snug and safe in a hospital room with the accident behind him, Mick couldn't see any good reason to give her a mental picture of her husband swinging dishrag limp at the end of a skinny rope twelve floors up. Sometimes a guy just needed to lie to his wife.

He looked like he'd been mugged—black and blue from one end to the other, nose the size and color of a plum, half his face bruised green and gold, a line of ragged stitches through his upper lip, and two front teeth missing. When he told her he fell off a wire reel she cut her eyes around at Danny for a truth check. Standing in the corner, Danny nodded, backing Mick up without so much as a glance, which was good because Layne didn't miss much. Anyway, it was the truth, technically—he really did fall off a wire reel. Besides that, Danny felt guilty. He was pretty sure he had caused the accident in the first place by going down and hard-cussing the crane operator, who got mad and snatched the beam off the deck, blind, without a flagman. Mick found out later they fired the operator.

Layne pressed him for details, but the fat lip and missing teeth made it hard to talk and he was slurring his S's pretty badly. She finally gave it up and just stood there holding his hand.

———

When he got home the next day the kids jumped him. Toad, the seven-year-old dynamo, flashed out of nowhere like a white-blond rocket and hit him square in the chest, which is why he didn't see her older brother coming. Ben charged in a step or two behind her and nailed his dad in the groin with his head. Dylan pulled up short. He took one look and refused to come any closer.

"Ith all right, thun," Mick said.

He was at eye level with Dylan, having dropped to his knees after Ben's headbutt. Dylan's brow furrowed, and when he heard a lisping imitation of his dad's voice coming out of that Frankenstein face he let out a little snarl. Mick waited, giving him space, and in that brief frozen moment he saw something he had not seen before. Deep in his son's eyes, behind the veil of suspicion and anger, he caught a glimpse of cold fear.

Layne's evil sister Lisa had come over to watch the kids while Layne brought Mick home from the hospital. Now Dylan sidled up to his aunt's legs, keeping a wary eye on this man who pretended to be his father.

Lisa lifted him to her chest and brushed the hair back from his dark eyes.

"It's your daddy," she crooned, with a triumphant little smirk. "He just looks a little . . . different, that's all. Maybe even better." Behind her back Mick generally referred to his sister-in-law as Lisa-Comma-PhD because she wouldn't even sign a restaurant check without tagging on the *PhD*. His arch-nemesis was enjoying this a little too much.

"Thank you, Lethal," he lisped, and as soon as he heard what he had said he knew that his fat lip and missing teeth had rendered something wonderful. "*Doctor* Lethal," he corrected himself, unable to keep from smiling despite the searing pain it brought to his lip. He saw the little flaring of her nostrils and made a mental note to keep calling her that.

Despite Doctor Lethal's urging, Dylan wouldn't go anywhere near his dad, but Ben and Toad hung on for a while, poking and prodding and asking questions about all the wonderful new injuries. Ben's wheels were always spinning, comparing what he heard to what he saw, and he wanted graphic details of the accident. Mick stuck to the short version, though it was even harder to sell a lie to Ben than to his mother. Toad just wanted to know if he cried.

———

Within a week the swelling was gone, along with all of the bruises except for a little dark yellow spot on one side of his chin. By the second week his knee was almost back to normal and he got a partial plate to replace his front teeth. Dylan, who had finally gotten used to the lisp and the gap in his dad's smile, backed off again, leery of front teeth that came and went. Dylan had a lisp of his own, and during the time of the missing front teeth he actually came to enjoy the fact that his dad had one too. Before Mick got his new teeth, Dylan would sometimes echo a word Mick lisped, repeating it over and over as if he were practicing sounding like his dad.

After a couple weeks Mick was itching to get back to work, so when Layne started making noises again about him staying home with the kids he dug his heels in.

"You might as well mark it down, hon," Mick told her. "As long as I've got a job and a truck, I ain't stayin' home. It'll never happen."

"Never is a long time," she said. At least she didn't bring God into it.

She made him nervous, acting like she knew something he didn't, and Monday couldn't come fast enough.

On Friday afternoon Mick was out in the garage tinkering with his brake lights when Ben climbed up in the bed of the truck and sprawled on his belly watching him back the screws out and line them up on the tailgate. Ben's eyes followed the whole process, his chin resting on his palms.

"Whatcha workin' on?" he asked.

"Brake lights."

"They busted?"

"No, they work. In fact, they work too much. They stay on all the time."

"Why do they stay on?"

"Don't know."

"Well, what makes them go on and off?"

"The brake pedal," Mick said, then went ahead and answered the next question. "The one that's sideways." He motioned toward the cab with his screwdriver. "They're supposed to come on when you mash the pedal and go off when you let go."

"But they don't?"

"No."

"Then it's got to be the pedal." Ben had a surprising grasp for an eight-year-old. Scary, sometimes.

"Well, I checked that first, but it looked to me like the switch was working okay, so I'm checking the wiring back here to see if maybe there's a short or something."

"Tell me about the accident again," Ben said.

Mick looked up, blinked. Ben had the attention span of a housefly, but he had laser focus. He'd seen Mick with his shirt off right after the accident, and something about it didn't add up.

"I told you, I fell off a wire reel." He took out the last screw and removed the taillight assembly. He'd already been over this a half dozen times, but for some reason Ben had sunk his teeth into it and wouldn't let go. "A *big* wire reel," Mick added, for emphasis.

Looking at that skeptical face, a memory flashed across his mind about something that happened in a camera store when Ben was little. Six years ago, but it seemed like only a week. Layne was holding one-year-old Toad, and Ben was cruising the lower shelves out on the floor while Mick talked to the guy at the counter. One of the clerks was watching Ben pretty closely. He was clearly nervous about a toddler handling the merchandise, so he went over to steer him away from the expensive stuff. Ben was only two, and small for his age. Bundled up in his snow jacket he looked barely old enough to walk. That young store clerk picked up a picture frame with a grinning cartoon dinosaur crawling around the edge of it, showed it to Ben and said, "Look, little dude! Do you know what this is?"

The clerk actually squeaked when he talked, the way most people do when they talk to an infant. He obviously didn't think Ben was old enough to talk, while in fact he was *born* talking in complex sentences. At two, he already knew how to run the computer and his favorite disc was a dinosaur program with a lot of moving pictures, roaring and sound effects.

Ben, not knowing the clerk mistook him for a child, assumed the man needed an expert opinion, so he took the picture frame in his little hands and studied it for a minute. Mick turned around just in time to hear him say, "I'm not sure. I guess it could be a diplodocus, but a diplodocus doesn't usually have these bumps on his back."

The clerk straightened up then, and looked over his shoulder with a kind of shocked half-smile on his face. He thought it was a setup. When Allen Funt didn't pop out of the shadows he just shook his head and walked away, left Ben standing there holding the picture frame.

That's how Ben was. When something caught his interest he locked on and learned everything there was to know about it. Things had to make sense. For Ben, his dad falling down and busting his face was fascinating stuff, but he saw something in it that didn't add up.

"It looked funny," he said, his head bobbing on his palms. "Like a big X on your back."

Mick took out the brake-light bulb and held it up. The filament looked okay. "I told you, my safety harness was too tight."

He was glad the phone rang when it did. He laid the screwdriver on the tailgate and ducked into the house to answer it.

What Mick heard over the phone came as such a shock that it wiped out everything else. Passing through the laundry room on his way back outside he bumped into Layne, folding clothes out of the dryer and dropping them into a basket.

"What's wrong?" she said, seeing the shock on his face. "Who was on the phone?"

"Bingham. The project manager. Apparently I won't be going back to work on Monday after all. They're letting me go."

She blinked, stopped folding. "Why?"

He shrugged. "Gross negligence, according to the safety report. They're *firing* me," he muttered, almost absently, still trying to get his mind around it.

"Negligence? For falling off of a wire reel?"

"Yeah, well, they're a little antsy about safety these days. A guy got killed a couple months ago. The safety nerds always go overboard for a while after something like that."

"I know some good lawyers," she said, but the twinkle in her eye told him she wasn't really thinking about helping him get his job back. She was thinking about that other thing.

He shook his head. "No, I don't want to sue anybody." He didn't want to get into a big long discussion with her, mainly because he was pretty sure the truth would come out if he did. She'd seen her share of cross examinations. He was beginning to wish he'd just told her the whole story in the first place.

She started to say something else, but she let it go. There would be time for questions later. She shook out another pair of jeans and let him slip out the door.

Ben was standing by the back of the truck with the screwdriver in his hand. When he heard Mick coming he laid it down real quick and jumped back a half step. Toad came flying up, white hair bouncing, jacket unzipped and flapping in the breeze. She skidded to a stop, grabbed her brother by the arm and spouted, "C'mon, Ben! Hap's cat's having kittens!"

Mick nodded, waved his consent. Ben took off, trailing his sister through the woods. When he picked up the screwdriver Mick saw there was nothing left to do because while he was gone his eight-year old son had fitted the tail-light assembly back in place and run all the screws in. Pity—his hands needed something to do right then. He just stood there for a long time tapping the screwdriver on the tailgate, thinking. It wasn't going to be so easy finding a job. Things had tightened up lately.

————

Later, after the kids were all bathed, pajamaed and packed into their beds, Layne looked over her book at him.

"So what are we going to do?" she asked.

He shook his head. "I guess I can ride workman's comp for another week or two while I make a few calls and see what's out there. I can tell you now, it doesn't look good. I'll probably have to take a pay cut. Even then, it might be a while."

"We can get by on what I make." She tossed this grenade very casually, while pretending to look at her book.

"I can scout around and maybe pick up a couple side jobs," Mick said, ignoring her ominous implication. "Room additions, garages." This was a real possibility. Like most construction workers, Mick knew more than just his own trade, and he had done remodeling work before in a pinch.

She sighed and kept her eyes on her book, but she was suspiciously calm, which was completely out of character. Women worried. Finally, she came out with it.

"Why can't you stay home, Mick? You're already out of work. It just makes sense."

"I told you, that's not happening. I'm not cut out to be a housewife. I don't even want to talk about it."

She lowered the book to her lap. "Why not? I mean, if it's about the money, we can tighten our belts a little. Besides, you remember we figured it up? It's a plain fact that after daycare, gas, lunch and all the expenses incurred by going to work every day, the second income doesn't amount to much."

Incurred. She spent entirely too much time with lawyers.

"Yeah, but the second income is *yours*," he said.

"Not anymore. My benefits are way better than yours, even when you're working, and right now we really need my health plan to cover Dylan." She was trying to hide the little catlike smile on her face. At least she had the decency not to point out that since the latest raise her check was bigger than his.

The television stayed on all the time whether anybody was watching or not. Neither of them was watching it right then, though they were both staring at it. What Mick was really seeing was the grin of a grizzled old man with stainless-steel hooks for hands, and he was hearing the words *"You don't know what the day will bring."* Alarms clanged in his head. Everything in him rebelled.

"Law's Miss Scahlet," Mick whined, doing his best Prissy impression, "I don't know nothin' 'bout birthin' no babies."

One of her eyebrows dropped, the other went up. "I've never seen anything you couldn't do if you put your mind to it," she said. "And besides, how many times have you told me a man could do a day's ration of housework in forty-five minutes?"

Anything you say can and will be used against you. For some reason it made him think of Layne's father. "In *my* day," her father had said—in fact, Mick was pretty sure everything his father-in-law ever said started with those three words—"a man didn't *have* to hang around the delivery room and catch the baby. In *my* day a man went out drinking with his buddies and smoked cigars until somebody come got him. A man never even had to *look* at a baby till it had a hat on its head."

That was then. This is now. Mick caught all three of his babies, and changed his share of dirty diapers, too. That incompetent buffoon in the movies with the tongs and the nose plugs didn't exist in real life. Not anymore. In *Mick's* day a man was expected to know how to coach his wife on counting and pushing and breathing and cleaning out a baby's nose with a suction bulb. His kids were all clear of bottles and diapers now, but he'd gotten his share of it. The care and feeding of children was not a whole new concept for him, and to tell the truth, it hadn't really been that hard taking care of babies. Babies were a lot like old trucks— they leaked and made noises. Clean up the mess, top off the fluids, and the noises usually stopped.

She was right, he could probably manage. It wasn't that Mick couldn't handle it, it was just that the whole idea of depending on his wife to bring home the bacon was completely unacceptable. Most of his childhood memories were of working alongside his brothers, cutting grass, sacking groceries, painting houses, digging stumps—anything to put food on the table. Because his father didn't.

He shook his head, finally, inspecting a callus on his palm. "No. No, thanks, but I'll find a way. I'll get us through this."

The darkness in his eyes betrayed his thoughts. She studied him for a minute, and a slight nod was all it took for him to know that she had gotten the message. It was a matter of honor. Of manhood. He had a right. She knew he was a man when she married him.

"Okay," she said.

4

Hap Harrelson.

THE NEXT morning Mick started looking for work. With the threat of housewifery looming, most any odd job would do. He went to see Hap.

Hap Harrelson owned the ten acres on one side of the Brannigan place and Aubrey Weems owned twenty on the other. Hap had been there the longest, having built his little bungalow back in the seventies. Mick and Layne had only been in the neighborhood for five years, Aubrey less than that. The next nearest house was almost a half-mile away, beyond a leased hunting preserve.

Hap had mentioned that he wanted a live-oak tree taken down. Dying from the inside out, the tree stood maybe ten feet from Hap's front porch and spread its thick arms over the house like an umbrella. Mick offered to take the tree down and cut it up for three hundred dollars if Hap would help drag the limbs off and split and stack the firewood. A tree service would have charged five times that much, and besides, an old country boy like Hap would never hire a tree service anyway. It just wasn't done.

Hap was a big, red-faced, slow-moving, pear-shaped bear of a man who wore bib overalls, always, and never buttoned the side buttons, claiming he needed the extra ventilation. He had some gray hair and he was getting bald on top, but most people never knew it because he never took that ragged red baseball cap off his head. As far as Mick could tell he never wore anything under his overalls, either. It wasn't a pretty sight. In the wintertime he'd put on a long-sleeved shirt, but that was about it.

The shop out behind his house was a big dark cave of a building that, apart from a little clear space on one side where he pulled cars in to work on them, was completely cluttered with stuff—motorcycles and lawnmowers and outboard engines mounted in fifty-five-gallon drums of water, all with cowls off, parts scattered across the floor and mingled with roughly a million tools on the workbenches along the outer walls. The workbenches were piled high with parts and pieces, tubing and wrenches, empty boxes, hoses and wires and jars of screws. The bare stud walls held a few tools, some coils of steel cable and rolls of copper wire, all hung on sixteen-penny nails in no particular order. The whole place smelled of old grease and mineral spirits.

Whenever anybody asked Hap what he did for a living he said, "I fix thangs," which was as good a job description as any. It was widely known that Hap could fix anything, so long as a person didn't insist on original parts and their only concern was to get whatever it was working again. People from as far away as Covington brought everything from clocks to corn binders and left them with Hap to fix, whenever he got around to it. An old wrecker sat under an awning at the far end of the building, but he didn't get a lot of calls for towing because he didn't advertise. He thought nothing of taking the wrecker to the grocery store if it hadn't been driven lately, although he always had two or three old cars and trucks scattered around the place in various stages of disassembly. He never called anybody when he was finished with a job, he just parked their washing machine or their car wherever he could find a spot, and sooner or later they would come and claim it. Hap kept his books in his head, but he always remembered what belonged to whom and how much they owed him for what he had done. He never charged much.

The one thing Hap would not touch was a chainsaw. Wouldn't use one, wouldn't fix one, wouldn't even pick one up. Mick asked him why once, and Hap pulled up the baggy leg of his overalls to reveal a deep purple scar running like a gulley up through the meat of his left calf. He'd been cutting the limbs from a downed tree, way back thirty years ago when he first built his house, and one of the limbs fooled him. He didn't read the lay of the tree correctly before he cut it loose. The weight of the entire tree lay against it, and when he cut through the limb it sprang back on him, swatting him down like a housefly. His own chainsaw fell on the back of his leg and took a massive bite before it stopped grinding. Not only that, but his all-time favorite dog, a pretty little springer spaniel named Rudy, was standing next to Hap and got his back broken by the same limb. It took a long time for Hap to extricate himself and stanch his own bleeding before he could put the dog out of his misery.

"Ol' Rudy was hollerin' something pitiful," Hap said, absently rubbing the back of his leg, and the remainder of the incident that still lived in his eyes was enough for Mick to see why he wouldn't have anything else to do with a chainsaw.

When Mick went over around noon to cut the tree, Hap was busy building a custom roll bar for a '69 MGB. The spotless little orange convertible had been restored to such a pristine state that it looked out of place in Hap's dark, grease-stained shop.

He grunted, pulling a U-shaped piece of heavy-gauge two-inch pipe out of the hydraulic bender. Nodding at the chainsaw Mick was carrying, he said, "I need to finish this. Reckon she'll wait a bit?"

Mick looked out the bay door at a fast-moving cloud bank. The big old oak was dying, and the limbs had started to turn gray and splinter off. Hovering as it was over Hap's house, the tree really needed to fall the right way. The weather worried him.

"I need to go ahead and get it down before the wind gets worse," Mick said.

"A'ight, then, suit yourself. Let me know if you need help." He took a felt-tip marker from his bib pocket, measured and ticked the legs of the roll bar, then hefted it to a shoulder and made for the band saw. There was something abrupt in the way he let his tape measure snap back, and it told Mick Hap would just as soon be absent while the chainsaw was running.

His kids fell in behind him like a row of ducklings as he

walked around to the front of the house with his chainsaw.

"What are you doing?" Ben asked.

"I'm taking down the big tree in the front."

Toad planted her feet and her hands flew up. "But that's our favorite climbing tree!"

"Yeah, well, it's dying. If we don't take it down pretty soon it's gonna be in Hap's living room."

He cranked the saw and cut a wedge out of the front of the tree, in the direction he wanted it to fall, and he was halfway through the backside when the blade struck metal and a shower of sparks shot out, bouncing off his jeans. The saw locked down. Mick goosed the throttle but the chain refused to budge, wedged tight. He hit the kill switch and straightened up. The kids gathered around, staring at the chainsaw sunk to the hilt in the base of a tree whose trunk was bigger around than their refrigerator.

"What's wrong?" Ben asked.

"It's stuck. I think it's jammed in under a big nail."

"What's a big nail doing in our climbing tree?" Toad asked.

"Deer hunters used to come here all the time back before I built the house," Hap said. He had come from around back to see what the silence was all about. "Musta been seventy-one, seventy-two. They had a tree stand here, and they drove big ol' spikes in it for a ladder. After a while the tree growed over the nails so you can't see 'em no more."

Ben leaned close, poked a finger into the cut. "Whatcha gonna do?"

"Get some dynamite and blast it," Toad suggested, dead serious.

"RIIIIING-ding-ding-ding-ding," Dylan said, doing a pretty good impression of a chainsaw while squatting in the dirt by the porch stabbing a pointed stick into the ground.

Hap went out to the shed and brought back an axe and a couple of steel wedges. They drove the wedges into the cut and finally got the chainsaw unstuck, but they broke the chain in the process.

Hap stood there with his hands on his hips looking up through the middle of that big old tree. The wind was starting to pick up and the trunk creaked and groaned a little. It was already cut three-quarters of the way around; if Mick could just finish the cut on the backside it would fall the way he wanted. If he did nothing, and if the wind pushed it the wrong way, it could topple onto the house any minute.

"Got another chain?" Hap asked.

"Nope." And he knew Hap wouldn't have one, either.

The wind gusted again and the upper limbs swayed. Hap shifted his feet and looked at his ramshackle house. It wasn't much of a house, but it was all he had.

"What are we gon' do?" he asked.

Mick shrugged, hefted the axe. "We could finish it by hand."

Hap shook his head. "I don't think she's gonna wait for us to do that. Besides, if you cut that big a wedge on the wrong side she's liable to come down on the house anyway."

"Blast it with dynamite," Toad repeated. She thought maybe they hadn't heard her the first time.

"Tie a rope and pull it with the truck," Ben offered.

This was probably the best idea yet, if only he'd thought of it sooner.

"We should have done that to start with," Mick said, looking up. "Climb up there now and you're taking your life in your hands." Lately Mick was feeling a little accident prone, and his knee started throbbing just thinking about it.

"Riiiing-ding-ding-ding-ding," Dylan said, still digging his hole.

"Y'all need to go on, now," Hap said, to the kids. "This old tree's liable to go any which away."

Mick pointed toward home. "He's right. Y'all scoot."

"I wanted to watch you cut the tree," Ben whined. "Can't we just stay for a little bit?"

"I think you should blast it," Toad said, still hoping.

Mick pointed again. "Go!" he said, raising his voice a notch and giving Ben *the look*. "Go find something that needs fixing."

Dylan got up dusting his palms and ran off ring-dinging after his brother and sister.

Mick scratched his head. "I don't get it, Hap. Layne says they don't pay any attention when she tells them to do something. They seem to mind me well enough."

Hap grinned. "She probly ain't totin' a axe."

He laid the axe on his shoulder, grinning. "That must be it. I'll tell her to start carrying it around the house with her."

The old tree shivered in the wind, and Mick looked up at it. "So what do we do, Hap? It's twenty miles to the nearest place where I can buy a new chain—an hour, round trip. We don't have that much time."

There was one option left, but Mick shuddered to think of it. Hap looked at the ground, hooked his thumbs in his bib, and Mick could tell by the mournful look on his face he was thinking the same thing.

"I reckon you could borry Aubrey's chainsaw," he said, wincing.

Even after the suggestion was out in the light it seemed a dark and perilous path.

"I don't know, Hap. You know how he is about his stuff."

5

Aubrey's chainsaw.

AUBREY and Celly Weems bought the twenty-acre plot on the other side of Mick's place four years earlier, then spent two years planning and designing and carefully choosing the right contractor to build their dream home. They'd only been living in it a year or so. From Mick's house, Aubrey's mansion could barely be seen through the woods in the summertime, which was a good thing because it also meant Aubrey could barely see Mick's. Aubrey had lived in upscale subdivisions all his adult life— the kind of places that have neighborhood associations—so he came to the woods with some stubborn notions about how often a man ought to cut his grass and what color he ought to paint his house.

Aubrey had built his wife a castle, a sprawling two-story brick Williamsburg with a three-car garage and a sweeping circular drive in front of it. They were in their fifties; both their kids were grown, the youngest off at college, so they had that big house to themselves. In the middle of the circle made by the driveway sat a manicured little garden that reminded Mick of the one in front of the bank. There was a pretty little Japanese maple hanging over a sculpted birdbath and a fancy bench carved out of Italian marble, the whole thing ringed about in the summertime with a dense thicket of flame-red salvia and in the winter with a million pansies. Like their house, that little garden island managed to be beautiful without being inviting. Mick just couldn't see anybody ever actually walking out there and sitting on that marble bench. Layne said their house was elegant, and she liked the way they decorated it at Christmas with one electric candle nestled in a garland of holly precisely centered in the bottom pane of each window, and a tasteful wreath on the front door lit by a spotlight hidden under the little marble bench. It made Mick want to sneak over there in the middle of the night and put up a big plastic Santa Claus with a hundred-watt bulb inside of it.

When Aubrey and his wife first moved in Mick and Hap got together and went over there one Saturday to help him clear brush from the back lot. Aubrey came out of the house wearing coveralls. Mick and Hap laughed about it for months and could never again work together on anything without one of them complaining about "soiling his jeans." Aubrey opened up a hard plastic case and pulled out a chainsaw that looked brand new—although he swore it wasn't. He just knew how to take care of his tools. He had to put oil and gas in it before he started, and he was really finicky about not spilling a drop. Later on, in the thick of the brush, Mick picked up Aubrey's chainsaw by mistake at one point and was about to crank it when Aubrey took it away from him and said, politely but firmly, "I'd rather you didn't."

When they got done Aubrey emptied every drop of oil and gas out of his chainsaw, took it apart, cleaned it with a toothbrush and a soft cloth, put it back together, sharpened and oiled the chain, enshrined it reverently in its plastic sarcophagus and then snapped a tiny padlock onto the latch. Aubrey was proud of all his stuff, but like Hap said, he was plumb stupid about that chainsaw.

Any other time Mick would rather have eaten a bowling ball than borrow Aubrey's chainsaw, but desperate times called for desperate measures.

"I don't see that we got any choice," Hap said. "If we don't do something d'reckly that old tree's comin' down all by herself."

He was right. They had no choice.

———

"I promise I'll take good care of it," Mick said. He had to do all the talking because Hap just flat wouldn't talk to Aubrey if he could get out of it. Said they didn't hardly speak the same language.

"Can't it wait?" Aubrey was middle-age pudgy—soft in the middle, with a comb-over. That day he was all dressed up in tangerine golf pants and pressed white polo shirt, and he glanced at his gold watch four times while they stood respectfully in his tastefully decorated foyer awaiting his decision. "I have to be at the club in a half-hour. Otherwise, I'd be happy to come over and cut it for you myself."

"What color is that?" Hap asked, touching a fingertip to the foyer wall.

"Hawk's Beak," Aubrey muttered, without looking. He kept jiggling the keys in his pocket and running a hand over his bulbous forehead, pushing his glasses up with a forefinger, looking this way and that, doing anything he could to keep from making eye contact.

Mick tried again. "It's an emergency, Aubrey. We've just got to cut through about this much of the trunk. Once the tree is on the ground we'll leave it until I can go get another chain, but there's no time. We've got to do something *right now*, before it falls on the house. We just need your saw for like two minutes, and then we'll clean it up and put it right back in the case. I swear."

Aubrey squirmed and grimaced like a kid about to wet himself. Mick thought for sure he was going to say no, but he didn't. In the end he took two keys from his key ring and handed them over. He almost pulled them back a couple times.

"It's out in the garage," he said. "In the top of the right-hand cabinet, on the shelf above the string trimmer, the edger and the electric hedge clippers. The big key unlocks the cabinet, the little one fits the padlock on the chainsaw case." His shoulders slumped and he looked like he was about to cry.

"We'll take good care of your chainsaw," Mick said gently. "I promise, we'll bring it back safe and sound." He meant every word of it, but a shudder ran down his spine when he said it. Mick Brannigan was learning to be wary of what the day would bring.

Neither of them said anything on the way back, but squatting in Hap's front yard unlocking the tiny lock on Aubrey's chainsaw case, Mick couldn't hold back any longer. He held up the little lock, impaled on its little key.

"That boy is a *bird*," he said, eyebrows raised.

"Yep. He's persnickety, all right." It was probably the only four-syllable word Hap knew, except maybe for *watermelon* and *Alabama*, but it was the right word. Aubrey was seriously persnickety. "I mean, what kind of fella would paint his garage floor with that shiny green paint? Looked like you coulda eat off of it."

"Same kind of fella that would wear those orange pants, I guess," Mick answered.

Aubrey's chainsaw, razor sharp and finely tuned as it was, cranked right up. Being careful not to hit the same nail, Mick ripped through the rest of the tree trunk in a less than a minute, but when Mick felt the blade cut through the last of the trunk, instead of falling the way it should, the tree leaned ever so slightly the wrong way and brought its full weight down on the backside, pinning the chainsaw blade. Mick couldn't budge it.

He killed the motor, straightened up and just stared at it.

Mick had done everything right—he was sure of it. He'd been cutting trees since he was a kid, and it was second nature to him. He had started by cutting a notch about a quarter of the way through the trunk facing precisely in the direction he wanted the tree to fall. Then he went around to the back and cut toward the notch from the other side, which should have eased the surface tension and let the tree shift its weight slowly until it fell, like every other tree he had ever cut in his whole life, toward the notch.

It should have. It had always been so, and there was no reason whatsoever to expect that the physical laws governing the felling of trees would be lifted in this one instance. But the heart of the old tree was black. A normal oak tree has a heart of pure, white, solid oak, but running up through the center of this one was a dead black place, all full of rotten leaves and squirrel droppings, and a black heart can be treacherous.

"Ain't never seen nothing like that," Hap said, his thumbs hooked in his galluses, staring up through the branches, looking for the first sign of movement. "She's cut all the way in two and she still ain't goin' down."

"I've never seen anything like that either. Just standing there."

"Well, there ain't nothin' we can do now. Sooner or later she's comin' down, and all we can do is get out of the way." They both knew better than to run. The safest place was right up next to the tree, where all they would have to do is sidestep the slow-falling trunk, whichever way it went.

The breeze had calmed over the last few minutes, but now the wind picked up and the limbs swayed. Mick grabbed the orange plastic handle of Aubrey's chainsaw and tugged hard, this way and that, but it was stuck fast.

And then the tree started to turn. Standing straight up, the old live-oak twisted very slowly in the wind. Balanced perfectly on top of the chainsaw bar, it pivoted off of its own stump, uncovering its black heart while the body of the saw crawled underneath the growing overhang. Mick winced, watching helplessly as the bar bent almost straight down.

I can buy another bar for it, he thought. Then a big piece of orange plastic popped off the housing and whizzed past his feet as the chainsaw motor slowly disappeared under the overhang.

They both took a soft step back and looked on with a kind of reverence. They understood already that they were witnessing a new thing. The tree continued in its delicate pirouette, balanced perfectly on the saw blade, twisting itself around and gradually exposing the stump underneath until it stood poised at the very edge, held up by a mere sliver.

Then, with a thunderous, earth-shaking crash, the tree dropped off the side of the stump, straight down, pile-driving the remains of Aubrey's chainsaw into the ground underneath its heel.

And still it didn't fall. The old tree stood straight up beside its own stump and kept twisting slowly in the wind, pushing up a little ridge of dirt around its base as it rotated like a monstrous weathervane, taking one last long look around.

The wind died. The tree stopped turning and hung there for a minute, dead still. Mick held his breath. There came a little groaning from the base as the old tree began to lean, very slowly at first and then picking up speed, right toward the middle of Hap's house.

The sheer weight and mass of the trunk cleaved the house clean in two, slicing straight through to the floor and filling the air with noise—the tangled shout of splintering wood, the deep crunch of old brittle limbs breaking at the shoulders, the shattering of rafters and joists, the popping of studs. As the thunder died a white dust-cloud rose up from the debris and curled itself calmly around the jumble of tree limbs, broken plasterboard and roofing shingles. There was a small sound of breaking glass as a sliver from what was left of the front window swung free and fell on what was left of the front porch.

Mick stood there with his hands splayed on top of his head and his mouth hanging open for no telling how long, until it finally occurred to him that Hap was still right there behind him.

Hap hadn't made a sound. He never even turned around. He glanced over his shoulder at his ruined house, once, the way anybody might look around out of idle curiosity to see where a loud noise came from, but he never even moved his feet. As the dust settled over the debris he just went back to staring at the ground where the tree had stood. It was a delicate moment for Mick, made even more awkward by Hap's strange behavior. He didn't seem to notice that his house had just been flattened, which struck Mick as the most frightening response imaginable. He eased up to Hap, hat literally in hand, his mind scrambling for the right words to begin an apology that might well take decades to finish. But it was too large—Mick couldn't get a handle on it right away, so he ended up just standing next to Hap and looking where Hap's eyes were looking.

Calmly sucking on a toothpick, gazing down into that big circle of hard-packed dirt where the tree had pulverized Aubrey's prize chainsaw and mashed the unrecognizable parts into a greasy swirl, a smile crept onto Hap's face as three words rolled out.

"Git 'em, Rudy."

When the long silence got too awkward Mick stammered some kind of pale apology and then said, hopelessly, "What are we gonna do?"

Hap sighed, glancing over his shoulder at the house, and said, "I reckon we'll need some tarps. And another blade for your chainsaw." He turned then, and surveyed the wreckage thoroughly for the first time. All he said was, "That's about a mess, ain't it."

Mick nodded, and tried again to apologize.

He shrugged. "It's all right. I got insurance." The toothpick switched sides and Hap's face brightened with an idea. "Hey, Mick, you can build a house, can't you?"

Mick grew up knowing how to swing a hammer, and he had framed his own house. "Well, yeah. Most all construction is just common sense."

"And you said you was looking for work, right?"

He nodded slowly.

"Well, there you go. We'll have to fix her."

"You want the guy that just smashed your house to rebuild it for you?"

"Why not? The insurance company'll pay you as good as anybody, and I'druther have you doin' it as somebody I don't know. You got yourself a payin' job right next door, if you want it."

———

There was plenty of daylight left. Mick went to buy a chainsaw blade and some tarps while Hap stayed there to shut off gas and electricity. He'd managed to remain calm around Hap, but Mick was acutely aware that he was in the middle of the worst run of luck since Job, and it was getting to him. Ever since Layne had started campaigning for him to stay home with the kids it was as if some invisible force had grabbed him in its fist like Cyclops and was flinging him against the wall, over and over. Up to that moment he had swallowed his frustration and just put up with it. He couldn't unload on Layne. Whenever things went south Mick was the one the whole family looked to—the stoic, the one with the big shoulders—and he couldn't very well gripe about his problems in front of a man whose house he had just turned into kindling. So he held it in, and the pressure mounted.

But as soon as he pulled out of the driveway on his way to the building supply place, Mick let loose. In his truck, alone, he screamed and spat and cussed, bounced up and down in the seat and banged on the steering wheel, even gave the bottom of the dash a couple of good swift kicks, venting a mountain of rage and coincidentally shaking loose a marble that one of the kids had dropped into the air vent three years ago. He shook his fist, pointed his finger, and poured out the full fury of his cross-grained, independent soul, railing against a wife he dearly loved but who had another think coming if she thought she was going to make a nanny out of Mick Brannigan. He railed against a homeless old man with no hands whose grin would not go away, and he screamed at any God who thought he could drive Mick Brannigan into a corner with one lousy lost job, a couple of weird accidents, a ground-up chainsaw and a smashed house. He would *not* be beaten down by a run of bad luck, he would *not* be painted into a corner while his options disappeared one by one, and he would NOT be forced into a life he did not choose for himself. As long as he had two good hands and a truck to carry him back and forth, Mick Brannigan would go to work.

Like a man.

The dirt road in front of his house ran fairly straight for about a mile and a half until it ended at the stop sign on Hampton Road—a small highway, but paved. Mick wasn't quite done ranting and railing when his truck roared down the hill toward the stop sign, leaving a long dust cloud in its wake, but he screamed for an entirely different reason when he stomped on the brake pedal and nothing happened. He pumped the pedal four times fast and stood on it with both feet, and still he shot past the stop sign and across the main road at sixty miles an hour. The truck left the ground briefly as it rocketed off the embankment on the other side of Hampton Road, then tore up some pasture grass when the nose came down and plowed through a barbed-wire fence, right before it launched off of a second embankment and belly-flopped heavily into Earl Jones's catfish pond. A flock of wintering geese, honking and squawking in protest, pedaled themselves into the air just ahead of a huge bow wave that rode up the mud bank on the far side like a miniature tsunami.

It happened so fast all Mick got was a series of mental snapshots—flying, screaming, plunging, a panicky fight with the window crank, brown water pouring in, swimming. There was just this furious series of insane snapshots, and then he was sitting on the bank staring down at that pond. He sat there hugging his knees for a minute or two before he even realized how cold the water had been. A fountain of bubbles boiled up in the middle of the pond, and a thin rainbow of oil had already started to spread across the surface. Curiously, the only part of his truck that remained visible was the tennis ball on the tip of the CB antenna still attached to the rear bumper, though the radio had been gone for years. The antenna reached precisely to the surface, so that the tennis ball sat there apparently unsupported yet oddly at peace on the turbulent pond.

He was freezing, and there was nothing he could do, so he got to his feet, turned around and set out for home, hugging a soggy denim jacket around him, his boots squishing with every step. Nobody passed him on the way, but if they had they would have taken him for a crazy man hurrying down the road all wet and bedraggled, hunched over and muttering to himself.

He walked briskly, partly because he was so cold and partly because, given the way things were going, he was half afraid somebody would pull up beside him and inform him that in his absence a great wind had come from across the wilderness and struck the four corners of his house and knocked it down on his family. But a long wet walk after a dunking in a muddy pond on a gray winter afternoon can change the way a man thinks, and Mick began to suspect he'd been putting himself in the wrong Bible story. Job, as Mick's admittedly limited understanding painted him, was a pawn in a cosmic game of "What If." Job got tossed into the frying pan as an experiment, to see how he would handle it. Mick, on the other hand, ever since the day of the accident, had lived with a gnawing suspicion that he wasn't being tested at all—he was being herded. The people in his life, not to mention cranes, trees, chainsaws, and the brakes on his truck, all seemed, at least to his half-frozen mind, to be conspiring to force him to quit work and stay home with the kids.

So far, he had refused. But Mick thought about these things as he walked home with his teeth chattering and the back of his neck aching from violent shivers, and he wondered quite seriously whether such bizarre ramblings might actually *be* the voice of God. He wanted to attribute it to hypothermia, but he was fairly sure that anybody capable of thinking of hypothermia probably didn't have it. Having been spit up onto the bank of Earl Jones's catfish pond and sent squishing toward home with his tail between his legs and water in his ears, Mick saw before him the knowing smile of the Man With No Hands, and he began to think that maybe he wasn't Job after all.

Maybe he was Jonah.

6

Caving in.

BY THE time he got back to the house Mick was a broken man. He wasn't looking forward to telling Layne what had happened, so when he saw that the black Explorer was missing from the garage he felt like he'd been paroled. She had left a note on the kitchen counter saying she had taken the kids to the store to get Toad a new winter coat. Toad's coats never could keep up—she went through two or three every winter.

There wasn't time for a shower if he was going to get his truck out of the pond before dark, so Mick just rubbed himself warm with a towel, put on dry clothes and headed back over to Hap's place.

Hap was out front with a shovel, happy as a puppy, prying pieces of Aubrey's chainsaw out of the ground and dropping them into a burlap sack. When Mick told him about the truck he laughed so hard he had to stop digging and wipe his eyes with his hat. Leaning on the shovel, he stomped his foot to clear his throat.

"Well, I reckon we better go pull him out," he said. "I hope you can fish better'n you can drive."

The tennis ball marked the back end of the truck so they didn't have to guess at it. Hap paid out slack in the winch cable while Mick rowed across the pond in a battered old johnboat and fished around until he snagged the trailer hitch with a loop of cable. It was the first bit of good luck he'd had all day. They winched the truck up to the edge of the pond, then snugged it to the back of the tow truck and dragged it to Hap's place for an overhaul. Even if the sudden jolt of cold water didn't crack the block, they were still going to have to break the motor down and clean it out.

"How come the brakes to give out?" Hap asked, shifting gears as the old wrecker rumbled up the dirt road.

Mick shook his head. "I got no idea." He was staring out the window at the gray winter woods, wondering. Obviously, things weren't making sense to Hap, either, so after a minute Mick just came right out and asked him.

"Hap, do you believe in God?"

He pondered this for no more than a second, then gave a little snort. "Don't everybody?"

"I guess. I don't know. Everybody sees it different."

"I reckon so," Hap said, in a way that somehow made it clear that it was okay to talk because he didn't get it anyway. One of the things Mick admired most about Hap was that he could say whatever he wanted to the man and it was perfectly safe because Hap didn't really listen. Layne took everything he said and broke it down, analyzed it, fretted and worried over it until he wished he'd kept his mouth shut. Not Hap. Most of the words people flung at Hap didn't stick, which is precisely why, if Mick absolutely had to talk to somebody, he'd pick a man over a woman any day. Men knew better than to listen.

"It's just, some people have this idea that God's got his fingers in everything," Mick said. "If Ben gets a bad grade Layne prays about it. You'd think God would have better things to do than fiddle with the study habits of a third grader. One out of eight million."

"Uh-huh," Hap said.

"That's just silly, is what it is."

"I reckon."

"You can't *see* God." Mick meant for it to be his last word on the subject, but apparently Hap had been listening after all. He leaned forward, pressing his chest against the steering wheel, rolled his eyes up and looked at the swaying pine tops along the roadside.

"Can't see the wind, neither," he said.

Mick retreated, and was staring silently out the passenger window when they passed Aubrey's place. He spotted the bumper of Aubrey's white BMW through the garage door and remembered with a sudden twinge that there was another grim task he would have to face before the day was done.

———

By the time they unhooked the truck in back of Hap's house most of the pond water had drained out, leaving two nice-sized catfish squirming and gasping on the floorboard. Hap took them as payment for the tow and carried them out back to nail them up and skin them, apparently oblivious to the fact that his kitchen lay under a pile of firewood.

Actually, his kitchen *was* a pile of firewood. Mick wormed his way in through a tangle of limbs to get a closer look. There wasn't much left. Hap had lived alone for the last five years, so his house was always a wreck, but now it was literally a disaster area. Cabinet doors, pots, roofing shingles, spoons, forks, shattered rafters, broken dishes and scraps of plasterboard were all tangled up with the busted remains of a maple dinette set under an impossible snarl of moss-draped oak branches and piles of fiberglass insulation. The refrigerator lay on its side, pinned down by a limb as thick as his waist, the door twisted half off. While he was gone Hap had cleared a path with an axe, and a wheelbarrow sat off to one side loaded with what looked like the contents of his freezer—mostly butcher-wrapped deer meat, hand-labeled with a felt-tip marker.

"See any plastic bags?" Hap's voice said from out in the yard. He held up the two dressed catfish.

Mick spotted a drawer, separate from any cabinet, almost under his feet. He reached down, plucked a box of freezer bags from the debris and threw it out to Hap, who stuffed the catfish into a bag and tossed it onto the wheelbarrow.

"Reckon I can put this stuff in your garage freezer?" Hap asked.

"Sure. Looks like you'll be staying with us for a bit anyway."

He nodded. "I 'preciate it. It'll just be for the night,

though. We can tow Uncle Dub's old house trailer over here tomorrow. That oughta hold me till we get her dried in." A little silence fell, and then Hap said quietly, "What we gonna do 'bout Aubrey's saw, pard?"

Looking over the wreckage, Mick's eye found the burlap bag in the front yard, still sitting on the stump, dripping oil down the side. He winced.

"I guess we better tie a couple tarps over this mess the best we can, and then go face the music."

———

Hap was standing out on Aubrey's manicured lawn holding the burlap bag when the porch lights came on and Aubrey swung open his heavy mahogany-and-leaded-glass front door. The bag dangled from Hap's fist and he held it a little away from him because it was dripping.

Mick faced Aubrey in the doorway, hands in pockets. Aubrey squinted past him at Hap, out there on the far edge of the light, but he couldn't make out what Hap was holding.

"Aubrey, I, uh . . . we had a little accident with your chainsaw this afternoon," Mick said.

Aubrey had apparently been eating dinner because he still had a light blue linen napkin tucked into the V of his white polo shirt. His eyes went from Hap to Mick and back, settling finally on the burlap bag. His brow furrowed and his mouth opened. Mick wasn't absolutely sure, but he could have sworn Aubrey's chin actually quivered. He pushed past Mick without a word and glided down the steps.

Hap held the bag up for him, solemnly. Aubrey reached

out with both hands and took it by the neck. Holding it as far as he could from his tangerine pants, Aubrey laid it out gently on the lawn. Pinching the bottom corners of the burlap carefully, so as not to get oil on his fingers, he shook out the contents of the bag and stood there clinching his fists, staring at a pile of grimy twisted metal and shattered orange plastic.

A seasoned lumberjack would not have known it for a chainsaw. For a moment, just one brief instant, Aubrey seemed confused. He stood there not saying anything for a minute, just looking. He stared at the wreckage, then looked up at Mick and Hap.

"We didn't even hardly use it," Hap said. "It was a accident. Somethin' went bad wrong."

For a few seconds the look on Aubrey's face hovered somewhere between curiosity, disbelief and rage. Mick started to tell him that of course he would replace the saw, but before he could get the words out, Hap, who had noticed Aubrey's pant leg about to brush against a piece of oil-soaked scrap metal, pointed and said, in perfect sincerity, "Careful there, boss, you're liable to soil them orange pants."

Maybe it was the deadpan seriousness of Hap's tone, or the look on Aubrey's face, or perhaps the soiled orange pants was the last straw, the overbalancing mite that tipped the towering pile of little tragedies the day had brought to Mick and sent them all crashing down into the realm of the absurd. But whatever the cause, Mick lost it. He started laughing. He tried to stop, but then he looked at Aubrey and Hap and lost it again. Doubling over, bracing one hand against a giant white column and waving at Aubrey with the other, wheezing, he tried to regain his composure enough to at least talk, to try and apologize and tell Aubrey that he really meant no offense. But when he looked at their faces again, the laughter doubled. He crumpled. He sank down until he was sitting on the Italian tile at the top of the steps with his arms propped across his knees, his head down, tears dripping from his nose, shaking, shrieking with laughter.

Hap stood it as long as he could, but then his shoulders started to shake and he lost it, too.

Communication was impossible. While Mick and Hap had plenty to say but couldn't say it, Aubrey was so angry he couldn't find the words at all. His eyes narrowed and his jaw clenched. He flung the burlap bag down at Hap's feet and strode quickly up onto the Italian tile of his porch, stepping over Mick's legs. He stood in the open door for a second, looking back at the two of them before he finally noticed the blue napkin hanging from his neck, snatched it off and held it in a shaking fist as he pointed at Mick.

His mouth opened to say something but he couldn't make it come out. In the end he just slammed his front door in their faces and sealed himself behind the walls of his castle. The porch light went out, leaving the two of them cackling in the dark.

Mick eventually regained his composure and started to knock on the door again, but then he thought better of it. The way he had seen this little scene played out in his mind, they'd show Aubrey the remains of his saw, tell him the remarkable, once-in-a-lifetime story of what had happened to it, and by the time it was all over they would promise Aubrey a new chainsaw and they would all have gotten a good laugh out of it, including Aubrey. But nothing ever played out the way Mick saw it in his mind.

"We best just go," Hap said. "Let him cool off. You can come back tomorrow and butter him up."

It was a good thing Hap went home with Mick that night. Hap's being there just may have saved Ben's life, because in the South it is generally considered impolite to kill one of your children in front of a guest.

Layne was cooking supper when they trundled over the wheelbarrow with the stuff Hap had salvaged from his freezer. From the kitchen she heard them talking and loading stuff into the freezer in her garage, so she came out to see what was going on. She and the kids had left before the tree fell and got home after dark, so they didn't know about Hap's house—or the drowned truck. Mick left the storytelling to Hap, since it was his house and he seemed to really enjoy telling her the part about Aubrey's chainsaw. Layne was spellbound, torn between laughing and crying while Hap told the story.

"But Hap!" she said, "Your house!"

"Aw, shoot," he said with a wave, "I been wantin' to remodel anyway." That part was a lie—Hap didn't even like the *word* remodel, let alone the task, but it did make a kind of sense. The house had been his wife's domain. Small though it was, Hap's ex-wife, Nadine, had supervised the building of it when they were young, and since then had chosen every scrap of carpet and paint, every cabinet and light fixture, every knickknack and picture frame in the cramped little four-room house. A born tyrant, she had run her house and husband like her own private fiefdom until five years ago, when she ran off with a house painter who, according to her, had more ambition than Hap—he owned his own business. After she left, there was no place Hap could look without seeing Nadine. It would never have occurred to him to destroy the house on purpose, but now that the deed was done he seemed relieved. Almost happy.

Layne fried a chicken for dinner, so while the oil was still hot she rolled Hap's catfish in some cornmeal and fried them, too. It was during dinner that Ben almost got himself killed. When they sat down to eat, Layne asked about the catfish.

"They looked fresh," she said. "Where'd you get fresh fish in the wintertime?"

"Out'n Mick's truck," Hap mumbled, his mouth full.

"Oh yeah," Mick said. "Layne, I meant to tell you about the truck." And then he told her the whole story, about how he came tearing down the hill toward Hampton Road and found out his brakes didn't work.

She was just sitting there, kind of stunned, when Ben muttered, "Musta been the Legos."

Mick's antenna went up. "What Legos?"

"The ones on the brakes," Ben said, cross-eyed, examining a chicken leg up close.

"Ben, what are you talking about?" Mick had a very bad feeling about this.

Ben looked up and noticed all of a sudden that all three grownups were staring hard at him and none of them were smiling.

"You *told* me to, Dad," he said, the pitch of his voice rising a notch in self-defense.

"Huh? What are you talking about, Ben? Spit it out."

"I fixed your brakes, Dad. You told me to go fix something. You *did*! You said the pedal made the lights stay on, so I thought maybe if I taped a stack of Legos to the back of the pedal with some of that black tape out of your toolbox . . ."

A stack of Legos would have kept the brake lights from coming on. They would also have kept the pedal from going all the way down.

Hap chuckled. "Yessir," he nodded, "that'd do her."

———

"You asleep?"

Layne stirred, rolled over to face him. "No."

It was late. Mick didn't know the hour, but he'd been lying awake for a long time, staring at the dark star that was the ceiling fan, thinking. His knee still hurt when he walked, his shoulder was still a little sore from a rotator-cuff tweak he got falling off a column-form last year, his lower back ached sometimes, and there were a half-dozen minor scars and old wounds that nagged him when the weather turned cold. Maybe it was time to take a break from work, stay home for a month or two. It might not be so bad. He couldn't even begin to untangle the economics of the situation but he knew he owed Hap big-time, and not just for the house. He also needed Hap to rebuild his drowned pickup truck. If he worked full time at it he figured he could have the house dried in before Christmas, and livable maybe a month after that. Maybe while they worked he and Hap could look after Dylan during the day and figure some kind of way to do this therapy that Layne wanted him to have.

"I changed my mind," Mick said softly. "I guess I'll stay home. For now."

A whisper. "Okay."

"For a while. I'll try it, just for a while."

"Sure."

"An experiment, that's all. Since I'm out of work anyway, I'll give it a shot and see how it goes for a month or two. After Christmas, if it isn't working out I'll go look for a job then. All right?"

"All right." Her voice came softly from the darkness, but Mick could hear her smiling. He felt like he was falling, like his whole life had been snatched from the top of a skyscraper.

7

Learning the trade.

A FEW years older than Layne, Mick was already a seasoned ironworker when he met her. She was in her junior year at the University of Georgia. At a movie theater one night he ran into a childhood friend who invited him to a Braves game the next week. Tip Turner's dad was the CEO of one of the smaller airlines, and salesmen were always giving him seats right down behind the dugout on the first base line.

There were eight of them at the game that day—five guys and three girls. Most of them were people Tip knew from UGA, where he was a senior. Mick the Ironworker felt out of place, big-time. College had changed these kids somehow, and he couldn't keep up. It wasn't that they were sophisticated or anything—they were going to *Georgia*, after all—it's just that the world they lived in every day was nothing like the one Mick lived in. They laughed, hard, at things he didn't see, and sometimes they talked in a shorthand he just didn't understand.

He ended up sitting between Tip and this girl. The girl came with the guy on the other side of her, a real clown with Harpo hair and a voice that was bigger than he was. He hollered at the batters constantly and his friends cracked up at everything he said. Some of it was even funny. When the left fielder made a spectacular diving catch to end a threat in the top of the third and then came up to bat first in the bottom of the inning, Harpo boomed out, "It was an okay catch, Zippy, but what have you done for us *lately*?" He really put on a show.

Mick had to force himself to concentrate on the game, not because it was a great game but because the girl sitting next to him was so strikingly pretty that it was hard to keep from sneaking glances at her. She was just a college girl in jeans and a blue sorority jersey, but she had heavy brown hair with traces of copper in it from the summer, and it rippled in the sun like liquid silk when she moved. She had deep green eyes, and when he looked into them it shook something in him that he didn't know was there. He tried to keep his mind on the game and forget about her. She was with Harpo, and she was way out of Mick's league anyway. He'd never thought of himself as ugly, but sitting next to her he was painfully aware of having inherited his old man's hook nose.

Late in the game the left-handed slugger for the Reds came up with the bases loaded. With a 3–0 count he got fooled on a changeup, swung from his heels and launched his bat over the dugout, straight toward the girl, a hundred miles an hour and twirling like a helicopter blade.

Mick didn't think about it—it was just a reflex. He lunged at the bat and somehow managed to stop it a foot in front of her face. The bat clattered down against the backs of the seats in front of them, and Harpo, who had ducked down behind the seats, ended up with it. He jumped up holding the bat aloft in his fists, hamming it up for the crowd. Half the stadium cheered.

But the girl. She was looking at Mick.

"Are you okay?" she said, just touching his shoulder.

"Oh yeah. It was nothing." He didn't tell her the little finger on his left hand was broken. Playing the hero. Anyway, it seemed like a small price to pay.

After the game, when everybody split up in the parking lot and they were walking away, she lagged behind her boyfriend a step, looked back, pulled that curtain of hair out of the way and flashed Mick a sideways smile that nearly buckled his knees. He knew right then he was seeing the rest of his life pass before his eyes, and he couldn't wait to get started on it. A gift like that could make a man believe in God, or at least cause him to make all sorts of promises.

He got her number from Tip and spent a lot of time that fall traveling back and forth to Athens on the weekends. She eventually cut her hair, and over the years it had changed color a time or two, but she still had those deep green eyes. Sometimes, even now, she could still buckle his knees just by looking at him.

Their marriage was pretty much blue skies and gentle breezes for the first ten years—minor squalls, but no hurricanes. Neither of them ever doubted that they had married the right one. For the first year, Mick worked while Layne finished her degree. She was planning on getting a job when she graduated; the second income would help buy a piece of land and build a little house out in the country, but before she could even get her resumé out they learned that Ben was on his way. Clarissa came the next year. Little Ben, whose mouth was only just starting to form words, christened his baby sister Toad, and it stuck. Mick got a kick out of it. Newborns had always looked like toads to him.

With two kids and one income money was always tight, and yet those were the best days of their lives, back when they were hanging by their fingernails, living from paycheck to paycheck. Layne planned on going to work as soon as the kids started school, but Dylan sprang himself on them when Toad was three. Mick was running a crew by then, and even with foreman's pay things were tight.

When Dylan was six months old they finally put the kids in daycare and Layne went to work with a law firm doing their research and legwork. Daycare and taxes ate most of her check, but the remainder was enough to make payments on a little piece of land down in the country. Even then, they would have been stuck in a cramped apartment for several more years if Layne's grandmother hadn't died. Layne had always been Granny Ima's favorite. When she died she left Layne her prized grand piano and enough money to pay off the land and make a down payment on a house. By doing the work himself, Mick saved enough money to put in a pool. Life was good.

But they were too busy. After a while they felt a little guilty about not being able to spend as much time with the kids, but that was life. Everybody was in the same shape. They were doing the best they could.

Now, suddenly and without warning, they were back down to one income, and it wasn't even Mick's. Their roles were reversed whether he liked it or not, and he didn't. Like most men, Mick drew a large part of his self-image from what he did for a living. Money issues aside, he couldn't help feeling that going from respected ironworker foreman to housewife was a major fall.

He had a very bad feeling about it.

────────

Layne started educating him right away. Now that he was committed to staying home for a while she made sure Mick knew everything there was to know about sensory integration dysfunction in general and Dylan's case in particular. It didn't take him long to figure out that there were just too many variables—too many ways and combinations of ways that the disorder might or might not affect various inputs from his eyes and ears and fingers. Common sense told him the first thing to do was get to know Dylan a lot better. If he was going to build something he needed to know a little about the ground under it.

Then she started teaching him housework, which turned out to be even more complicated than Dylan's problem. Mick was going to have to do it all, and she wanted to give him every last secret, every last trick of the trade discovered and passed down by a thousand generations of housewives. She showed him which cleanser to use on the toilet bowl—but not on the tub because it would dull the finish. She showed him how to get a spot out of the carpet. She taught him the intricacies of sweeping and mopping and dusting. She went through a dozen different soaps and waxes and polishes and told him which ones to use on furniture, on glass, or on a hardwood floor.

His eyes glazed over after a while. Most of this stuff was written right on the labels, and Mick knew he wouldn't remember half of what she told him anyway. Make a guy read the whole encyclopedia and he's not going to remember much of it. Mick knew the guy stuff—how to run a vacuum cleaner and wash dishes, how to cook a hamburger. He knew nothing about laundry and very little about cooking, but he did know that a man learns best by doing.

She went on forever about the clothes, all about laundry detergents and fabric softeners, how to work the washer and dryer. When she saw she was losing him she even wrote down a list of instructions on a piece of paper and taped it to the cabinet door above the washing machine. Hot water and bleach for the white stuff; most everything else warm, no bleach. Watch the labels for cold water wash.

He had quit listening by then, confident that he could figure it all out anyway. If he could erect a sixty-story highrise he could manage a little housework.

But then she took him to the closet in the bedroom—actually dragged him back there by the shirt sleeve and pointed to the hamper against the back wall of the closet.

"The house is yours," she said, "and you can do whatever you want, except for one thing. You will not touch the hamper in the center of this closet. It is *mine*, and you cannot wash a woman's clothes." She warned him sternly, solemnly, that he must not touch it nor wash the things in it, for in the day that he did he would surely die. She didn't care if he washed *his* clothes, or even the kids' clothes, but she drew the line at *her* clothes.

This was odd. *Clothes is clothes,* he thought, *and one kind is not that different from another.* But whatever. If she wanted him to stay away from her stuff, it would just be one less thing to do.

————

He woke up early the next morning, like always. Mick was always the first one out of bed anyway, but normally he would be in a hurry to get out the door. Construction jobs cranked up at seven. The drive to downtown Atlanta took nearly an hour, so he always had to leave by six. Staying home, he woke up at five and then had time to kill before he got the rest of the family up.

"Time for school," he said, poking his head into his oldest son's room and flipping the light switch. Ben sat bolt upright, a pajama-clad question mark, squinting at the strange voice in his doorway and wondering what had happened to his mother.

"You'll get used to it," Mick told him, and went to wake up Toad.

He looked at the list on the refrigerator door, checked off the next item and counted out lunch money for two kids. It was cold out, so he took Layne's keys out of her pocketbook and cranked her car so it would be nice and warm by the time she was ready to go. This was too easy. There was a twinge of guilty pleasure in knowing he wouldn't have to drive downtown or spend the day out in the cold. He turned on the kitchen radio to hear the morning traffic report, just for fun.

The kids were sitting at the table moping over their

oatmeal when Layne breezed out of the bedroom in a new pinstriped suit.

She stopped, leaned down and looked under the table. "Where's Dylan?"

"He's asleep. He's staying home with me now, remember? No more daycare." Mick said this a little smugly, but the look on Layne's face gave him the sinking feeling that he'd really stepped in it, somehow. She came to him then, smiling patiently, and cupped his face in her hands.

"Please tell me you're not going to leave my four-year-old asleep in bed while you're taking Ben and Toad to school."

It was a natural law. Everybody had to be dressed and ready and the car loaded with all the apparatus and paraphernalia necessary for the life support of three munchkins—car seats strapped in, noses wiped, shoes tied—before anybody could go anywhere. Gone were the days when he and Layne could just say "Let's go somewhere" and then jump in the car and go. His mind flashed back to the time Before Kids, when he'd gotten laid off for a week, unexpectedly. It had taken them about five minutes to throw some camping gear in the Jeep and take off to the Florida Keys with three hundred dollars in their pockets and not a care in the world.

They were free in those days.

Now a simple trip to the store was a logistical nightmare involving forty-five minutes of dressing, packing and loading before the car was even cranked. Mick knew this. He had merely suffered a momentary lapse while trying to remember a dozen things at once. His first test. His first failing grade.

"Why not?" he said, trying to make a joke of it, but he caught the look on Toad's face when he said it. His daughter grinned, lowering her face, and a little trail of milk escaped down her chin. Even Toad knew he'd blown it.

Layne was still holding his face in her hands, and there was laughter in the corners of her eyes.

"Why not? Because he'll wake up alone in the house and he'll freak, and then he'll end up thirty years from now trying to explain you to his therapist, is why not."

Mick went and got Dylan out of bed, carried him into the dining room in his pajamas, all warm and limp, legs dangling, head lolling on his dad's shoulder. Four years old and he still smelled like milk.

Layne appeared in the kitchen door sipping coffee from a stainless-steel travel cup.

"You need to lay out their clothes in the morning, or at least *check* them," she said patiently. "Toad, you know you can't wear that dress."

He hadn't noticed. Toad had always loved plain cotton dresses. She was a full-throttle kid, and a loose cotton dress was all about freedom of movement. It took a long time just to convince her to wear shorts under it if she planned to climb any trees.

"And Ben, I know that's your favorite T-shirt, but it's a rag. Put on the new one I got you—the one with the pirate. And you'll need another layer. It's cold today."

Neither of the kids looked to their dad for a reprieve. They knew who was really in charge.

Mick went out to move the car seat from her Explorer to the Datsun pickup he'd borrowed from Hap. On his way back in Layne brushed past him, tossing a peck at his cheek without slowing down, and he knew she was hurrying because she didn't want to cry in front of the kids. She never said it, but deep down he knew. What she really wanted all along was to be home with her kids herself, but things just hadn't worked out that way.

Despite the rough start, nothing about his new job seemed difficult to Mick. There was no real work here, no tough decisions, no pressure—just baby-sitting and house-cleaning. After fifteen years of construction work it felt like a vacation. The toughest thing he had to do was work on Hap's house, and that would be a piece of cake. It was right in his happy zone.

———

Whatever the task, Mick believed in doing the hard part first. A man could do any sort of job if he could break it down into parts and then deal with the hardest part first. The way he saw it, his toughest job that first morning was to go get Aubrey a new chainsaw and take it to him, so he dropped off Ben and Toad and then headed up the express-way with Dylan strapped in next to him. An hour later he parked Hap's old Datsun on Aubrey's spotless circular drive and grabbed a new chainsaw out of the back, still in a shiny new orange plastic case with the tags hanging from the handle. It looked a lot like the one they smashed, except it was a newer model—a little more horsepower and with a cylinder release button to make it easier to crank. He figured he owed Aubrey an upgrade for pain and suffer-ing, mental anguish. He even bought a new little padlock to put on it.

He ran up the steps to Aubrey's front porch and was

about to ring the doorbell when he saw there wasn't one, there was just a brass plate with speaker holes in it and a button at the bottom—an intercom. Mick had always been cursed when it came to electronics. Layne said he emitted an electrostatic field. If he bought a new stereo it would self-destruct within a week, and if it didn't, lightning would hit it and take the television out for good measure. So it didn't come as any surprise to Mick when he pushed the button on the brass-plated intercom next to Aubrey's beveled-glass-and-mahogany front door and the speaker went nuts. It crackled and spat a couple times, and then he could hear Aubrey and his wife talking. It sounded distant, like they were down a well, but plain as day. They must have been sitting at the kitchen table having a second cup of coffee because they were talking quietly and there were comfortable little spaces in the conversation.

"Well, you musn't make too much of it, Aubrey. It's not that important, really," Celly Weems said, leaving the R out of "important". She wouldn't pronounce an R unless she had to. Celly was a Rutherford—local aristocracy for as far back as anybody could remember because they owned the biggest lumberyard in the county. She pronounced it "Ruthuhfuhd." Her family tree was dotted with lawyers in white linen suits, county commissioners and state representatives whose favorite family story was about how they rebuilt the lumber business after Sherman burned it up. They told the story as if they'd done it just last week, themselves, and not some other long-dead generation of iron-willed Rutherfords.

Celly was the celebrated beauty queen of her generation. Her high cheekbones, long neck and Roman nose gave her an elegance to match the graceful way she moved. She spoke with the leisurely drawl of Old South high society, and always formally introduced herself to people by offering limp fingertips and rolling out her full name— "Celestine Rutherford Weems." Layne liked the way she talked; she called it languorous. Mick had another word for it.

There was a long pause and then Aubrey said, "It's the principle of the thing, Celly. I have *tried* to be neighborly."

"Well, of *course* you have," she said quietly, splitting the word into two syllables. "These are country folks, sugar, and they're common. We knew they were trash when we moved here—Mister Harrelson with his junk cars and those Brannigans with all those barefoot young'uns, livin' in pure squalor."

She reminded her husband that it wasn't she who had been drawn in by the bargain price of land on this side of the expressway, but now that they were here she felt perhaps they had an obligation to bring some culture to the less fortunate folks in this backward part of the county.

Mick suddenly realized he'd been standing there the whole time with his finger poised to hit the button again. His hand came down and he backed away slowly. Leaving Aubrey's new chainsaw on the porch, he eased back out to the truck.

8

Of kids and dogs.

MICK spent the rest of the morning cutting away limbs while Hap winched the trimmed logs out of his house. He waited awhile before he told Hap what Celly Weems had said because, frankly, it flew all over him and he figured it was better to let it settle a bit. But the more he thought about it the madder he got. By the time he told Hap about it he was ready to go over there and tear off a chunk of somebody.

They had a fire going in the back, and Hap was feeding limbs into it. He didn't even break stride when Mick told him what Celly said, he just laughed.

"Well," he said, "you get lookin' too deep into somebody else's low opinion and you might find out they're right. Anyways, what them people think of me ain't none of my business, old buddy. Yours, neither."

Mick shook his head. "I wish it was that simple, Hap,

but I can't get it out of my head. *'Trash,'* she called us. *'Living in squalor.'* You think we live in squalor, Hap?"

Hap paused, frowned, scratched his chin. "Not that I know of," he said thoughtfully. "My mailin' address is Hampton."

Mick let it go; to define the word now would only embarrass him. "Well, right now the last thing I need is something like that to chew on, but I can't shake it. It grates on me, that's all."

Hap laughed that easy laugh of his. He never worried about anything. "Ain't no use to get your hackles up over somethin' like that, old buddy. Everything's gonna be all right. You'll see. Ain't nothin' ever as good or bad as you think it is. What you need is a hobby. Somethin' to take your mind off of things."

Hap's whole life looked like a hobby to Mick. He'd had his share of bad luck, what with his wife running off and all, but nothing bothered him much. Maybe he was right. Maybe a hobby was what Mick needed.

———

After lunch they towed Uncle Dub's trailer in and set it up, hooked up the water and electricity. It was a busy day, especially since Mick had to keep an eye on Dylan the whole time. He wasn't used to it. Among the many things doctors had told them in recent weeks was that Dylan suffered from attention deficit disorder, but on this particular afternoon it was his father's attention deficit that invited disaster.

Dylan loved being outdoors but he lived in his own little world. He had to be watched constantly because he'd wander off. Mick had noticed in the past that when there were other kids playing games and chasing each other around the yard, Dylan would be off by himself squatting in the woods investigating a hole in the ground or throwing rocks or wrestling with their dog, Andy, but it had never seemed particularly important before. The kid was just a loner, that's all.

Several times that day, when Mick was preoccupied with cutting up the tree, he would look up and Dylan would be halfway to the woods. He headed off into a neighboring soybean field once, and Mick would have completely lost sight of him if it hadn't been for Andy's tail waving like a flag.

Andy was Dylan's best friend, a lop-eared yellow lab with a disarming grin that hid a diabolical intelligence and a genius for problem-solving. Mick suspected the term *lab*, in Andy's case, referred not to his bloodlines but to his place of origin; he *had* to have been a genetic experiment. His tail was grafted from an otter and mounted precisely at tabletop height so he could back up to a table and sweep it clean of drinking glasses and lamps. Then he would grin and try to look stupid, but he knew exactly what he was doing—Mick could see it in his eyes. The dog understood English. Sometimes Mick suspected he could read.

Hap entertained Dylan most of the morning, letting him throw limbs and scrap lumber into the fire. In that respect, at least, Dylan was no different from any other boy; he could play with a fire for hours on end. After lunch Mick tried giving him a board and a hammer and showing him how to drive nails. He hit his fingers. Even when Mick started a row of nails for him he still couldn't hit them.

Choking up on the hammer didn't help. Every time Dylan missed he got a little more frustrated and swung a little harder, which made his aim worse. He finally lost his temper and threw the hammer as far as he could throw it. Andy ran after it and brought it back. Dylan threw it again.

Mick spent the afternoon carving up the last of the tree trunk in Hap's kitchen, creating his own little storm of noise and sawdust. It was a thick trunk, and Mick didn't realize how much time had passed before he looked up. When he finally did, Dylan was gone. The fire had burned itself down some, and Hap was busy picking up the unburned remains of limbs around the perimeter and tossing them onto the coals.

Mick killed the chainsaw, put it down.

"Hap, where's Dylan?"

Hap tossed a limb, straightened up, hooked his thumbs in his galluses, looked all around.

"I don't see him," he said calmly.

Mick worked his way through a pile of cut limbs out into the backyard, and scanned the property as far as he could see. He shouted Dylan's name and waited for an answer. Nothing.

Hap shouted. His voice was a bit bigger, but there was still no answer. Neither boy nor dog was anywhere in sight. Both men stared at the ominously dark woods, which seemed now to have moved closer. They both called out again, cupping hands around mouths and trying different directions, listening. Still nothing.

Then Hap, probably because it was not his son missing and his mind was therefore working a bit more clearly, boomed out in his best foghorn voice, "AAAANDYYYYY! COME HERE, BOY!"

They listened but heard no bark. They waited for a minute, and right when Hap was raising his hands to his face to shout again they heard the quick, light steps pattering through the dry grass out behind the shop, coming up from the direction of the pond. Andy loped around the corner of the shop and trotted up to them with his tongue hanging out and his tail wagging. His legs were covered with black muck, and mud hung in clumps from the fur on his belly.

Mick didn't say a word, he just started running. He was getting up to speed when he rounded the corner of Hap's shop. The pasture gate was ajar from the post, and he burst through the narrow gap, bouncing off the gate, running downhill across the pasture toward the pond.

It wasn't exactly a pond. Hap had borrowed a bulldozer years ago and scooped out a catch basin down at the low end of his property to hold rainwater runoff and give his cows a place to drink. But there was a layer of shale near the bottom that let the water out, so most of the time the pond held only a bottom full of composted black, stinking, slimy, mosquito-clouded muck. Mick didn't know how deep the mud went—didn't know for sure if it was deep enough to kill a four-year-old. A hundred yards before he reached the upper lip of the pond he saw the blue coat, the shirt, the pants tossed on the winter-brown pasture grass, and the break in the weeds where the trail led over and down.

He skidded to a stop at the top of the bank, six feet above a black expanse of mud. Out in the middle was a small shallow pool of dark water maybe twenty feet across. The rest of the bottom was nothing but black, wet muck. Dylan was there, out near the middle, mired up to his naked chest, screaming and crying and flailing about with his arms, struggling, straining against a frustrating enemy that took his struggles and used them to pull him farther down. Except for his eyes he was completely covered in black.

"Dylan!!" Mick screamed.

He stopped flailing and looked up at his dad.

Mick held his hands out, palms down. "Stop moving around, son. Just be still. I'll come get you."

He sat down at the top of the bank and pulled his boots off, then slid down to the bottom and started wading out. He hadn't gone three steps, up to his knees in muck, when Hap showed up. Hap, in his commonsense way, had seen the same thing Mick saw when the dog turned up with pond mud on him, but he'd taken the time to think it through, and now he was standing at the top of the bank with an armload of one-by-eight planks.

Even with the planks it took ten minutes of fierce effort to free Dylan from the cloying muck and drag him to safety. It turned out that Dylan had thrown the hammer out into the middle of the pond, where it plopped into the mud and disappeared. When Andy couldn't get to it, Dylan took off his clothes and went after it himself. He was afraid of water because he couldn't swim, but this was not water. It was more like pudding, and there was nothing in the world Dylan loved more than butterscotch pudding, although he wouldn't eat it. He liked to take his clothes off and smear it all over himself. It would never occur to him that a pond full of pudding might kill him.

After he and Dylan cleaned up and changed clothes, Mick locked both Dylan and Andy in the dog run with Hap's beagles. There were nine of them—Hap was a rabbit hunter—and they loved company. Dylan loved it, too. Sometimes he'd lay his head on a dog's belly and just rub his cheek back and forth over it, feeling that fur on his face.

That evening, as soon as Layne walked in the door from work Dylan told her, proudly, that he'd spent the afternoon locked in the dog pen. She handled the news fairly well until Mick explained to her exactly *why* he was in the dog pen.

She blanched, and sat down rather heavily at the dining room table. "He could have been killed. My baby could have *died*," she whispered, bringing her fingers to her mouth.

Mick winced, shrugged. "Well, it wasn't all that . . . Okay, it was pretty bad, but everything's all right now. He's fine. And believe me, it won't happen again." He sat down and took her hands across the corner of the table.

"I saw, today," he said. "I don't know all the big words for it or anything, but today I got a good look at what's different about Dylan and what can happen because of it. I saw it in his eyes out there in that pond, and I want you to know I understand a lot better now, that's all. I understand, now, that he doesn't see the world the way everybody else does, and it can get him in trouble. I want you to know I'll take care of him, Layne. I'll protect him, even from himself."

———

Over the next few weeks a lot of things began to sink in. Mick's world had shrunk. He rarely left the property except to go over to Hap's every day and work on the house, and while it wasn't bad hanging out with Hap and Dylan and the dogs, he began to miss the rest of the world. He missed the guys—dogging each other out at lunch and talking about old times, other jobs and friends they had in common. He didn't realize how bad he missed the guys until he ran into Gruber's wife in the grocery store one afternoon. Gruber was an old ironworker buddy, and Mick recognized his wife from the company Christmas party. Word about him must have gotten around because Deb Gruber already knew he was staying home with the kids.

"It's an experiment," Mick told her. "Just temporary."

She seemed happy about it at first, all smiling and nice. Deb Gruber was a terminally perky blonde with a lot of teeth, and she had on a red sweatshirt with a gold glitter Santa Claus on it. She always wore roughly a pound of diamonds, and earrings the size of hubcaps. Some of the guys called her Bangles behind her back. Dylan was sitting up in the cart with his legs hanging through. He was wearing pink fuzzy earmuffs.

"Those are mighty cute little earmuffs," she said. She was grinning at Dylan, wrinkling her nose and talking squeaky. She pulled one side of the earmuffs out from his head, then let it go a little too hard. He clapped his hands over his ears and gave her his death stare.

"They're Toad's, but we found out he likes them," Mick said. "He hears too much, and they help filter out some of the noise. He's a lot calmer when he's wearing them."

She kept poking at Dylan, trying to get him to laugh.

His chin jutted and he started breathing hard. She was lucky he didn't have his light saber with him. Mick just knew any minute he was going to bite her finger off, but in the end it wasn't Dylan who bit her.

"It's *hard*, isn't it?" she asked. "Staying home with the kids."

He thought about it for maybe a half-second and then, like an idiot, told her the truth.

"Nah. I don't know what all the fuss is about. Any reasonably intelligent adult ought to be able to stay on top of a couple kids. And when you been doing construction work all your life, housework is a piece of cake. There's nothing to it."

Right then, for Mick at least, it was true. He'd only been home for a few weeks—nowhere near long enough to understand where she was coming from.

She went kind of slit-eyed on him, and it was like a curtain dropping on a stage. All of a sudden she was in a big hurry to get the rest of her grocery shopping done. It took him a while to figure out that Bangles Gruber had actually been trying to sort of welcome him into the housewife club, and he had body-slammed her. After she huffed off he wanted to call her back. Not that he minded offending her—he'd been offending people all his life—but Mick genuinely wished that she could have just stood around and talked a little longer. A grownup. Any grownup.

They left the store that day with a ton of groceries dumped into those filmy, weightless little plastic bags by an obnoxious spiky-haired kid wearing five or six eyebrow rings. In *Mick's* day groceries got bagged in good, stiff, useful paper sacks that would stand up under the sink and hold garbage. He hated the filmy plastic bags, but it never seemed all that important until they were flying down the back roads on the way home and he started hearing a weird noise. The afternoon had turned off warm, and Mick had rolled the window down and hung his arm out. That's when he heard it.

Flup.

He listened hard, trying to tell whether the noise was coming from the engine or the rear end. He was still driving Hap's old Datsun pickup, and he was always hearing new noises from it.

Flup.

Definitely the rear end, but this was a sound he'd never heard a truck make before. He knew he wasn't imagining things because Dylan started imitating it.

"Flup," Dylan said.

He finally looked in the rearview mirror at just the right instant to catch an empty bag at the peak of a graceful arc fifteen feet above the road, billowing out like a spinnaker and then collapsing, rolling, dancing on the backwash of the truck and swooping low to snag on the windshield wiper of the police car behind him, where it streamlined itself and buzzed like a rattlesnake.

When that red hair, stern face and aviator sunglasses appeared in his window with a clipboard, and the cop asked for his license in a no-nonsense drill-sergeant tone, Mick knew there was no point in arguing with him. The man clearly had no sense of humor. Littering. Not since Arlo Guthrie had anybody actually gotten a ticket for littering.

While Officer Bowers wrote the ticket, Dylan stood up

in the seat with his palms pressed against the back glass marveling at the sight of a week's worth of bagless groceries awash in the bed of the truck. Mick made a mental note: in the future, he would risk the loathing of the kid with the eyebrow rings by demanding paper bags.

Driving away from the scene Mick had some choice words for Officer Bowers, and some of them came back to haunt him the next Sunday afternoon. When Layne and the kids came home from church she seemed kind of tight-lipped. Like an idiot, Mick asked her what was wrong.

"Strangest thing happened this morning in Sunday school," she said. "The kids were all gathered around and I was reading them a story."

She'd been teaching the four-year-old Sunday school class for years. Dylan was in her class this year.

"There was a picture of three men on an elevator, and when I read the part where it said 'The elevator came to a stop with a jerk' your *son* leaned over my shoulder and looked real close at the picture. Then he put his finger on the man in the middle, the one with red hair and sunglasses, and said, 'That one right there. *He's* the jerk.'"

9

Christmas.

MICK Brannigan had never been a big fan of Christmas. He wouldn't have called it depression, but a kind of weight always settled on him around Thanksgiving and stayed with him until January. He couldn't possibly have picked a worse time to quit his job. The holidays rolled over him like a truck, as usual, only it was worse this time because he was out of work.

Then Ben and Toad got out of school a week before Christmas. One of the things—one of many things—Mick didn't understand about staying home with the kids was that there was no such thing as a vacation. No holidays. The definition of a holiday for a stay-at-home parent was "a day when all the kids are out of school and your workload triples." He hadn't counted on that. Three times as many cups of juice to pour and three times as many empty cups to round up—constantly. Piddly stuff, but endless. He couldn't believe how much juice three kids could drink in one day.

He didn't know about the Rain Rule, either. He was completely unaware that there was a law of nature that said, "If the kids are out of school, it *shall* rain." When the rain set in, he and Hap covered the unfinished house with blue plastic tarps and hunkered down to wait it out.

Stuck indoors, the kids were bored. They watched Disney movies, played video games, spilled juice, strewed toys and fought while Mick cleaned up after them and kept the peanut butter and jelly sandwiches flowing. He never realized how demanding kids could be until he got trapped in the house with three of them for two weeks. The kitchen alone ate up half his day. He told Hap he felt like a life support system for a brood of rug rats.

And they were territorial beasts. Cooped up together, the day would always turn into one long property-rights dispute, so Mick had to be a lawyer, too. The fighting was mostly between Ben and Toad. Because they were close to the same age, they liked the same stuff, and Dylan tended to argue with his light saber. In close quarters he could be a little short-tempered. There wasn't much they could do about it—he was mean as a snake but he was too little for a fair fight.

Mick blamed his old man for his attitude about the holidays. He'd never had a lot of patience with whiners, and he knew very well that everybody blamed their parents for one thing or another, but he would have put his old man up against any of them, especially at Christmas. Mick's daddy was bad to drink anyway, but when December rolled around he was always happy to embrace a legitmate excuse to celebrate.

The last year Mick's father was home he took to hauling Mick and his brother around with him on his route the week before Christmas. He drove a truck for a uniform rental company, delivering clean uniforms and picking up dirty ones. It was an industrial route, and he always took second shift so he could be at work when the house was full of noisy kids. He'd sleep as late as he wanted and then leave right before they got home from school to go run his route. Sweatshop Row he called it—mechanic shops and assembly plants—places where the guys get pretty ripe. When they got out of school for Christmas break and he couldn't avoid them, he took Mick and his brother with him on his route. Mick was twelve that year, his brother thirteen, but they learned the job well enough so that the old man didn't even have to get out of the truck when they were with him.

They were quicker than he was, too, and the time they shaved off his route he naturally chose to spend sitting in a bar. He'd leave them locked in the truck, and it would get cold five minutes after he left. Sometimes he'd stay gone half the night and they'd have to crawl in the back and burrow down into those stinking uniforms just to stay warm. Most nights they'd fall asleep that way.

When he finally came back to the truck in the wee hours he'd be limping, always. He had a bum knee from a wreck when he was a kid. He didn't favor it much when he was sober but he limped badly when he was drunk. Even without the limp they could always tell when he was hammered by the way he held his head tilted over against his shoulder as if he had a crick in his neck. Mick figured it helped him see a little better, brought the two images in line with each other somehow.

———

While Mick's kids were out of school for Christmas, the rain never stopped. Sometimes it would ease up to a fine drizzle, but it never stopped. He did his best to entertain the kids without spending any money, but a couple days before Christmas he got cabin fever so bad he caved in and took them to a matinee.

The movie was okay, as far as Mick could tell. It was a kids' movie. Robin Williams flaunted his patented schizophrenia, joy and pain fighting for control of his face. Coming out, Ben and Toad ran ahead, burning off the caffeine and sugar they got from a large Coke that cost him about five bucks. They were jumping and dancing, being silly, being kids, thudding down the broad promenade past posters of coming attractions spaced like presidents on the wall. Dylan flailed along behind trying to imitate them until he tripped over his own feet—boy and popcorn spilling across the carpet.

Mick stopped at the glass doors, hands in pockets, staring out at a wet, gray parking lot. Rain before the movie, rain after—a cold, steady, pitiless rain from an aluminum sky. Toad bounced up beside him, pressed her forehead to the cool glass, breathed a big fog spot, wrote her name in it with a fingertip. Dylan tugged at his sleeve and said what any four-year-old would say after two hours of drinking Coke:

"I dotta doe pee."

The new theater complex was plush—even the bathrooms were state-of-the-art. Mick waited across from the sinks while the boys did what they had to do. Leaning his head back against the tile, he stared at his tired reflection in the mirror on the opposite wall and wondered if it was the monotonous rain, the loneliness, or the meaningless-ness of what passed for Christmas that made him feel so drained and hopeless.

Dylan got done with his business before Ben and came out to wash his hands. His mama trained him well. Mick watched his son in the mirror as he stood on tiptoe peeking over the lip of the counter, looking for something on the long row of sinks.

Handles. The faucets didn't have handles. He wanted to wash his hands but he couldn't see how to turn on the water. Finally, he raised a shoulder and stuck out his little hand to feel around and see what he could find.

Mick watched his face.

When his hand swept past the motion sensor the water leaped out, warm and ample. One second it was off and the next, on.

He gasped. Those bright eyes widened and a smile shot across his face. There for just a second shined a pure child-like wonder, like a flash of light spilling out of a brand-new soul who sees every day as an adventure, a voyage of dis-covery. *Every day is a present to be opened.* Mick glanced up at his own reflection and was shocked to see the same smile—the exact same one—as if it had stowed away on the light reflected between them, as if that childlike won-der was as contagious as light itself.

There, he thought. Right there. *That* is Christmas.

He felt better after that. Something in that moment left

its mark on him. Thinking about it on the drive home, replaying it in his mind, it occurred to him that maybe what a man saw was just a matter of where he looked.

There was a Christmas Eve service at Layne's church and the whole family went to it. It was nice. Mick normally didn't attend church with her and the kids but he always liked the candlelight service on Christmas Eve. It was simple and quiet, and with the candles and the music there was something *sweet* about it, although no self-respecting ironworker would have used that word out loud.

———

There was nothing in the world quite like the excitement of three little kids on Christmas morning. They still believed, and it was amazing. They could have lit a city off of the energy. Everybody had a grand time. Layne got down in the floor in her flannel pajamas right in among the kids, and before long the room was waist deep in wrapping paper and torn boxes. Santa had been there. He'd even eaten the cookies and left a letter for the kids:

Dear Ben, Toad, and Dylan,

 Sorry about not leaving you one of those Galaxy 200 games like you wanted, Ben, but the truth is my elves refused to make the Galaxy 200 because it's a piece of junk, so the only way I could get one was to order it myself from that cheesy advertisement on TV, which I wasn't about to do because, well, I'm Santa, and I have a reputation. Besides, I can see you've already got a computer, so I brought you a couple games for that. There's a nifty multi-tool in your stocking that has a folding knife blade in it. Treat it with care—a knife is not a toy. You're growing up. Be responsible.

Toad, in case you're wondering, the Barbie doll was your mother's idea. Even Santa can't win an argument with your mom. Be careful with the magnifying glass. I gave one of those to your dad when he was little and he tormented ants with it. Don't do that. I think you'll like the slot cars, but don't do like your dad and his brother did. They figured out how to reverse one of the engines so they could have head-on collisions. Never let grownups play with your toys.

Dylan, I know how you like to dig, so I brought you a folding shovel. When you get about halfway down to China, stop and wave. The North Pole will be on your left.

Apart from the toys in the rain gutters and the PB&J in the VCR, you were all pretty good this year.

Merry Christmas!
Santa Claus

P.S. Dylan, here's the list of bad names you wanted. But you have to promise not to call your brother and sister any of these in front of anybody.

skankbelly	hogface
hornet-head	mumblemouth
scuzzyteeth	addle-brained marmaloot
catfish-breath	engineer
lawyer	chicken lips
tater-toes	bedpan-head
skimbleshanks	poodlepants
bilgemonkey	

Santa was careful not to list any names that started with G.

Layne read the letter out loud and just about wet herself laughing. Nothing on earth was more beautiful than Layne when she was laughing. When she laughed the sun shined and all was right with the world—it was all Mick ever really wanted from her.

Afterward, she went to the kitchen to cook a huge breakfast with pancakes and sausage while Ben and Toad put together the slot car track. Mick went in the kitchen to help, and while he was cooking a pan of sausages Layne sidled up next to him, put her arm around him and said, "Have you thought any more about whether you're going to keep staying home after Christmas?"

He shrugged. Didn't look at her. He thought about his old man, and what he would have said in the same circumstances. He wanted to say no, he really did, but for whatever reason he kept seeing Dylan's face—the light in his eyes that day in the bathroom mirror at the theater. The joy. As strange as it seemed, that was the thing that changed Mick's mind. He'd gotten a glimpse of something real and worthwhile that he thought might just be lost if he didn't let go of what Mick wanted for a while and do what was best for the kids.

"I guess I can stick it out a while longer," he heard himself say. "If you're sure that's what you want."

10

The gift.

THAT afternoon, while Mick was stretched out in the recliner watching a football game and recovering from a turkey dinner, the doorbell rang. He heard Layne open the front door—which was surprising in itself since nobody but the Jehovah's Witnesses ever came to the front door—and then he heard Celly Weems' sugary drawl in the foyer. He got up and went to see what was going on.

One glance at Celly and Aubrey told Mick all he needed to know. Celly had her Christmas face on, and Aubrey was standing behind her holding three wrapped presents. He gave Mick a little nod, barely noticeable, and then focused his attention on the wives. His face was stone. Mount Rushmore. Mick hadn't seen Aubrey at all since the night they returned his mangled chainsaw, but that one little conciliatory nod told him the score. Celly must have figured Christmas Day was the perfect time to make peace with the neighbors, so she drug her husband over with presents for the kids to make up for his slamming the door in Mick's face the night of the chainsaw incident. Mick had, after all, replaced the saw. Celly had no way of knowing that it wasn't what Aubrey did that stuck in Mick's craw. Given the way things played out that night, Aubrey's reaction was perfectly understandable, but Mick wouldn't soon forget what he heard over the intercom the next day. *"Trash."*

"I'm sorry my house is such a wreck," Layne was saying. It didn't even occur to her that keeping it clean wasn't her job anymore. Mick was pretty sure he could keep house for a hundred years and she'd still feel guilty about the mess.

Celly waved her off. "Aw shoot, it's Christmas, sugar. It's supposed to be messy." But while she was saying it her eyes swept the foyer, lingering for a split second on a cobweb in the corner of the ceiling. Mick could have sworn she cringed the tiniest little bit, but it could have just been his own prejudice at work. He fought back the urge to say something about "living in squalor."

"Seems like months since we've seen y'all," Celly went on, "so I thought we'd just drop by and give the children a little something, if that's all right." She was dripping southern charm so badly Mick was afraid for the carpet.

All three kids came running without being called. They clustered up under their mother, grinning like idiots at Celly and Aubrey, who had raised a couple of polite children and therefore thought these were being polite. Mick knew better. His kids could smell a Christmas present a mile off.

Celly took the gifts from Aubrey and handed them out to the kids, who scattered and ripped into them. Ben got a weird little RC car that went zipping around the room at light speed. When it ran into something it would do a backflip and go the other way. Toad—Celly made a point of calling her Clarissa, which was, after all, her name—got another Barbie doll. Mick was right proud that Toad managed to squeeze out a thank you between clenched teeth. He felt sorry for Barbie. That doll hadn't done anything to deserve the afternoon it was in for. They gave Dylan some kind of plastic thing that he could strap on his arm and spray purple foam like Spiderman, and he tore off down the hall decorating the walls and ceiling.

Layne dragged Celly off into the kitchen for a cup of coffee, but before she left she glanced back at her husband. It was only for a split second, but in that second her plastic smile wavered and her eyes panned down to Aubrey's feet. As fleeting as it was, the command was unmistakable: Stay.

Mick didn't know what to say so he just stood there. Aubrey fidgeted, shifted his feet, glanced at the ceiling, shoved his empty hands into his pockets, took a breath and said, "Ah, about the night you and Mr. Harrelson brought back the saw—"

Mick shrugged it off. "Forget about it. Heat of the moment and all."

"No. No, I shouldn't have lost my temper like that. I was just upset, that's all. I'd had kind of a bad day."

Mick couldn't help it. He started laughing again, and Aubrey shot him a hard look. But this time he managed to bring it under control.

"*You* had a bad day!" Mick said, still chuckling. "Listen,

let me tell you what really happened to your chainsaw, but you better come in here and sit down first. This is gonna take a little while."

He steered Aubrey into the living room, the little front room dominated by Layne's piano and the desk—the only room left after Christmas morning that wasn't totally trashed—and told him the story of the chainsaw's demise. Aubrey sat in the desk chair while Mick perched on the piano stool and spun his yarn. He and Hap had had time to embellish the story a little, and Mick left nothing out.

Aubrey started to chuckle when he told him about the tree pinning the blade underneath it, turning off of its own stump, and he laughed out loud when Mick held his arms up and mimed the great tree twisting slowly in the wind, grinding the remains of the saw into the dirt and falling on Hap's house.

Then he told him about sailing his truck off into Earl Jones's catfish pond, and by the time he was done Aubrey had to take off his glasses and wipe his eyes.

"Now I understand why you couldn't stop laughing that night," Aubrey said, putting his glasses back on.

"Yeah, well, I tried."

"You know, when I drove by the next morning I saw the tree on Mr. Harrelson's house, but I had no idea. The chainsaw story is priceless—and the *pond*!" He slapped his palms down on his knees and started laughing again. "You really did have a bad day, didn't you."

"I've had better," Mick said. And then, suddenly, awkwardly, there was nothing else to say. In the end the two men had virtually nothing in common, and the emptiness crept back in between them. Fingers drummed lightly on knees. Heads turned, looking at walls, at nothing. In the quiet interval they could hear Celly talking in the other room. Aubrey's gaze drifted to the door for a moment, and there was a trace of sadness in his eyes.

"So, did the new chainsaw work out okay for you?" Mick asked, mostly to break the silence. "Because, I mean, I wanted it to be—"

"Oh, it's fine," Aubrey said, shifting in the desk chair. "It's great, thank you. In fact, it's better than the other one. Newer model."

"Really?" He knew, but Aubrey wanted to tell it.

"Oh yeah. The old one was a 310. The new one's a 350. More horsepower, and there's a compression release button—much easier to crank."

"Wow, okay. Didn't know that," Mick lied.

"So, what's happening with Mr. Harrelson's house?" Nobody but Aubrey ever called Hap "Mister Harrelson." "Are you two rebuilding it yourselves?" Aubrey was the sort who hired most things done despite the fact that he owned every tool known to man. Mick figured he just collected tools and preferred to keep them clean and new by not using them.

"Yeah, well, I'm doing most of the framing and he's rebuilding my truck engine for me."

"So who's paying whom?" For some reason this seemed to be an important point with Aubrey; his eyebrows were almost touching in the middle.

"Nobody, right now. We'll just get it all done and then settle up. Like as not, in the end there won't be a whole lot of money changing hands."

"I see," Aubrey said, and Mick could tell from the frown

he didn't see it at all. "So the two of you just barter work for work?"

"Not exactly, no. Me and Hap do things for each other without necessarily keeping score, that's all. It's just . . . we're *neighbors*, Aubrey. Around here, that's what neighbors do."

While Mick was talking, Aubrey glanced over his shoulder at the computer screen. The monitor was looping a slideshow of the pictures of Layne and the kids Mick had shot that morning with the digital camera. It captured Aubrey's attention.

"These are good," he said.

"What, the pictures?"

Aubrey nodded.

"Well, you know. Christmas morning. How you gonna mess that up?"

"No, I mean they're really good. You know how to frame a shot." He turned and propped his elbows on the desk.

Mick shrugged. "Pure luck. I'm not even sure what you're talking about."

"I'm talking about composition," Aubrey said, pushing his glasses up and leaning closer to the screen, pointing. "Look at this. Everything's in thirds. There's a kind of balance, and your eye is drawn to the right place. Where did you learn to take pictures like this?"

"I didn't. I told you, it's just luck."

"Well, then you're a natural. I've been into photography since my college days. Just a hobby, really, but I've been dabbling for a long time. I've taken classes, read books, bought all the right equipment, and I still can't compose a shot as consistently as this," Aubrey said, waving a hand at the screen. "What else do you have?"

Mick went to the cabinet under the bookshelf and dug out a couple old albums of stuff he'd shot with film before he got the digital.

Aubrey sat flipping pages for a while, stopping occasionally to lean over and look closely.

"You never went to school?"

"Not for photography, no." For some reason Mick wanted to sound like he'd been to school for something else.

"Well, you have some rough edges, technically, but you can *learn* technique. The thing is, you have an eye for the story, you know what I mean?"

Mick shook his head and chuckled. "Not a clue."

"All right. Let me see if I can explain it. I had an instructor once who said you can teach a child how to use a camera—it's just X amount of light for Y amount of time—but you can't teach anybody how to tell a story. How to *see* the story in front of them while it's happening."

Aubrey was really into this stuff. It was the first time Mick had ever seen him get remotely passionate about anything—except for his chainsaw. He looked down as he was flipping a page in the album and then, pausing, he looked back up at Mick.

"Did you take this?" he asked, pointing to a photo at the top of the page.

Mick leaned over his shoulder to look at it. "Oh, yeah. I shot that. Probably the best one I ever took. Dumb luck, I guess."

It was a picture of Dylan shot within seconds after he

was born. The midwife held him up the instant they cut him loose, all red and slimy with his arms flung out and his mouth open, screaming, and that's when Mick shot the picture. Exposure, framing, focus—everything was dead center perfect, for once, and the way the light hit him everything else faded to black—even the midwife's arms. There were just these two hands reaching out of darkness, holding a brand new life in the center of the light. Even now, he could look at that picture and *hear* the light, like angels singing.

"It's a great shot," Aubrey said, and there was a wistfulness in the way he was staring at it. "Brings back memories."

"You mean about when your kids were born?"

"Oh, no. About when I was in college and I thought I wanted to be a photographer. There was a picture I took that just . . . *inspired* me. Made me think I was destined for artistic immortality—for about a week."

Somehow, Mick couldn't picture Aubrey as an artist. The image just didn't fit. "So how come you didn't pursue it?"

"Ah, well . . . it just wasn't in me." He twisted around, squirming in the little desk chair as if he was suddenly embarrassed at revealing so much of himself, but he smiled a little, his eyes still remembering. "I majored in accounting. I don't believe I could have done otherwise, but until the day I die I will wonder what might have been."

It was right about then that Dylan came screaming through the room wearing nothing but his fuzzy pink earmuffs—buck naked and painted purple from head to toe. Running kind of flop-legged but still making pretty good speed, he banked off the desk and disappeared around the corner into the kitchen, from whence came screams and crashing sounds. Mick had seen he was clutching something in his hands, but he didn't know what it was until Ben came skidding through the room after him. Ben was carrying the remote for his new RC car, the antenna whipping from side to side as he ran, yelling, after Dylan.

Aubrey blinked, and his head tilted. "Purple?"

"Yeah. Must be that foam stuff. He likes bright colors. We have to hide Kool-Aid packets because he'll dump them in the sink, mix enough water in it to make a paste, and then rub it all over. You gotta admit the purple goes nice with the pink earmuffs, though."

11

Fribbles and penguins.

CHRISTMAS finally passed, and so did the rain. Mick was glad to see both of them gone. Georgia winters always cycled from warm and wet to cold and dry, so as soon as the rain passed and the blanket of clouds moved off, the night temperatures dropped into the twenties. But the days were beautiful. Mick went at it full bore and finished Hap's framing in a week. After Ben and Toad went back to school Mick could work pretty much all day, except for Tuesdays, when he took Dylan to the therapist and bought groceries. Hap's nephew, an out-of-work commercial form carpenter, came by most days to help, which freed up Hap to get Mick's engine rebuilt. By mid-January they had the house dried in and Mick got his truck back. It smelled a little mildewy, but he was glad to have it just the same.

It turned off nice and warm one afternoon, up into the

sixties. Mick was in his shirtsleeves up on the roof nailing down shingles when Aubrey came over. Mick was in a rhythm, so he didn't even notice Aubrey till he hollered up at him.

Aubrey worked in the headquarters of his father-in-law's building supply place over in McDonough, so he didn't usually get home before five. When Aubrey called to Mick he straightened up and looked at his watch. Seemed like no more than fifteen minutes since the kids got off the bus, but it had actually been two hours. He had worked way past quitting time. He unplugged the air hose, carried the nail gun down the ladder, then took off his pouch and wrapped the belt around it while he walked over to see what Aubrey wanted.

"I can't believe how fast that thing went up," Aubrey said, looking up at the roof. For a guy who worked in the building supply business, he didn't know a lot about building.

"Yeah, well it's just the framing, really, and it ain't the first time I've done it," Mick said. "Wouldn't have taken this long except that Hap wanted it a little bigger and we had to pour footings in the back. What's up?" He was thinking about having to go cook supper before Layne got home, and the kids probably had homework. A housewife's work is never done.

Aubrey avoided the mud, stepping on lumber scraps, trying to keep his good shoes dry while he made his way up onto Hap's new front porch. He was wearing a camera around his neck, a plain old-fashioned black SLR.

"Oh, I uh, well—" Once he made it onto the porch he was looking all around, checking out their framing. Mick thought for a minute he'd gotten distracted and forgot what he was going to say, but it wasn't that at all. He just didn't know how to say it.

"Ah, you see, Celly gave me a new camera for Christmas—latest and greatest, with all the bells and whistles—and I was thinking, you know, after you showed me some of your photographs, I just thought maybe you'd be interested in my old one."

"Your old what?"

He held up the camera that was hanging from his neck.

Mick winced. "Oh, I don't know, Aubrey. I'm sure it's a good camera but I'm a little short on cash right now."

"No, no, no, you misunderstand me. I wasn't trying to *sell* it to you, I just wanted you to have it."

Mick eyed him suspiciously.

"It's a good camera," Aubrey said. "A Nikon F3. It's not fancy, and it's got a lot of miles on it, but it's got a good solid metal body, virtually indestructible, a real workhorse. It just occurred to me I'll probably never use this one again—"

"You want to *give* it to me? You don't owe me anything, Aubrey." Mick tried not to act too surprised, but Aubrey had never seemed like the type to give anything away.

Aubrey stood there for a minute, turning that camera over in his hands, looking at it. His voice dropped a little when he said, "Well, all right, maybe I felt bad about you buying me an expensive chainsaw when you're unemployed. But I'm really not going to use this camera anymore and I just think you have the potential to be a good photographer with the right equipment. I *want* you to have it." He slipped the cord off his neck and held out the camera.

Mick took it and stood there studying it for a minute, not sure what to say. It felt solid and heavy and balanced in his hands, a real serious piece of equipment.

"Thanks," he finally said. "This is nice. This is more camera than I've ever owned."

"Don't mention it. Really. Go shoot a bunch of rolls, and bring the pictures over to me if you like. I'd be happy to give you a pointer or two. Better yet, if you shoot black-and-white I can develop them for you."

"Oh, I don't know, Aubrey. I appreciate the camera, really, but that sounds like a lot of trouble. I mean, like I said, you really don't owe me anything, you know?" It seemed like a little too much, a little over the top.

But Aubrey didn't appear to be listening anymore. He was watching Hap play with Mick's kids in the roughed-in living room. Hap and Ben and Toad were taking turns piling roofing shingles on Dylan, who was lying spread-eagle on his back on the sawdust-covered plywood subfloor, giggling. All you could see was his head and feet because the pile was getting pretty big. Most kids would have gone nuts, but Dylan loved it. He knew exactly where his arms and legs were when they were pressed under a pile of shingles.

"I know," Aubrey said quietly, still watching Hap play with the kids. Apparently he'd been listening after all. "I know I don't owe you anything, Mick. I just thought, you know . . . we're neighbors. It's what neighbors do."

———

The pictures in the album that had so impressed
Aubrey were taken with the camera Layne gave Mick for
his birthday right before Ben was born—a cheap 35 milli-
meter automatic, the kind that fit in his pocket. It was one
of those backwards presents, like when a guy gives his wife
a new shotgun because it's what *he* wants. Layne wanted
pictures, but she was a technophobe who didn't want to
mess with a camera. She just wanted to be able to sit and
leaf through snapshots of her kids in their Sunday clothes
holding Easter baskets, watching them grow from page to
page.

A closet romantic, Mick had always preferred the memory to the snapshot. If he got to thinking about the striper
he caught up at Lanier and went digging in the family
album, the fish in the picture always seemed small. Snapshots were too uncompromising. It was that way with
people, too—their pictures always looked worse than his
memory of them.

He liked landscapes. He'd always had a soft spot for old
barns and dilapidated houses leaning a few degrees out of
plumb, with holes in the roof, gray wood curling up and
peeling off—maybe with an old rusty truck parked up
against one end, forgotten, tires flat and weeds growing out
from under it. There were ghosts in places like that—
stories hidden in the shadows and deep in the grain of old
boards that real people with callused hands once measured
and sawed and nailed together on purpose to make a home,
boards that they sat on and leaned against every day for so
long that now they were full of the memory of laughing
and crying, the murmurs of lovers and the barking of dogs.

Old barns and empty houses, they remembered. Those

were the pictures Mick secretly longed to take, and that's what he was thinking about when he went home that afternoon with Aubrey's camera. He sat down at the desk and opened up the photo album to The Picture—the one of Dylan in the light—and just sat there staring at it.

He could still hear the angels.

————

When Layne got home from work Mick was still sitting at the desk fiddling with the camera, looking through the viewfinder, snapping the shutter. He really hadn't been paying attention to the kids. They were in the den watching wrestling on one of the fuzzy channels. Mick didn't even know Layne was home until he heard her talking to the kids.

He put the camera down and went to the doorway.

"What is this you're watching?" She was standing over them with her arms crossed.

"Wrasslin'," Toad answered without taking her eyes from the TV. Some guy with cartoonishly large arms and shoulders was right then body-slamming a bald-headed, tattooed fat guy. The one with the arms had his face painted in black-and-white tiger stripes. His hair was Elvis black and tied up like a shock of corn. Gothic.

"Turbo's gonna win," Ben said from the couch. "He's got a very scientific technique."

Dylan was sitting next to his sister, three feet out from the tube. He pointed. "He's dot black fingernails and earrings in his fribbles. He's the dood duy." He just couldn't make his palate wrap around a G. *Fribble* was Dylan's word for breast—he had his own words for some things. When

Layne saw Mick in the doorway she gave him one of those sideways looks and her tongue forced itself into her cheek.

"Change . . . the channel," she said, turning to Mick. She grabbed him by the ears and locked onto his eyes while she spoke to the kids. "I can't believe your father lets you watch that garbage."

"Sorry, I didn't know they were watching that. *Now hear this!*" he announced, "Henceforth, anyone caught watching professional wrasslin' will be summarily executed. And then flogged."

Ben giggled and changed the channel—he understood not only his dad's words but also his sense of humor. Toad and Dylan stared open-mouthed from their father to their mother, waiting for a definition.

"Big trouble," Layne told them. "No wrestling, okay?"

Mick didn't say anything else, he just slipped away to the kitchen and started cooking dinner. He was late for that, too.

This stuff was all new to Mick. He had run lots of construction jobs, so he was used to having a crew under him and having to answer to the boss for what they did. Managing a crew of hardhats came naturally to him, even when half of them had done serious jail time for one form of mischief or another, so how come he couldn't manage three little kids?

The conversation at dinner didn't help matters much.

"I'm glad I'm not a baby penguin," Ben said around a mouthful of mashed potatoes.

Toad stopped pushing English peas around her plate and looked at him. "Huh?"

"They have to eat their mother's barf," he explained.

Toad nodded, real slow. It was a serious conversation. Layne put her fork down and leaned forward to say something, but she got in a hurry and choked so that nothing came out.

"They prolly like it," Dylan said, staring cross-eyed at a forkful of meatloaf, as if it were covered with fungus.

Toad started laughing, warming to the subject. Layne's eyes bugged out, and she still couldn't talk. She grabbed her iced tea to clear her throat.

"Yeah," Ben giggled. "The penguins probably brag about it when they're old like Dad. 'My mom had the *best barf*!'"

"'*Your* mom!'" Toad hollered. "'Nobody could barf like *my* mom!'"

Mick was having a big time. He was laughing right with them, thoroughly enjoying his free-spirited and original-thinking children, when Layne got her voice back and shouted down the rebellion. Silence held for a second or two while she turned and gave Mick the slit-eyed look, but right in the middle of that little silence Dylan reeled off a letter-perfect imitation of a cat coughing up a hairball, and Layne lost it. Putting down a rebellion required dignity, and not even Layne could pull it off while she was laughing.

———

The next day, while Ben and Toad were at school, Mick got a fresh roll of film for the camera Aubrey had given him, and he and Dylan went to shoot some pictures of an old abandoned house down the dirt road a ways, back in among some old ivy-covered oaks. The light was all wrong, but Mick couldn't figure out why. When he got the pictures back he thought about showing them to Aubrey, but he just couldn't make himself do it. He was beholden enough. It was clear that Aubrey knew something about photography, and he said he'd be happy to share it with him, but Mick just couldn't do it. He couldn't make himself give that much ground. According to Hap, Mick always had been an independent cuss.

12

The Man With No Hands.

IT TOOK a while, but by the time Mick got done rebuilding Hap's house he was beginning to get used to the whole stay-at-home-dad thing. His fifteen-year routine had finally begun to fade and he rarely even thought about the high steel, or the crane, or the Man With No Hands. But in the first week of February they called him back up to the job for a hearing. Mick wouldn't have even bothered to go except that Bingham, the project manager who called him, said if a review panel found that Mick wasn't negligent he could end up getting back pay. He figured he could use the money, so he went. The hearing turned out to be a waste of time—nothing but office politics, and completely one-sided. It was all about covering their butts. Mick never had a chance.

It was cloudy and dreary when he got out of the meeting, the kind of damp cold that crept down the back of his neck. He zipped up his coat and was heading for his truck when he saw a raggedy little man in a hard hat shuffling off through the parking lot with a brand new right-angle grinder on his shoulder. When the guy looked back and saw Mick his pace picked up a bit. Obviously, he was stealing the grinder and heading back home with it—to Overpass Plantation.

The little grin on his face when he looked over his shoulder instantly reminded Mick of the Man With No Hands—the way he was looking over the wall and smiling when Mick was swinging. He decided on the spot to follow the guy, just wander down to Overpass Plantation and see if he could look up the Man With No Hands. He never realized until he found himself following the raggedy man down through weedy lots and shadowy places toward those bridges that he was actually a little bit afraid of the Man With No Hands, but there was something in him that always reacted to a deep-down fear by walking straight at it. He couldn't help it. Besides, Dr. Lethal was watching Dylan for him and he hadn't told her when he'd be back. He had the afternoon off. No need to hurry home.

Overpass Plantation was a regular small town of boxes and tents thrown together up under a couple of parallel bridges. They were good-sized, stout concrete bridges with a broad street running under them, but the traffic was all on top. Not many cars passed through underneath, which was probably why such a big homeless community was allowed to exist. Mick followed the guy with the grinder all the way down the slope by the nearest bridge, down to the edge of the street. He would have followed him right on across, but he got intercepted on the near side by a very tall woman in a very short red-sequined dress. She stopped right in his path, a few paces ahead, and waited for him. Mick couldn't help noticing the too-broad shoulders and the too-narrow hips as she slipped her pocketbook to the crook of an elbow and held up a hand, palm out.

"Where you goin', man?" The voice, not to mention the adam's apple, didn't belong to any lady.

The guy with the grinder had already crossed the street, and he glanced back with a little grin when he saw Red Dress intercept Mick.

"Nowhere," Mick shrugged. "Well, actually I was kind of looking for the Man With No Hands."

"Preacher? He up there." He pointed to the slope of concrete under the second bridge, on the near side of the street. "What you want wi' him?"

"Just talk. Just wanted to see him." Mick kept his hands out of his pockets, in plain sight.

Red Dress was watching his face closely. "Okay, you go on then. But you best not do no dirt to the Preacher, you hear me? And I wouldn't go over *there* if I was you." He pointed across the street. "The *devil* stay over there."

Mick wanted to ask him what he meant by that, but he hesitated a little too long and Red Dress sashayed on down the street, pocketbook swinging. Mick took his advice and didn't cross to the other side.

There were people all over the place—mostly men, but a couple of women and a few kids. Most of them were pretty scruffy and a few of them had to be either drunk or crazy, but for the most part they were just people. Their houses, if you want to call them that, were mainly wooden boxes built out of scrap lumber, but there were also a couple of tents and a few cardboard boxes—cast-off people and cast-off junk, all jumbled together and packed in under the bridges where at least the rain didn't get to them. Mick saw a recliner with the footrest missing from the frame, the seat piled with rolled-up clothes and plastic bags of what looked like loaf bread. Behind that was a grocery cart full of paint cans. The paint cans were shiny clean, the labels all peeled off—no telling what was in them.

There was a bigger than average box near the bottom with a little makeshift stovepipe sticking out the top. A toothless old woman wearing a mound of blankets stood next to it, pulling down a dirty sheet that looked like it might have been hung on the side of the box to dry. Mick asked her where he could find the Preacher. She pointed. The Man With No Hands was sitting in front of a small campfire near the bottom of the weedy shoulder of the second bridge. Mick had already looked there, but didn't recognize him because he wasn't wearing a hard hat. He wore an old-fashioned felt hat like men used to wear in the Depression, and it suited him. There were two other guys by the fire with him, all of them sitting on inverted five-gallon buckets they must have pilfered from the job. One of them rose from his bucket when Mick walked up, and he just kept unfolding. Mick figured he was about seven feet tall. The giant had a sock hat pulled down low over his eyes so that he had to lean his head back a little, even from that height, to look Mick over. He wasn't wearing a belt and his hands stayed busy constantly hitching his pants, front and back, while he stared at Mick like a boxer in an opposing corner.

"Mick!" the Man With No Hands called out, to give him safe passage, most likely.

"I'm surprised you remembered me," Mick said. "We only met that one time, but come to think of it I guess it was a pretty memorable meeting."

"That it was," the Man With No Hands said, and smiled. "That it was."

The giant hitched his pants one last time, then sat back down and quit staring at him.

A little guy with a red face and puffy eyes got up and left. The Man With No Hands motioned for Mick to take his bucket, so he sat down by the fire and acted like he was warming his hands. Somebody had made a little grill out of rebar and tie-wire, and a sooty aluminum coffeepot perked over the coals.

"Not too many outsiders have the nerve to come down here," the Man said. "But then, if I remember right, you do have a backbone."

"More backbone than brain, most of the time," Mick chuckled.

"I never did hear how you came out. None the worse for wear, I see."

Mick clicked his partial plate out with his tongue and grinned his missing teeth at him. The old man laughed, and the giant looked confused.

"Mick here is the ironworker I told you about who took a ride off the top of the building a couple months ago," he explained. Now the giant laughed, a big rumbling laugh, rubbing his hands on his knees.

"So, what brings you down here?" the Man asked. He kept his hooks in his jacket pockets.

Mick stared at the fire, shook his head, shrugged. "I don't know. Man, you wouldn't believe what all's happened since the last time I saw you. Up there." Mick pointed with his eyes. The giant giggled, made a little swinging motion with his hand. "I guess I just wanted to make sure you were real."

The Man took his hooks out of his pockets and spread his arms. "Well?"

"I don't know. The guys think you're some kind of spook—a miracle worker, or worse."

"Do you believe in miracles?" He had that little half grin on his face again, like he was toying with Mick.

"No."

"Well, then there aren't any. There. That was easy enough."

"Yeah, maybe too easy." Mick shook a finger at him. "There's something about you that makes people, I don't know, *scared* or something. Like the guy in the red dress down there—"

"Oh, you met Sheila."

"Yeah, he told me not to cross the street because the devil lives on the other side. What was that all about?"

"Oh, well, our little community has its social strata, the same as any other, except that the dividing line here is drugs. We've got our share of winos and potheads on this side, but the serious drug users live on the other side of the street."

"And prostitutes," the giant said. He rolled the R. Sounded Russian.

The Man With No Hands nodded. "It's all about AIDS, really. There's a lot of it on the street, especially among hookers and IV drug users. People are afraid, so they keep their distance."

"I see," Mick said. "So the devil doesn't really live over there."

"Sure he does. Unless you don't believe in the devil."

"No, I'm not gonna argue with you there. Matter of fact, I was in a meeting with him just a little while ago." He had to admit the Man With No Hands seemed a lot more human and personable in his own world than on the outside. Made Mick wonder if maybe it was the outside world that had a problem.

"But you didn't answer my question," Mick said. "How come people are scared of you?"

"Is no fear," the giant said quietly. "Is respect. Is love." He reached over and squeezed the Man's shoulder. "Tell story," he said, and gave him a gentle nudge. "Tell story, please."

"It's kind of a long story," the Man With No Hands said, leaning forward, propping his elbows on his knees and gazing into the fire. "But maybe I can hit the high points. See, I used to live on the other side of the street. I know the devil well. In my first life I was a chef, and a good one. I was the youngest chef at the Chateau in those days, and my future looked bright. I made friends with a lot of pretty people who had money and time on their hands, went to a lot of penthouse parties. First it was just a little cocaine, but one thing leads to another. I had a good wife and a future, and in the end I sold it all for the next fix—same story as every other junkie, I suppose. It took a couple years to make the whole trip, but basically it started at a party and ended up in an alley, lying in my own filth, wondering how

I got there and where my life went. Funny, I don't much remember the years between the party and the alley. It's all a blur. The devil shows you some sweet pleasure and you chase it to the end of the earth, but you can't catch it. One day, there you are at the end of the earth, with nothing. It happens to you so easily—so *incrementally*, you know? You just never really see the spiral you're in. After a while it's all about the fix, and you'll do anything to get high. Anything."

So far, the story was nothing he hadn't heard before, and Mick had never been prone to addiction of any kind, so he couldn't relate. He shook his head. "Doesn't fit. You don't talk like any junkie I ever met."

"Well, it can happen to anybody—trust me. You can take any road to any place. It just depends on where you turn."

"But you're clean now, right?"

"Oh, yeah, that was a long time ago. Another life."

"So, what happened?"

"A predator." He chuckled, pinching a red plastic cup out of his jacket pocket and pouring himself a cup of coffee. "There are predators out there, and they pick off the sick and the lame, like jackals. They've always plagued the homeless—everything from teenage boys clubbing winos for fun to twisted perverts who find guys passed out and set fire to them because they get off on the screams."

He took a sip of black coffee and was quiet for a minute. When he spoke again he didn't look at Mick anymore. "I don't remember much about what happened that night. I know I was high, and then there was this bright light and the earth was shaking."

Mick hadn't forgotten that everybody called him Preacher. He figured this was the part where the preacher would make the standard Jesus speech. Probably hallucinated some angels and walked the aisle at a tent meeting or a homeless mission.

"I remember an air horn, too," the Man said. "Close. Really close. Something hit me, and the next thing I knew I was in the hospital."

"You got hit by a truck?"

"Train," he said. "I found out later it was a guy they called the Stick. Friend of mine saw him drag me up to the track and lay my hands up there. My friend tried to get to me but he didn't make it—he was somewhat impaired himself. He saw the Stick over by the wall jumping up and down, laughing."

Mick pointed loosely at the hooks. "You mean somebody did this to you on purpose?"

"Oh, yeah, it happens all the time. It's just that homeless people aren't news—unless of course you get it on film. People love to watch."

He let out a low whistle. This was *not* what he had expected, but what could he say?

"That wasn't the worst of it," the Man continued. "Not by a long shot. The real hell was after that, in the hospital. When all you've got is bandaged stumps where your hands used to be, you can't do anything. I mean, think about it. You can't feed yourself, can't brush your own teeth. You can't even go to the bathroom by yourself."

"Can't pick nose," the giant said, miming the act.

"There's a lot of things you can't do. You sure can't shoot up, so on top of the sheer horror of losing my hands,

I was going through withdrawal and was in intense pain at the same time."

"But you were in a hospital. They gave you something for pain, right?"

"Yes, but what they gave me was nowhere near the level of narcotics I was accustomed to. They gave me all they could legally give me and it didn't make a dent. We're talking excruciating pain, here, and it went on for a long time. Soon as the grafts healed over the stumps I ended up strapped to a bed at Atlanta Regional."

Mick had heard of it. There was a detox unit there.

"Strapped down. You try to kill yourself or something?"

He nodded. "Couple times. I tried to go out a window on the sixth floor. I couldn't open it with my teeth, so I just backed up, got a running start, and tried to dive through the glass. But apparently I wasn't the first to try it. That window was bulletproof or something. When I came to I was lying in the floor bleeding, with a couple orderlies leaning over me, laughing. After that they kept me restrained. I remember some long nights. A lot of screaming."

"But obviously you got over it. So what happened?"

"Oh, eventually I got well enough to be fitted with these prosthetics, and when they ran out of bed space they declared me healed and put me back on the street. I remember standing there in front of the place thinking, *Which way?* It was crunch time. I mean, I knew. I knew beyond a shadow of a doubt if I went back "home" I'd find a way to score some smack inside of an hour, and I knew people who would push the plunger for me if I couldn't handle it.

"But right then I was clean, and stone-cold sober. Right then, in that lucid interval, I knew for a fact that I would never have a better chance to turn around and walk the other way. If I went back where I came from, I knew what would happen. It was just plain ugly suicide, and I wouldn't be able to resist it. Just thinking about that led me to the third option, which was to go down to the tracks and let the train have the rest of me. Get it over quick."

He wrinkled his nose, glared into his nearly empty coffee cup, flung the dregs on the ground and stuck the cup back in his jacket pocket.

"It was one of those stormy, gray summer afternoons," he said, locking his hooks together and settling his elbows onto his knees again.

"Been there," Mick said. "Pop-up thunderstorms rolling around, threatening to bust wide open any minute. Nervous times, up in the steel."

"I can't tell you . . . I don't think anybody can imagine the mental anguish I felt right then, standing at the intersection waiting for the light, literally at the crossroads of life and death, and knowing it for what it was. It's like the clock stopped for a moment—all the noise and thunder and voices went away, and the universe itself whispered to me and said, *'Well? What are you going to do?'* But I was worn out. I just wanted somebody else to take it off of me, to make a decision for me right then—either way—so I could turn my brain off and maybe not hurt so bad."

This was starting to sound familiar.

"I just couldn't hold it anymore, couldn't contain it. I looked up at those rolling black clouds. I didn't actually say any words, but it's as if all the pain and angst and confusion and guilt, along with everything I ever wondered about life and death and right and wrong, it all just sort of coiled itself together and sprang out of me right then and there. I know it sounds crazy, but that's how it felt."

Mick chuckled, but nervously, because he hadn't forgotten that morning at dawn, the day of the accident, when he was up in the steel alone.

"So, did you hear any voices?" he asked. He *must* have. Mick's throat was a little dry.

"Wait," the giant said, grinning. "Is good."

"No, I didn't hear a thing. I stood there for a minute or two, and then the light changed. I started to step off the curb, heading down to where I knew the train would come through, but before my front foot landed in the street a bolt of lightning hit the YIELD sign on the other side of the intersection."

"You're kidding."

"I'm dead serious. Lightning. BAM!! Just like that. It hadn't even started raining yet. You know how you jump when something like that happens—I nearly jumped out of my skin. It was just a reflex, but I came down heading in the other direction without even thinking about it, half blind, with a jagged blue line burned into my vision. And you know what else? I never looked back."

"So where did you go?"

He smiled a little, and his eyes looked at nothing. "It's a long, roundabout story, but the short version is I ended up at a monastery for three years."

"No way. You stayed straight?"

"As an arrow."

"Okay. I see," Mick snorted, and he did. He saw where

this was going. "You got religion."

"Religion," the Man With No Hands said quietly, staring at his feet. "Religion is what regular people get in order to stay out of hell. People who have already been to hell don't want religion, they just want to know God."

Mick raised an eyebrow. The things the Man said made a kind of sense, but they left another question. A big one. "You're telling me you came back here to live under a bridge, on purpose, just so you could preach to crackheads and junkies?"

A shrug. "These are my people."

"You gotta be kidding me."

He smiled, watching the fire. "Yeah. Sounds crazy, doesn't it."

"Sorry," Mick said. "I just . . ."

"It's okay." The old man glanced across the street, chuckling, and said, "I'll take an honest skeptic over a hypocrite any day, and in the context of the wider world you're a fairly soft-spoken skeptic."

"It just seems risky to me. I mean, for a recovering junkie to come *here* and try to rehabilitate other junkies. Seems more likely they'd drag you back in."

The Man thought about this for a second. "I worried about that at first, I guess, but the desire was gone. I didn't just kick a habit, my whole nature changed. I was clean, as if none of it had ever happened. The funny thing is, when I came back here after three years I still recognized some faces. There's a pretty big turnover—a lot of them dead or in jail, some of them just moved on—but there were still a few people who knew me from before. People I used to run with. I was braced for an argument, but they didn't even try."

He looked Mick square in the eye and said, "At first I thought maybe these hooks had bought me a little space, but it wasn't that at all. These people, they watched me. They waited, and watched to see if I was real, and for a while they didn't say anything at all. Once they made up their minds they fitted me back into their world, but here's the thing—when they saw I was clean, and *staying* clean, none of them ever asked me why. Not one. All they ever asked me was *how*."

Mick couldn't help admiring any man who refused to let people tell him how to run his life, and if what the Man With No Hands said was true then he was a man of strength and independence. But Mick's admiration only went so far. He admired the Man With No Hands, but that didn't change how he felt about the rest of them. Mick had always seen homeless people in general as failures, not victims, and nothing he'd witnessed here had changed his mind. They were real to him now—he'd gotten close enough to smell them and hear them talk and see the fear in their posture and the hunger in their eyes—but as far as Mick was concerned they had earned their troubles, same as he did. They had brought their troubles on themselves, one way or another.

Just the same, he went home and hugged his kids. Hard.

13

Snapshots.

IT DIDN'T take long for Mick to fall in love with the Nikon Aubrey gave him. He had to get used to all the manual options—play with the F-stops and figure out exposure times—but he could shoot with it all right. He carried it with him on Tuesday mornings when he took Dylan to his therapist, and on the way home he'd drive down back roads looking for old barns. Sometimes, if he found one he liked, he'd stop and shoot a roll of film, but when he got the pictures developed they were always just okay. When he laid them alongside professional landscape pictures he found in magazines they seemed flat and lifeless. Aubrey was right—there was something he didn't understand about lighting. He just couldn't see it. He showed a batch of them to Layne one afternoon while she was down in the floor reading *Yertle the Turtle* to Dylan. She flipped through them and handed them back.

"There are no people in them," she said. "What's the point?"

"I just thought you might be able to help me figure out what's wrong with them."

She lifted her chin from her palms to look up at him. "I told you, there aren't any people. That's what's wrong."

"I'm not taking snapshots, Layne. I'm trying to shoot photographs."

She tilted her head and looked at him kind of sideways. It was a little embarrassing, to tell the truth—a construction worker trying to explain to his wife that he was trying to be some kind of artist. It felt like a dirty secret.

"I see. Well, honey, I sure can't help you. I don't know anything about serious photography. You need to go see Aubrey."

He just stood there slapping his pictures against his leg. Seeing the look on his face, Layne handed *Yertle* to Dylan, stood up, put her arms around his neck and whispered in his ear.

"It's okay, Mick. There's nothing wrong with wanting to be creative, and it's perfectly all right to accept help from another human being."

"Aubrey doesn't really want me hanging around there," he mumbled.

She pulled back to face him, their noses an inch apart. "Yes. He does. He's our neighbor, and he's trying to be your friend. You just don't like him."

"He's kind of a nerd."

"You haven't given him a chance."

"He's just so . . . well-dressed and educated and *polite*."

"So am I."

He gave her a little squeeze. "That's different. You're built better."

"He can't help being rich, dear. You need to overcome a few of your prejudices. Some of them. Maybe."

———

No matter how much he adored his wife, no matter how persuasive she could be, Mick couldn't make himself go asking Aubrey for favors. He'd already gone too far just taking the camera from him. The balance sheet in his head told him things were just fine the way they were, and he didn't want to owe Aubrey any more than he already did. What he needed to know about photography he figured he could learn from magazines and how-to books.

He managed to get away from Layne without making any promises about Aubrey, and he already had plans for after supper. It was skate night. Normally Layne liked to do the nighttime extra-curricular stuff with the kids herself—the PTO meetings and dances and such—but she hated skate night, so Mick always went in her place.

Skate night was held at the indoor rink over in Stockbridge—a great big slick concrete oval with lots of spotlights and a glitter ball overhead, too-loud teenybopper rock music blaring from state-of-the-art speakers and a snack bar specializing in the three main food groups—hamburgers, pizza and Coke. Toad could skate like a pro. She just needed a ride to the rink; after she got there she didn't need help with anything. So that night Mick took Dylan along to see if he could handle a pair of skates. He figured it might force the kid to focus on where his feet met the ground.

When Mick first strapped the skates on Dylan he couldn't even stand up by himself. Mick tried to hold his hands loosely as they lurched around the rink, giving him enough slack to learn—and to fall. Every few seconds Dylan would do a split or a half-gainer and Mick's fists would flinch, catching him just in time to soften the fall. There was a kind of sense in what they were doing, and Mick marked it down in the little parenting guide he was building in the back of his mind.

Give him room to fall, but soften the landing.

He never knew what would happen with Dylan. Some things came easy. Other things that appeared to use the same muscles were completely impossible. Dylan couldn't jump a rope to save his life, so Mick figured there wasn't much chance of his being able to skate. He helped him around the rink most of the night, and then, finally, toward the end, something clicked and Dylan suddenly took off on his own. He staggered, he floundered, he waved his arms and fell down every ten feet, but he never quit. Once he got the merest glimpse of success, of possibility, his natural tenacity took over and he kept getting up until he didn't fall down anymore. By the time the rink closed he could actually skate a little bit. It wasn't pretty, but he stayed up.

While Mick was helping Dylan he noticed a bunch of kids skating in a cluster. When they rounded the far end and turned to face him Mick saw they were ganged up behind a wheelchair, pushing it. The kid in the wheelchair was skinny, and his knees and ankles looked kind of twisted. The whole group was having a wild time, zipping around the rink, hair flying, laughing hysterically. There were kids of all sizes, shapes and colors, all shoulder to shoulder pushing this wheelchair. The kid in the chair was laughing harder than anybody. The faces behind the wheelchair kept changing—some dropped off, others joined in, sometimes there would be six behind him and sometimes only one or two, but the kid in the wheelchair never stopped grinning.

Mick had his hands full with Dylan, so it was a long time before he noticed that the kids behind the chair seemed to be coasting, and that the wheelchair and its tires looked oddly heavy, and that the kid in the chair gripped a small joystick in his hand.

Motorized.

He was bitterly disappointed. The shine on that little cluster of kids dimmed considerably and his whole opinion of them changed. They weren't pushing, they were hitchhiking. They weren't looking to show the handicapped kid a good time, they just wanted a free ride.

But he kept watching. There was a spotlight pointed down on an angle at his end of the floor, and every time the wheelchair boy passed by he would charge out of the darkness and flash through that spotlight right in front of Mick. More than once he wished he'd brought his camera, just to try and catch that grin all lit up. The boy in the wheelchair was having the time of his life. It finally dawned on Mick that the boy wouldn't have had half as much fun if he hadn't been the one doing the pulling. For once in his life he was the one with an advantage, something special that gave him an edge and made him everybody's friend. The kids who hung on and let him tow them around the rink actually gave him more than if they had pushed him.

Mick couldn't get that boy's face out of his mind, even

after the last turn around the rink, after he pulled the skates off his kids, handed them in, laced Dylan's shoes and headed for his truck carrying Dylan and dragging Toad. The gleam in the wheelchair boy's eyes spoke to Mick. Driving home, one thought spilled into another and he started thinking about Aubrey again.

It had seemed strange to Mick, especially for a guy who didn't normally just give things away, that Aubrey would give him a perfectly good Nikon camera. Even his old one. And then he had offered to teach him about photography and even develop prints for him. It was too much. Like the kid in school who didn't have any friends, Aubrey seemed to be trying too hard. But after watching the boy in the wheelchair Mick began to wonder if maybe—just maybe—Aubrey *needed* somebody to ask him for help.

"When did you shoot these?" Aubrey asked when Mick took his pictures to him the next day. He was dressed for golf again. Loud plaid.

"Last week."

"No, I mean what time of day?"

"Oh. 'Bout noon, I guess. We were on the way back from the therapist."

"Yes, of course. That would explain it. Look, see the way the colors are all washed out? That's because the sun is directly overhead and the light's coming straight down. You have to take advantage of slanting light to create contrast."

He was pretty annoying, gesturing with his hands like he was making a speech at the club or something, but Mick could tell he knew what he was talking about.

"If you want to shoot landscapes you're going to have to do it early in the morning or late in the afternoon, Mick. Pound this into your head—*nothing* comes alive without contrast."

14

Expectations great and small.

LIKE a lot of men, Mick's calendar year was divided into only two seasons—baseball and football. He was never into basketball, so there was a hole, a great empty void in his year between the Super Bowl and the beginning of spring training—roughly from early February to late March. Every fourth year the Winter Olympics would come along and plug the hole if he could tolerate the figure skating, but the winter he came home to stay with the kids wasn't one of those years. Stuck at home with no games to look forward to and no grownups to talk to, the dead of winter was just that—dead as a hammer.

He and Dylan took to riding around looking for pictures in the mornings after they dropped off Ben and Toad at school. After he bought an equipment bag he started keeping the camera in the truck, along with plenty of black-and-white film. Morning light was magic. Evenings were always tied up with dinner and homework, but it didn't take long to figure out Aubrey was exactly right about the morning light. It was much better for pictures, he'd just been too busy to notice.

One morning, way back down a dirt road alongside the railroad tracks, they found an old abandoned shack covered up by kudzu. The world was winter-bare. No evergreen came near, and the old house was completely consumed with ropy, brown, naked vines, laced all across the windows and doors, climbing over the roof and running back down the other side. The house itself was built low to start with, and now it sat waist-deep in an impossible tangle of vines like a forgotten prisoner, lost and hopeless. The morning sunlight laid across it and made the window and door holes look even blacker and more forbidding through the vines.

"Probably snake infested," Mick said when he got out of the truck. Dylan pulled the door closed and retreated to the middle of the seat. Mick didn't tell him snakes weren't a problem in the winter.

———

Even in February the afternoons warmed up enough most of the time so that he and Dylan and Andy could get out and ramble in the woods a little bit. Sometimes they'd cut firewood or dig up a stump, but it was too cold to swim and there really wasn't that much to do when the yard was hibernating. It was Dylan's idea to build a tree house.

In the olden days when Mick was young, children would sally forth into the forest by themselves, without any grownups, and making use of whatever scrap lumber they could scrounge around the neighborhood and whatever bent nails they could forage, they would hammer a few short boards up the side of a tree for a ladder, then build a platform. No sides or anything, just a platform, rickety and crooked, and they'd spend ages playing there.

Kids didn't do stuff like that anymore—mostly, Mick figured, because it was too dangerous. Modern children, set loose with hammer and nails to build their own roost twenty or thirty feet up in a tree, completely unsupervised, would surely kill themselves. They'd saw their arms off, contract all manner of tropical fevers from rusty nails and spider bites, hammer their fingernails off, fall out of the tree and break their necks, and then some social worker would come haul away the survivors. He figured every generation of parents in history was equally horrified by the thought of their children doing the things they did when they were kids, and it never occurred to any of the parents that those were the very things that made them who they were.

They worked on the playhouse mostly after school. He'd pick up Ben and Toad, and the four of them would go out back and work for a couple hours before Mick had to go in and cook supper. He started out with the notion that they'd all build it together, but then there was that safety thing, and he soon discovered that the kids just weren't capable of doing work that was up to his professional standards. It had to be plumb and level, and strong enough to survive a hurricane or a major earthquake. In the beginning they helped a little, but Mick took the handsaw away from Toad when she gummed it up sawing on pine saplings, and he took the hammer away from Ben because he was using up all the nails driving them into tree trunks for fun. After the chainsaw incident at Hap's, Mick was pretty finicky about nails in trees. Eventually, the kids got tired of him taking the tools away from them and griping about the quality of their work, so they wandered off to do unproductive things like climbing trees and playing in the mud with Andy. Mick didn't really notice. He was building the fortress that he wished he could have had when he was a kid.

It started out simple enough, just a little house on four-by-four stilts attached to the side of an oak tree. But when Mick saw how much scrap lumber was left over from Hap's he decided they needed an annex with a footbridge so he could hang a couple of swings from it. Danny Baez came by one afternoon, and when he saw what Mick was doing he brought a bunch of rope. The safety man on the job had made them dump half a truckload of perfectly good rope just because it was frayed in a couple places. Mick made a cargo net out of it and fashioned rope handrails along both sides of the bridge. One of the guys from church, whose kids had grown up, gave him an old slide. He attached it to the annex to make an emergency exit. He used good stout three-quarter-inch pipe for the ladder, and made the rungs close together so Dylan wouldn't have any trouble climbing it.

When he was done he stood back and looked at his fortress. There was a hatch in the floor with a pole to slide down, and windows for looking out over their domain and defending themselves from attackers. It was grand. He rounded up the kids and took them up there to show it to them.

"You know, with the bridge and the ropes and everything, I think it looks a little bit like a pirate ship," he said, and waited for the applause.

"Cool," Ben said. "Can we go play now?"

Ben and Toad slid down the pole and disappeared. Dylan studied the pole for a minute with that dark look on his face, then crossed the bridge and went down the slide. He was afraid of heights, and he didn't trust his own arms and legs to get him down that pole without falling. The roof was low—kid height—so after they left Mick was standing there sort of hunched over, trying to figure out what had just happened. Andy was sitting in front of him with his big hind feet out to one side, staring at him.

"Where'd I go wrong?" Mick asked the dog.

Andy sighed, then got up and trotted across the bridge, slid down the slide and went to find the kids. It didn't even occur to him at the time to wonder how the dog got up there in the first place.

It was a little late when Mick came in from the play-house, so he was just getting things cranked up in the kitchen when Layne came home from work. When he saw the look on her face he thought she was unhappy because he was late getting dinner started.

"I've been out back finishing up the playhouse," he explained. "We're having pork chops. It won't take long."

Her mouth was kind of skewed to one side. "The kids are out in the front yard. Do you know what they're doing?"

He could tell by her tone it wasn't good. He went to the window.

"Looks like Dylan and Andy are digging a grave. Ben

and Toad are sword fighting. Hey, at least they're getting exercise, right?"

"And what are they using for swords?" One eyebrow went up sharply.

He turned to the window again. "Ah, it looks like the brass pedal-rods out from under your piano." Layne was extremely protective of her piano. The ebony six-foot Steinway bequeathed to her by her grandmother was the most valuable thing in the house. "I'll, uh, I'll just go out there and get them, okay?"

The kids followed him back in, and with a little prompting apologized meekly for dismantling the piano. Layne still had her travel cup in her hand, and she went to put it in the sink while they were groveling.

"What's all this Tupperware doing in the sink?" she asked.

Toad lit up like a Christmas tree. "OH! We were playing Taheckizzat! It's a awesome game, and I won! I guessed the green beans!"

"Taheckizzat?" Layne said, turning to Mick.

"A game we, uh, you know . . . a game we play when we clean out the refrigerator."

Now she was glaring.

"I guess you sort of had to be there. It really is kind of fun," Mick mumbled.

"How often *do* you clean out the refrigerator?"

"Whenever it needs it," he lied. "Okay, whenever we run out of Tupperware." Things were going from bad to worse.

She shook her head, chuckled, and started to walk out without saying anything else. He thought he'd heard the last of it, but when she was almost out of the room she stepped in an old dried juice spill on the tile, and when she lifted her foot it made that ripping sound.

She stopped. Looked over her shoulder at him.

"How often do you mop the floor?" she asked.

He shrugged. "Whenever it pulls my socks off?"

———————

That evening he left the kids home with Layne and escaped over to Aubrey's for a while. Standing in the red light of his darkroom he watched while Aubrey prepared to develop the negatives. The darkroom was bigger than Mick's kitchen, and probably better equipped. There were cabinets and countertops down both sides of the room, which Mick learned were divided into a dry side and a wet side. There were trays and beakers, funnels, measuring cups, canisters of chemicals, an enlarger that looked a lot like a drill press, timers and blowers and drying lights and magnifying glasses—he had every toy known to photography.

The first thing Aubrey did was take out a stainless-steel container the size of a pint jar.

"Developing tank," he explained, then he showed Mick some little spools. "First we wind the film onto these spirals, then put them in the tank for a few minutes. This part has to be done in the dark."

He flipped off the light. In total darkness he rolled the negatives onto the spindles, dropped them into the tank, and sealed the lid on the light-tight tank.

He turned on the red overhead light—dim, but better than pitch black. Then he unscrewed a smaller cap in the top of the tank and poured in the developer fluid. Every minute or so he would grab the tank by the ends and shake it to get the bubbles off the film.

"It's chilly in here," Mick said, rubbing his arms.

Aubrey nodded. "Sixty-eight degrees. The room is climate controlled. Temperature is important."

Perfectionist. When the timer dinged Aubrey funneled the developer back into the jug it came from and poured in a different chemical.

"An acid solution," he said. "It's called a stop bath because it stops the developing process."

A couple minutes later he changed the chemical again, to something he called a fixer. Two or three minutes later he dumped that out, pulled the lid off the tank and ran tap water directly into it.

"We have to let it rinse for a half-hour," he said, flipping on the fluorescent overhead light. "While we're waiting, let me show you a couple things. What do you want to do?"

"What do you mean?"

"What kind of photography are you most interested in? What gets you excited?"

"Oh. Old houses and barns. Landscapes, I guess. That's mostly what's on this roll."

Aubrey pulled two books down from a high shelf and laid them on the counter. Photography books. He spent the entire half-hour going over the essentials of landscape and architecture photography, talking about how to best reveal the "essence" of a place and its atmosphere.

"You're not just making a recording of what you see," he said, "you're trying to capture what you feel when you

see it. Like I told you before, you're telling a story, convey-
ing a mood."

"Um, Aubrey, this is all a little rich for me, you know?
I'm trying to follow you, but—"

"It's an art, Mick. You have to treat it like an art."

Mick scratched his head, winced. "Right. Maybe . . .
Listen, when you were at my house on Christmas Day you
were telling me about a picture you took. You said it
inspired you, made you want to take up a career in photography, but you never told me what it was. Maybe that
would be a good place to start."

Aubrey leaned back against the counter and eyed him
for a long moment, biting his lip. He didn't say anything,
yet there was a wariness in his eyes and Mick sensed it was
a question of trust. Then he pulled an album down from a
shelf and opened it. From the first sleeve he pulled an
eight-by-ten black-and-white glossy photograph and
handed it to Mick.

"I shot this in college. I'd just gotten my first Nikon,"
Aubrey said. "The one I gave you. I was downtown with a
couple friends on a Saturday afternoon and happened to
have my camera in the car. We ran into a traffic snarl—
police cars all over the place, yellow tape, crime scene. So I
pulled over, grabbed the camera and ran up to the second
floor of an abandoned warehouse across the street to see
what I could get."

Mick was drawn into the photograph. A ring of uni-
formed police held a crowd back from a man lying on the
sidewalk, face down, his arms out in front of him and a
handgun just beyond his reach. There was a little nook
where the façade of one building stuck out farther than the

other one, and a kid stood with his back in the corner, staring down at the man on the sidewalk. The camera zoomed in at a perfect angle, just over the heads of the police, drawing Mick's eye straight to the face of the boy backed into the corner. He was maybe ten years old, wiry, a little too streetwise for his age, and the look on his face was not one of sadness. He was angry. There was a sense of loss in his eyes, but it was an angry loss. A loss of betrayal. His eyes said, *"How dare you get killed."*

Aubrey waited, silent.

Mick looked up, met his solemn gaze. "It was his father, wasn't it."

Aubrey nodded slowly. "I don't know, maybe it was dumb luck, but that picture captured whole lifetimes in an instant. Generations. Eternity. It's all there."

Mick studied the picture, the boy's face, the rigid posture. "Yeah," he said softly. "Twenty years later it'll happen again."

"One way or another. There's power in story, Mick. In being able to capture a truth like that in one quick snap. *That's* what I'm talking about."

The picture explained a lot, not only about the power of photography, but why it meant so much to Aubrey.

"I still don't understand why you didn't follow up on it," Mick said. "It's clear from *this*"—he raised the photograph—"that you care, a lot, about photography. Why didn't you stay with it, do it for a living?"

The merest flash of pain came into Aubrey's eyes then, and he turned his back to shake the tank one more time. His shoulders shrugged and he said quietly, "I guess it was because there weren't any guarantees. I have to have order,

Mick. I have to know things are in their places and tomorrow is all planned and paid for, that's all. I admire the art, but I could never live the life."

———————

When the negatives were ready Aubrey unrolled them and hung the strip up in a long cabinet in the corner, clipping a clothespin to the bottom to keep the strip from curling as it dried. Then he took some kind of scissor-like squeegee from a drawer and wiped it down to take off the excess water. When the negatives were dry enough to suit him he fitted them into the top of the enlarger and fastened a sheet of print paper into the flat bottom.

Mick had never seen it done before, so the whole process was like magic to him. Aubrey kept up a steady lecture while he developed a stack of prints and fed them into a drum dryer that looked for the world like an old mimeograph machine. He said there were all sorts of tricks, things he could do during the developing process to change the way a finished print would look. He held his hands in the way of the projector beam on one print just to show Mick how the light could be altered.

The prints came out of the dryer curled up, so he laid them out on the counters to flatten. Then he started going down the line examining them with a magnifying glass. He went over them pretty quickly until he got to the ones of the kudzu house.

"Where did you find this place?" he asked.

"Down that little access road off of Highway 3, close to Tara Boulevard. By the tracks."

"Amazing. I've been through there a hundred times and

never noticed this. You have an uncanny eye."

"So, you like the pictures?"

"No, I like the subject. The pictures are overexposed. Have you ever heard of the Sunny 16 Rule?"

"No."

"Okay, back to basics. Basic daylight. If you're shooting a front-lit subject in full sun, set the shutter speed to 1/100, assuming you're using 100 speed film, and F–16. Got it?"

Mick had spent hours fiddling with the camera and knew the knobs and switches pretty well by then. "There is no 100 on the shutter speed dial of the F3," he said.

Aubrey frowned. "That's true, but get as close as you can. Set it to 125. If you'll make a habit of switching to manual exposure mode and locking in those settings, you'll do fine in direct sunlight. What happens to a lot of amateurs when they use automatic settings is the camera's internal light meter gets fooled. If you go to manual you bypass the meter." His eyebrows went up and he raised a finger, just like a schoolteacher. "*But!* If the subject is lit from the side, like this one here, you want to increase exposure one stop. That's why this one's not quite as over-exposed. Do you know how to bracket a shot?"

He pulled his new camera from the shelf and showed Mick how to do it. He told him where to start from, and how to compensate for a dozen different variables, all depending on angles and intensity of light—way more information than Mick was capable of absorbing in one sitting. But it helped. Mick didn't understand half of what Aubrey told him about light and exposure, but he did get the Sunny 16 Rule and how to bracket a shot. He figured he could work out the rest. Eventually.

15

The road to hell is paved with tourist dollars.

THE KIDS were out of school for a week in February for no apparent reason, except that the school board had decided to give them more time off during the winter—the latest move in the ongoing battle to force kids to go to school year round so working moms wouldn't have to feel guilty about summers. Mick didn't see the vacation coming, but Layne did. She cheated. She looked at the school calendar. She had scheduled the week off for herself before she even knew Mick was going to be out of work. Now, since they were all free at the same time for once in their lives, she planned a real vacation.

He'd never actually laid eyes on it, but Mick knew that *somewhere*—probably in the Library of Congress or someplace like that—there existed a Supreme Parenting Handbook. It was carved out of stone, and chiseled somewhere on the first tablet was a law that stated very clearly, "While your children are still young enough to believe in Santa Claus, you *must* take them on a vacation to that shining city in central Florida." It was Law. He wasn't sure what would happen if they failed to comply with The Law, because as far as he knew, no one had ever had the guts to deliberately flaunt it.

He tried. Mick didn't think they needed to spend the money, so he put up a valiant fight, but in the end The Law won. In the end, he discovered he couldn't win an argument about money because he wasn't making any.

So it was inevitable. They would make a pilgrimage to that vast playground where fantasy reigns and the surly bonds of earth are temporarily lifted, along with your wallet.

The friction started early, when Mick began referring to the place as Hell. He had developed a bit of an attitude.

Layne planned their trip to Hell like a military campaign, mapping out weeks in advance where they would stay and which theme park they would target each day. She felt sure late February was a perfect time to go because nobody else would be there and the Brannigans would have the parks pretty much to themselves. Much later, Mick would point out that her reasoning was probably sound because the greater part of New York City and a fair portion of Massachusetts, Pennsylvania, Canada, the Dominican Republic and South America had thought precisely the same thing.

They drove all day Saturday and stopped about an hour short of Hell, where they checked forty or fifty places before finding a vacancy at the Oasis Motel. The sign said *Free H O, contl bkfst*. Mick stood in line thirty minutes to get to the desk, where the night guy informed him, while digging in his ear with his car key and running a finger down his dwindling list of rooms, that the next day was the biggest race of the year at Daytona, and he was in possession of what he was pretty sure were the last two available rooms between Atlanta and Miami. He would be very happy to provide Mick with a clean room—although there were no nonsmoking rooms left—but if he wanted to think about the price he needed to step aside because the gentleman behind him already had his Platinum Card out of his wallet.

———

Mick flicked a dead roach from the pillow. "Isn't that supposed to be a mint?"

"In some countries, but I'm not sure about Florida. Mustn't be prejudiced," Layne said.

He stomped a bug into an asterisk on the carpet and went to get a Kleenex, but when he came back he couldn't find the asterisk. Apparently the shag carpet had been chosen for its camouflaging properties.

"And the TV doesn't work, either," he growled. "Yessir, free HBO."

Layne shrugged. "The sign said 'Free H-*blank*-O'. Maybe it was supposed to be a 2."

The next morning they turned down the free "contl bkfst" and ate at the Waffle House, after which a toll booth got them in the spirit of the place by charging two dollars for the privilege of driving down the highway to Hell. They had reservations for the rest of their stay, and since they couldn't check in until later Layne decided they would go straight to one of the parks and spend the day frolicking—put the bad start behind them. While they sat in a two-mile line of cars watching the engine overheat they learned from the radio that they'd fetched up in Hell during the biggest convention week in the area's long, proud, convention-mongering history. Forty-five minutes and seven dollars later they parked the car and started the long hike to the ticket office, where they stood in line for twenty minutes to hand over a mortgage payment for a three-park pass, then stood in line another fifteen minutes for the tram ride to the actual gates of the park, where there was a ten-minute line to get in.

Once inside, the lines vanished. A line requires definition—it isn't a line if no one can tell where it starts or where it ends, or who's in it and who's not. Inside, there was only a great, oozing, shifting sea of humanity as far as the eye could see. They didn't exactly walk, they just drifted like jellyfish from one attraction to the next. Every now and then Mick got a glimpse of the trappings of the park itself, and from what he could see over the heads of the crowd it was magnificent, a wonderland of brightly colored plastic.

Mick started making up his own names for the rides. They inadvertently waited ninety minutes to ride The Spleen Buster—to be fair, they didn't know they were in line for the first hour—and then found out at the door that Dylan wasn't tall enough. All was not lost, though. Mick spent most of the ninety minutes with his nose pressed to the shoulder blade of a three-hundred-pound cabbie from Brooklyn who turned out to be a really nice guy. He promised to write.

It was just as well they didn't make it onto The Spleen Buster. Dylan had been on a roller coaster once and hated it. He wanted nothing to do with any so-called amusement that went clacking up into the sky and then plummeted back to earth. He only wanted to ride the kiddie rides—the little teacups and such. He started crawfishing at the sight of the roller coaster. And then they lost Layne in the crush.

After they regrouped—Layne spotted them by shinnying up a lamppost—Ben said he was thirsty, so Mick fought his way to a pop stand where he gave the guy a twenty for five bottles of Coke. The guy rolled his eyes, muttered something about "hicks" and told Mick he was short four dollars. Later, when she got knocked down and trampled, Toad was lucky enough to land on top of a map somebody had thrown away. From the map Mick learned that the park consisted of six major rides—by *major* they meant no pregnant women, heart patients, neck braces, small children or sissies—six kiddie rides, eighteen brassy, obnoxious, Broadway-style reviews, four hundred and thirteen "restaurants" where you could buy a small Coke for nine dollars and a hotdog for seventeen, and nine hundred and six trinket shops where you could buy cheap plastic souvenirs for a king's ransom. In spite of the prices, it seemed everywhere Mick went he could hear some fat guy in plaid Bermuda shorts, dress shoes, brown socks and a pork-pie hat braying about how cheap everything was.

They had to hurt a few people to do it but they finally made it onto two of the major rides before the park closed. Actually, it was just Toad, Ben and Mick riding the first one because Dylan dug his heels in and started screaming. Layne took him to the teacups while the rest of them stood in line for a sadistic roller coaster Mick called Permanent Brain Damage. Most of the people coming off the ride stopped in the gift shop and bought a T-shirt with the name printed on it. Every major ride had a gift shop at the end so people couldn't escape without winding their way through a maze of T-shirts, key chains and coffee mugs, all with the name of the ride printed on them. It was a great marketing strategy because it allowed parents, who couldn't possibly make it to daylight without their kids dragging stuff off the shelves and begging to buy it, to shell out several hundred more dollars for the privilege of advertising the place.

The other ride they managed to fight their way onto was a nice relaxing river float where their boat drifted past an assortment of rubber dinosaurs roaring at them from the banks, then plunged over a two-hundred-foot cliff into a pond. The name of that one was either Compressed Vertebra or Death by Drowning—Mick vacillated because his short-term memory was getting a little spotty by then. Dylan rode that one with them. He got on the ride before he found out about the plunge over the cliff, but when that boat tilted up and started clacking he knew what was about to happen. Mick had to hold him down hard to keep him from jumping out. He thought for a minute Dylan was having a seizure.

The combined effect of the full day was a bit like being mugged by a motorcycle gang, keelhauled, robbed and left for dead, but the weather was nice. Bloody but unbowed, they hobbled the six miles back to the Explorer. The drive to the motel turned out to be a leisurely two-hour crawl in bumper-to-bumper traffic through eight miles of potholes, striped plastic barrels, jackhammers and flashing yellow lights.

"All things considered," Mick said, "a lot more relaxing than the park. But for another two hundred a night we could have stayed inside and avoided all this."

"Relax," Layne said, winking and nodding toward the kids. "This is supposed to be fun." She'd been reading the brochures again.

They checked into their deluxe accommodations—the room came with a little refrigerator—then went out for dinner at the same time as everybody else in the western hemisphere. They waited an hour for a table, then paid a car note for some spectacularly mediocre spaghetti.

The next morning they got up early and waited an hour for a breakfast table, then muddled through rush-hour traffic to the next park on the list. It was pretty much the same as the first one, except the lines were longer. For the whole two hours Mick spent waiting in line to ride Soiled Trousers there was a tattooed pagan girl from the Bronx pressed so hard against his back he was afraid he'd have permanent imprints from various body rings. She slapped him once, but he assured her he was just checking to make sure his wallet was still there.

The most popular ride in the park was the one where a rubber shark roared at them and simulated cannon splashes filled their shoes with water.

After the first couple days Mick learned to carry a backpack full of iced-down soft drinks with him. He figured it saved roughly a hundred and fifty dollars a day, plus it dripped ice water down the back of his pants, which cooled him off, and it prevented any further body-ring imprints on his back. Two days in the trenches had taught him well. He was a battle-hardened veteran.

The last morning, while the Explorer was stuck in traffic on the way to yet another theme park, it started to rain. Hard. Mick looked around at the faces. They looked like a Marine recon platoon on the way back from Vietnam. Out of the blue, Layne turned to the kids and asked, "What do you say we just go home?"

Ben, who was looking kind of shell-shocked until she said that, sat up.

"I want to go home and sit on the couch and watch TV."

"I wanna doe play with Andy," Dylan said.

"I miss my climbing tree," Toad chirped.

Layne saw Mick's chin quivering and misunderstood. She put her hand on his arm, gently.

"It's okay," she said. "We can use the last day on our pass anytime. It never expires. We'll just save it for the next time we're down this way."

He thought about this for a long time, trying to find the right words. It was not easy, and they had left Hell far behind before he spoke again. The windshield wipers were slapping softly and the kids were unconscious in the back, sleeping off the sensory overload.

"Layne?"

"Yes?"

"Um, about using our pass the next time we come this way?"

"Yes?" She was smiling, bless her heart.

"I'd rather be staked out naked to a fire-ant bed and forced to watch soap operas while a patch-eyed pirate with

Parkinson's removes my pancreas with a sharp stick. Yo-ho, yo-ho."

It was a bull's-eye, and like a thousand other times in his life he immediately wished he hadn't said it. Layne's lips disappeared.

"You've done your best to ruin this trip for all of us," she said quietly. "I wish you wouldn't complain so much."

Pride got the better of him, and he joined battle. Like two old warships, they sat there and let each other have it, broadside, driving up the expressway. They didn't notice when Dylan woke up and let himself out of his car seat, or even when he climbed up between them—they just kept firing over his head. He sat down on the console, staring out the front of the car, and started singing the Barney song. When they ignored him, he sang louder.

Dylan didn't sing particularly well but he was definitely loud. He drowned them out. When Layne told him to get back in his car seat he ignored her and sang louder. When Mick threatened him he sang louder still. Finally, they went to neutral corners—Mick kneading the steering wheel and muttering to himself, Layne steaming up the window on the passenger side. When they stopped fighting, Dylan stopped singing. For maybe another five minutes he just sat there between them on the console holding his knees, then he turned around, climbed back into his seat and latched himself in.

16

Livestock.

MAYBE it was the first signs of spring—
daffodils, little clumps of lavender thrift blooming at the
ends of the driveways, clouds of redbuds lining the roads.
Whatever caused it, Mick got a case of spring fever. If he'd
had any sense he'd have gone fishing, but the malady man-
ifests itself in a thousand different ways, and he ended up
buying chickens instead. Hap's brother sold them to him,
six of them. They were shiny, black, healthy-looking laying
hens, and Mick brought them home in a crate and let them
run loose in the backyard while he and Dylan rounded up
some pipe and roofing tin, and borrowed a bender from
Hap. It took the better part of a day to build a good solid
chicken coop on the edge of the woods down behind the
house—two plywood sides to keep the wind off, with
chicken wire around the rest, a tin roof, a place to roost and
a long shelf where they could lay eggs.

For the first two weeks he kept them penned in the coop so they'd get used to laying their eggs there and not scatter them all over the woods. Then he started letting them out during the day and spent the next two weeks trying to convince Andy they weren't his private hunting stock.

Those chickens were weird. He couldn't tell what it was they were eating, but they were always pecking at something. They'd pounce on the handfuls of chicken feed Dylan scattered on the ground every morning, but then they'd clean that up pretty quick and go right back to bugs and grass. Sometimes, on up in the warm part of the day, they'd dig holes in the dry dirt up against the house behind the shrubbery, then squirm down in there and fling dirt all up in the air.

He never did figure out why, but they hated the nice comfortable chicken coop he built for them, and they would only go in it at sunset when they were ready to climb up on the roost for the night. They laid eggs behind the bushes, under the deck, in the woodpile, under the swing set—everywhere but in the nesting place he'd built for them in the coop. Every day was an egg hunt, and Dylan loved it. It took a while to figure out that a couple of them were laying their eggs in the doghouse. Mick had built the doghouse when Andy was a pup, and like everything else, he overdid it. He roofed it with leftover shingles from the house, insulated the walls with Styrofoam, lined the floor with carpet, cut a vent in the back and put it in the shade up under the deck so it would stay cool in the summertime.

Andy wouldn't go near it. He hated that doghouse, but

the chickens loved it. They paraded in and out all day long like it was a convenience store or something. Mick tore out the carpet and put straw in it. Crawling in the doghouse and looking for eggs was the highlight of Dylan's day. Sometimes he'd just sit in there for a while, holding a chicken, stroking its feathers, rubbing his face against its back. The chickens didn't seem to mind, and whenever Mick found something Dylan liked he tried to let him do it. His therapist said it was important to give Dylan some slack and let him "seek out sensory experiences commensurate with his level of development." So Mick let him play with the chickens all he wanted. He was way too clumsy to catch them in the open, but when he hemmed one of them up in the doghouse he'd sit in there and pet it for an hour.

Dylan was afraid of a lot of things. Some of his fears were so strange it took a while to figure out what they were. Besides normal stuff like rats and heights he was scared of antiques, clowns, anything bright yellow, and anybody dressed up like an animal. When they went to Hell there were people walking around dressed up like cartoon characters, and when the big duck tried to come up and shake hands with Dylan he bolted screaming between Mick's legs, scampered up his back like a monkey and latched onto his neck. Almost choked him to death. But the darkness and tight spaces inside the doghouse never bothered him at all. It was as if he needed close confinement sometimes, as if his world needed closer horizons.

Dylan liked the chickens so much that when Hap told Mick his brother had a goat he wanted to get rid of Mick took it without a second thought and put it in the backyard. It was a small goat, some kind of dwarf, the color of a deer except for a white saddle across her back, and she loved Dylan right from the start. Whenever she saw him in the yard she'd run to him, put her face under his arm and let him scratch behind her ears. She didn't do that with anybody else, just Dylan. He didn't give her a name, though, he just called her "the doat."

Andy liked the doat, too. After he got yelled at once or twice he wouldn't give chase while Mick was around, but as soon as Mick turned his back he'd hear bleating and hoofbeats and he'd know Andy was at it again. He kept a pretty close eye on the sliding glass door, too, because once or twice the goat bolted for it when Andy was after her. He didn't even want to think about what might happen if the two of them got loose in the house.

Apart from that, the goat wasn't much trouble. Mick didn't even have to build a house for her because the goat immediately seized on the empty chicken house and claimed the laying shelf for her own. She spent most of her time eating the flowers and shrubs out of the backyard— the chickens had already pulled up most all of the grass— but when she got tired she'd go in the chicken coop and hop up on the laying shelf for a nap. Mick was out back trimming what was left of the shrubs one afternoon and missed Dylan. He'd last seen him going into the chicken coop, so he went down there and found Dylan and his doat curled up together on the shelf, sound asleep.

He got a great picture.

17

Spring break.

IT RAINED during spring break. When the clouds finally broke Mick threw the kids out of the house and they brought that red Georgia mud back in with them. He made a mental note to take a jar of mud with him the next time he went to buy carpet, and color-match it.

He'd been home for several months by then, and his sanity was starting to slip. He'd always had a boss, all his life. Half the time his boss had been a nut bag, but he was still the boss. There had always been clearly defined goals complete with blueprints, and they were always at least somewhat predictable. He knew when he went to work in the morning that he would be tying down a slab, or building columns, or flying in I-beams that day.

But now *everybody* was his boss—including his wife, three kids, a dog, a goat and a bunch of chickens. He never knew from one minute to the next what kind of madness lay around the corner. He drank his coffee in cold half cups and couldn't remember eating lunch. Sometimes he'd find a moldy half cup of coffee sitting on a shelf where he had set it down when he stopped to pick up the shards of a picture frame smashed by a stray football three days earlier.

There was one particular day when Mick got up at six thirty, got dressed, made coffee, started Layne's oatmeal, and then picked up a basket of dirty clothes and headed for the laundry room. On the way past the living room he spotted a pair of socks in the floor—probably Toad's—so he put the basket down in the foyer by the front door and went to pick up the socks.

Since he was already in there by the desk, he checked the e-mail because sometimes the lawyers at Layne's office changed her plans in the middle of the night and sent her off to do some of their legwork. The dial-up was painfully slow, and while it was still bonging and hissing he heard Layne calling to him from the bedroom door. There were no towels. He ran to get one out of the pile he'd washed the day before, still in the laundry room.

On the way back through the kitchen he noticed the oatmeal was boiling over. By the time he gave Layne her towel and cleaned up the oatmeal mess, Ben and Toad were up, in their pajamas in the middle of the den, fighting over the remote. While he was settling the fight he happened to look out through the sliding glass door and noticed that during the night Andy had brought home a sizable chunk of a deer's hindquarter in a fairly advanced state of decomposition, and dragged it up onto the deck. He put his shoes on and went out to deal with the deer carcass. While he was out there he noticed he had forgotten to put the sealer on the new section of the deck.

Between meals and floors and dishes and juice cups and spill control, he dipped a drowned rat out of the pool, sprayed weed killer on the poison ivy, filled in the hole Andy dug under the fence, cut the grass, hauled the garbage out to the road, finished building the new steps to the deck, fertilized and bug-sprayed the flower beds, fixed the latch on the back gate, went to the building supply place for sealer, the pool place for chemicals, and the grocery store for something to cook for supper.

When Layne got home from work, supper was on the stove and Mick was helping Ben with his history project. School was starting back in a couple days and Ben had waited until the last minute to tell his dad he was supposed to be using some of his vacation time to build a replica of the *Merrimac*. Mick, of course, went overboard. In the beginning he was just going to cut out a piece of quarter-inch plywood for a base, but then he got carried away.

Ben finally brought him back to earth when he rolled his eyes and said, "Dad, it's just a report. The cannons don't have to have real smoke coming out of them."

Layne, just coming in from work, hanging up her pocketbook and pulling off her earrings, wanted to know why the phone had been off the hook all day.

Mick looked up, puzzled. "Oh yeah," he said absently. "The e-mail."

"And why is there a basket of dirty clothes in the foyer?"

"I was on my way to the laundry room with them."

"But dear," she said patiently, "that basket of clothes

was sitting right there in that same spot when I left the house this morning. What have you been doing all day?"

————

The weather turned off gorgeous on the last day of spring break. The kids watched *Wanda's World* that morning while they slopped cereal on the carpet. Wanda was one of those irritatingly perky moms who grinned all the time and constantly looked surprised, as if her eyelids were stapled to her forehead, and she flitted from project to project like a hummingbird on speed. She made Martha Stewart look like a slug, and she made Mick wish he was still an ironworker. That morning, after demonstrating "How to build an herbal terrarium from the weeds in your yard," "Forty-nine fun things you can make from a broken umbrella," "How to make a battleship out of toilet paper tubes," and "Paris—an origami replica," she explained how you could keep your kids from soiling Aunt Minnie's fine upholstered dining room chairs by sewing ribbons to the corners of a handkerchief to make a seat cover and using a pillowcase to cover the back. Somewhere in the middle of all that she showed the kids how to make a kite out of a Hefty bag.

They'd had kites before, but Layne always just took them to Wal-Mart and bought the ones with cartoons on them—Spiderman and Sponge Bob. In Mick's day they used to make kites all the time out of paper grocery sacks, so he knew more or less how to go about it. He found some stiff plastic tubing and a big roll of construction twine among the junk in the garage, and they put it all together with duct tape. Ben kind of did his own thing, but Mick had to help Toad and Dylan build theirs.

"I really need to aerate the lawn and throw some seed," Mick said, looking up at the sky. "I finally get a couple days of decent weather and here I am, building *kites*."

He did resent it a little. There were things he really needed to get done, but with three kids demanding his attention he never seemed to know from one minute to the next what he was going to be doing. There were days, still, when he just didn't want to be a mother. He wanted his old life back.

Toad was down in the floor putting a cross of duct tape in the middle of a bag, getting ready to punch holes for the braces, when Mick snapped at her for about the fourth time because she was doing it all wrong. She stopped and looked up at him with an earnestness that only a seven-year-old girl can own, and said, "Dad, you just don't know how to have fun, do you?"

"Maybe not," he muttered, feeling a little ashamed. "Not sure I remember it."

He took them up to the big field on the other side of Hap's place to fly the kites. The first half-hour was a back-breaker because the wind was too strong and the kites kept nose-diving into the ground. There were three kids and only one dad, so he spent a lot of time sprinting to which-ever kid squawked the loudest and getting his kite airborne again. He finally sent Ben back to the house for some old pantyhose to make tails out of. Later in the day, after Layne got home, he found himself wishing he'd paid closer atten-tion when Ben came running back into the field with a big handful of pantyhose. If he'd been on top of things Mick would have asked Ben exactly where he got them from.

But he didn't. Though they did seem remarkably runless for ragbag pantyhose, the honest truth was that he was too busy to notice it at the time. He cut them in half with his pocketknife and knotted them together. It took three or four lengths to keep a kite straight in that wind, but then it worked great.

The kids had a blast. They cut sticks for handles and wound the strings around them, then flew their homemade kites all the way out to the end of the string and held onto the stick, arms bobbing, for a half hour or so. Mick kept looking at his watch, thinking about the lawn.

When Dylan let go of his stick—which was inevitable, really, just a matter of time—Mick got a little irritated. He'd spent all morning helping build that kite, and then Dylan let it go, just like that. But there was nothing he could do about it, so he said nothing.

"Look at that!" Ben cried. "It's gonna go right into the stratosphere!"

He was right. With a long pantyhose tail and fifty yards of string anchored by a stick, the kite was incredibly stable. It sat there steady as a rock, facing into the wind without a twitch, climbing serenely away.

Then he saw the second kite pulling away, with its string hanging down, an untended stick twirling slowly at the end of it. Toad had let go. Thirty seconds later there were three, as Ben liberated his kite, and they formed a staggered line up into the blue. For Mick, it was frustration cubed. He couldn't quite understand why they'd put so much work into something like that and then just let it go.

But then he looked at Dylan's face.

His mouth was open. His hands were clasped in front

of him and he actually shivered with excitement, watching that thing climb like a helium balloon. Toad and Ben were caught up in it, too.

He'd almost forgotten the camera. He'd already taken a couple long shots of the kids with the kites, but he knew they weren't any good; the perspective was all wrong. Then he saw those faces, looking up at the sky, watching the kites.

There was magic in their faces, he just hadn't noticed it before. All three of his kids were up there, right then, in that moment, *with* those kites. They were soaring. They could feel the cold high wind on their faces, and they could see the quilted farmland passing beneath them. He shot the whole roll, tight on their faces. When he ran out of film he looked up at the kites—just dots now, high and far—and suddenly he was there, too, like an ant perched on the nose of the kite, feeling the hum of dead-center perfection.

They jumped in the truck and roared down dirt roads chasing the kites until they disappeared. The last they saw of them there was a star-crossed buzzard circling the little formation as it climbed out of sight over the expressway.

In the truck, chasing kites down the wind with three children, laughing and pointing, Mick kept thinking about what the Man With No Hands said to him.

"You don't know what the day will bring."

Sometimes the day brought magic.

When Layne got home and saw her underwear drawer still hanging open, plastic eggs halved all over the floor and her new pantyhose missing, the shriek from the bedroom brought Mick back to reality. And Ben, of course, threw him under the train.

"Dad told me to," he said—the little traitor.

Mick opened his mouth to argue, but then he recalled that he hadn't specifically told Ben to get the ones from the ragbag. It was his own fault. He drove Layne to the department store after supper and entertained the kids while she restocked her hose drawer. While he was waiting he dropped off the pictures he'd shot that afternoon. She was a little upset about the pantyhose at first—it had been a long day—but when he showed her the pictures of her kids she melted.

A few pairs of pantyhose was a small price to pay.

18

Aubrey's notion.

ONE EVENING after the kids went back to school Mick took several rolls of film over to Aubrey's and helped develop them. Aubrey was impressed. He kept going through them, studying them with a magnifying glass.

"I see you were paying attention," he said, and there was a weight to the way he said it. "These aren't perfect, but they're pretty good."

Mick had gone back to the kudzu shack early one morning and shot it in ground fog. This time he bracketed the exposures and apparently got some of them right, although it was still hard for him to tell the difference. Aubrey liked those a lot, and he also said good things about the ones Mick took of an old barn listing ten degrees to starboard in the process of collapsing, but the ones he kept going back to were the prints Mick had already gotten developed—the pictures of the kids watching their kites. He raved about those.

"Technically, these aren't landscapes, but they're still good," Aubrey said. "There's just a couple things," he said, still going over them with his magnifying glass. "Do you have a tripod?"

"No, why?"

"Because they're not razor sharp. Close, but close isn't good enough. You're great with composition and you're getting better with light, but you can't hold a camera still enough in your hand. Not if you want your photos to be up to contemporary professional standards."

"It's a hobby, Aubrey. It's just something I do to keep from . . . disappearing. I mean, why do I need to be up to contemporary professional standards?"

Aubrey lowered his glass and stared. He looked puzzled, as if Mick had missed something obvious. "I don't think you realize how good these are, Mick. If you'll fine-tune a few details your pictures can hang with anybody's. And I mean *anybody*. Start shooting with a tripod. Bring me perfection and I'll get you a show."

"A show?" Mick had no idea what he was talking about.

He nodded. "I'm on the board at Arts Clayton, the art museum in Jonesboro. They have a juried show every summer with judges from all over. It'll be a great experience for you."

While he was talking Aubrey pulled a tripod down from the shelf and handed it to him. "Use this. And start using fine-grain film—it's good for landscapes. Bring me perfection and I'll show you what to do with it. What you have, Mick, is not a hobby. It's a gift."

Closed up, the telescoping tripod was about the size of a loaf of bread. Mick pulled out one of the legs, fidgeted with the knobs. Matte black finish, precise fits—everything Aubrey owned was top quality.

"I, uh . . ."

"Keep it. I have another one," Aubrey said. "And shoot more pictures. Film is relatively cheap, and a good photo—a really *great* photo—is always one part preparation and one part blind luck. Give yourself a chance to get lucky."

He was starting to like Aubrey in spite of himself.

19

Self portrait.

ONE EVENING after supper Mick went over to Hap's to do some welding. Hap had contracted to build a couple of engine pullers for a trucking place and he wanted the welds to look professional. Hap could weld, but he couldn't make it pretty.

While Mick welded the frame together, Hap sat on a milk crate and made small talk.

"So how's things goin', old buddy? You 'bout to get used to not workin'?"

Mick raised his hood, shook his head. "I don't know, man. I think I'm starting to understand what Bangles Gruber was talking about when she said it was hard."

Hap's brows furrowed, confused. "Hard. Ain't nothin' hard about it that I can see. Heaviest thing you got to lift is a laundry basket."

Mick clamped another rod in the stinger, flipped his

hood down, struck an arc, and ran another bead. In a few minutes the nervous blue glow ceased, he raised his hood and slung the spent rod from the stinger.

"It's not the same kind of hard, Hap," he said. "It's not like swinging a pickaxe in August, but see, when a man puts the pickaxe down at quitting time, he's done. He kicks back and relaxes, and he's entitled to it because he's *working*. What a housewife does isn't hard—none of it's hard— but it never stops. It's all day long, every single day, and all night, too. No holidays or sick days or vacations. If the baby gets sick she stays up all night tending him, and tries not to wake up her husband because he's *working* and he needs his rest. It's not hard—it just never stops. And there's no dignity in it."

Hap eyed him suspiciously. "Old buddy, you ain't turnin' feminist on me, are you?"

"Nah." Mick snapped his hood back down and his voice echoed from behind it as the blue arc flashed and he started another bead. "I just feel a little hollow sometimes, that's all."

That hollow feeling might have had something to do with what happened in the parking lot at McDonald's the next day. It was Tuesday. They left the therapist's office at lunchtime and Dylan kept fussing about being hungry, so Mick pulled into the burger joint just short of the expressway. He was waiting in line with Dylan up on his shoulders, minding his own business, when a bunch of iron- workers came in for lunch and lined up behind him. One of them started right away mouthing off at the girl behind the counter, griping about the long line. Mick thought he recognized the voice, so he looked over his shoulder.

Sure enough, it was Randy Tewksbury, a guy he'd worked in his crew a time or two. Tewk was a pretty good hand, but he'd always been an obnoxious pain in the butt. The last time Mick saw him was the day he fired him for cussing Mick out in front of the crew. Tewk thought he was a tough guy. He liked to play the part, wearing a confederate do-rag and sunglasses, indoors or out, and he always cut the sleeves off his T-shirt to show off his tattooed shoulders. Mick didn't say anything at first, but about the third time Tewk popped off at the girl he could see it was getting to her, so he turned around and stared.

"Why don't you lighten up, Tewk? It's not her fault the place is crowded. It's lunchtime." Mick said it as politely as he knew how, but as soon as Tewk recognized him that smirk spread over his face and he started bobbing his head, all cocky.

"Hey! Look, guys! It's the *nanny*!" Then he started in on Mick, giving him the cleverest lines he could come up with. Things like, "Ooooh, what you gonna do, nanny? Hit me with your purse?"

Mick knew three of the four ironworkers in line behind him. The other guys were all okay, it was just Tewk. His buddies couldn't decide whether Tewk was funny or embarrassing, so they stuck their hands in their pockets and watched. Mick let it go, turned his back on them. Tewk was all mouth. Now, at least, he was leaving the girl alone.

That would have been the end of it except that Tewk never did know when to shut up. He kept razzing Mick behind his back. Dylan's grip on his forehead tightened up, and Mick could feel him turning around to stare at Tewk. He muttered, "Where's a light saber when you need one? Huh, pal?"

He got the tray with the burgers on it and put Dylan in a booster seat. Sure enough, a minute or two later Tewk and his buddies sat down right across the aisle from him. All through lunch, anytime Tewk thought of a clever *nanny* line he'd belt it out around a mouthful of fries and then pound on the table laughing at himself. Mick ignored him. Once or twice he heard Tewk's buddies trying to get him to lighten up, but he just wouldn't quit. Dylan could hardly eat his Happy Meal for watching him.

Mick kept his head down and somehow made it through lunch. Tewk and his friends straggled out into the parking lot while Mick was strapping Dylan in his car seat. Tewk stopped at the back of Mick's truck to light a cigarette. The other three stopped, too, but they were looking antsy, edging toward their truck.

"Yo, *nanny*, you gonna take your kid swingin'? I heard you like to swing." Talking about Mick's little accident. Clever.

Mick closed the passenger door and brushed past Tewk as he walked around the back of the truck, trying hard to ignore him. But right when he was opening his door, about to get in and drive away and leave the jackass standing alone in the McDonald's parking lot, Tewk said the wrong thing.

"Hey, Mick, I heard you quit your job so you could stay home and take care of a little *re*tard. Is that him?"

Mick leaned in and told Dylan, "I'll be back in a minute."

He closed the door gently and walked right up to Tewk, who blew smoke in his face.

"What did you say?" Mick asked it very calmly, which, if Tewk had any sense, would have made him pay closer attention.

His buddies were standing back finishing their biggie-size drinks, sucking on straws. Grinning over his shoulder at them, Tewk mouthed, "Ooooh, Nanny's mad! I think he's gonna spank me!"

When he turned back around Mick hit him square in the teeth. His sunglasses flew off and he staggered back a step.

Tewk wiped fingertips across his lips, looked at the blood and tossed his cigarette away. If he'd still been grinning at that point Mick would have been worried, but he wasn't. Tewk glanced at his buddies, and for just a second there was uncertainty in his eyes. That was all Mick needed to know.

Tewk came at him hard but he didn't know what he was doing, throwing roundhouse punches. Tewk was taller and his arms were longer, so Mick covered up and slipped a few punches to get inside. The first solid uppercut buckled Tewk's knees, then Mick caught him with an overhand right on the way down. It was all over in about thirty seconds.

Flat on his back in the parking lot with Mick standing over him and a crowd starting to gather, Tewk looked out of his good eye at his buddies like he thought they were supposed to help him out or something. All three of them just stood there with one hand in a pocket, still sucking on straws, kind of half smiling at him. They knew where the line was, and they knew he had stepped way over it when he bad-mouthed Mick's kid. He had it coming. And he hadn't heard the last of it, either. Mick almost felt sorry for him when they all got back to the job. Randy Tewksbury was in for a long afternoon.

Just to make sure they had plenty of ammunition, he bent over, grabbed a fistful of T-shirt, lifted Tewk a little so their faces were inches apart, and said, "Who's your nanny?"

When he got in the truck he had to put Dylan back in his seat. He'd unbuckled himself and watched the whole thing through the back glass. Driving off, watching Tewk's buddies help him to his feet, Mick could tell by their faces they were already razzing him, using that line on him. He was going to hear it a lot.

Dylan had a little smile on his face, a look of pure admiration. "You won," he said. "You're the dood duy."

"Yeah, right," he smirked. "I'm the good guy."

It killed him that Dylan saw what happened. Something the therapist had said that very afternoon came back to haunt him, something about how Dylan "tended to process visual information much more readily than auditory."

It ain't what he hears you say, it's what he sees you do. He felt like he'd let his son down, like he'd shown him something that ran against everything else they were trying to teach him. Sure, Tewk had it coming, but deep down Mick knew that didn't stack up against the picture he'd planted in a four-year-old boy's mind. A picture that said if somebody got on your nerves it was okay to clean his clock.

Then there was Tewk. Deep down Mick knew, he and Tewk were more alike than he cared to admit.

20

Still life with children.

AUBREY made four-by-six prints from the latest batch of negatives, and Layne naturally fell in love with the pictures of the kids. She just flipped past the ones of the barn, even though Mick told her from a purist standpoint he thought they were better. That was an Aubrey word—*purist*—but the ironworker in Mick got a kick out of wearing a label like that.

"See," she said. "I *told* you. Pictures need people in them." She had a maddening way of being right for the wrong reasons. Once, when he was working on the ignition in his truck, frustrated because he'd spent all morning trying to get it to crank, Layne walked by, pointed out a missing screw in the license plate frame and said maybe that was the problem. He explained very patiently that the license plate screw had absolutely nothing to do with the ignition, but she wouldn't give it up. Finally, just to shut her up, he found a screw, ran it into the license plate, and then turned the key. That no-good truck fired right up. There was no way to convince her it was a coincidence.

He didn't want to take pictures of the kids. Even Aubrey liked the pictures with kids in them, but Mick knew what he wanted to do. He didn't want to shoot snapshots, he wanted to take *photographs* of barns and old houses. Landscapes. In his entire life this was his first and only attempt at artistic expression, and he knew exactly how he wanted to go about it.

He tried to explain artistic expression to Danny Baez the next weekend when he took Ben fishing down at Danny's place on Jackson Lake. But even Danny didn't see any point in taking pictures without people in them.

"I don't know," he said. "Sounds to me like you're just being the same old stubborn Mick. I been trying to tell you for years, you need to loosen up and think outside the box. Like that time at the Ford plant. . . ."

And so it went.

They were in Danny's bass boat, and on the way back to the dock Danny said he needed to pull his boat out and take it to a guy to work on the motor, so after they unloaded the boat Mick helped him put it on the trailer and haul it out. Danny lived on a little wedge-shaped lot at the back of a cove. He had been feuding with his neighbor over the property line, and his neighbor had just put up a six-foot fence right on the line, all the way down to the water. When Danny tried to drive out, he learned that the boat trailer wouldn't fit between the house and the neighbor's new fence. It was a big boat. The truck would go through all right, but the trailer was too wide.

They stood around scratching their heads for a while, debating about whether to tear the fence down or knock the back wall out of Danny's garage. The neighbor was watching. The first idea would have gotten Danny locked up. The second would have been a disaster. Finally, Ben tugged at his sleeve.

"Will the boat float with the trailer under it?" Ben asked.

It was a brilliant solution, but it took a kid to come up with it. Danny drove his truck around to the public ramp while Mick and Ben puttered down the lake in a bass boat with a trailer strapped to the bottom of it. Ben reminded his dad two or three times that it had been his idea.

Fortunately, Mick had tossed his camera bag into the boat with his fishing gear, and he took it out now. Ben's chin was up, proud. The red setting sun sparkled the water and lit Ben's profile, standing up there like a commodore in the front of the boat. For a moment Mick saw his own face through the camera lens, the clear expression of hope and pride he'd worn when he was Ben's age, and he didn't know whether to feel pride or pity.

They got some strange looks when they pulled the boat up to the ramp with the trailer already strapped to it, but Mick just nodded and acted like they did it that way all the time. His kids had a way of changing how he saw things— like Danny said, thinking outside the box. He thought about it a lot on the ride home, and it spilled over into the photography part of his brain. Sometimes a guy just had to swallow his pride. Purist or not, Mick would start taking the kids with him when he went to shoot landscapes.

One sparkling Saturday in late spring it paid off, big-time.

There was an old homeplace not far away where a friend of Mick's grew up. His friend's father had died and his mother, in her eighties, ended up in a nursing home. The vacant homeplace had been up for sale for nearly a year. The old house sat in a grove of big V-shaped pecan trees, and the leaves were just starting to bud out. Somebody had planted those trees and spent years caring for them—somebody with kids and dogs and dreams, and a family name that would soon fade from the land. Set back among those pecan trees, the deserted farmhouse looked lonely and old, and full of stories it wanted to tell. Mick shot a few pictures with the morning sun slanting through the trees and across the covered porch with its two empty rocking chairs—a lot of sharp angles and high contrast. Somebody had left the front door open and the windows up. Lace curtains ruffled against the black emptiness inside. He set up the tripod and bracketed a couple shots of the front of the house before he noticed a face peeking out the corner of the right-hand window; Ben had slipped in through a back door to look around. He wasn't smiling or anything, and all Mick could see was that face, staring out like a question mark, but somehow it made the shot come alive.

He set up to take some pictures angling down the porch from the side, centering on the empty rockers, the unswept leaves blown across the boards and in drifts against the wall, the screen door hanging from one hinge. Right before Mick snapped the picture, Toad stuck her head out the door. She was holding onto both sides of the frame and leaning out, looking right at him when the shutter snapped. Barefooted, with her white-blond hair tied back, and wearing that old cotton dress, he knew in the black-and-white stills she would come out looking like a ghost child from the past.

"Freeze," Mick said. "Don't move a muscle. NO! Do not grin. Put your face back like it was." As she obeyed he noticed for the first time how thin she was and how the whites of her eyes made her look hungry, like a depression-era kid. He shot six pictures, a range of exposures, and he knew he had something special.

After he shot the house the kids dragged him around back to the barn. They'd already been playing in it. It was a huge barn, old but solid, with most of the brick-red paint still on the outside, although it was flaking and peeling pretty badly. The outside wasn't much to look at—too old for a postcard and too new for art, but the kids had a ball playing in the hay. Somebody had dumped a mound of hay in front of the loft, and Ben and Toad saw right away that they could climb up and jump from the loft onto the haystack and slide down the sides. Dylan wanted no part of the loft. When they started climbing and jumping he latched onto Mick's thigh like he was afraid somebody would try to force him to climb up there.

The big loading door up high on the front of the barn was wide open and a shaft of morning sunlight angled right in on the haystack, so Mick decided to set up the tripod and try to get some shots of them jumping. He set the shutter speed high and opened the aperture wide, but he wasn't used to action shots so he didn't expect much. When he thought he had shot enough he left the camera on the tripod and went over by the haystack to round up the kids. Toad, who happened to be in the loft right then, stood up and yelled, "Catch me!"

She flung herself out into space and Mick threw his arms up to catch her.

There was not one ounce of fear in that girl.

––––––––––

Mick was standing next to Aubrey waiting to see his reaction when he took the prints out of the dryer and laid them out to flatten. Going down the line Aubrey leaned close to them, nodded once or twice and said, "Mm-hmm."

They developed three rolls. He got through the whole first roll with not much more than a nod, but when he got to the ones of Ben looking out the front window he took his glasses off and wiped them with a lens cloth, put them back on, leaned even closer and let out a low whistle. There were three photos just alike but shot at different exposures. Aubrey picked up the magnifying glass and bored in on the middle one. When he straightened up he ticked the bottom of the picture with a forefinger.

"This one's excellent," he said. "Striking."

Three or four pictures later he blinked and his eyes went wide. "Another one!" he said, and then did a close study of the one with Toad leaning out the front door.

"Two out of seventy-two." Mick shrugged. "Not a real high percentage."

Aubrey shook his head. "I don't think you understand the odds, Mick. A lot of photographers will shoot for a month just trying to get one picture of this quality. You've got two on the same roll."

He didn't say much else while he scanned the rest of them, until he got to the very last print. Mick didn't see what it was before he snatched it up.

"Oh my." Aubrey said it very quietly, but the look on his face—Mick thought he was about to cry.

"This one," he said, shaking the picture lightly. "This is the *grail*, Mick."

"Let me see it." Mick hadn't seen it before Aubrey snatched it up, so he didn't know which one he was talking about. Aubrey ignored him and picked up the magnifying glass. Mick finally moved in and looked over his shoulder.

It was a picture of Toad flying through a shaft of light. Her arms were flung wide, her head back, her hair dancing wild and that cotton dress pressed against her by the wind of her flight. It was absolutely crystal clear. He could see specks of dust drifting in the sunlight and little scraps of hay frozen in midair all around her. Her face, tilted up toward the light, had a look Mick could only describe as pure childlike joy, and her eyes were closed. He remembered the moment well, but not the picture.

"I didn't take that," Mick said.

He frowned. "You didn't?"

"No. See the hands in the bottom right?" It was just his outstretched hands; the rest of him was out of the frame.

"Yes."

"Those are my hands."

A shrug. "I thought maybe you set the timer."

"Right. In precisely ten seconds my daughter is going to be flying through this exact spot. 'Fraid not. It must have been Dylan."

"Your four-year-old?" One eyebrow went up.

"Well, look. There were only the four of us there. Here are my hands, and if you look close—right up here—you can see one of Ben's feet hanging off the edge of the loft. There's no way Dylan *meant* to do this. I don't know, I guess he must have been playing with the switch and took it by accident."

"Wow," Aubrey said softly, staring at the picture. "I've always heard it's better to be lucky than good. This one's a winner, I guarantee it."

"You serious?"

"Deadly. You never know what judges are looking for, but *nobody* could ignore this. It's . . . *surreal*."

"But I didn't shoot it, Aubrey. I can't enter a contest with a picture I didn't take."

"Did you set it up? Aim the camera, set the shutter speed and F-stop?"

"Yeah."

"Then no matter who your assistant is, it's your photo. You have three fine pictures here, Mick, and one of them is a drop-dead stunner. But for a juried show we need to submit six. They might not all make it in front of the judges, but you're allowed six. Bring me three more the same caliber as these and you're on your way. Maybe you'll be able to quit your day job."

"Right," Mick snorted. "My day job has a no-quit clause in the contract."

"Oh, and another thing. You need to start thinking about titles."

"Titles?"

"For the photos. When you submit a group of photos for a show they have to be titled. Individually."

"Man. That's gonna be harder than taking the pictures. I'm no good at stuff like that. I'll ask Dylan—maybe he'll get lucky again."

Aubrey couldn't quit staring at that picture. "An accident," he whispered. "Wow."

For better or worse, Mick's whole life felt like an accident.

"You never know what the day will bring," he muttered.

21

Banana pudding and pine trees.

LAYNE'S church held their annual spring picnic at a local park when the dogwoods were in bloom. It was a gorgeous place, a picture of Georgia in the spring-time—little islands of pine trees here and there surrounded by clusters of pink and white azaleas in full blossom, wide stretches of well-kept grass and some really fancy play-ground equipment for the kids. It was an Easter kind of day, all sunshine and crystal blue skies—and warm, but not the kind of stifling heat they knew they'd be getting in a month or two. Mick didn't know many people there, but they made him feel right at home.

First, he got talking sports with a bunch of guys while their wives were putting out fried chicken, potato salad, baked beans, and green bean casseroles. He'd always loved baseball. Five or six of the guys were pitching horseshoes and talking about the season that was about to start. It all seemed friendly enough, just men talking. Next thing Mick knew, he had promised to sign up Ben and Toad for Little League ball, and somehow—he never did figure out quite how it happened—he managed to get roped into coaching a team. They were short of coaches. It would be fun, they said. His guard was down. They caught him in a moment of weakness.

Then when he was helping Layne fix plates for the kids, Mick looked over at what she was doing. She was dabbing half-spoons of baked beans and potato salad onto a paper plate.

"Is that for Dylan?" he asked.

She nodded.

"He won't touch it."

"Well, he's got to eat something, Mick."

"But the potato salad has celery in it. He hates celery."

"All right, then he doesn't have to eat the potato salad."

"You don't understand, Layne. He won't eat anything on the plate if there's celery on it, he hates it that bad. It's the texture."

She scraped the potato salad off of Dylan's plate onto her own and didn't say anything else about it, but he could tell it upset her a little. It was tricky sometimes, working around her feelings. More than once she had told him she felt like she was missing out on her kids' lives. Her husband wasn't supposed to know more about her own children than she did.

After lunch, while everybody was enjoying a wide array of desserts, they fell to talking about a food and clothing drive that had been going on at the church. Mick was an outsider; he didn't know anything about it. It was just a drive the youth at church had organized for a homeless mission in Atlanta, so he minded his own business and paid loving attention to a Styrofoam bowl of Lois Freeman's renowned banana pudding. On the edge of the conversation, Mick was only vaguely aware there was a problem.

"Closed down?" Layne said. "Why would the homeless mission close down?"

"Dooley got sick," Tom Herman said, shoveling the last of a giant piece of strawberry pie into his mouth. Tom was the big bald-headed guy who had conned Mick into coaching a Little League team. "Roy Dooley's been running the place pretty much by himself for the last ten years, and now he's got lymphoma. He's doing okay, I guess, but he doesn't have the energy to run the mission anymore and nobody else has stepped up."

"That's a shame," Lois Freeman said. Lois had actual blue hair, all glued into a hard, swirling sculpture. Not a hair would dare move. "What will we tell the young people? They were so looking forward to the trip to the mission."

Tom shrugged. "Yeah, it's a shame. They've got a whole big truckload of stuff piled in the storeroom at the church. They worked hard. I hate to just give it to the Salvation Army, but Beal Street Mission is the only homeless place I know."

"You don't have to go to a mission to find homeless people," Mick said. He wasn't even thinking about it, he was just scraping his bowl.

"That's right, I hadn't thought of that," Layne said. "Mick has a friend in a homeless community downtown."

Tom chuckled. "A homeless *community?* Isn't that an oxymoron?"

Mick shook his head, wiped a little pudding from the corner of his mouth with the back of his hand. "It's just a couple bridges, but there's like a whole little city under there. They live there, all the time."

He was just volunteering information, or so he thought. Turned out he was volunteering to head up a mercy mission to Overpass Plantation. There were times when he really wished he could learn to keep his mouth shut.

They were all writing down phone numbers and plans and finalizing a caravan for the following weekend when Layne's head went up and she looked around to see where the kids were. It was a mommy thing; she did it every few minutes, as if she was on a timer. Mick knew there was going to be trouble when her gaze locked on something and her eyes went wide.

"DYLAN!" she screamed. Everybody at the picnic table looked up.

Mick whipped around expecting to see his youngest son impaled on a fencepost or something, but he was just peeing on a pine tree. The problem was, there were two little girls, one on either side of him, watching in wide-eyed amazement while he demonstrated what a boy can do and how high up on the tree he could do it. Dylan was reared back and grinning. Proud.

Mick tried to explain on the way home.

"It wasn't really his fault," he said. "We spend a lot of time out in the woods—you know, just me and him and

Andy. How was he supposed to know the difference? To a four-year-old, a tree is a tree."

"You're right," she said. "It's not his fault."

She didn't say anything else. She didn't need to.

22

Toad's backpack.

MICK went down to Overpass Plantation a couple days ahead of time and told the Man With No Hands what the church group was planning. Word spread, so when they pulled off next to the bridge that Saturday morning with Mick's truck, two vans and a car loaded with food and clothes, a crowd started gathering right away.

Mick had never put much stock in giveaways because his own experience had taught him that giving somebody a handout rarely changed their life for the better. He'd always belonged to the "Teach 'em to fish" school—if a man wanted a job Mick was more than willing to let him prove himself. Not only that, but it always seemed to Mick that the real reason people organized charity drives like this one was so they could pat themselves on the back. That Saturday at Overpass Plantation it was one of his kids who showed him another side to the equation. By the end of the day he was just glad he had the foresight to bring his camera.

There were ten of them in all—Mick, Tom and Joanie Herman, plus four teenagers and three kids. Two of the kids were Mick's. Dylan and Toad came with him—Ben was home sick with his mother.

The Man With No Hands met the group and took over. He let the little kids hand out loaves of bread and canned goods to whoever wanted it, but he told them only two cans to a customer, and watch out for repeat customers. Mick noticed Joanie Herman was keeping a really close eye on the little ones, and he figured it was out of fear. Dylan stayed right up under him the whole time, usually holding onto him one way or another.

"Clowns," he whispered once, and Mick knew what he meant. He didn't mean they *looked* like clowns, but they gave him the same feeling. Dylan wasn't sure the outside of them was real, as if somebody might be hiding inside that exterior. It was definitely a rough neighborhood. Mick had only seen homeless people in the context of other homeless people, or mixed with construction workers. But now he was seeing them next to Tom and Joanie Herman— Mr. and Mrs. Straight-laced Clean-cut Churchpeople. Most of the people coming up the hill hadn't had a bath in recent memory; there was dirt ground into the creases on their faces and black lines across the backs of their necks. They smelled foul, and most of them hadn't had a haircut in years. Some of them were stoned, some of them were mentally or physically handicapped one way or another, and some were just plain crazy. One wild-haired guy with an eye-patch squatted down behind Mick's truck and kept peeking around it like he was scared of something. Mick tried to talk him out into the open but he just put a finger to his lips and motioned him away, muttering something about the KGB.

"That's Bond," the Man With No Hands said. "James Bond. He's harmless. He'll forget after a while, and then he'll come out. This is one of his bad days. Come around tomorrow and he'll have the patch on his other eye."

Homeless people wandered up the hill one at a time and went first, always, to the food van. Some of them carried bags—everything from a grimy Saks Fifth Avenue shopping bag to a black plastic garbage bag, but the garbage bag seemed to be the standard. They'd get a loaf of bread, some canned goods and maybe some peanut butter from the kids, stuff it all in their bag and move on to the clothes truck, where the teenagers would try to fit them with a pair of jeans. Dylan spent the first hour hanging onto Mick, one arm wrapped around his thigh, but after a while he decided these clowns were just people after all and he started getting into the spirit of the thing. Mick got a couple really good pictures of Dylan handing out canned goods. He noticed quite a few of them hit Dylan up for seconds. He was an easy mark.

Mick learned from Tom and Joanie that the teenagers from the church—most of whom were the mop-haired, ragged-jeans-and-T-shirts variety—had collected about five hundred dollars and used it to fill up a van with jeans and shirts and coats they bought dirt cheap at a thrift store. The clothes they were handing out looked a lot like what they were wearing, and it wasn't until later Mick found out that the teenagers bought their own clothes at the same thrift store, not because they were cheap but because it was fashionable. Go figure.

A couple times a whole family came up the hill together—a mother and father and a child or two. Little kids. Mick hurt for the kids, though for the most part the little ones seemed happy enough. He figured they just weren't old enough to know how poor they were. Most of the parents seemed a little ashamed of taking a handout, but they were also the most grateful for it. The teenagers treated them well, playing with the kids and joking around. Mick talked to a couple of the parents, and the stories were remarkably similar. They had used their last dime getting to Atlanta for a job and then lost it somehow, couldn't find another job and didn't have enough money to go someplace else and start over. They seemed decent enough. More than anything else they seemed surprised to find themselves in such a fix.

One of the teenagers, a gangly kid named Rob, with black hair down in his eyes, was handing out backpacks. They were brand new backpacks made for carrying books and school supplies, but they would be handy for a homeless guy who needed a way to carry his stuff around. They even came with a little water bottle. According to Tom, Rob found them on clearance someplace, and after he told the store manager what he planned to do with them the manager let him have the whole stock at wholesale. He must have brought fifteen of them in the trunk of his car and was doling them out to anybody who asked for one. They went pretty fast once word got around. After the backpacks were all gone a doe-eyed little black kid came up the hill by himself and stood there at the back of Rob's car peeking into the trunk, wringing his hands. This kid was wearing a dirty T-shirt four sizes too big and two left tennis shoes, one black and one white. He mumbled something when Rob walked by, but he was very timid and Rob had to get down on his knees to hear.

Rob shook his head, slung his hair out of his eyes and put his hand on the kid's shoulder. "I'm sorry, man, you got here too late. They're all gone."

The kid just nodded and started to turn away. His head hung and his shoulders drooped. He hadn't even looked at the clothes or the groceries in the other vans.

Toad was standing on Rob's back bumper, holding onto the open trunk lid and bouncing, making his shocks squeak. Mick didn't think she even heard what was being said until she turned around, jumped down and called out to the kid.

"Wait a minute," Toad said. "We got one more." She ran around to the passenger side of Mick's truck, yanked the door open and leaned in. Mick went and peeked over her shoulder to see what she was up to. His daughter was cleaning out a really nice, nearly new Nike backpack on the front seat, dumping out pencils and pens, a pile of wadded-up papers, a couple of books and folders, an old sandwich, some rocks, and a headless, naked Barbie doll. She snatched a water bottle from the cup holder on the console and stuck it in the little webbed pocket on the side of the backpack, then closed the door and ran—literally *ran*—back over to Rob's car and shoved the thing into the kid's hands. She didn't say a word, just gave it to him.

Mick shot a close-up of that kid's face. The kid never saw the camera. He hugged that backpack to his chest like it was the finest thing he'd ever owned, and then turned and took off down the hill as fast as he could run. Mick, for whom the joy on the boy's face had seemed as close and clear as his own hands, watched him go and understood something that perhaps no one else even thought about. In his growing up, lost among all the million things that would happen to that kid in his life, he would forget this. It was just a backpack. Ten years later maybe that kid wouldn't even remember it. It was entirely possible that Toad wouldn't remember it, either. But Mick would. And judging from the look on his face, he figured Rob would, too.

The Man With No Hands saw what happened. He watched Mick shoot the picture, saw the look on his face. Mick didn't even know he was standing there until he spoke up.

"Children. They know how to preach," he said.

Mick just nodded. He was astonished, sometimes, at the things he saw in his kids. Toad was just a simple, straightforward girl with a straightforward heart. It struck him that he must have had a heart himself at some point, and he wondered what happened to it. He figured it was one of the many things that got beaten out of a man one way or another before he grew up, but at the moment his daughter had him wondering if there was any way to get it back.

When they were loading up to leave, the Man With No Hands came up to say thanks for about the tenth time.

Mick said, "Listen, is there anything else I can do for you?" He didn't know why he said it. Or maybe he did.

"No. Thanks, but you've done quite a lot already. It was kind of you to bring these people down here. It makes a difference, you know."

"Well, that's nice, but what I meant was, is there anything I can do for *you*, personally. It must be tough sometimes, living here and all."

He chuckled. "It's not that hard once you get used to it. There's a shelter I can get to when the weather's too cold, or sometimes just for a hot meal and a shower. There is one thing, though . . ."

"Name it," Mick said, and he meant it. He actually *wanted* to do something to help this man.

"Well, you can see I have no transportation. Once in a while I need to go someplace too far to walk, and it's not always easy to arrange a ride."

Mick dug in his pocket and came up with a grocery store receipt. He scribbled his number on the back and handed it to the Man.

"You got a way to call me?"

The old man nodded, tucking the paper into his shirt pocket. "There's a pay phone."

"Good. You need a ride, anytime, day or night, you call me, okay?"

Mick figured he'd never hear from him again, but at least he made the offer.

23

Ick's Fish.

THE WEEK before the Little League season started up, Tom Herman called about the preseason planning meeting. On Mick's list of fun things to do, a planning meeting was right up there with a vasectomy.

There must have been fifty men gathered in the new county annex building, and listening to the talk Mick knew he was in over his head even before the meeting started. He was the only rookie there—the rest were seasoned coaches who talked about kids by their first names as if they were big league stars. These people were serious. The first order of business was to find fresh meat to coach teams. Mick thought about laying low and slipping out the back door, but Tom canceled that plan right away.

"Mick wants to coach a team," the big man said, his folding chair complaining as he stood. "He's not working, so he's got lots of time."

Mick didn't let it get to him. The kids' school had already taught him that anybody who wasn't working was a prime target for everybody's projects.

Ben and Toad both landed in the seven-eight age bracket, so that's where Mick coached. He didn't know enough to take advantage of the draft, nor did he understand just how dead serious all the other coaches were, so Mick went into it with the naïve notion that Little League baseball wasn't so much about winning trophies as letting the kids have a good time and earn some memories. He didn't scout or recruit like the other coaches, so he ended up with a team full of kids who had never played before. This drew snickers from the hard-core set because it was common knowledge that a kid needed to start playing two seasons a year at the age of four if he was ever going to amount to anything.

Ben was the only eight-year-old on the Marlins—the rest were all seven—so they were always playing kids a head taller. Most of the teams in their bracket were hard-driven, winning-is-everything, semi-pro, two-uniform, twice-a-week-at-the-batting-cage, double-play-turning, custom-bat-toting, chewing, spitting testosterone rockets. They had blazing fast base runners who stole every base at every opportunity, including home, even when the pitcher was holding the ball and the Marlins were down by seventeen runs.

Other teams had kids who brought their own monogrammed equipment bags, complete with batting gloves, and could hit with power from either side of the plate. Eight years old, and they would dig in, keep their head down, focus on the ball with cat-like intensity and smash line drives off the fences.

The Marlins had kids—two of them—who would drop the bat as soon as the pitcher started his windup, turn on their heels and bolt from the batter's box grabbing their head with both hands, and by the time the ball crossed the plate they were crouching, whimpering, by the backstop.

Mick was getting ready for a game one afternoon when he noticed the M was peeling off the back of his team jersey where it said COACH MICK. He figured they just didn't iron it on well enough, so he turned the iron to High and spread the shirt over the ironing board. By then Mick was an old hand with an iron. He knew better than to put a hot iron directly on top of one of those stick-on letters, so he grabbed a pair of boxers from the laundry basket and spread them on top, between the jersey and the iron. Turned out the reason the letter didn't stick in the first place was that they originally applied it with the sticky side out. He did a really thorough job of ironing the initial onto his shorts, so he ended up with a jersey that said COACH ICK and a pair of red boxers with a big white M on the front.

Layne enjoyed the whole thing a little too much. The boxers had her screaming with laughter. "Good idea, Coach Ick. Why don't you put your initials on *all* your shorts? Then you'll always be able to tell the front from the back."

Before long, everybody was calling him Coach Ick. The team came to be known as Ick's Fish, which seemed appropriate for a team that played baseball about as well as the average trout. There was one kid he was pretty sure had never tried to *run* before, let alone play baseball. About halfway through the season a pitch accidentally hit his bat and the shortstop picked it up and threw it into the stands. The chubby little guy rounded first, waddled halfway to second, stopped, turned around, took his helmet off, scratched his head, looked back at Mick, who was coaching first base, and asked if he was going the right way. Not having been there before, he was unfamiliar with the route. The team parents put their heads together and told Mick he should iron numbers on the bases to help the kids remember which one was which.

Ben never took the bat off his shoulder the whole season. He didn't bail out, he just never swung at a pitch. Not once. Nobody could convince him the pitch was a strike, ever, and anyway he liked arguing with the umpire better than running the bases. But Ben was short for his age and when he went into a crouch he had a very small strike zone, so he led the league in walks. Toad, on the other hand, swung at everything. They could throw the ball over the backstop and she'd swing at it. She struck out most of the time. When she did get on base she always tried to steal second because she liked to try to spike the shortstop. She led the league in fist-fights.

Defense? Ick's Fish used the Bob Uecker method: wait till it stops rolling and pick it up. Mick tried to teach them to hold onto the ball after they picked it up—just run it in and stand on home plate—but they wouldn't do it. Every time one of them got his hands on the ball he'd throw it into the outfield or the dugout. They gave up several grand-slam bunts that year. They also had a deaf outfielder—great kid, but stone deaf. He didn't pay attention any better than any other seven-year-old, so sometimes he wouldn't see a ball hit over his head and he'd just stand there with this puzzled look on his face trying to figure out why everybody in the bleachers was jumping up and down and pointing.

Whenever Layne could get off work in time she came to the games. She made sure Mick brought his camera so he could record Ben and Toad's baseball experience, but the pictures didn't turn out very well. He used the long lens and got a good close-up of Toad landing a punch, and another one of Ben looking up at a ball in the outfield right before it hit him, but Layne wanted pictures of them sliding into home plate, so they faked a couple after a game. There wasn't much chance of catching Ben or Toad sliding into home during a real game.

24

Rounding out the six.

AUBREY got excited the night he developed the pictures from Overpass Plantation. Mick had never seen him that animated; he was usually pretty reserved. Aubrey went through the whole stack with a magnifying glass and there were a number of pictures he liked, but he found two that blew him away. Mick could have predicted he'd like the close-up of the kid hugging the backpack. That one was a no-brainer. Only the very top of the backpack showed; it was just a picture of a kid's face, glowing. Even without Toad in the shot, the boy's face told a story. But the one that surprised Mick was one he had forgotten taking, probably because the light was weird and he didn't think it would turn out.

The photo was a silhouette. They had gone down to the street below the bridge at one point—Mick, the Man With No Hands, and Dylan—figuring there were a few people who couldn't or wouldn't make it up the hill. Mick carried a sack full of groceries to hand out. He shot a few pictures while he was down there, but not many. Mostly faces. There were some real characters, but for the most part the shadows were too deep. He never shot with a flash, and besides, he got the feeling there were people down there who didn't want their picture taken. But there was this one old guy—really old, with a long, grimy, gray beard—who came up and started talking to Dylan. A tall man, he walked with a cane, very slowly, swinging one leg out because the knee wouldn't bend. Mick kept an eye on Dylan, thinking any minute he was going to bolt and run between his daddy's legs, but he never did. The old guy stopped and talked to Dylan as if he were a grownup. No baby talk. Called him "young man." There was something in his smile and that deep formal voice that fascinated Dylan. Mick could see it in his eyes.

They were standing in semidarkness under the bridge, but the street was wet and the sunlight bounced off the pavement toward him from the other end. When Dylan held up a loaf of bread with both hands the old guy hung his cane on his arm and bent stiffly at the waist to take it. That's when Mick shot the picture. He wasn't prepared for shooting into the light like that, and he didn't have time to fiddle with the settings; he just shot from the hip and forgot about it. He didn't figure it would come out.

But when Aubrey developed the picture it jumped off the page.

"Oh, this is *perfect*," he said.

Dylan and the old man were in almost complete silhouette. Only the old man's face caught some of the light reflected up from the wet street. He was smiling, and something in that wrinkled smile and formal posture spoke of warmth and kindliness. He had a kind of dignity about him. Dylan was looking up at him, leaning back a little as if the bread was heavy.

"Look at the symmetry of it!" Aubrey said. "And the way the light comes from a vanishing point to engulf them. It's like it *connects* them, somehow. Astonishing."

He got excited then, pulled out the top drawer of his filing cabinet and started leafing through folders. Being the kind of meticulous nerd that he was, Aubrey had made contact prints of all Mick's pictures—the ones they hadn't culled—twelve to a page, and sorted and labeled them and filed them neatly so that in less than a minute he had Mick's whole portfolio spread out in front of them.

Aubrey had already circled the ones on the contact prints that he thought were the best, so within minutes he had pulled the negatives and started setting up to print eight-by-tens of his top choices. He couldn't contain himself. As soon as the prints were dry he rushed upstairs to show them to Celly. Mick followed.

She was sitting at the sun table by the bay window off the kitchen, sipping tea from a china cup. Eight o'clock and she was already in her robe. She looked tired. Celly Weems could be charming when she wanted to be, like when she brought Christmas presents over for the kids, but Mick figured it was the kind of charm she could turn on and off like a light switch. On her home turf, she was imposing. Even sitting at her kitchen table in her robe she was the kind of person that made him uncomfortable.

Aubrey coddled her, talked to her like a child, called

her Baby. When he spread the eight-by-tens out on the table in front of her she made no move to touch any of them, she just placed her teacup on the saucer very gracefully and laid a finger against her chin.

"Mr. Brannigan, did you take all of these photos?"

"Yes, ma'am." He couldn't help it, it just came out that way. She was older than him, but not old enough to be a ma'am.

"They're quite nice," she said. "Your children photograph so well."

"Oh, they're terrific!" Aubrey said, with an enthusiasm she didn't seem to share. "We're going to enter these in the Clayton show. I have a hunch Larry Mac's not going to run away with it this year."

"They're very nice," she repeated, and Mick got the distinct impression he and Aubrey were being dismissed. She lifted her teacup and looked out the window at the twilight woods.

"Can I get you anything, Baby?" Aubrey asked softly as he picked up the pictures.

"No. Thank you, I'm fine." She didn't look at him.

———

By the time they got back down to the darkroom Aubrey didn't seem so excited anymore, as if his wife had taken all the starch out of him. Mick just came right out and asked him, "Is Celly okay?"

Aubrey hesitated, pushing his glasses up onto his forehead and pinching the bridge of his nose. "Well, yes and no. It's a long story."

He meant it was a private story. Mick knew enough not

to ask any more questions. Aubrey put the pictures into a manila folder, and then, while his hands were busy straightening up the darkroom, he must have decided he needed to talk.

"She suffers from depression sometimes," he said quietly, swabbing the sink with a cloth.

Mick hadn't expected that. He thought she was just snooty. He let it lay there for a minute, but then he couldn't help asking.

"What has *she* got to be depressed about? I mean, Celly's an attractive woman and you're comfortable financially," which they both knew was code for *stinking rich*. "She's got a husband who's crazy about her, your kid is doing well at college, and you don't even have to worry about how to pay for it! I would have figured if anybody was content, Celly would be. She's got it made."

Aubrey glanced at the door then, and dropped his voice a notch. "Well, she's had her share of problems. Now it's mostly empty nest syndrome, I think. Our youngest is off at school, as you know, but he's going through that whole 'breaking away' phase. Tanner called his mother yesterday and said some things about how we're screwing up his life. I know it's just a phase and he didn't really mean it, but Celly takes things like that pretty hard. I just don't get it, Mick. We've done everything for our kids. We're *still* doing everything. Where'd we go wrong?"

Mick shrugged. "I couldn't tell you, Aubrey. At the moment I'm busy screwing up my own kids' lives."

That drew a laugh out of Aubrey. Apparently it was what he needed because he sighed with his whole body, and when he looked up it was as if he had turned a page.

He picked up the folder with the pictures.

"Names," he said, slapping the folder against Mick's chest. "You've got to put titles on these. Apart from actually shooting the pictures, it's the one thing I can't do for you. The deadline for entry is only a couple weeks away, and the only thing left is titles. Give it some thought. Try to keep it simple and tight, but appropriate."

25

Looking for answers.

WHEN he got home from Aubrey's with the folder Mick went off by himself and just sat at the desk for a long time staring at them. The kids were in bed and Layne was reading. The house was quiet.

Aubrey had picked what he said were the best six pictures—the one of Toad flying through the air over the haystack, a close-up of Ben's face gazing up at an unseen kite, another of Ben peeking out the window of the old house, the one of Toad leaning out the door, Dylan handing a loaf of bread to an old man, and the close-up of the homeless kid hugging Toad's pack.

They were good pictures, and he believed in them, but this photography contest scared him half to death. Like everything else that had happened to him lately, it was an accident. It wasn't his plan. He started out thinking he would take a few pictures for fun, just to see how they turned out. If anybody had told him in the beginning that he would end up with framed, matted, titled photographs hanging in a gallery being judged by people in suits, people with education and refinement and discriminating taste, he would have run the other way as fast as he could. It scared him a *lot* worse than the high steel in a thunderstorm. Even in the quiet, sitting alone at his desk, he couldn't quite get his mind around it.

In his insecurity, he wondered if Aubrey was just toying with him. What if Aubrey was just telling him he was a good photographer so he could gather around with his rich friends at the gallery and horselaugh him? But no. Aubrey might be a nerd but he was a *serious* nerd—he didn't know how to be insincere. And yet, what if he was just wrong, and the pictures were no good? Aubrey wanted this for himself, anybody could see that. He'd wanted it for years and couldn't get there. Maybe he was projecting his fantasies onto Mick, and it was all just wishful thinking. Mick believed his pictures were good, but didn't everybody? Didn't everybody think their own work was the best?

He needed a second opinion.

He went into the den, sat down on the couch next to Layne and handed her the folder. She put her book down and gave each of the six pictures a long look. They were eight-by-tens, and she studied them for a long time. Mick didn't say anything, he just sat there twiddling his thumbs. He didn't want to prejudice her. By the time she was done he noticed there were tears in her eyes.

She closed the folder and wrapped him in a hug. "These are wonderful," she whispered.

"You really think so? They're that good?"

"Oh, absolutely! We have such beautiful children. Do you have any pictures where they're smiling?"

So much for an objective opinion. To Layne, these were just good snapshots of the kids. Very good, but snapshots all the same. He knew without further discussion that she was never going to see beyond the faces of her children. She was too much of a mom.

The next day he took the folder over to Hap. He was in his shop, under the hood of a candy-apple red '56 Ford pickup. Hap wiped his hands on a greasy rag and sat his big self down on a tool chest to look at them.

"Pretty pictures," he said. "I like that'n of Toad. That girl's about a whirligig, ain't she? When you gonna get yourself a *color* camera?"

He loved Hap, but there were times when he wished he were a touch more sophisticated.

The folder rode around on the dashboard of his truck for a couple days and Mick's insecurities only grew. He still didn't know for sure if they were any good, and he certainly couldn't come up with any titles for them.

That Friday afternoon Ick's Fish had a big game. There was one other team as bad as the Fish, and the highlight of the whole season was the next to last game, when the two worst teams played each other. Neither of them had won a game, so the outcome was terribly important. Ick's Fish kept their record intact, losing four to three.

Mick took the team to the Dairy Barn for ice cream after the game. The kids were whooping and hollering and cutting up, flipping ice cream all over the place with those long plastic spoons and giving each other hot-fudge wet willies. Mick stayed by the garbage can, out of the line of fire, sucking on a butterscotch shake.

Danny Baez walked into the place in the middle of the party. He'd been working overtime and was on his way home, all rusty and dirty. Danny didn't recognize Mick right away because he was wearing his Marlins cap and COACH ICK shirt, but he finally spotted him and threw a hand up. After he got his sack he came over to say hello, dodging a stray missile of chocolate ice cream on the way.

"Hey, Mick, I didn't know you were coaching a team," he said. "Those little guys party hard. They win the championship?"

"Nope. Lost," Mick said. "Haven't won a game all year."

"Wow. Then what are they celebrating?"

Mick shrugged. "Free ice cream. And they get to keep the uniforms."

"Cool," Danny said, nodding, flashing a wide smile. "Kids got their priorities straight, man."

He was right. Win or lose, seven-year-olds knew how to have a good time. Watching them made Mick think about the pictures. *Everything* made Mick think about the pictures.

"Say, Danny, can I ask you for a favor? If you got a minute, I want you to come out to the truck and take a look at something."

There were plenty of other parents hovering around the edge of the melee trying to control the kids, so Mick and Danny slipped out the door and went to the truck. Danny pulled the tailgate down and sat up on it unwrapping his burgers and fries while Mick got the folder off the dash.

Danny wiped his hands on his jeans and went through the pictures without saying anything, just a chuckle here and there. While he was looking at them, Mick filled him in a little, told him about the juried show Aubrey wanted him to enter. When Danny closed the folder and handed it back he shook his head and said, "Man, I wish I could do something like that. Those are like art."

"You really think so?"

Danny shrugged, bit into a burger, talked around a mouthful. "Well. If you want to talk about art, you're way over my head, Mick. I think they're good, but that's just me. I'm a rod-buster, not an art critic."

An old yellow biplane passed overhead, on a final for Bear Creek. "That's that Steerman out of Williamson," Danny said, watching the plane. Mick waited. There was something else on Danny's mind, he could see it in his face. Danny finally got still for a minute, staring at the ground, and said something not at all like a rod-buster.

"All I can tell you is those pictures make me feel something, Mick. Every one of them. When I look at them I *feel* something. They leave questions, like a good story. Is that what you wanted to know?"

Mick nodded. "Yeah. That's a big chunk of it."

They sat quietly for a minute, Mick pulling on a shake and Danny dipping fries in ketchup.

"Listen, Danny, there's one other thing. I've got to name them. If I enter these pictures in the show I've got to put titles on them. You got any suggestions?"

Danny shook his head. "Shoot, I ain't got a clue. You're on your own there, pard."

The phone rang right after Mick got home that evening. Everybody else must have been busy because Dylan picked it up. Mick was putting chemicals in the pool when Dylan brought the cordless out to him.

"Hook," Dylan said, handing him the phone.

It was the Man With No Hands. After he got the small talk out of the way he asked if Mick could give him a ride someplace.

"Sure. Just tell me where and when."

"I need to go out to Conyers. It's about an hour from here."

"I know where Conyers is. What time?"

"Uh, well, we need to leave early. Is there any way you could pick me up at the bridge at five thirty?"

"Five thirty in the morning?" He'd caught Mick by surprise. He'd figured they were talking about a doctor's office or something, maybe nine or ten o'clock.

"Yes," the Man said. "I know it's early, but it's important."

Saturday morning. Layne would be home with the kids.

"Well, yeah, okay. I can do that. Five thirty, by the bridge."

Mick spotted him in the headlights as he drove across the bridge, waiting patiently, alone in the darkest part of town. He punched the Off button to kill the radio before he pulled onto the shoulder.

Driving east in the darkness on a deserted Saturday morning expressway, Mick asked the obvious question.

"Where are we going?"

"The monastery," the Man With No Hands said. He was dressed in his usual khakis. Didn't look like he was going to church.

"What for?"

He was silent for a minute. "Well, ah . . . you'll see."

Mick might have been a little ticked if anybody else had gotten him up in the middle of the night, made him drive out to a church in the middle of nowhere, and then had the nerve to be all mysterious about it. But he'd been around the Man With No Hands long enough to know that there was usually a good reason for the things he did. Besides, there was a *presence* about him. Mick trusted him.

"So, are you like . . . a monk?" Mick asked. He wasn't even really sure what that meant.

A chuckle. "No, I never took a vow. I'm treated more like a guest these days."

High streetlights swept by on the sides of the expressway, light coming and going.

"You're a strange man," Mick said.

"Oh? How so?"

"Living the way you do. You don't belong in that world."

"None of us belongs in this world," the Man said. "We're just passing through."

"I meant the world under those bridges. The homeless world. And you're preaching again—I hate when you do that."

"I preach all the time," he explained. "I just don't use words most of the time."

Mick had to smile at that. He was beginning to understand the Man. "What I meant was, I still don't really understand why you live down there. You're not a junkie anymore—you could make a life for yourself. At the very least you could have stayed at the monastery. Why do you do what you do?"

"Gratitude," he said. He had the answer right there, as strange as it was, and it rolled out without a second's hesitation.

"Gratitude," Mick repeated. Switching to the left lane to pass a semi, he glanced at the smile on the old man's face. He was dead serious. "For *what?* Having hooks on the ends of your arms?"

He laughed out loud at that. "Yes, I suppose so. That's actually a pretty good analogy."

Mick waited, figuring he would explain. He did.

"This place, where we're going—I learned things. When I first got there I couldn't do much of anything with these hooks. I was clumsy, inept, frustrated. They took me in, and then they put me to work. They taught me to use these hands for simple tasks at first, and then harder ones. They gave me patience, perseverance and dexterity. In their silence, they taught me the meaning of love beyond judgment."

He held his hooks up in front of him and stared at them with a kind of reverence.

"So, yes, as strange as it may sound, I *am* grateful for these hands. They've never held a syringe. They're stainless. Indestructible. What I choose to do with them, I do out of gratitude."

Driving on in silence, the lights flashing past, it occurred to Mick that the Man was a pretty good preacher, even when he used words.

They pulled down a long drive lined with low trees and parked off to the right, in the parking lot of a little gift shop. No other cars were there. The shop was closed and dark.

Ahead of them, beyond a scattering of poplars on a manicured lawn, sat an imposing structure, tall and white and pointed, with a square bell tower on the left side.

"The abbey church," the Man With No Hands said. "The brothers came here in the forties and built most of this with their own hands. They believe in hard work."

A small light mounted up high near the bell tower gave just enough light so they could see their way across the lawn to the front of the church. The massive front doors were bolted, so the Man With No Hands led Mick around to a side door and into a stairwell leading up to the balcony.

Mick had never been in a church building like that one. It was one of those places where the inside was bigger than the outside. The ceiling curved to a point high above, supported by a series of graceful arches. The same simple arch pattern repeated itself again and again down the side aisles and in the two rows of stained-glass windows, one high and one low. The windows were dark. The two of them were alone there, and the sanctuary—the Man called it "the nave"—was lit only by a few candles on tables near the corners and a small candelabra down in front. Just enough light. There was a stillness about the place, a towering silence that made Mick want to walk on the edges of his feet and hold his breath. When they sat down in the front of the balcony the old hardwood pew gave out a groan that echoed from the rafters like thunder.

"They'll be in presently," the Man whispered. "The morning service starts at seven."

"Early risers," Mick said.

A smile. "This is the *second* service for the brothers. They rise for vigils at four. Listen, you can stay here if you like. I'm going down there for a bit. I'll be back."

Leaving MIck alone in the balcony, the old man retraced his steps down the back stairwell they had just come up, and emerged below in the broad aisle running down the center of the church. He walked very softly as he made his way past a few rows of pews at the back, past two long rows of raised seats facing each other in the middle, and right down to where the aisle ended and the dais began. He got down on his knees there, alone in the front of that huge place, and lowered his head.

Mick turned off his cell phone. Even that little chirp seemed to rattle around the top of the arches like a cannon shot.

The Man With No Hands knelt down front without making a move or a sound for a good twenty minutes. Sitting up there alone in the balcony with his elbows on the rail and looking out over that cavernous place, the quiet got to Mick. It felt to him as if the silence itself came and wrapped softly around him and took everything away, just stripped away all the craziness and busyness—the kids and chickens and goats and dogs—and left him nothing but quiet. Right then he felt like he could have reached out and touched God, and deep down he knew—if God was anywhere, he was in that silence.

Then, as the upper level of stained-glass windows

started turning from black to purple, the houselights came up a little. The monks in their robes began to file in and find their places in the raised seats on the sides, a few regular people straggled in to sit in the pews, and the Man With No Hands struggled to his feet and ambled back down the aisle with the swaying, precarious walk of a man whose legs are half asleep. A lot of the monks waved to him as he passed, and one or two came out and put an arm around him.

Mick didn't remember much about the service. Somebody read from the Bible, a trio of monks sang some kind of chant without accompaniment, everybody recited words back and forth, and one guy—the head monk, Mick figured—stood at a little lectern down front and spoke. Later Mick would not remember what the head monk talked about, but he would remember thinking that the man was intelligent and well-spoken, and he had worthwhile things to say. It was all very quiet and orderly. Dignified. Nothing at all like the church Mick remembered from his childhood. The Man With No Hands sat beside him through the whole thing but Mick didn't ask any questions because he didn't want to bother him. He figured this must have been what the Man came here for.

But beyond the silence and the dignity and the strangely beautiful music, the thing that impressed Mick the most was the light. As the sun came up, the stained glass came to life and he noticed that the arched windows were made of a million little colored glass triangles held together by veins of lead. In the beginning the sunlight infused the windows themselves with iridescence, and Mick sat and stared at them like works of art, which they were. But as the sun rose higher a million shards of glass fired color into the air until the rafters sang with an incredible blue and red and purple light. Mick pretty much forgot what was going on down below. Except for the Man With No Hands, he was alone in the balcony at the back, and it felt to him as if the dignified, reverent things they were doing down there belonged to someone else.

The light was for him. And it was singing.

Walking outside later the Man With No Hands asked him what he thought of the service.

He shrugged. "I liked the music, and the light. Never seen anything quite like that light. Apart from that, I didn't understand much of it."

"Yes. I suppose the rituals are different from what you're accustomed to."

"To tell you the truth, I'm not much on ritual of any kind," Mick said.

The Man's eyebrows went up. "Everybody needs rituals. They help people feel safe and secure."

He showed Mick around the grounds and told him a little about the building of the place.

"The guesthouse was the first building to go up," he said. "There's a story the brothers tell about a man from the town hired to help with the construction. He had a very large voice and a particularly colorful vocabulary, and whenever one of his coworkers tried to get him to curb his profanity he would just get louder. But every time he let fly with an expletive there was this one brother who would just bow his head for a moment. Whatever he was doing, he would just stop and bow his head. He never said a word, but after a while the carpenter stopped swearing."

He smiled, thinking about it. "It was here that I learned a man doesn't have to preach. All he has to do is bow."

The sun was well up when they arrived in the bonsai gardens—rows of windswept miniature trees on long worktables. Some of them had little handwritten tags pinned into the moss at their feet telling who had planted them, how long ago, and what kind of tree it was. Some of them were very old.

"This is where I worked most of the time," he said. "These are my friends." There were people around, a few monks and a few visitors, but Mick understood the Man With No Hands was talking about the trees. "I learned patience in this place, how to trim and prune—and wait. I helped to shape some of these trees, and they helped to shape me."

―――――

They stopped for breakfast after they left the monastery, and then hit the expressway heading back toward town. They were almost home before Mick remembered the manila folder on the dash. His pictures. He pulled the folder down, laid it on the seat between them and explained about the juried show.

"I still don't have much confidence in them," Mick said. "Start talking about art galleries and professional critics, and I'm out of my element."

The Man With No Hands laid the folder open on the seat and picked them up one at a time, holding each photograph between his hooks and studying it for a long time.

"Extraordinary," he said quietly. "God has his hand on you."

"Huh?"

"This," he said, touching a hook to the stack. "This is a gift."

"Yeah, that's what Aubrey says. But what's that got to do with God?"

He laughed. "A gift, by definition, has to come from someplace. Let me ask you something, Mick. Have you felt, lately, as if your life and circumstances were being . . . steered?"

The question troubled him, and he didn't answer right away. He was busy turning off the expressway ramp and merging into street traffic, and he was glad for the interruption. The bridge was only a few blocks away.

"Well?" The Man kept watching him, waiting.

"I don't know," Mick lied. "Look, I'm just an ordinary guy trying to live an ordinary life."

He shook his head, laughing again. "There *are* no ordinary guys, Mick."

As he said that Mick was slowing the truck, pulling onto the shoulder of the road at the end of the bridge. From where they were sitting they could look down the hill and see the hive of homeless people under the bridge.

"The people around here look plenty ordinary to me," Mick said.

"I'm talking about potential. Do you think these people have found their gifts? Reached their potential? I believe every one of us was designed—in his mother's womb, before birth—to do something extraordinary. The trick, if I may call it that, is in avoiding all the distractions, learning to hear and recognize the voice that guides you into your gift."

Mick switched off the engine. "You're preaching again."

"Yes, I am. You see that thin man down there whipping the column with a broken fishing rod?"

"Uh-huh." Young. Barefoot. Shirtless. A ton of hair. He was wearing that column out.

"His name's Bill. Eight years ago he was the youngest man ever to pass the state bar. But he had to stay up nights cramming, and he discovered the magic of speed. He never sleeps anymore. He's also not a lawyer anymore—he doesn't even know who he is anymore, and it's just a matter of time until his heart collapses under the strain. He wasn't designed to be ordinary. The man could have been a senator if he hadn't sold his soul for amphetamines."

"Sold his soul. Is that what you call it? I don't know, preacher, it seems to me you go out of your way to make everything a God story. In the real world, people don't sell their souls."

"Sure they do."

"Only in the movies. And then only so they can get rich and famous, or incredibly talented, or powerful—not so they can live under a bridge."

"Right, but in the movies it's always a lie, isn't it? Most people *do* sell their soul, they just can't get their price." His eyes were watching Bill whip the column with the remains of a fishing rod.

Mick's fingers drummed on the steering wheel. "So, what's your point?"

"You have to let go, Mick. You have to *give* your soul away, let it go—because it's not a matter of commerce, it's a matter of faith." He looked Mick in the eye and wiggled one of his hooks at him when he said this. It sent a chill through him and made him look away.

"Anyway," Mick said, in a blatant attempt to change the subject and draw attention back to the pictures, "Aubrey wants me to come up with titles for some of these for the show. I ain't got a clue."

"Really? It doesn't seem hard at all. You have only to see the story behind the picture."

Mick thumbed through the stack and handed him the one of Ben watching his kite soar away. It was a head shot. Ben had his hands together, looking up at the distant sky, and his eyes were positively *lit*.

"He was watching a kite," he explained. He didn't bother with the rest of the story; he wanted to know what the picture said on its own.

"That's *hope*," the Man With No Hands said, just like that. He recognized it instantly, the way Mick might have recognized a picture of a baseball and said, "Oh, that's a baseball."

Mick took the photograph back, pulled a pen out of the pocket in the dash and wrote HOPE across the back. Then he handed him the one of the old home with the empty rockers on the porch and Ben peeking out the right-hand window.

"*Emptiness*," the Man said. Again, instantly.

"Why emptiness?"

"The rockers, the house. The aftertaste of death and loss."

"But it's not empty." Mick pointed to Ben's face. "See?"

He nodded. "Yes, I saw that. There's always hope.

Death and loss is never the end of the story. They always leave something behind. That's what makes this a great picture."

He scribbled EMPTINESS on the back.

When Mick handed him the picture of the little black kid hugging the pack the Man With No Hands laughed out loud. "They call him Dirt," he said. "I love that kid. I hope he makes it. This one's easy—it's *joy*."

The one of Dylan handing the loaf of bread to the old guy under the bridge he called *charity*. That one Mick could have almost done himself. The one of Toad leaning out the door of the old house in her faded cotton dress he called *hunger*.

When Mick handed him the picture of Toad flying through the air toward his outstretched hands he had the weirdest reaction of all. He busted out in a bright, celebratory laugh, the way Mick would laugh if his clean-up hitter hit a ninth-inning walk-off home run. It was a laugh of pure joy.

"I can't believe you don't see this one," he said, still laughing. "This one's a snap."

Mick took the picture back, looked at it for a long time, and finally conceded. "I'm afraid I just don't see whatever it is you're seeing."

"It's *faith*. Children are full of uncluttered, unbroken, unembarrassed faith. They just have it in them, like they're born with it. We lose it somehow, growing up. Life drives it down like a nail, and we forget. We grow up, we learn the reasons behind things, we see the springs in the clock, and bit by bit we forget how to believe in something we can't explain. I'm old now. I own the wisdom of bitter experience, but you know what? I'd trade thirty years of experience for thirty seconds of a child's faith."

Mick looked at the picture again.

"Her eyes are closed," he said.

"Exactly."

Mick laid it facedown on the seat and wrote FAITH across the back.

26

The thief.

IT WAS a beautiful day with a bright breeze and high, thin clouds, and Mick was feeling frisky for some reason after he dropped off the Man With No Hands. He didn't want to go straight home and dive into Saturday chores, and he had some mad money in his wallet that he'd rat-holed from side jobs here and there. He stopped off at the camera store in the mall on the way home. The long lens he wanted was still out of his price range, so he settled for a couple filters.

When he finally got home around noon the house was deserted. Layne had left a note saying she was taking the kids shopping for new bathing suits. Oddly, the back door was unlocked. Layne never went off without locking all the doors. Then Mick noticed a couple of drawers hanging open and flour all over the kitchen counter, the Tupperware flour bin sitting on the counter open.

He started looking around, then, and noticed other things out of the ordinary. The door to the hall closet was open and some of the coats had been thrown in the floor. The walk-in closet in his bedroom had been ransacked, clothes strewn all over the place. Even the hamper against the back wall, the one with Layne's stuff in it, had been dumped out and left overturned.

Somebody had been in the house. Then he saw that Layne's jewelry box on the dresser had been cleaned out. In the kids' rooms he found the remains of broken piggy banks on the floor. The stereo was still in its place, and his guns remained untouched. Whoever had broken into the house apparently wanted only jewelry and cash. Mick called the police.

Of all the cops in the world they could have sent, Officer Bowers showed up—he of the red hair and sunglasses. The jerk who tagged Mick for littering last fall. Mick was in the kitchen talking to him when Layne showed up. Coming home and finding a police car in her driveway, she barged in all breathless and hysterical. Officer Bowers was probably forty-five years old, and he'd been a policeman more than half that time. He was leaning against the kitchen counter with a toothpick in his mouth, smiling, unperturbed.

"What did they get?" she asked, clutching the kids up under her and staring around wild-eyed, like she thought the burglar might still be in the house.

"The biggest thing was your jewelry," Mick said. "And the kids' piggy-bank money." His jaw tightened and his nostrils flared. This was his turf, and he'd been invaded. He would have strangled somebody if he'd known where to start, but he didn't. In the end, he remembered that it was his job to calm Layne down.

"Did you have a lot of expensive jewelry?" Bowers asked.

"Not really," she said. "There were a couple of opal rings my mother left me, and a pair of diamond stud earrings."

"Have you noticed anybody hanging around watching the house lately?" The cop swiped a finger through the flour mess on the counter.

"No, not that I recall," Mick said.

"There's that kid on the motorcycle," Layne said. "He's been riding through the woods around here the last couple days."

Mick had forgotten about him. "Just some teenager on a dirt bike," he said. "Probably from one of the subdivisions a mile or two up the road."

Bowers nodded, picked up his hat and made a move toward the door. "Okay. I'll take care of it. Odds are you won't get any of your stuff back, but I'll go lean on him. I can guarantee he won't come back here."

He knew. Bowers had already figured out who did it. It was obvious he had a history with this kid. Mick wanted a name. He wanted a piece of biker boy.

"You know who it is, don't you?" he said.

"Oh yeah, I knew right away. This isn't my first trip around the block. I keep tabs on all the aspiring young criminals around here. This particular one likes to circle the house at a distance first and look for cars. If all the cars are gone, he'll come up and ring the doorbell. If anybody comes to the door he'll just ask to borrow some gas for his bike. But if nobody's home he'll jimmy the back door and make a quick grab for cash and jewelry—whatever he can stick in his pockets. He knows enough not to take guns. I don't know why, but he always looks in the flour bin—probably where his mother hides her stash."

"I want a name," Mick said. He didn't try to hide his intentions. He felt sure he could persuade the little delinquent to give them back their stuff—and maybe some of his own.

"Not a chance," Bowers laughed. "I told you I'll take care of it. Make a complete list and report it to your insurance company. And, ma'am, I'll try to get your jewelry back, but don't count on it. He's a tough kid."

Toad had gone into the living room and squatted down in front of the open cabinet where the DVDs were stored when they weren't scattered all over the floor.

"There's a couple movies missing," she said.

"Superheroes?" Bowers asked.

Toad nodded. "Batman and Daredevil."

Bowers nodded. "That's him." He was watching Mick pretty closely and noticed him flexing his fists. "And Mister Brannigan, you'd best let this go. I don't want to have to lock you up for assault, you hear?"

———

"I feel so violated," Layne said after the cop left. "What if we'd been home?"

"He wouldn't have done it if we'd been home," Mick said. He had calmed down a little by then.

Layne stopped pacing for a second and asked, "Where

were you, anyway? I tried calling you but you didn't answer your cell phone."

"I turned it off. I'm sorry. I would have been home earlier but I went by the camera store. How much do you think was in their piggy banks?" he asked.

"About fifty dollars apiece, mostly in two-dollar bills. Birthday money from their grandparents. What are we going to do, Mick?"

She was distraught, and he could understand it. Her home had been invaded by a stranger and she felt helpless, defenseless. Mick's family's safety was his first priority, and even though biker boy hadn't taken anything of his it felt like he'd lost more than anyone else. He was his family's last line of defense and he had let them down.

He was spitting mad, but at least he had sense enough to see how shaken Layne was. Even the kids picked up on it. Dylan shadowed him. He didn't say anything, but there was fear in his eyes; he kept wringing his hands and asking Mick to pick him up. Toad followed her mother around asking a million questions.

"You really think it was the boy on the bike? Why didn't he take the other Batman movie? Do you have a piggy bank, Mom?"

There was one question Toad asked more than once. Several times she took a breath and asked her mother in a hushed tone, "Do you think he'll come back?"

Ben was being really quiet, a disturbing sign. He swept up the broken pieces of his piggy bank, laid them out on the dining room table, and sat there turning chunks around and fitting them together like a puzzle, thinking about glue. It would never work—the thing was too badly shattered.

Layne finally called everybody together in the dining room. She knelt down where she could look the kids in the eye and talk straight to them.

"This is exactly why you don't put your confidence in *stuff*. It all goes away sooner or later, one way or another," she said. "There's moths and rust and bad people who break in your house while you're not at home, and stuff just goes away. You can't trust *stuff*."

Dylan clung to his dad, buried his face in Mick's neck.

"We need to do something," Toad said.

"Like what?" Mick asked. He had some ideas himself, but most of them involved yet another crime.

"We could walk around," Ben said.

"Walk around?" Mick asked. They were already walking around—like scared rabbits.

"When Cameron's TV and stuff got stole they walked around the house. Seven times."

"Let's do it!" Layne said. She knew right away it was what they needed. Mick sensed it, too.

They all went out into the yard and took each other's hands.

"We have to pray," Ben said. So while they walked, they asked God to protect them and make their house safe again. Even Mick said some words. He wasn't sure if the words went anyplace, but he said them anyway. Dylan, in his own odd way, even prayed for the burglar. He asked God to give biker boy "some stuff of his own so he won't come and take ours anymore."

It seemed like such a simple thing but it had a calming effect, even on Mick. Somehow, it took away the rage. In the end he thought maybe the Man With No Hands was right. Maybe rituals really did have a way of making people feel safe and secure.

————

The kids were out of school for the summer, so as soon as the bank opened on Monday morning Mick loaded all three of them into the truck and drove up there. On the way he explained to them that it might take a while for the justice system to make biker boy give them back their money, so he was going to replace it and let them pay him back later.

He sat Dylan up on the counter and made the teller give each of them their piggy-bank money in the same denominations that were stolen. She got a huge kick out of the story. She went all over the bank rounding up two-dollar bills and telling people about it. By the time they left, the kids could have had a job there if they'd wanted it.

27

When frogs and crawfish fly.

SUMMER. The real test.

When the kids went out to play Andy couldn't stand being locked in the backyard with the rest of the livestock, even though it was three acres. His mission in life was to find a way to get out—when he wasn't chasing the goat or working alongside the chickens to unearth the foundation of the house so rain could drain in under it.

He loved to get into Hap's pond. He wouldn't swim in the pool because he was afraid of the steep sides, but he'd tunnel out of the yard, run through a quarter-mile of woods and climb Hap's pasture fence to get to the stinking, swampy muck hole Hap called a pond. Andy thought it was heaven. He'd escape, and after a while he'd come prancing home, black on the bottom and yellow on top, proud as a two-tone Buick and smelling like a swamp. It was then that he particularly liked to find an open door into the house.

The only thing he couldn't do was get back *inside* the fence, where they kept his food and water. Mick provided dog food strictly for appearances; he didn't think Andy ever actually ate any of it. He foraged. He'd eat absolutely anything except dog food. Mick knew this because Andy was very careful to vomit only on the sidewalk around the pool—never in the woods. He'd go off and eat somebody's weed-whacker, a basketball and maybe a whisk broom, and then, when goat fare disagreed with him, he'd come home and ralph on the concrete by the pool where the kids could squat next to it, poke it with sticks and speculate about what it used to be:

"Looks like part of a pencil, a couple Legos, a Hefty bag and some yellow junk . . . squash, maybe?"

"Oooh, no! Yuck! Even Andy wouldn't eat squash."

What he didn't eat he destroyed, and left the remains scattered in the grass or the flower bed—doormats, car-washing utensils, toys, tools, other people's newspapers, shoes, begonias. He also liked to invite his friends over for a good romp and wrestle, always in the nice, soft, damp flower beds in front of the house. And he was a world-class digger. Mick came home from the store one hot day to see a black nose poking out of a Volkswagen-sized hole up against the house in the front flower bed.

In hot weather Andy would belly down on the pool steps to cool off. He wouldn't get all the way in, he'd just lay down on the top step. On the rare occasions that Mick managed to plug all the holes and keep him in the backyard for a day or two, the kids would leave the pool gate open and Andy would spend all day traipsing back and forth between his red-dirt digs under the deck and the pool steps. He'd get good and muddy, then leave a trail to the pool and a bushel of red mud on the steps. He could also destroy as many as nine flotation devices, three inflatable balls and seven plastic squirt guns in a single afternoon when he had access to the pool. Once in a while a lizard would scurry under the fence and Andy would hunker down with those big webbed feet and broad shoulders, hiking dirt and gravel into the pool at the rate of about fifteen pounds a minute. If nobody was around when the gate got left open, the goat would add his trail of raisins and the chickens would leave their mark.

Of course, with three kids "working" full time, there was no chance of keeping things put away where the dog couldn't get them, and no hope of keeping gates and doors closed. There were seven gates and doors that had to be controlled. On one side there were three kids, six chickens, a goat and a diabolically intelligent dog. On the other side was a tired old ironworker.

Mick was losing, and getting tired.

But he had to admit the pool was worth it, for the kids. He put in an hour or so every day keeping it clean and keeping up the chemicals, but the kids loved it. Since they didn't have to be in daycare all summer long and there were no other kids in the neighborhood for them to play with, they practically lived in the pool. Ben and Toad swam like otters, and before long all three of them were brown as crowder peas.

But Dylan couldn't swim, or at least he claimed he couldn't, so Mick worked with him. Every day, while Ben and Toad were playing games in the deep end and showing off on the diving board shouting "Watch me!" every five seconds, Mick was in the shallow end holding Dylan up so he could beat the water into submission. Layne worried constantly about Dylan and the pool. She insisted on keeping the rope across the shallow end, and she told Dylan if he ever crossed that rope he would surely die. Anytime Mick went to the deep end Dylan would just stand there on his side of the rope and whine until he came back. More than once it occurred to Mick that his own father would have just chunked him in the deep end and gone in the house. But Mick was not his old man.

He took Dylan to the therapist once a week, where she did all the weird exercises with the big ball and the weighted blanket and such, none of which really accomplished a whole lot as far as he could tell. Dylan still wore his pink fuzzy earmuffs half the time and he still couldn't pronounce a G, but she did say his hand-eye coordination was a little better. She always seemed a little disappointed, and every week she made a point of encouraging him to do a more consistent job with Dylan's home-therapy regimen. Mick was doing the best he could, but he wasn't much of a mother. The truth was, Dylan didn't like his therapy exercises; he hated them almost as much as Mick did. He'd much rather spend time playing in what he called his "net"—a makeshift swing Hap and Mick had made from an old hammock and hung from a white oak out in the woods—or rolling around in a short section of drainpipe they found out behind Hap's workshop. With everything else Mick had to do he was just too busy to remember Dylan's therapy every day, but they were always together. After the near disaster in Hap's pond, he never let Dylan out of his sight. Dylan had become Mick's number one sidekick, and he tried to emulate every move his dad made. He was getting pretty good at swinging a hammer, but Mick felt sure that was not the sort of thing a therapist would want to hear.

———

One afternoon in late June they walked down to Honeysuckle Creek—Mick and his kids and Andy. There was a wide place in the creek where it crossed under the road about a mile from the house, and the current had scooped out a little shallow pond in a bend. The kids loved to go down there and get filthy. Andy liked it, too. There was nothing he liked better than going for a swim in muddy water.

Ben made a spear out of a reed and spent the afternoon trying to harpoon bream with it. He had no chance, but he had fun trying. Dylan made a handgun out of a dead pine limb—to a boy, everything was a potential weapon—and Toad threw rocks. Andy got into the shallows down below the pond and started chasing crawfish. He'd paw at a rock until a crawfish darted out so he could chase it, then he'd splash through ankle-deep water with his nose tracking back and forth just above the surface until he caught up and pounced. He'd stick his whole head down in the water and come up with a crawfish in his teeth, but he must have gotten pinched once because he wouldn't keep it long. He'd fling it twenty feet in the air and then splash over to wherever it landed and start the chase all over again. Mick would have given anything for a close-up shot of the look on that crawfish's face.

He was sitting on the edge of the old wooden bridge

laughing at Andy when Aubrey's BMW pulled off the road and stopped. Mick hadn't seen him in a few weeks, since giving him the titles for the pictures. Aubrey had called once to tell him he had submitted the six photos to the museum for the show, but Mick had almost forgotten about it. He figured Ben could spear a boxcar load of bream before he got a photo picked by a panel of judges—professional photographers and museum curators. It was all just Aubrey's wishful thinking. When Aubrey got out of the car he didn't look happy, so Mick figured he must have gotten the word. He came over and sat down beside him on the bridge, letting his legs dangle.

"I got a call from a friend of mine at Arts Clayton this afternoon," Aubrey said.

"So, did they pick one of my pictures for the show?"

"No." Now Aubrey smiled. "They picked three."

"Get outta here."

"No, seriously. You'll be getting a letter from them in a day or two—that's the normal routine. I only got a phone call because the curator is a personal friend."

"Which three?"

"Let's see . . . I know he mentioned the one of Toad flying through the air. I think the other two were the close-up of Ben watching his kite and the silhouette of Dylan with the old man under the bridge."

"Wow. That's amazing. I never in a million years . . . *Three?*"

Aubrey nodded, grinning at him. "You know what that means?"

Mick shrugged, shook his head. "Never done anything like this before."

"The thing is, you submit up to six pictures and a panel of judges goes through them with an extremely critical eye. If you're lucky, they pick *one* of your photos. I've had one of mine selected on three different occasions—out of nine shows. One year they picked two of mine, but in all the years I've been doing this they've never taken three. It means they like your work. A lot."

———

Walking back up the dirt road toward home he felt like his feet weren't touching the ground. Nothing like this had ever happened to him, and it felt like he was living somebody else's life. He couldn't wait for Layne to get home so he'd have somebody to brag to, but his kids had a way of bringing him back to earth. Ben found a sailfrog on the side of the road, and Mick showed him how to throw it.

It was a good, big sailfrog, nice and flat from being run over by a thousand cars, parched hard and dry by the summer sun. In Mick's day they played with sailfrogs all the time; it was sort of a country boy's Frisbee. Toad and Ben got the hang of it right away and were having a blast flinging that thing back and forth across the road, but the first time Mick turned his back he heard both of them yelling at Dylan. What he saw when he turned around made him scream.

"DYLAN!! DO NOT BITE THE SAILFROG!!"

Dylan got his feelings hurt and started bawling, so Mick had to carry him on his shoulders the rest of the way home, wondering how his life had come to such a place. He felt like he was losing his mind. For years he'd commanded the respect of grown men in a trade where such respect wasn't easy to come by. Now he heard himself yelling things no man in his right mind should hear coming from his own mouth, and booming out these absurdities with all the conviction of Winston Churchill getting up volunteers for Dunkirk. He walked home fuming, spitting and muttering, replaying in his mind all the things he'd heard himself shout.

"Those are *NOT* Frisbees, they're compact discs!"

"You agreed to eat seven green beans, and you will have *NO* snack until you have eaten *SEVEN GREEN BEANS!*"

"How many times do I have to tell you, you will *not* put jelly-toast in the VCR, you will *not* put furniture in the pool, and you will *never, ever, ever, ever again* put tadpoles in the blender!!"

Now he could add a new gem to the list.

Layne got home from work while he was putting supper on the table. He had calmed down by then and couldn't stop thinking about what Aubrey had told him. He was proud as a puppy when he broke the news to Layne about getting three of his pictures picked for the show. She was pleased at first, although she knew even less than Mick about photography and juried shows and what it all meant. But then Toad tugged on her arm.

"Dylan bit a sailfrog," she said. She just ran it right out there, the little tattletale. She was kind of happy about it.

"Sailfrog?" Layne gave him a sideways glance.

Bacteriology was a major issue with Layne. New rules concerning the biting of sailfrogs dominated the dinner conversation while Mick's photography show faded into obscurity.

28

Of shoes and ships.

HE WAS out cutting grass when Layne heard the lawnmower running and decided it would be a good time to have a chat. It had always seemed to Mick that she preferred to talk to him when the vacuum cleaner was running or she was at the other end of the house. They would sit in the same room for two hours while she read a book and he watched a ball game, with neither of them saying a word. But then she'd lay her book down, get up, go all the way back to the bedroom and start talking to him in a normal tone of voice. A minute later, she'd come back down to the den and ask why he didn't answer her. She told people he was hard of hearing.

She fell in step beside him while he pushed the mower.

"Have you been washing my"—she ducked as the lawnmower plucked a blue plastic toy from the lawn and whisked it past her head—"*things?*" she screamed over the roar of the mower.

He shook his head. He never touched the hamper in the center of the closet. It was forbidden.

"Well, some of my underwear is—"

She yelped and hopped sideways as the mower fired a piece of orange plastic between her feet. Mick loosely calculated that they owned roughly four tons of assorted, unidentifiable, brightly colored plastic doodads, each a part of some long-forgotten plastic doodad set. Hap said their front yard looked like a Fisher-Price cargo plane crashed in it. The kids couldn't help it; it was in their genes—they had to take everything apart. And scatter the parts. Zorf the Alien Ninja Leprechaun could be found naked, armless, and buried head down in the sandbox, his battle-axe stuffed between the couch cushions, and his hauberk stopping up the downspout on the southeast corner of the house.

"—missing!" she shouted.

The lawnmower roared on for a few more feet before it clanged and clattered as if it had sucked up a pipe wrench and ground abruptly to a stop. Mick shoved the mower out of the way, bent down and pulled something from the grass.

"I wondered where this got to," he said, wiping off his pipe wrench. He nodded toward the mower. "If I find your bloomers out here they aren't likely to be worth much."

"It's not just that," she said, gripping his forearm with that worried look on her face. "A couple of my shoes are gone, and there are other things missing. Weird things—a toilet brush, the top to the humidifier, one of my new red shoes. I'm just afraid our little friend is back."

She meant biker boy, the burglar-in-training. But what

would he want with a toilet brush? Mick couldn't picture him breaking into somebody's house and cleaning their toilet.

"Any cash missing?" he asked.

"No."

"Diamond stud earrings?"

She shook her head.

"Cartoon videos, superhero action figures?"

"There's no way to know for sure without an exhaustive inventory, but I don't think so."

"Then it's not him. We need to look closer to home. The kids are probably just gathering parts to build a spaceship or something."

"My underwear?"

He shrugged. "Bungee-launched spaceship?"

———

Over the next few days the pilfering increased. When the spark-plug wire from the mower disappeared Mick began to suspect Andy, even though he didn't find the wire next to the pool. When one of his rankest old tennis shoes went AWOL Mick was sure Andy was the culprit since he'd always shown a fondness for the smell. The kids swore they were innocent, and for once he believed them, so the four of them mounted a massive search for the missing items. They moved mountains and looked under beds. They searched the yard, the garage, Hap's pond, the doghouse and the chicken house.

"The goat might have ate that stuff," Toad said. "He eats everything."

This was true. He even ate the junipers. "But the goat

hasn't been in the house, as far as I know," Mick told her. The goat left telltale signs everywhere he went.

They found nothing. No trace of the missing items.

Ben talked about wormholes in the fabric of time and space, doors to other dimensions. They cornered Andy in the garage and gave him the third degree, but he wouldn't talk. He just grinned. He was a tough dog. He only had one weakness:

He was terrified of thunder and lightning.

When the storm first rumbled in from the east the hardwoods slapped each other's shoulders, the light dimmed to a dusky yellow and the temperature nose-dived. Mick stopped for a minute by the sliding glass door and watched Andy pace back and forth on the deck, tail tucked, nervous as a cockroach at *Riverdance*. Their eyes met. The dog pleaded.

"No," Mick whispered. "You can't come in. You have a doghouse—go there. Thief."

Fat chance. Mick played computer games with the kids and forgot about the dog. When it rained they always watched movies and played games. There was this one game they played on the computer where they fought off an invasion and shot a lot of aliens. Dylan loved it. He'd sit on Mick's lap and work the Fire button while Mick did all the complicated moving and dodging. What Dylan liked best were the lunatics running around waving their arms and yelling a lot of nonsense.

"They're everywhere!"

"KILL ME!"

"I'm out of ammo!"

And Dylan's personal favorite "Frog less a pin core!"

It was complete nonsense, but the kids got a huge kick out of it. Dylan started mimicking the lunatic lines first, but pretty soon they were all doing it. Mick would be putting clothes in the washer when, from out by the pool, he'd hear, "Kill me!" Then an answering shout would come from the backyard, "I'm out of ammo!"

Then Dylan would chime in, "Frog less a pin core!"

"We didn't have all this stuff when I was a kid," Mick once told them.

"All what stuff?" Ben asked.

"Computers, video games, DVD players."

Ben's eyes went wide. "What did you *do*?"

"We played outside. We stayed outside till dark every night, and all day Saturday." It was true. He told them all about how there were always lots of kids outside back in the olden days, but they had to invent things to do. They played baseball every day until cold weather set in, then switched to football. He could remember wearing the cover off of a baseball, then wrapping it with electrical tape to keep the string from unraveling, duct-taping a cracked wooden bat, sharing gloves, using rocks for bases.

They couldn't imagine such a world. He tried, but he knew for a fact that no child of his would ever understand what he was talking about when he told them how highly prized was a brand-new baseball. They looked at him like he was crazy, but there was no doubt in his mind it was their loss. There was a golden sense of community in those days—a time when kids could play outside without parents having to watch for predators.

"Did your dad teach you to play ball?" Ben asked, and a memory came flooding back. It hit him like a brick—the memory of his father's face, laughing. Mick could hear his actual voice in his head, though he hadn't heard it in years.

"*Catch it in the pocket, son. You have to learn to use the pocket.*"

He remembered very clearly the first time he caught the ball in the pocket of the glove—how it felt and how satisfying it was. It triggered something inside Mick the child, like a light coming on. He had loved baseball ever since, and way down deep some part of him knew that he loved baseball because his father loved baseball. It was the only good memory Mick had of him. The only clear one. Mick wasn't afraid of his father's hands so long as he had a ball and glove in them.

"Yeah," Mick said, nodding slowly. "He did. My dad taught me to play."

The thunderstorm swept through in great rolling waves so thick Mick couldn't see more than fifty feet in any direction. At the height of the storm lightning shattered the woods close to the house a dozen times, and only then, with a stab of regret, did Mick remember about the dog. He went to the picture window in the den because it commanded a wide view of the backyard, but he couldn't see Andy anywhere. He could see the goat curled up asleep on the laying shelf in the henhouse, and he could see a chicken's behind poking out the door of the doghouse. All was right with the world, except he couldn't see Andy anywhere. The doghouse and the chicken house were the only safe, dry places in the whole backyard—well, except for the tree house.

He stood by the picture window staring out at the playhouse, up there on its stilts. Such a waste. The kids never played there. Mick still thought it looked like a pirate ship with all those timbers and ropes, the heavy-duty bolts and sixteen-penny galvanized nails, the camouflaged roof, and . . . the child-size door with a dog's nose sticking out of it. . . .

———

They found all the missing stuff up there—the shoes, the spark-plug wire, Layne's underwear, the top to the humidifier. He was pretty sure Andy ate the toilet brush. When he asked Ben why he hadn't noticed the mound of unusual chew toys the dog had accumulated, he just shrugged.

"I haven't been up here in months," he said. "There's no TV."

Mick wouldn't have believed it if he hadn't seen it himself. Andy had figured out how to climb a ladder. He must have decided that he liked the look of the tree house, sized up the ladder and thought, "I can do this." So he did. It was no easy climb, either—six feet high and practically straight up, with rungs of three-quarter pipe.

While Mick and the kids were up there, they called Andy. He was sitting in the sandbox watching them, wagging that big otter tail. He never hesitated, he just hooked his shoulders into the ladder, scrabbled for a hold with his back feet and up he came, all by himself. When he was ready to come down he used the sliding board.

Mick loved that dog. At least he had good taste in housing.

Late that night Layne woke him up because she heard a noise.

"I think there's somebody on the roof," she whispered.

"It's probably just the dog," Mick muttered. "Go back to sleep."

29

The show.

ARTS Clayton held the photography show on the weekend of July 4th. Layne dressed Mick in a new suit and made him put on a tie. She said he needed to look professional. She even made the kids dress up, and they didn't like it a bit. They had an unwritten law about not dressing up in the summertime, but she insisted that they attend. In Layne's mind, Arts Clayton was having a photography show so people could see pictures of her kids.

They picked up Aubrey, and on the way to the gallery he told Mick what to expect.

"The panel of judges probably won't be there today," he said. "They choose the winners when nobody's around. Today is the culmination of that whole process—the awards ceremony where they announce the winners."

"Is Daddy gonna win?" Toad asked from the back seat.

Aubrey chuckled. "Well, I suppose anything's possible."

"Yeah, right," Mick said. He still didn't share Aubrey's confidence.

"Don't sell yourself short, Mick. We already know the judges liked your style. Still, it's good not to get your hopes up—there are some very good photographers out there. I've been getting my hopes up for years and so far I've only got two honorable mentions. Just relax and keep in mind this isn't the big leagues. It's not the High Museum, it's only a small-town juried show. There are hundreds of these around the country every year. Think of it as a good place to test your mettle, to see how your work stacks up against professionals. A good place to start. Plus, there will be a lot of art patrons at the show. If you're lucky, maybe you can sell a few prints. Sometimes they go for two or three hundred dollars."

"Apiece?" This was surprising. He really didn't expect to win anything, but if he could come away with a little money in his pocket he figured the trip might be worth it after all. Every now and then it still hit him that apart from the occasional side job he wasn't bringing home a paycheck.

"Yes, apiece," Aubrey answered, laughing. "And you never know what else might happen. I've heard stories about people from the big museums nosing around these little shows looking for local talent. I've even known people who got magazine contracts out of events like this one."

———

The gallery was in a brick building on Main Street in Jonesboro, a typical old southern town whose main claim to fame was its connection with *Gone With the Wind*. Anybody in town could tell you, and would if you stood still long enough, about the love affair between Doc Holliday and his cousin, who spurned him and ran off to a convent. She was the real-life inspiration for Melly in the novel. The building housing the gallery had actually been rebuilt on the original foundation after Sherman burned it. Down in the basement there were still some hand-hewn beams with charred places on them. In Jonesboro, nobody ever forgot "the war of northern aggression."

The curator, a matronly lady named Lillian, spotted Aubrey at the reception desk as soon as they came in, and rushed over to say hello. She was nice, but she made the mistake of guiding all three of the kids to a side room and showing them a table loaded with cookies and punch.

Aubrey dragged Mick and Layne around introducing them to people for a while. There were clusters of folks in suits and Sunday dresses, standing around sipping punch from little crystal cups and chatting politely. It made Mick nervous. He couldn't recall ever in his life standing around in a crowd like this one, chatting politely. He wasn't quite sure how to go about it so he kept quiet, smiled, nodded a lot, and followed Layne's lead. She seemed to be enjoying herself. Mick kept looking over his shoulder to see what the kids were up to.

There were pictures hung around the walls, each one given its own space and lighting. In keeping with the slightly rustic Civil War theme of the town, they had left the old brick walls bare and the rafters exposed. Rows of pinpoint track lights accented the photos on display without drawing attention to the lights themselves. Mick's three pictures, which Aubrey had developed and matted and framed just for the show, had been hung one above the other on one of the freestanding walls in the middle of the floor. Aubrey had doctored the final prints to make them even better—bringing up the background details without losing the contrast or dimming the focal point. They looked fantastic.

The gallery had even made up a nice little card for each photo, with the title and a byline. Mick stood there for a long time just admiring the card next to the picture of Toad.

"Faith"
by
Mick Brannigan

It looked classy. It made him feel like somebody, at least until he looked around at the rest of the crowd. He kept tugging at his collar, feeling a bit like an ironworker in an art gallery, but he did manage to spot one guy in the crowd who looked as badly out of place as himself. He was a big old boy, bald on top but with a stark white braided ponytail hanging down his back, wearing a western-style suit and a string tie. His coat was open because it wouldn't wrap around his gut, which hung over a big round rodeo belt buckle. His boots came to a point, and he carried a Stetson hat at his side. A real character. He made Mick feel a lot better.

Layne and Aubrey were off with Lillian talking to some tall blond woman. Dylan, who was perhaps the only person in the room who hated crowds worse than his father, was snugged up to Layne, literally hiding behind her skirts. By the way Layne stroked his dark hair and looked down at him while she talked, Mick knew she was talking about her kids. Toad and Ben showed up out of nowhere to bring him a cup of punch and a cookie.

"They're quite delicious," Ben said, trying to live up to his fancy clothes.

"Excuse me," a deep voice said. The big cowboy had come up behind Mick while he was distracted. He nodded at Mick's pictures. "Are you by any chance the photographer?"

"Uh, yeah. Mick Brannigan." He shifted the cookie and punch so he could shake the cowboy's massive hand.

"Name's A.J. I was admiring your pictures earlier. You're good."

Mick mumbled thanks. He wasn't sure, but he might have even blushed.

A.J. smiled at Toad. "Is this your daughter?"

"Uh, yeah. Clarissa."

"Very photogenic," he laughed. "And now she's a celebrity."

He bent down and shook her hand. She grinned.

"I haven't seen your name before," he said to Mick. "Are you new?"

"Yeah, I'm new." *I guess that's one way of putting it*, Mick thought. "I just started doing this. A friend of mine suggested entering the show." He nodded in Aubrey's direction.

"Well, sometimes inexperience yields a fresh approach, and technique is secondary to vision, I always say. I like the personal touch. Your work speaks to me, and that's not an easy thing to do."

Mick mumbled thanks again. He had no idea how to talk the talk, so he didn't try.

"Do you have a portfolio?" the cowboy asked.

He wasn't entirely sure what that meant, but he nodded anyway. "Sure, I've, uh . . . I've got some other stuff at home."

"Do you have a card?"

He patted his pockets. "I, no, I'm afraid I must have left them at home," he lied.

"Well, give me a call sometime. I'd like to see what else you've got." A.J. pinched a card out of his coat pocket and handed it to Mick, who stuck the card in his shirt without looking at it.

Layne came up right then with Dylan in tow, and Mick introduced her to A.J. Mick was distracted, so he didn't notice what Ben was doing until it was too late. Ben had gotten down on his hands and knees in the floor right in front of A.J., staring up under that belly. Mick opened his mouth to tell Ben to get up from there, but he was a split second too late.

"I *love* that belt buckle," Ben said.

Layne's mouth opened but she couldn't speak. She looked like she might pass out.

Fortunately, the old guy had a sense of humor. He hitched up his pants, threw his head back and laughed a big booming laugh that sounded really out of place in a crowd of rich people politely chatting. He made Mick feel a *lot* better.

"A.J., meet Ben," Mick said.

Lillian stepped up to a little podium they had set up at one end of the room and tapped on the microphone. "Can I have everyone's attention, please?"

She made a short speech—something about the importance of art in the life of the community, to which Mick was not listening—and then said, "Now, the moment we've all been waiting for. First, I want to thank all the entrants, and I'd like to say that each and every one of them is a winner in my book. The judging this time was very, very difficult, because there were so many wonderful photos."

Polite applause.

She held up a purple ribbon. "Honorable Mention goes to Rue Vaughn, for the evocative piece titled "Winter Night." Polite applause while some little guy took the purple ribbon from Lillian, went over and pinned it up next to a very nice blue-tinted photo of some moonlit pine woods under a heavy blanket of snow.

Third prize went to a color photo of sailboats at anchor in a quaint little harbor. Razor-sharp reflections. Looked like a postcard.

Up to that point Mick had been paying attention. In fact, he had even been a little nervous, because some small part of him believed what Aubrey said—that his pictures could rival anybody's. But being a realist, his highest aspiration was the lowest prize, so when third place went to the sailboats he knew he was out of the running. He looked around to make sure all three kids were accounted for, then squatted down and licked his thumb to wipe a chocolate-chip smear off Dylan's chin. He wasn't really listening anymore, so when he heard Lillian's voice say, ". . . to Mick Brannigan, for his stunning black-and-white photograph, 'Faith'," he wasn't sure he'd heard right until Toad did a backflip. In a dress.

Aubrey grabbed the shoulder of his coat and hauled him to his feet.

"I *told* you it was good!" Aubrey whispered, grinning. Caught up in the moment, he actually threw his arms around Mick's shoulders and gave him a hug. Layne lifted Toad off her feet in a congratulatory hug—it was, after all, Toad's picture—and then reached up to give Mick a kiss on the cheek.

"Now do you believe?" she asked.

He didn't answer her right away because, frankly, he didn't believe it until the little guy took the red ribbon from Lillian, made his way through the crowd and actually pinned it up beside Toad's picture.

It really was more than Mick ever expected. Second place, in his first show. Not bad for an ironworker.

First prize went to a shot of an osprey caught in mid-flight, snatching a fish out of a lake. Another great picture.

"He must have had a thousand-dollar lens to get that shot as clear as he did," Aubrey muttered. He was right. There were drops of water frozen in flight, and he could count the feathers on the osprey's wings.

A color photograph titled "Cote d'Azur" took Best of Show. It was an angled shot of a door and window in the front of what looked like an old adobe house with the sun slanting across it. There were red flowers in a blue window box. The shadows, the light and the colors were really striking. It was a good picture but it wouldn't have been Mick's first choice. He started to ask Aubrey what it was that made it a great picture, then thought better of it. It could wait.

As Lillian closed the ceremonies and left the podium the Musak came back on and people started easing toward the door, still chatting politely. Several of them stopped to congratulate Mick and pat Toad on the head before they left.

Afterward, he and the other winners had to do a couple of interviews for *arts&expressions* magazine and the local paper, then pose for pictures. It was nice to be the center of attention for a change, but he had to scratch his head when the reporter asked him what he did for a living.

"I'm in construction," he said, mostly because it sounded better than "I'm an unemployed ironworker." It didn't even occur to him to tell them he was a stay-at-home dad.

It was Aubrey who came and pulled him away. "Lillian wants to see you for a second," he said. Something was up. Aubrey had a gleam in his eye. He led Mick to an office in the back, where Lillian stood waiting by her desk.

She shook his hand and congratulated him, then said, "Mr. Brannigan, the gallery would like to buy your photo," she said. "We normally only purchase the Best of Show, but personally I find your picture very distinctive and . . . compelling. Mr. Weems said he thought you might be amenable."

"The picture of Toad?" he asked, confused.

Lillian frowned, turned to Aubrey. "Toad?"

"His daughter," Aubrey explained. "The girl in the picture."

"Yes," she said, smiling a little too broadly now. "The picture of Toad. We'd like to place it on permanent display if it's all right with you."

It was all right with Mick.

———

Having been forced into their best behavior for a couple hours, the kids went nuts on the way home. Aubrey insisted they all go someplace and celebrate, and since the kids were with them it seemed perfectly natural that they ended up at the Dairy Barn. Layne didn't even seem to mind when Dylan dripped chocolate syrup down the front of his dad's new suit.

Riding home, Aubrey couldn't stop talking about it. He was more excited than any of them, including Mick.

"It was just second place," Mick said. "Beginners luck."

Aubrey shook his head, laughing. "*Beginners luck?* Mick, I've been at this for years and only managed Honorable Mention a couple times. And I'm a major contributor to the gallery. I'm telling you, you've got talent." He sounded almost insulted.

Mick stared at him for a second, and saw no jealousy in him. He was as proud as if his own child had done well, and it finally began to seep into Mick's brain that Aubrey's interest in him was purely unselfish. Aubrey saw himself as a mentor, and Mick's success, in a way, as his own.

Mick cleared his throat, keeping his eyes on the road ahead. "I, uh, I don't know if I ever thanked you for this, Aubrey," he said. "Of course it means a lot to me. I guess it just hasn't sunk in yet. I couldn't have done any of it— wouldn't have known it *could* be done—if it weren't for you. Thank you."

"Don't mention it," Aubrey said quietly. "I haven't had this much fun in years. By the way, did you make any contacts at the show?"

"Nah, I kind of kept to myself most of the time," Mick said.

"Yes, I could see you were a little uncomfortable. That's all right. It'll happen. Sooner or later some high roller from a magazine is going to ask to see your portfolio."

"Well, actually, one guy did," Mick said. The mention of a portfolio reminded him of it. "But it was just that cowboy character. Nice guy, but a little eccentric."

"Yes, I noticed him talking to you. I don't recall ever seeing him there before. I assumed he was a friend of yours from . . . work. He asked to see your portfolio?"

"Yeah. Well, he asked if I had one. I lied and told him I did."

"Who was he?"

"I don't know. A.J., I think it was. Oh, wait—" Mick stuck two fingers into his shirt pocket, found A.J.'s card and handed it to Aubrey. Busy dodging traffic, Mick didn't look at it.

Aubrey sat there holding that card in his two hands for a long time, just staring at it. Finally, very quietly, he said, "Mick, do you know who this is?"

"No, I never saw him before."

"Albert Joss Ecklund," he read slowly, and then lowered the card to his lap and sat staring out the front window for a minute as if he was in shock.

"Name doesn't ring a bell," Mick said. "Should I know him?"

Aubrey just laughed, shaking his head. "I suppose not, but everybody else does. Or at least they know *about* him. A.J. Ecklund started out as a photojournalist with the wire services in Vietnam, then went on to do freelance work for major magazines. He's done covers for *Time, Newsweek, Life, National Geographic*—all the big ones. He's something of a legend in photography circles. Now he's semi-retired, and according to this card, consulting for the High Museum."

"In Atlanta?"

"Yes. In Atlanta. So what you're telling me is that A.J.—*the* Albert Joss Ecklund—asked to see your portfolio?"

Mick shrugged. "Yeah, I guess. Do I have a portfolio?"

"Hardly."

"Then what do I do?"

"You're going to get busy, is what you're going to do. People wait their whole lives for an opportunity like this." He shook the card at Mick. "You can't let it go to waste. You've got to put together a portfolio before Mr. Ecklund forgets who you are."

Pure blind luck, every bit of it. More than ever, Mick had the feeling he was being driven down a course he didn't set and could never in a million years have planned. He had no idea where to go or what to shoot next, but he was beginning to get comfortable with the notion that somebody—or some bizarre accident—would tell him.

30

The next level.

MICK went out a couple times that week and shot barn pictures with the kids in the early morning and late afternoon while the light was on a slant, but when he took them over to Aubrey's to get them developed, Aubrey was not impressed. There were a couple decent shots, but nothing spectacular. High summer had turned the Georgia sky white and hazy, diffusing the light and making it nearly impossible to get a decent landscape shot. As soon as the prints were dry he and Aubrey took them upstairs and spread them out on a marble dining room table, under a chandelier that would have filled the back of Mick's truck.

"Some of these are good, Mick, but not good enough. If you want to impress A.J. Ecklund, they have to be great. There's no spark here, nothing new. You've already done a show using your kids. You've got to find something else."

"Like what?"

Aubrey raised his eyebrows and blew a breath out through pursed lips, stumped.

"I don't know," he said. "*You're* the golden child. I've always been a little short on imagination, myself—come to think of it, maybe that's my problem. I only know that good isn't good enough. Not for the High. If you're going there, you've got to bring your A game, and it better be something new."

"Well, with the kids out of school for the summer there's only so much I can do. There's only so far I can travel. I'm afraid we're stuck with the landscapes."

Aubrey bit his lip. "How are you on nature photography?"

"Never tried it, but from what I've read it's a whole different set of problems. I don't think this is the time to learn."

"Good point. What about your homeless friends? Maybe you can do more of that kind of thing."

Mick snorted. "Right. Imagine yourself trying to shoot pictures in hell's kitchen while trying to keep an eye on my three kids. It can't be done, Aubrey. There's no way."

He heard a noise and looked around to see Celly standing in the doorway in her robe, brushing her hair. Without her makeup he could see the dark circles under her eyes. When he said hello she just kind of nodded and turned away without saying anything. He could hear her puttering around in the kitchen.

"Is she okay?" he muttered to Aubrey after she left the room.

Aubrey nodded, but he made a rocking motion with his hand. "She has good days and bad days," he said quietly.

31

Beal Street Mission.

THAT Sunday, as usual, Layne asked him to go to church with her and the kids. She always asked, and most of the time he declined. It had become sort of a Sunday morning ritual. The simple truth was that Layne's church reminded him too much of the one he grew up in— a squat little red-brick place where the song leader did the tomahawk chop to the same old hymns out of the same old blue hymnbook while the preacher's wife pounded an upright piano, and then the preacher dragged out the same tired jokes and worn-out sermons week after week while old people nodded off and fluttered their funeral-home fans. Mick's mother made the family go to church all the time—everybody but his old man. She let him sleep. She said it was because he worked night shift, but even when Mick was little he knew better. If she ever even mentioned church to Mick's father he'd start bad-mouthing her friends. He loved to hit her with the old line about how you could spot the churchpeople—they were the ones who didn't wave to each other in the liquor store.

Mick didn't agree with his old man about anything, but he did like his freedom on Sunday mornings. After he started staying home with the kids, Sunday morning was the only time he had to himself. Layne said he should be setting a better example, but what kind of example would he be if he went to church just because his wife made him? It never seemed that important as long as he was working, but now that Layne was the breadwinner, little issues like that took on a whole new significance. Little issues like that were starting to add up, like bricks.

When Mick told her he was going downtown to shoot some pictures she didn't say anything. Lately, she'd been not saying anything with increasing frequency. He left the house before Layne and the kids, but he knew it was already too late to find the light.

Driving up the expressway he turned the radio off. He'd gotten to where he did that a lot lately, because the quiet felt so good. He could think when it was quiet, and there was something else, too. He didn't understand it at the time, but after the trip to the monastery, whenever something ate at him, he looked for quiet. With three kids it wasn't that easy. He never considered himself much of a thinker, but he had begun to look for the odd ten minutes here and there where he could just be alone and sort things out in complete silence.

The difference was subtle, yet pivotal—since his little field trip to the monastery, for the first time in Mick's life he had the feeling he wasn't *alone* in the silence. God had always been a mystery to him, and way beyond anybody's reckoning—especially the people who claimed they knew all about him. But for the first time in his life Mick felt, with a quiet certainty, that God was *there*. If he was being honest, the most he would have ever claimed before was that he didn't *not* believe, but the morning he sat in the blue and purple light next to the Man With No Hands in the balcony of the abbey church, things changed. It seemed small at the time—the perception of an Other, a Presence in the silence. Sometimes, now, when he was quiet, Mick found himself talking to God, or not; the awareness was there, even if he had no words. Sometimes he asked questions and sometimes he just thought whatever he was thinking, but he was aware. He wouldn't have called it prayer—not like the gravy-cooling blessing Deacon Hanratty put on the food at the picnic or the rumbling, musical, thee-and-thou prayers the pastor preached at the end of his sermons when Mick was a kid—but what difference did it make what he called it? Anyway, there weren't any answers, or if there were Mick couldn't hear them. That didn't matter, either. His experience with Dylan's sensory integration dysfunction had taught him that just because he couldn't see or hear a thing didn't mean it wasn't there.

———

Things were pretty quiet under the bridges that Sunday morning, which was a little spooky when Mick went down there by himself. He didn't see the Man With No Hands anywhere, but coming back up the bank he ran into the tall cross-dresser that he had first seen wearing a red-sequined dress. This time Sheila was decked out in a royal blue evening gown, limping down the hill after what must have been a rough night. His dress was torn and dirty, and one of the straps hung down the front. He looked like he'd been in a fight. He had broken a heel but was still walking on the other one—up, down, up, down.

"Seen the preacher?" Mick asked.

"I ain't been here," he said, stopping, looking sideways at Mick. "But it's Sunday. He'll be over to the Beal Street Mission."

"I thought the mission shut down."

He nodded, tucking in his bra strap. "Did, but it's open again. Dooley's kid's runnin' it, what I heard."

———

Mick found the mission five blocks over, in the old warehouse district. Being Sunday morning, the world was deserted except for the occasional dark figure shuffling across a street or over the tracks, moving in the general direction of the mission. The place looked like an old brick church building except for the missing steeple and the whitewashed plywood in all the arched holes where stained glass windows used to be. Mick left his truck in the nearly empty parking lot, checking twice to make sure the doors were locked, and headed for the chapel. He could hear singing from inside. Up close, he could see gray wood where the white paint was flaking off the doors and little worms of shrunken calk curling up out of the corners.

While he was standing in the doorway trying to make up his mind about whether to go in, a bum tottered past him clutching at walls and doorframes on his way to the nearest chair. Still drunk—Mick could smell it on him. He wondered who else was out there and what they were up to, so he stepped back into the sunlight for a second and peeked around the corner. Already, some guy had his face pressed up against the driver's side window of his truck. Mick strolled out there casually, with his hands in his pockets. When the guy saw Mick he backed away from the truck, then turned around and ambled past him toward the door of the mission like nothing was up.

Mick unlocked the truck, got his camera bag off the seat and hung it on his shoulder. Nothing else inside the truck was worth stealing, so he rolled the windows down and left it unlocked. He figured it might save him a busted window.

Once inside, he still didn't see the Man With No Hands anyplace. He had fully expected him to be up there preaching. There were stairs leading down from the vestibule, but some young guy with long red hair all in his face was sitting at a table blocking the way to the stairs and tapping on a laptop computer. When Mick paused and glanced over at the stairs, Red looked up. His lip curled and he shook his head.

"After church," he said. Obviously, he thought Mick was one of *them*.

He stood in the back of the church and looked the crowd over from behind. Mostly men, and mostly black or Hispanic. They were standing up singing when Mick came in, but a few sat slumped in the folding chairs. No pews, no carpet, just scuffed hardwood floors and rows of metal folding chairs with BSM stenciled across the back. They were singing old hymns out of hymnbooks, and the singing was better than Mick would have thought. Stronger, with a lot of bass. Uninhibited.

In that confined space the combination of smells was overwhelming—a lot of body odor, which Mick had expected, laced with whiffs of urine and vomit, which he hadn't. A lot of these guys slept wherever they fell, and their clothes didn't get washed much. There was a lot of long, dark, scraggly hair, and a lot of grime. Industrial grunge had worn their jeans slick and shiny and ground itself into the creases in the backs of their necks. Without really thinking about it Mick pulled out the camera and shot a few pictures. He kept an eye on the young preacher who was up front alone, leading the singing while a woman who must have been his wife played the piano. Some things never changed. The young preacher looked his way a few times but didn't say anything and didn't seem to mind him taking pictures, so he moved around to the side and kept shooting.

Looking down the rows Mick noticed right away there was a scattering of church kids among the street people. He could tell by the clothes. The church kids were clean— volunteers from someplace else. Some nice clean suburb with good schools, manicured lawns.

He got some great pictures. One guy was singing his heart out—dirty gray face uplifted, eyes closed, hands raised—while an equally grungy guy in the chair right next to him sat slumped over with his chin on his chest, sound asleep. Another man, with dark black skin and shiny scars all over his face, scowled in the general direction of the preacher while a young white boy, obviously a volunteer, stared up at him unnoticed. The kid's eyes were full of teenage curiosity but his mouth had a little twist in it, like he couldn't completely hide his disgust.

When the singing stopped and everybody sat down Mick found an empty chair near the back and took a seat holding his camera bag on his lap. He knew better than to put it under his chair. On the back row alone he counted four guys with backpacks, and every one of them was holding it on his lap, guarding it. He had learned from the Man With No Hands that a backpack—or a camera bag, for that matter—was a prize possession because it replaced the usual black garbage bag with something that could carry a man's stuff while leaving his hands free. It could also be used for a pillow, and in a pinch could be traded for a bottle of wine or maybe even a rock. He didn't dare leave it unguarded.

He could smell spaghetti cooking someplace, probably downstairs since there was no room for a kitchen up behind the dais. The sanctuary was nearly full, and Mick figured most of these men came for a hot meal and a handout. The young preacher was talking about choices, decisions, but Mick wasn't listening, he was watching people, checking out faces and body language. Some of them were really into it, like they came there hurting and were serious about getting help. Others nodded off. They were just there for lunch and a goody bag. Mick didn't hang around long; he had come there looking for the Man With No Hands but didn't see him in the crowd, so as soon as the preacher got cranking he slipped out.

The red-headed sentry was still sitting at the head of the stairs, tapping his laptop. He warned Mick off without even looking up.

"I told you, man. After church. You know the drill."

"I'm looking for the Man With No Hands."

"Oh. You a volunteer?" Red looked him up and down then and relaxed a little. Even in his work clothes Mick figured he was too clean to be mistaken for homeless.

"Uh, yeah, I guess," Mick said. "Whatever. I just wanted to talk to him, but I can hang around and help out if you need me to."

Red jerked his head. "Go on down, then. He'll be back in the kitchen."

———

The basement of the old church could have been a thrift store, except it was a lot more crowded, like a warehouse in a phone booth. Rows of old coats hung on racks jammed up against racks of pants jammed up against industrial metal shelving full of all kinds of shoes with the laces tied together and handwritten paper tags hanging from them. There were sweatshirts and T-shirts and underwear and socks, toothpaste and brushes and mouthwash and soap, all sorted and stacked and labeled. Mick squeezed between the racks and wormed his way to the back. From the other side of a swinging door came the sound of pots clashing. The scent of spaghetti drifted over the musty odor of old clothes.

There were three volunteers in the kitchen with him, two boys and a girl. High-school kids. Mick stood in the door for a minute or two, watching the Man With No Hands run the kitchen like it was an orchestra. He was clearly in his element, and he had those kids synchronized. It was a typical church kitchen, six-burner gas stove with an industrial vent-hood roaring over it, a walk-in cooler at the far end and a large worktable down the middle—everything stainless steel. The girl was chopping a mountain of salad on the worktable while one of the boys stirred a cauldron of spaghetti sauce and another hustled a two-handled pot of water over to the stove. The Man With No Hands opened the door to a stacked oven and snatched out two trays of rolls. Mick couldn't help chuckling at that—anybody else would have had to use a potholder.

When he turned around to slide the trays into a standing rack he spotted Mick.

"Mick! I'm glad you're here! We can use some help."

Mick unslung his camera bag and glanced around for a place to put it.

"Set it anywhere," he said. "It's safe. Nobody's allowed down here except for volunteers and staff."

The Man knew how to run a kitchen. For the next half hour Mick filled paper plates, poured tea into Styrofoam cups and loaded meals onto rolling carts that fit neatly into a dumbwaiter that took them upstairs. While he worked, he told the Man With No Hands all about the show at Arts Clayton, how he took second place and opened a door with A.J. Ecklund. Only after he told the story, and after the Man was suitably impressed, did Mick realize that it mattered to him. He wanted the Man With No Hands to be impressed.

The young preacher, who turned out to be Robert Dooley, son of the man who had been running the place for years, came down himself to tell them when it was time to serve lunch. Once the preaching was over they converted the sanctuary upstairs to a lunchroom. They hauled everything up to the front through the dumbwaiter; then the guys in the sanctuary came up front for a plate and took it back to their seats to eat.

After lunch Mick found out what Red's laptop was all about. It was their tracking system. All the homeless guys were required to register in the system, and they were given an ID card.

"Keeps them honest," the Man With No Hands told him while overseeing the distribution process in the vestibule. Volunteers—mostly high-school kids on the day Mick was there—circulated through the crowd asking each man what he needed and checking his ID. Then they brought the card to the table with the laptop, and if the database agreed with the order they'd send a volunteer downstairs to fill it.

"You can only get a pair of work boots every other month," the Man With No Hands said. "Same with backpacks, when we have them. Otherwise, they'll just sell them on the street."

Mick didn't know where to find anything, but it didn't matter. There were volunteers who stayed downstairs and pulled stuff from the shelves. Mick took an order down and handed it off, and a minute later he came back up the steps with a black garbage bag containing a shirt and a pair of pants in the size requested, a couple cans of fruit cocktail, a hygiene kit and a couple of aspirins. He couldn't help noticing the aspirins were always in small quantities.

When he got back upstairs with the bag he asked the Man what to do next.

He waved a hook toward the sanctuary. "Take it up front and call out the guy's name. When he comes up to get it, check his ID before you give it to him."

He could handle that.

"Then ask him if he wants you to pray with him."

Mick just stared at him. He was afraid something like this might happen. He hadn't signed up for this; he only came to shoot some pictures. He certainly didn't feel qualified to be praying for anybody.

A little smile came into the Man's eyes as if he'd read his mind. He laid a hook on Mick's shoulder.

"Just do it," he said. "It's okay."

So he did.

He got lucky at first. The first couple guys came up there with dull eyes, wobbling a little, and when Mick mumbled something about praying with them they shook him off.

"Just gimme the bag."

He was relieved. Felt like he'd dodged a bullet.

But the third guy Mick waited on came up there with something else in his eyes. He was wide awake and he looked scared. When he took the bag his hand was shaking.

"Is there something I can pray for?" Mick asked, hoping the guy would blow him off and slide out the door like the others.

But he nodded.

Uh-oh. "Well . . . okay, what?"

"Everything," he whispered.

Mick hesitated, not knowing exactly what to say.

The man's eyes wandered, lost, and he went on, "I don't know. I don't know nothin' no more. I used to. I really did—I used to be okay. I had a job, a car, my own house. Last night I sold my jacket. For a rock," he said, his face twisted with pain. He looked down at himself. "This ain't what I started out to be. How'd I get *here?*"

There was desperation in his eyes and he looked like he was fighting back tears. Mick waited.

"Look, bro . . . if you know God," the man said, "I wish you'd tell him to show me somethin', cause I don't know nothin' no more. I'm wasted, man."

It wasn't as hard as Mick thought. He already knew the words to that prayer, so long as God didn't expect him to sound like a preacher.

Before the man walked off he gripped Mick's hands, looked into his eyes and said, "Thanks, man."

Mick couldn't say anything. He just stood there and watched him go.

The next one brought him back to earth. He was a big guy with a stone face and gray hair spread out loose over the shoulders of a T-shirt that said *Another Brick In The Wall.* Mick had seen him hanging around outside during the service, smoking cigarettes, waiting for it to be over. The look in his eye said he was just working the system. It was in his face and his posture.

"Just gimme the bag," he said, then opened it right away and started digging in it while he walked back through the sanctuary. There were others waiting their turns, so Mick went out to the vestibule for another card.

The big guy turned around at the outside door, spotted Mick and said, "Hey, these ain't the boots I wanted. I said eleven. These are eleven and a half."

Mick went over to him and looked at the tag.

"Okay. Wait here and I'll go down and get it straight."

The kid downstairs who pulled the order, a pimply

teenager with a buzz cut and glasses, looked at the boots and said, "Right. We're out of elevens. That's the best I can do."

Mick took the boots back upstairs.

"I don't want these. I'll take some athletic shoes instead. Size ee-lev-ven."

Back downstairs, back up.

"Here. Sneakers. Size eleven." Mick tried not to show his irritation.

The shaggy gray head shook side to side. "I don't want no canvas sneakers. *Athletic* shoes. And clean. These are dirty."

Mick figured clean ones would sell better on the street.

"Right. And what would be your preference, sir? Nike? Adidas? Reebok?"

The man leaned toward him, a little too close. Mick got a whiff of liquor.

"I just want some *decent* shoes, man. Why you want to bust my chops? I don't see you messin' with nobody else." There was a lot of activity in the vestibule, volunteers going and coming, the Man With No Hands directing traffic. In that moment it seemed like everybody had stopped and was staring at Mick.

Mick had to remind himself where he was, and that it was not his place to argue.

"All right," he said, through clenched teeth.

He brought up a pair of leather athletic shoes.

"Clean. Size *ee-lev-ven*," he said. But now the big guy had pulled the shirt from his bag and was holding it up by the corners.

"I don't want this. I want a sweatshirt," he growled.

Mick had worked guys like this a hundred times. But people were watching and it was a church, after all. He took the shirt downstairs without a word and brought back a sweatshirt—double X.

The man took one look at it and got right in Mick's face, bobbing that head.

"Wrong color," he sneered. "I want blue."

He was pushing all the wrong buttons. "Listen to me—*sir*," Mick said, his voice shaking. "You got *shoes*, and you got a *sweatshirt*. That's what you got, and it's all you're gonna get. You want 'em or not?"

Silence fell like a blanket over the vestibule.

The man saw people watching, changed his tactics and sulled up like a child. "I don't know why you're givin' *me* grief," he said, and his voice even had a little whine in it. He was a pro. "I'm just a guy down on his luck, and it seems like you'd have a little Christian compassion."

He glanced around, judged that he had the sympathy of the crowd, and went on the offensive again. "But you don't care, *do* you?" he snarled. "You're just like my old man."

Mick wasn't sure exactly how it happened, but the next thing he knew his forearm was pinning the man and his bag and his athletic shoes and his sweatshirt to the wall between the back doors—with considerable force. Their faces were inches apart. There was fear in the homeless man's eyes, and this time he wasn't faking it.

"Let me tell you something," Mick said, intentionally keeping his voice low because he knew it would feed the fear. "You ain't the only one with a rough old man—I'll swap stories with you all day long, pal. But the truth is, it wasn't your old man that made all the choices that put you on the street. You did that yourself. And until you figure that out, you'll *stay* on the street. Right this second, your best choice would be to take your goody bag and go."

Mick was still locked onto the man's eyes when he felt the gentle tug of a steel hook on his shoulder and eased off. As soon as he let go the man bolted out the door. He kept running, all the way across the street and on out of sight.

The Man With No Hands and the young preacher were both standing right behind him. Like a committee. Mick held his hands up, palm out.

"I'm sorry," he said. "I'll go now."

He pushed past everybody and went downstairs to get his camera bag. A bunch of kids were down there cleaning up the kitchen, wiping off counters, putting away pots and bagging up garbage. He picked up his camera bag and left. He had to shade his eyes when he went out from the dark church building into the bright sunshine of the parking lot. About the time he reached his truck he heard steps behind him and turned around.

It was the Man With No Hands.

"We need to talk," he said. He didn't even look mad.

Mick threw his camera bag on the seat and leaned back against the side of the truck. "Go ahead," he said. "Let me have it."

"Let you have what?"

"The speech. Lower the boom. Tell me how I need to control my temper, and how when you asked me to help take care of homeless people you weren't talking about assault and battery. Tell me how wrong that was, like I don't already know."

He crossed his hooks on his chest and stared.

"What you said to that guy—was it the truth?"

"What?"

"That he should take responsibility for his own choices instead of blaming his failure on somebody else. Was that the truth?"

Mick shrugged. "Yeah, I guess."

"And if he was clearly manipulating everybody around him for the purpose of feeding his self-destructive habits, and you knew it, would it have served him for you to ignore it and let him get away with it, thinking that nobody cared enough to challenge him?"

Mick had to think about that one for a minute. "No," he finally said. "I guess not."

"Then what did you do that was so wrong?"

"Oh, I don't know. Maybe . . . putting him up against a wall and threatening his life?"

"You didn't threaten his life."

"Yes I did—I just didn't use words."

He smiled then, shaking his head. "Desperate times, desperate measures. My point is, that guy's been working us for years, and this is the first time anybody's ever gotten through to him. Your methods may be a little unorthodox, Mick, but your message was better than a lot of sermons. Sometimes it takes a jolt to clear a man's head."

"You mean like a train?"

The Man With No Hands chuckled softly. "Yes, exactly. Or a crane."

The midday sun beat down out of a blinding white sky. Even the black asphalt parking lot made Mick squint. He snagged a cap from the dash of the truck and clapped it on his head.

"Tell me something, Preacher," he said. "You think everybody gets hit by a train sooner or later?"

"Maybe," he nodded. "I don't know. I do know this much—everything depends on what you choose to do after that. How you deal with it. What you choose, right then, after the train, decides who you are."

Mick shook his head, chuckling. "Well, then I must have made a wrong turn because things ain't workin' out so great."

The Man's eyebrows went up in surprise. "Really? What about the photography? Sounds to me like things are going fine."

"Yeah, the photography thing is nice, but everything else . . ." He turned a thumb down. "It's mostly the staying-at-home thing. The house is always a wreck, my kids are turning into savages, Dylan's not doing so great with his therapy, and my wife isn't real happy with me. Truth is, I'm not much of a mother."

"No," the Man said, laughing. "You're not. That's good. That's progress."

"Progress? How you figure that?"

"You may not be much of a mother, but from where I'm standing you're a pretty decent father. The trouble is, you're always trying to fit into somebody else's mold. The only time you followed your heart was when you had a camera in your hands, and look how that turned out." He waved a hook toward the church building. "There's a place for you here, and you don't have to be somebody else to fit into it. It's perfectly all right to be Mick Brannigan. I told you before, God's got his hand on you, Mick. God designed you, and he had something in mind when he did it."

"Yeah, well I wish he'd let me in on it."

"Oh, I suspect he has. You just don't see it yet." He said this with a wry smile that made Mick nervous, and made him want to steer the conversation someplace else.

"Yeah, well, if God's gonna give me a portfolio for the High Museum I wish he'd get on with it. Time's a'wastin'."

The Man stared at the ground for a minute, reaching up and scratching his head with the tip of a hook. "You know, sometimes you seem to be making it hard on purpose. What are you afraid of?"

"I'm not afraid of anything," Mick said. "I just don't know what to do."

"Pictures are just stories, Mick. What are the stories you know best?"

He laughed. "The only thing I've ever known is construction work. I can guarantee you, nobody wants to see pictures of that."

"Why?"

"Why? Because it's . . . because nobody . . . Who wants to look at a bunch of construction workers?"

"Right. And who wants to look at pictures of your kids? Or homeless people?"

"Aw, come on, Preacher. It's not the same thing. Turn on a television and you'll see that a construction worker is an ignorant redneck with a beer gut sitting on a wall harassing women and showing four inches of crack."

The Man With No Hands stared evenly, letting the assertion hang between them for a minute. Without taking his eyes from Mick's face, he asked quietly, "Is that the construction worker you know?"

Mick wasn't sure why, but the question conjured pictures in his mind. He could see Mike Dover standing on a crane hook thirty stories in the air, sucking on a lollipop and holding onto the cable with his other hand, grinning. He could see big old Butch Hinton, the toughest man he ever met, squatting in the gravel by the trailer feeding half a tuna sandwich to a stray kitten. A dozen images ran through his head just that quick—pictures of men he'd known and things he'd seen them do. None of them were ignorant, at least not on certain subjects, and none of them went around wearing their pants too low in the back.

"No," he said quietly. "That's not the construction worker I know."

"Then show people things they've never seen before. There's your portfolio. Tell the stories you *know*."

32

Marco Polo.

IT RAINED the first couple days that week and the things the Man With No Hands said on Sunday afternoon got drowned out by a houseful of wild children. Two days of movies, fighting over toys, spilling juice . . . and boredom.

"I'm bored."

"What do you feel like doing? Want to play a game?"

"Let's shoot some aliens," Ben said.

"Frog less a pin core!" Mick shouted.

"KILL ME!" Dylan answered, from the living room.

"I'm out of ammo!" Toad hollered from her bedroom.

"They're everywhere!" Ben giggled.

They took turns sitting on his lap blasting aliens all afternoon. Mick had a feeling Layne wouldn't approve, but the kids were having a ball and getting along with each other for a change. After a couple days of rain, he'd use whatever he could.

By Wednesday the sun had come out. He had to vacuum the pool and cut the grass, but it felt great to get the kids out of the house again. By the time he finished mowing the lawn he was hot and ready to hit the pool.

Ben and Toad started begging him to come play Marco Polo with them in the deep end.

"Can't," Mick said. "Gotta work with Dylan." He was trying really hard to be conscientious about Dylan and his therapy, and he knew in his gut that swimming would be the best thing in the world for him if he could just get him to do it.

But all he ever did was hold Dylan up in the shallow end, on his side of the rope, and let him club away at the water. His hands and feet splashed a lot but he wasn't really trying to swim. Whenever Mick stopped supporting him he'd keep clubbing the water and pretending, but he'd instantly put a leg down and hold himself up with a toe. He never actually swam an inch. Mick wasn't sure if he was afraid of it for some reason or if he just liked the attention, but after a month of it he was pretty sure it was the latter.

When Mick ducked under the rope and did a turn through the deep end to cool off, Dylan started squawking. He stood on his side of the rope and fussed and whined the whole time, wringing his hands and begging his dad to come back and work with him.

"Come on, Dad. Me and Toad want to play Marco Polo," Ben said.

"I *neeeeed* to swim," Dylan whined. Whenever he got desperate for something he didn't just want it anymore, he *neeeeeded* it.

Mick swam up toward the shallow end but stopped at

the rope. Dylan lit up, and actually started clapping his hands. But when Mick unhooked the rope from the little chrome eye on the side of the pool Dylan stopped clapping. When he waded across to the other side, coiling the rope around his forearm, Dylan frowned and started wringing his hands again. When he unhooked the other end and climbed up out of the water Dylan latched on to the side and stood there looking over his shoulder at where the rope had been, as if it confused him. Mick thought for a minute he was going to cloud up and cry. He hung the coiled rope on the fence and knelt down in front of his youngest son.

Dylan looked up at him and said, very deliberately, "Mom said we dotta keep the rope on."

Mick wasn't expecting the twinge of pain he got from it, but he knew it had to be done. He leaned down close to Dylan's face and said, "I'm not your mom."

And then Mick dove into the deep end and ignored him. They played Marco Polo, he and Ben and Toad, and ignored Dylan's yelling. He yelled and pleaded and threatened for five or ten minutes, insisting that he *neeeeeded* to swim and he *neeeeeeeded* his dad to help him. When that didn't work he threatened to tell his mom. When that didn't work, he cried. Mick ignored him while he cried softly, huddling in the corner of the shallow end, and he ignored him when he screamed and beat the water, bellowing loud enough for Layne to hear him at work. Dylan eventually gave up on that, too, and squatted down with his back against the wall, just his eyes and nose showing above the waterline.

Mick watched him from the corner of his eye. He didn't want Dylan to *know* he was being watched, but he kept pretty close tabs on him. He'd spent so much time with that boy Mick knew how his mind worked. Dylan was thinking. He knew for a solid-gold fact Dylan wouldn't have stayed in the water this long unless he was thinking about it. If he ever gave up, he'd get out of the pool.

But he didn't get out. He sat there by himself, up against the wall, watching.

They kept playing Marco Polo. It must have been half an hour later when Mick popped up in the middle of the deep end with his eyes closed. He was "it."

"Marco," he sang out.

"Polo," came Toad's voice from over by the ladder. She liked it there because she could push off in any direction if he came after her.

"Polo." Ben, hanging under the diving board. He liked to drop deep and shove off. Both of them were quick as frogs. Mick was about to make his move when he heard hands splashing, *behind* him, and getting closer.

He wanted to turn around. He wanted to very badly, but he didn't. He kept his eyes closed and stayed where he was, treading water for a few more seconds, until a little hand grabbed his shoulder. Then another. Two skinny arms wrapped around his neck from behind.

"Polo," Dylan said.

―――――

That same evening, while they were cleaning up the kitchen after supper, Layne asked him what was happening with the portfolio.

"Nothing much," Mick said, scraping a plate into the garbage. "I got a few shots Sunday morning but they didn't turn out all that good. Interesting faces, but the light's all wrong inside that old church building. I've got to come up with something better. Something new."

"So do it," she said, opening the dishwasher. "Aubrey said you needed to take lots of pictures, and soon. The man from the High Museum won't wait forever."

"When?" Mick asked, handing her a salad bowl for the dishwasher. "I'm busy yelling at kids, trying to keep the goat out of the flower beds and trying to figure out where the chickens are laying their eggs this week. Did you know I found a nest under the four-wheeler in the shed the other day?"

"That's your excuse? That you're too busy with the kids to take pictures?"

"It's not an excuse, Layne. It's just the truth. I guess I could run downtown and shoot homeless people in the evening, but by the time we're done with supper and the dishes are washed it's always too late to go."

"So shoot in the morning."

"I can't take three kids to Overpass Plantation. Do you know what it's like around there?"

"So take pictures of something else. It doesn't have to be homeless people, does it?"

He was wiping off the last of the counters. "You know, now that you mention it, the Man With No Hands thinks I should be doing a whole spread on construction workers."

Dylan had come in with *The Cat in the Hat* under his arm and was dragging Layne toward her reading chair. She stopped, turned around, jammed a hand in her hair.

"That's *brilliant!*" she said. "The places you've been, the people you know. Mick, that could be really good."

"Maybe, but it's still outside. I need to shoot in the morning when the light's good. Downtown. Construction site. What do I do with the kids?"

She let out an exasperated sigh. "Work with me here, Mick. Sometimes I get the feeling you really don't want to do this. What are you afraid of?"

Again with that question. As far as he knew he wasn't afraid of anything, and he was getting tired of people asking him that. He was about to tell her so when the phone rang and she escaped into the den to answer it.

Ben was painting a model airplane on the dining room table, an exact scale replica of a World War II vintage P–51 Mustang. He'd made a mess of the paint job but he wanted his dad to show him how to do the decals. Mick put some water in a jar lid and was showing him how to slide a wet decal off the card when Layne called him back to the bedroom and closed the door behind them.

"That was the strangest thing," she said. "You know the discussion we were just having about how you needed to go shoot pictures in the morning, but you couldn't go because of the kids?"

"Uh-huh."

"Well, that was Celly Weems on the phone. She said she heard you and Aubrey talking about that very thing, and she wants to keep the kids for you a couple mornings a week so you can go take pictures. What do you think?"

He wasn't sure he wanted to say what he really thought. Layne hadn't seen the private Celly.

"I don't know, Layne. What do you think?"

"Oh, I think it would be fine if she really wants to do it. Don't you?"

"Well, for one thing," Mick said, "they'd kill her. Our kids can get a little wound up. And for another thing, I'm not too sure about Celly. I mean, she's not the same when there's nobody around. She's kind of . . . depressed. And depressing."

"Yes, I'm aware of that," Layne said. "She has good reason, you know. She doesn't go around telling people, but she had a mastectomy eight years ago. On top of that, now she's going through menopause."

"They got drugs for that," he said. He'd heard about it from older guys he worked with.

"Yes, but she can't take any of them because of her history of cancer. She was handling all of it okay until her youngest son left for college, but now she's alone in the house all the time. Put yourself in her shoes, Mick. She doesn't feel like much of a woman anymore. I think it might actually be good for her to come over here a couple mornings a week and stay with our kids."

He nodded grudgingly. "I still think they'll kill her," he mumbled.

"She's stronger than you think. We all are." She put her arms around his neck and smiled that little smile that made his knees buckle.

"Yeah," he said. "Sometimes I get little glimpses."

"It'll be fine, you'll see. I think it'll be good for *both* of you. Now you can go downtown a couple mornings a week and shoot pictures of your buddies hanging by their knees from a skyscraper if you want."

There went his last excuse. The rope was off. There was nothing left for him but to just go and do it. Win or lose. Glorious victory or humiliating defeat.

She looked into his eyes and saw the hesitation there.

"What is it, Mick? Talk to me, honey. We're all trying to help you, trying to give you a chance to do something special, and you're moping around. Why are you so . . . reluctant?"

Marco.

He shook his head. It was hard to look at her.

"I don't know. Maybe I really am scared. I mean, come on—the High Museum? I'm an ironworker, Layne."

"What difference does that make? It's a *gift*, Mick. It's all in how you see the world, sweetheart. If you think everything is just pure dumb luck, of course you're afraid. Luck is capricious. But if you believe there's a greater hand, a greater mind guiding things, opening and closing doors, then you don't have to be afraid of what's happening. You can live in fear, or you can live in faith. It's up to you."

She held him there, and looking into his eyes she said, "I believe in you, Mick. You're good, and you're strong. There's *nothing* you can't do."

He loved that woman. Her belief in him meant more than anything else in the world. It always had.

He nodded slowly. "That's all I ever needed from you," he said. "All right. I'll go downtown and take pictures. I'll do the best I can. Even if it's a wild goose, I'll chase it. For you."

Polo.

33

Goats and dogs and highborn ladies.

MICK called Danny Baez the next day and told him what he was up to, sidling up to the idea at first because he figured Danny would think the whole notion of doing artsy photographs to try and impress some guy at the High Museum was a little froufrou. But Danny surprised him. He ragged him about being a "famous photographer" but Mick could tell he was excited about the idea. After checking the weather they set it up for the next Tuesday morning. Danny was running a crew on a high-rise on the north side of Atlanta.

"Now, you know the safety man's gonna run you off if he catches you. You're not on the payroll. Uninsured," Danny said. "You'll have to wear your hard hat and go incognito, but if anybody gets curious I'll cover for you. You think you can manage to look like an ironworker?"

"Yeah. I think I can probably fake that."

On Tuesday morning Mick loaded his camera equipment in the truck and took off before daylight. The kids wouldn't be up for an hour or two, and Layne was still in her robe.

He still felt funny about leaving his kids with Celly. Going out the door he asked Layne if she was sure Celly would show. He was afraid the woman would come to her senses at some point and back out.

"She'll be here," Layne said. "Everything is going to be fine. She has my number at work, and your cell number is written on the fridge. Go. Take pictures. Do good. And quit worrying—that's *my* job."

He met up with Danny in the parking lot and walked onto the job as if he belonged there, with his camera equipment in a tool bag and the extra film in a lunchbox to keep it cool. Unless somebody recognized his face there was no chance he'd get tagged as an outsider. After nearly eight months away it felt good walking back onto the job with a bunch of guys, riding up in a crowded man-lift. Nobody talked much. It was still half dark, the daylight just starting to creep in from the east, and most of the guys were still half asleep. He had forgotten how cool it felt up there in the morning, even in summer. Invigorating.

He kept pretty much to himself that morning because he didn't want people posing for pictures. Danny didn't tell anybody what Mick was up to, and they didn't ask. Mick already knew a couple of Danny's men. He'd worked with them before. There was a guy named Ralph who wore a pair of green goggles all the time—the little round ones like they issued for torch work, with an elastic strap. He wore them day and night, mostly because they made him look tough. Mick got up in the steel when Ralph wasn't looking and got a shot of him way up high by himself, just standing free in the middle of a beam with one hand in his pocket, staring at the city. Using a long lens and bracing the camera against a vertical beam, Mick was able to zoom in and get the side-lit city in striking detail reflected in the lenses of his goggles. He also happened to catch him taking a bite out of a Twinkie.

Mick didn't go in with a plan, he just kept his eyes open and took lots of pictures. Everywhere he looked, stories appeared in front of his camera. Mick got several low-angle shots of an old electrician dragging a heavy cable out across the slab by himself, leaning into his work like a plow horse with the skyline of the city rising over him in the background. At break time he got pictures of guys laughing at each other's lies—faces lined with work and sun, callused hands holding foil-wrapped cake from home, drinking coffee from plastic cups, opening a bottle with a pair of worn-out side-cutters. Good faces. Solid, tough, trustworthy hands. When he left, right before lunch, Mick didn't know what was in the bag, but he knew some of it was good.

After he got on the job and started shooting pictures, Mick clean forgot about leaving his kids with Celly. He never gave it another thought until he was on his way back down the expressway in his truck. As he drove through downtown Atlanta the noon news said something about a baby-sitter in Colorado being killed in a bizarre household accident, and that's when he thought about Celly. He picked up the cell phone and called home to check on the kids. That's what he told himself, anyway. The truth was, he was afraid for Celly.

Ben answered.

"HELLO!!" He was screaming into the phone; probably because he thought Mick couldn't hear him over the noise. There was an impossible racket in the background. It sounded the way Mick imagined the inside of the *Poseidon* sounded while it was rolling over—furniture crashing, glass breaking—that sort of thing. Above all the other insanity he could hear dogs barking. Lots of dogs. In the house.

"What's going on?!" he shouted.

"WHAT?" Ben couldn't hear. Mick could picture him putting a hand over his other ear.

"I SAID, WHERE'S MISS CELLY?!!"

"SHE'S TRYING TO GET THE DOGS OUT OF THE HOUSE!"

Crash, rumble, the baying of hounds.

They only owned one dog.

"WHAT DOGS?" Mick had to repeat the question because it sounded like Ben ducked and dropped the phone.

"HAP'S DOGS!" he yelled. *"THEY CAME OVER TO PLAY!"*

Nine of them. Hap had nine beagles. Plus Andy, the large yellow leader of the pack.

"WHAT ARE THE DOGS DOING IN THE HOUSE?"

"THEY'RE CHASING THE GOAT!!"

And then the line went dead. Mick calmly closed his cell phone, laid it on the seat, and drove a little faster.

———

He half expected to find Celly floating facedown in the pool when he got home, or hanging from the oak tree out front, or being loaded into an ambulance. But when he got there all the farm animals and packs of hounds had been routed. The doors were closed and the house was still standing.

He found Celly in the den, feet planted, hands on hips, directing traffic while the kids—the *kids*—put the house back together. Her hair, or some of it anyway, was tied up on top of her head. She gave Mick a glance when he closed the back door, blew a strand of hair out of her face, rolled her eyes and turned her attention right back to the kids. Toad was sweeping up the remains of some porcelain figurines in the foyer, Dylan was vacuuming the living room, and Ben was picking up papers from the floor, thumping them into tight little piles and stacking the piles on the desk. Neatly.

Mick eased up next to Celly, cautious of her mental state. There were goat pellets and hoof scratches on the dining room table and muddy paw prints all over the new sofa. The computer keyboard dangled off the desk by the cord, half its keys missing. Celly still hadn't said a word, but she didn't look like a sick woman on the verge of collapse. There was fire in her eyes and color in her cheeks. If anything, she looked *defiant*. Like a queen who had just put down a rebellion.

"What happened?" Mick asked gently.

She tossed her head to sling a ragged wisp of hair back from her face. Funny how she could pack pride into a little gesture like that, but it was unmistakable.

"Mister Harrelson said he let his dogs loose for some

sort of hunting excursion, but one of your children had left the back gate open and *your* dog, Andy"—she lipped the name in three syllables, *A-yin-dy*, with fairly obvious disgust—"was at that moment indulging himself in chasing that *animal.*" Meaning the goat. More disgust. Her aristocratic southern drawl got even more pronounced when she was mad.

"Mister Harrelson's pack of *hounds* heard the animal bleating and decided to join in the revelry. Meanwhile, another of your progeny opened the pool gate and a third, hearing all the commotion, opened the sliding glass door at *precisely* the wrong moment, whereupon he was bowled over by the aforementioned goat, who, fearing for his very life, bolted into the house hotly pursued by half the dogs in the county. Only after the entire slobbering horde had begun chasing itself in a circle through the den, the living room, the foyer, the dining room, and back through the den, did the child have the presence of mind to pick himself up and close the door, thereby preventing them from finding their way back *out* of the house."

"I see," Mick said, and he really did. It made perfect sense. He couldn't figure out why it had never happened before. "Well, you handled it better than I would have, Celly. I'd have lost it."

She gave a satisfied little sniff and raised her nose a notch. "I know a man who can clean that sofa. Just have Layne call me. Dylan! Honey, you missed a spot. Over by the chair."

Dylan couldn't really hear her over the high-pitched whine of the vacuum cleaner. When he looked up to see what she was saying he saw his dad and came running.

Didn't even turn off the vacuum, just left it.

Soon as Mick scooped him up Dylan shot a suspicious look at Miz Weems and said into his ear, "I wanta swim."

Mick didn't know all the details of what had passed between his kids and Celly, but the facts were fairly obvious: She was standing her ground, and Dylan was trying to go over her head. It was a test.

"Okay," he said. "We'll go swimming. Just as soon as y'all get done cleaning up this mess." Then he put him down and shoved him gently him toward the still-running vacuum.

"Thank you," Celly said quietly.

There was magic happening here. If this had happened on Mick's watch he would have been fussing at the kids and cleaning up the whole mess himself. Celly was just standing there supervising.

He waved a hand in the general direction of the kids. "How did you get them to, uh. . . ?"

She gave him one of those down-the-nose looks.

"Mister Brannigan," she said, "it's simply a matter of letting them know who's in control. A child *needs* to know who's in charge. If they think for one minute there's no one bigger than them in control of things, it only frightens them."

It was a beautiful thing, and he could never have worked it out himself. Aristocracy, it seemed, had its strengths.

34

The mold.

THE NEXT Sunday morning Mick went downtown again. He told Layne he was going there to shoot pictures, and he did shoot pictures, but mainly he went for church. Not that Robert Dooley was a great preacher or anything—it's just that when Mick was at the Beal Street Mission he felt useful. He could actually do something. It took him a little while to figure out that the main thing he never liked about church was that he couldn't get in. When he was a kid he always thought church was like going to the movies: they took your money and put on a show. All he had to do was sit there, and sometimes pretend to sing. There was nothing for him to do, no way to be a part of what was going on.

He did try to help Layne with the four-year-olds at her church—once. There was a little monster named Kevin who went around all morning bonking kids over the head with a pot. When church let out and Kevin's mother came to the door to pick him up, Mick didn't see him anyplace, but they could hear him bawling. Little Kevin was all folded up inside a cardboard box, and one of the kids he'd been bonking all morning was sitting on the lid. Bouncing. Laughing. Poor darling Kevin's mother was shaking mad. Mick was afraid she would sue. Later, when he told Layne he thought the little demon got what he had coming, she said Mick probably wasn't cut out to work in the nursery. It was always like that. He didn't fit in anyplace.

But when he went to Beal Street he knew what to do. There were things that needed doing, and Mick knew how to do them. Nobody at Beal Street expected him to talk a certain way or dress a certain way; there was just all this work that needed doing, and he knew how to work. The volunteer kids were all new, and yet anytime a kid had trouble with a homeless guy he'd come get Mick. Word must have gotten around on the street, because they didn't try to con him anymore. The big guy—the one he put up against the wall the week before—came back as if nothing had happened, except that he was very polite and didn't try to push Mick's buttons anymore.

When Mick first got there that morning he snapped a few pictures outside, but it was an overcast day and the light was diffused. He was still carrying the camera when he got down to the kitchen, where the Man With No Hands was orchestrating lunch, and he happened to catch one of those freak moments, completely by accident.

There were three kids in the kitchen helping, including a girl who was frying a big pan of chicken on the stove—a tall wisp of a girl, her blond hair tied back with one of those gauzy scarves. She went to turn the chicken, and when she leaned over her cross necklace broke and fell right in the pan. She let out a little yelp and panicked, started sloshing the pan around and trying to fish her necklace out with the spatula she was holding. A bit of grease slopped over the side, caught fire, and the whole pan blazed up. She let go, screeching, and jumped back.

But the Man With No Hands was watching. He moved in, smiling, and calmly reached right into the flames with his bare hook, picked out the necklace, raised it dripping out of the way and laid a cookie sheet over the frying pan to snuff out the fire. It all happened very quickly, but Mick managed to raise his camera and get one good shot, a close-up of a hook with that cross dangling from it, all shiny with grease, with flames in the background. There was an eerie beauty about it.

After all the homeless people had been preached to and fed and given their staples for the week, and all the dishes were done and all the pots washed and put away, Mick took out the prints of the pictures he'd shot on Danny's job and spread them on the steel worktable in the kitchen. The Man With No Hands liked them a lot, but he seemed preoccupied. He finally just came out and asked Mick for a ride up to Grady Hospital.

On the way, Mick asked who they were going to see.

"Bond," he said. "James Bond. He's a little . . . eccentric. You met him when the group from your church came down that time."

"Oh right, the guy with the eye patch, hiding behind the cars. Yeah, *eccentric* is a polite word. What happened to him?" Mick figured a heart attack, or an overdose.

"Well, the information I got was kind of sketchy, but I heard he was panhandling up by Piedmont Park when some stranger offered him a drink of something out of the back of his car."

"And he drank it?"

"Well, yes. Around here, that would be the normal thing to do. When Bond came to he was naked, tied upside-down to a tree in the middle of the woods. The stranger had poured acid on him."

Mick steeled himself, but when they got to the hospital it turned out that James Bond wasn't hurt as badly as they expected. From the sound of the Man's description Mick figured he would be unconscious and in critical condition, but James Bond was walking the halls in his hospital gown, still wearing his eye patch. He was doing a kind of spraddle-legged duck walk and didn't seem to notice, or care, that his gown was flapping open in the back.

"They were KGB," he said, lifting his patch to peek around a corner, then dropping his voice to a whisper. "They got me in the privates. Wanta play cards?"

They ended up back in the tub room at a little card table, teamed up against Bond and a wiry little black woman who had spilled flaming grease down the front of her legs and then ruined her hands trying to beat out the flames. She was fierce, and hugely entertaining. She'd slap a trump six down with a bandaged hand and then dare Mick to overtrump.

"Don't you *mess* with that six!"

Mick thoroughly enjoyed the game. Bond kept tilting and squirming in his seat, trying to get comfortable, and the Man With No Hands fumbled a bit when he tried to pick up his cards, but nobody whined. They were happy and forgetful for a time, slapping cards down and talking trash. Mick got some great pictures—some of them with his camera.

———

Later, driving back to Overpass Plantation, Mick sensed that the hospital visit had brought back the Man's own hospital memories. He was very quiet, and his thoughts were written on his face. Finally, Mick said to him, "People are strong, aren't they."

"Yes they are," he nodded. "And weak. We need each other, if only for a card game."

Mick drove on in silence for a minute, then said, "You're sure not like any preacher I ever met. You don't fit the mold."

The Man With No Hands smiled. "There's only one mold that matters."

They were passing through an old part of town, three- and four-story brick office buildings mixed with decrepit storefronts and weed-choked vacant lots, when Mick spotted an old homeless man coming down the sidewalk pushing a grocery cart full of junk. Wild gray hair hung down and crowded in on his face, and his clothes were ragged out worse than most. He was filthy. But the sun had come out, and now it lay across the homeless man at a perfect angle. Mick whipped the truck over to the curb and grabbed his camera, snapping it up to his eye and dialing in the focus.

Looking at the man through the long lens while he was still a block and a half away, Mick saw something he could never have predicted. The man was bent and old, and leaning heavily into his grocery cart, but he kept turning his head and looking over his shoulder as if something was after him. That's when Mick saw the nose. Just a flash in the sunlight, and with the hair Mick never got more than a glimpse of the rest of his face, but that nose had a distinct hook in it. The old man quickened his pace, and Mick saw that he was favoring his right leg, limping. His head was down, pushing that cart uphill with an awkward limp, but once Mick got him dialed in he saw that when he was facing forward he kept his head tilted over against his left shoulder.

The way his father had always done.

He lowered the camera without taking a picture, his mind filled with confusing and conflicting emotions. He couldn't think straight.

Then he saw why the old man kept looking back over his shoulder. Three young punks emerged from the alley he'd just left, about a half-block behind him. They were yelling and waving at him, laughing and taunting. When he picked up speed they broke into a trot and gained on him. Mick opened his door and got out of the truck.

"What's going on?" the Man With No Hands asked, but Mick didn't answer him. Mick saw what was coming and broke into a run.

The punks reached him before Mick did. The old man was passing a vacant lot strewn with rubble from a torn-down building when one of the punks shot past the old man, grabbed his grocery cart and flung it off the sidewalk onto a pile of bricks. A second one grabbed the old man from behind and whipped him off his feet, tossing him like a toy. He hit between junk piles and rolled. Running up the sidewalk, all Mick could see were his feet sticking out when the third one ran up to him and started kicking. The other two joined him and the homeless man's feet drew up out of sight.

Mick yelled at them when he was still thirty or forty yards away. The biggest one stopped kicking and looked up, then punched his buddy in the arm and pointed. The second one looked up, saw Mick closing on them and turned toward him, grinning. He was the smallest of the three, but even on a dead run Mick could see he was the ringleader. The other two took a half-step back and waited.

In the few seconds it took Mick to close the interval, he saw the punk's hand go to his back pocket. Saw his wrist flick.

But the young man, in his inexperience, made several mistakes. He underestimated the resolve of the man bearing down on him as badly as he underestimated the weight of a Nikon F3 and the length of its neck strap.

Mick let the strap slide through his fingers until he was holding the camera like a sling behind his back, then put on the brakes and feinted left. The punk's eyes went where Mick wanted them to.

It only took one swing. He was pretty sure he broke the kid's jaw.

The other two took off right then, just turned tail and booked up the street. The little guy crabbed away and staggered to his feet as quick as he could while holding his jaw together. He held Mick in a rancid glare for a few seconds, then turned and staggered off after his friends, leaving his knife behind.

The old man was still curled in a ball, moaning and rocking himself on the ground. Mick knelt down, touched his shoulder.

"Dad?" he said. His hands were shaking. "Are you all right?"

The head turned. He looked up at Mick then, and the hair fell away from his face.

" 'Oo are you?" he asked, wheezing.

It wasn't his old man's voice. This guy's accent was distinctly British, and his face, now that Mick saw it up close, was not the face of his father.

"I dunno you," the old man said. There was fear in his eyes, and confusion.

The Man With No Hands caught up with him then, and knelt down beside him. The old bum wheezed and coughed, spat blood onto the sand.

"He could have a punctured lung," the Man With No Hands said.

Mick was still too confused to say much, still breathing hard, still dealing with adrenaline rush and a half dozen other things. He nodded. "I'll get the truck."

They picked him up, gingerly, and laid him in the bed of the truck. The Man With No Hands sat back there holding the old man's head on the way to the hospital.

Later, after they dropped him off at the emergency room and headed back toward Overpass Plantation, the Man With No Hands asked Mick about what happened. About why, without a second's hesitation, he had charged in against three younger men.

"I thought he was my dad," Mick said softly.

"I see." He let the words hang in the air for half a block, and then said, "You were trying to save him."

"Yeah," Mick said, his eyes on the street in front of him. "Imagine that."

35

Pretend cigars.

CELLY stayed with the kids on Tuesdays and Thursdays, and over the next couple weeks Mick shot nearly a thousand pictures—some of them at Overpass and the Beal Street Mission, some of them at Danny's high-rise. He spent several late evenings in Aubrey's darkroom developing prints, picking out the better ones and setting them aside.

After a couple weeks he had a sizable collection of keepers. Aubrey took the pile upstairs, spread pictures all over his dining room table and started going over them with a magnifying glass. There must have been sixty or seventy prints. After a while he straightened up and took his glasses off.

"I think we can find a portfolio here," he said, wiping his eyes with the back of a wrist. "I'll start developing final prints tomorrow. Some of them need adjusting—a little burning and dodging here and there to bring up the back-ground detail—but make no mistake, this is a *very* nice group. One other thing, though. I need to order a binder, a nice leather one with your name embossed on the front—Michael Brannigan."

"The name's Mick."

"Well, yes, but Michael sounds a little more . . . profes-sional, don't you think?"

"It's Mick, Aubrey. If you put my name on the front of the book I want *my* name, not somebody else's. The name's Mick."

Aubrey's mouth went crooked for a second, but he gave it up. "All right, then, Mick it is. I also need to buy some boards to mount eight-by-tens, but don't worry about pay-ing for it—I'll keep up with everything and take it out of your first big sale."

"It's your money." He chuckled, still refusing to pretend there would ever be a big sale.

Celly had come in with a cup of hot tea on a china sau-cer and was just standing there checking out the pictures. Mick didn't see it right away, but after a while he noticed she looked better than she had the last time he saw her at her house.

She sipped her tea and raised an eyebrow, looking over the spread.

"These *are* very nice, Mick. They get right up off the table and talk. But then, as Paul Theroux pointed out, a picture is only worth about a thousand words." A wry smile. She had actually made a joke.

After she left, Aubrey leaned close to him and, almost whispering, said, "I can't thank you enough, Mick."

"For what?"

"For letting Celly keep your kids. They've worked a miracle on her."

He thought about it for a few seconds and nodded. "Yeah. They've been known to do that."

———

The next night he had planned to go over and help Aubrey with the final prints, but Layne's aunt Essie died. Layne couldn't get off work for the funeral the next day, so that evening they had to make a two-hour drive down to a dinky little farm town close to Columbus and put in an appearance at the funeral home. Layne called her sister to see if she could keep the kids for an evening, but Lisa had a social engagement so they ended up taking the kids with them to south Georgia. Big mistake.

Things had been going well for the last couple weeks. Mick had managed to stay out of trouble somehow, and everybody was all excited about him and Aubrey putting together a presentation for the High Museum.

On top of that, Dylan was swimming. Once he got over his fear he took off. They spent three or four hours a day in the pool, always in the deep end. Dylan wouldn't go near the shallow end anymore—he said it was for *little* kids—and in a few short weeks he had blossomed into an otter just like his brother and sister. Skinny as he was, Dylan shot through the water like a needle. Life was good, and Mick was on a roll until the night they went to see Aunt Essie.

They only spent about an hour at the funeral home after a two-hour drive down there. They didn't know Aunt

Essie all that well. She was actually Layne's great aunt, her grandmother's sister. Aunt Essie sent her a card once or twice a year, always out of season. Like as not, she'd send Layne a Mother's Day card in November, and it was always covered from corner to corner on the inside with completely illegible handwriting, as if she'd written it while riding a bicycle down a dirt road. Aunt Essie did come to their wedding. Mick could still remember Layne cutting up over the antique waffle iron she gave them. He was pretty sure it was one of Aunt Essie's own wedding gifts, from seventy years ago.

The funeral home was set up like a little church, with pews and a pulpit and the open casket down front. Cousins and second cousins and aunts and uncles came from all over Georgia, and there were a bunch of them Layne hadn't seen or talked to since the last funeral. People were quiet and reverent when they first came in. They'd go down front for a minute or two and gaze solemnly on Aunt Essie's earthly remains, then troop to the back pews to sit down and gab, catch up on the family.

Mick didn't know anybody there except for one or two of the cousins, so it fell to him to keep the kids entertained on the back pew—keep them out of trouble while Layne caught up on family gossip. Everything was going fine until he got up to go to the bathroom, and on the way back he bumped into Uncle Sid, who recognized him as Layne's husband.

"So, what do you do?" Uncle Sid asked. He was a wiry little retired farmer who had a head like a tomato with glasses on it and a navy blue nose with an oxygen tube in it.

"Well, I'm an ironworker by trade, but right now I'm staying home with the kids."

The tomato head recoiled a little and Uncle Sid looked like he'd just bitten into a bad persimmon.

"Pshaw! You mean you don't *work*?"

"Well, no, sir, but it's just temporary. I plan to go back in a few weeks, as soon as the kids are in school." *Come follow me around one day, you old coot, and see if I don't work.*

"How long you been out of work?"

"Let's see . . . It's been since before Christmas, so I guess—"

"Since *Christmas*? Pshaw! How you put food on the table?"

"Um, well, Layne has a pretty good job. Good benefits." *I put food on the table with potholders, Gramps, right after I buy it, bring it home, and cook it.*

"But you ain't *workin'*?"

Mick could see it all in that sour-persimmon look. Uncle Sid was thinking how in his day he'd have set the Klan on him. Mick was all set to spar with him, but he happened to look across right then and see what the kids were doing.

Layne was sitting in a pew with her back to him, catching up on old times with her cousin Alicia. Layne's head was down, laughing at something her cousin had said, so she didn't see the look of horror on Alicia's face. She was staring past Layne at the kids.

While Mick was gone they had apparently amused themselves by digging in their mother's pocketbook. Now they were standing up in the pew behind Layne's back, all three of them, in the rear of a funeral home with a hundred people watching, puffing away on the pretend cigars they had found in Layne's pocketbook. Oh, they were having a big time, grinning and puffing, everybody watching them, laughing and pointing.

Somebody tapped Layne's shoulder and whispered to her, and before Mick could get over there she had snatched the tampons out of their hands and jerked all three of them down into the pew.

They left right after that. It was a long, chilly ride home.

36

The heart of the matter.

AUBREY bought all the hardware he needed to put together a portfolio—a stack of boards and matting material for sandwiching the prints, all in matching shades of blue, and a rich-looking leather binder with *Mick Brannigan* etched in gold on the front. He had gone through the pictures until he'd narrowed the field down to twenty-seven shots, and he had them all spread out on the dining room table. Most of them had been shot on the job, construction workers doing their thing. The rest were a mix of homeless people and old barns and houses.

"What I've done so far," Aubrey said, "is go through and sort out what's great photography and what isn't. I've had to be absolutely ruthless in sorting them out because one mediocre picture can bring down Ecklund's impression of the whole lot. I've spent hours going through them, and I'm confident that the ones we have here on the table are your very best, from an art critic's point of view. But I won't make final decisions about what to present. You have to do that yourself."

Mick scratched his head, gave him a sort of Stan Laurel wince.

"I don't know how these artsy people think," he said. "How many do we actually need for the portfolio?"

"I'm thinking twelve to fifteen. More than that can get confusing or monotonous. Less, and it looks like you don't have much to show. The main thing I think you have to do is decide on a theme. Your presentation needs to be focused. You want to have something to say—something that nobody else is saying, or at least something you say *better* than anybody else. One thing that ties it all together. Once you know what you're looking for, the selection process gets easier."

"So, what do *you* think I'm saying, Aubrey?" This kind of stuff was just *out there* for Mick.

Aubrey shook his head. "It's not up to me. I have my opinions, but yours is the one that matters."

Mick planted his fists on the edge of the table and leaned over the pictures, studying them, for a long time. Aubrey had burned and dodged and tweaked the final prints, brought out the best in them. Mick saw them with new eyes. He saw homeless people and children and working-men—wonder and confusion and fear and disappointment and triumph in all kinds of faces.

Aubrey stirred first. "What do they tell you?" he asked quietly.

"I don't know," Mick said, still leaning on the table. "All I see is people trying to make sense out of things, trying to make it through the day and wondering why. There are more questions here than answers, but maybe that's just me. Maybe that's how I see my ownself."

Aubrey stared at him for a minute, then leaned on the table beside him, poring over the pictures.

"Yes," he said, finally. "There's no pretense here, quite possibly because you don't know how to pretend. But there has to be a common factor, a thread that ties these pictures together."

The picture of Toad flying through the air over the hay-stack was not there—Mick had sold it to the gallery and no longer owned it—but it kept flashing across his mind anyway as he looked over the body of work in front of him. The picture of the electrician dragging out a cable with the skyline rising behind him, the ironworker eating a Twinkie with the same city reflected in his goggles, the silhouette of Dylan handing a loaf of bread to an old homeless man, a close-up of a guy in church with his hands raised, his eyes closed, and the trail of a tear on a grimy cheek—all of them reminded him of Toad, flying through the air with her eyes closed. It occurred to him all at once that his own life reminded him of the same thing. He was, at that moment, in the act of building a portfolio for the High Museum— doing something totally foreign to him, something completely out of his experience and comfort zone, for the purpose of flinging it out there with a kiss and a prayer.

"What about faith?" Mick said.

"What about it?" Aubrey was still staring at the pictures, thinking.

"*Faith,*" Mick repeated. "It's what I see here. People believing in something bigger than themselves, or at least hoping. People all blind and confused, but reaching for something anyway. Working, walking, trying—putting one foot in front of the other and pressing on. Not churchy faith. Faith at street level."

Aubrey straightened up then, took his glasses off and chewed on the end of them. Slowly he began to nod, and a smile came into his eyes.

"Yes. I can see that. *Street Faith*. That's good. That's *very* good."

It still took two hours to cull the pictures that didn't fit, but the finding of the theme was the key. The job became doable. At some point Celly got in on it. Mick and Aubrey explained what they were looking for, and then the three of them argued endlessly about what fit and what didn't. They had a grand time, and finally agreed on twelve pictures. After they cleared away everything else, they lined up the final twelve and argued about what order they should be in.

But they got her done. In a day or two, when Aubrey and Celly were finished matting the pictures and arranging them in the binder, they would send them to A.J. Ecklund at the address on his card, with a cover letter that Aubrey would write and Mick would sign. And then they would all wait.

Mick didn't know how to thank Aubrey and Celly. He tried, but he just didn't much know what to say.

"It's all right," Aubrey told him. "We're having fun. Besides, it's what neighbors do."

37

Clothes is clothes.

HE NEVER should have done it. Mick never quite understood what pushed him to it, unless it was simply that he was trying to find a way to restore himself in his wife's eyes after the funeral-home fiasco. He should have listened to his instinct, that grim sense of foreboding that sat like a brick in his gut whenever he looked at that hamper—the one in the middle of the closet.

But it ate at him, that one forbidden thing. Day after day it sat there in the back of the closet and watched him, waiting. It caught his eye and began to challenge him; then it taunted him, and then it beckoned him. Over time the hamper in the back of the closet appealed to his pride and called to him, precisely because it was forbidden. She said she'd kill him graveyard dead if he touched the clothes in there, but Mick suspected that the only reason she wouldn't let him wash her clothes was that she didn't *want* him to know everything she knew. She was jealous of her knowledge.

He would show her. She would be proud. She would say that he was the smartest man in all the earth.

He flung open the closet door and stood in the opening. Clothes hung down opposite sides of the dark closet—mute, withholding judgment. There, in the center, at the far end of the closet sat his judge, squat and dark, a deeper shadow at the end of shadows. He could have sworn it bulged and pulsed. Through the open window came the sharp warning hack of a blue jay, and a chill ran up his spine.

He flipped on the light. The hamper did bulge—it was full. The lid yawned back against the wall, trapped there by a limp mound of dresses and pants and bras and sweaters. Cotton blouses and silk nightgowns spilled in a tangle to the floor.

"Just clothes," Mick muttered, jacking up his courage. But he didn't move. He shuddered, vacillating; they were a *woman's* clothes.

I can do this, he thought. *Cotton, wool, polyester, colored, white. Ain't no hill for a climber. I cook, I buy groceries—I even mop, for cryin' out loud. I wash my clothes; I wash the kids' clothes; I can wash a woman's clothes.*

He got a laundry basket, plunked it down in the middle of the closet and started flinging things into it. He tossed the white stuff aside for the moment, smug in the lofty knowledge that white stuff, for whatever reason, had to be washed separately. Anything with the faintest trace of white in it went into a separate pile—underwear, a white shirt with a brown collar and pocket flaps, a white sweater with red stripes.

An obscure bit of laundry lore nagged the back of his mind, something about the little tags. He stopped, straightened up and studied the tag inside the neck of a cashmere sweater, but the print was so tiny he couldn't make it out. He started to go get his reading glasses from the desk, but thought better of it.

You call yourself a man? Next thing you know you'll be stopping at gas stations to ask directions. Buck up, man. Have you no pride?

He would not be the slave of a care tag. Clothes is clothes. If it had not a speck of white in it, into the basket it went. The culling of the white stuff was the only taxing part of the process. The rest was easy: White stuff, hot. Everything else, warm. Piece-o-cake.

He did everything right, he was sure of it, but the minions of the dark hamper ranged far in the absence of a woman, and evil was afoot. When the first load came out of the washing machine everything had taken on the same dark shade of pink.

It's because they're wet, he told himself. *This is just the color women's clothes take on when they're wet.*

The white stuff, when it came out of the washer, confirmed his theory. Everything was a much lighter shade of pink—except, for some strange reason, the red sweater, which had turned a sort of mauve. He was reassured by the fact that the white stripes were a very light pink, as they should be. He figured he needed to cook all the pink color out, so he dumped everything in the dryer, set the heat to High and the timer on extra long.

But he really started to sweat when he took the first load out of the dryer. The pink hadn't gone away. Must not have dried them long enough.

He ran them through again.

When he took them out of the drier the second time Mick learned that pinkness wasn't the worst of it. While the clothes tumbled, some imp had spirited away some of Layne's best dresses and left others in their places. They *looked* like Layne's dresses but they were smaller. Much smaller. These might fit Toad.

Still, he thought these dresses might actually be larger than they appeared because they were so deeply wrinkled, like wads of dark pink tissue paper. He figured if he could iron out all the wrinkles they might grow back to their original size. Maybe she wouldn't notice. Maybe she'd just think she was gaining weight.

Mick knew how to use an iron. He'd been ironing his own cotton clothes for a long time and considered himself something of an expert. Pour in a little water, turn the dial all the way up, and wait. When the iron gets hot enough to light a cigarette you're good to go.

He started with a cotton blouse, confident, self-assured. But none of the lines in the blouse were straight like a man's shirt. Everything was bent and curved and refused to lay flat on the ironing board. Not only that, but the blouse had beads on it. All down the front of the blouse was some kind of artsy design made from a hundred little white beads, like pearls, and Mick couldn't get the iron in between them. He mashed the iron down hard on the beaded section, pressed the Extra Steam button, and held it there long enough for the steam to do its work.

When he lifted the iron the shirt came with it. He slung the whole mess up and down a few times, but the shirt clung tight, flapping like a signal flag. He lost his temper, grabbed a handful of shirt and ripped it off the iron. He heard a little *"tsst"* when the shirt lashed back and fused itself to his forearm.

Holding his arm under cold tap water, he didn't worry so much about the geometric pattern of tiny blisters on his arm as he did about the flat plastic beads on the front of Layne's blouse, now garnished with hundreds of little arm hairs.

He tried ironing out one of the balled-up dresses, but it just melted and stuck to the iron. By then Mick's sanity was ratcheting close to the brink. He was defeated and he knew it. He threw away the worst of the evidence and put everything else back in the hamper like he found it. The dark hamper, with its lid thrown back, looked for all the world like it was laughing at him.

Dylan was standing in the bedroom when Mick flipped off the closet light. A breeze from the open window pushed against the closet door and swung it slowly shut. The hinges squeaked and gave off a long, high-pitched giggle. Dylan picked up the sound and mimicked it perfectly.

"Wiiiiii-imp," he said, with a little cry in his voice, dropping from high to low just like the hinge.

"Shut up," Mick muttered. "Just shut up."

38

Games.

THEY did a lot of shopping over the next few days. Layne had already begun buying new school clothes for the kids, and now she needed to pick up a few things for herself, to replace the items her "nearly departed" husband had washed. She bought everything from a new cashmere sweater to Autumn Russet hair coloring with built-in highlights and moisturizing conditioners for that fuller look. He tried teasing her about it, tried to lighten the mood by telling her that all this time he thought she just dyed the roots gray. She was not amused. Lately, since he'd violated the Hamper, it had been hard to make her laugh.

They took Layne's Explorer to the superstore that night because they couldn't all fit in Mick's truck. He didn't drive her car often, and she never noticed when something was amiss. The engine didn't sound quite right. He cocked

362 | W. DALE CRAMER

an ear, frowning, and Layne asked him what was wrong.

"Not sure," Mick said. "Could be the timing chain."

"I don't hear anything," she said. "What does it sound like?"

She wouldn't have heard it. In the first place the kids were making too much racket in the back seat. Second, as Mick was well aware, the part of the male brain that proc-essed engine noises had been assigned other duties in women. Maybe it was the part that slapped a mother awake at two o'clock in the morning at the sound of a single muffled cough in the bedroom across the hall.

He tried to explain. "You know how your car sounds when it's running right?"

"Yes," she lied.

"Well, it doesn't sound like that."

"I don't see how you can tell," she shouted, glancing over her shoulder at the source of the blood-curdling screams, machine-gun sounds and gurgling, theatrical, death-rattle noises.

She was getting that look. He'd seen it a lot in the last three days—that tight-lipped, slit-eyed look.

"What?" They always played out the ritual the same way. He'd see the look, ask what was wrong and get a terse "Nothing" in reply. They'd usually repeat this pattern until he stopped asking, and then she'd tell him. This time he didn't have long to wait.

"It's that game," she growled. "Can't you hear what they're doing?"

"FROG LESS A PIN CORE!" Ben belted out.

Dylan answered with a perfect impression of a Mark–9

rocket launcher being primed and fired, then screamed, "I'M OUT OF AMMO!"

Toad shrilled, "KILL ME!"

He knew she disapproved of the video game, but the kids didn't play it often, and then only while sitting on his lap. But such games had gotten a bad rap as the favorite pastime of dark, brooding teenagers who daydreamed about shooting real bullets at their classmates.

"Games don't kill people," Mick mumbled. "People kill people."

"Right. Games just teach them how much fun it is."

He could hear his father's voice in his head. *"Son, you need to sit down and shut up."* This once, discretion got the better of him, and Mick shut up. The game had never been particularly important to him. It was a minor amusement, and not worth fighting about.

The kids were their usual manic selves in the super-store, grabbing things off the shelves and begging. Their behavior normally would not have bothered Mick a whole lot, but on that particular night it seemed important for them to calm down, just once, and show their mother what little angels he was raising. Mick tried giving them "the look," but they watched TV—they knew that if he beat them in public he'd be arrested. As soon as Layne turned her back he got their attention, narrowed his eyes and drew a forefinger across his throat, but for some reason they thought it was outrageously funny and started doing it to total strangers in the aisles.

Layne stopped to look at pantyhose, dozens of little boxes of different shades and sizes of pantyhose. Dylan appeared beside her for a second, staring at the pictures of underwear-clad models on the boxes.

"Lookin' for fribble covers?" he asked. He meant bras. She ignored him, bent on examining each and every one of the hundred or so boxes before deciding not to buy any of them, then moved on to the fingernail polish.

"Listen," Mick said, "I'll just take the kids over to the magazine section, okay? They like looking at magazines. Keeps 'em quiet."

Layne nodded. "Okay. I'll catch up in a bit," she said, distracted.

Mick browsed the racks while the kids flipped through magazines on the floor. Dylan loved to look at pictures of grotesquely over-muscled superheroes in weird paint schemes, so he picked a wrestling magazine. Toad picked out a comic book with a snarling T-rex on the cover and Ben flipped through *Popular Mechanics* because there was a picture of a bizarre machine on the front and he thought it might be a time machine.

Mick's eye always went to the do-it-yourself magazines, all about how to build everything from your own house to your own airplane. He was looking through one of those, mostly at the pictures, when he ran across a picture of a guy in jungle fatigues riding a zip line across a river gorge. It caught his attention, and the next thing he knew he was completely absorbed in reading an article on how to build a zip line—everything from optimum fall rates to detailed instructions on what size cable to use, how to clamp it and how to build the trolley.

As Mick was reading the article, picturing angles and distances and fall rates in his mind, it came to him slowly that the tree house—Andy's House, the kids called it now—was right in line with the swimming pool, about forty feet straight out from the shallow end. Dead center at the back of the tree house stood a good stout white oak tree, and at the far end of the pool was a diving board, fastened to the top of a heavy steel pedestal, which was bolted into the concrete. The plan came together in his mind, whole and complete, and he could see it—an eighty-foot cable from the top of the tree house over a short stretch of grass, traversing the deck, sloping down the entire length of the pool to the deep end, and anchored at last to the diving board pedestal. He knew for a fact he could scrounge up all the parts he needed and fabricate a trolley in Hap's shop.

It was a beautiful plan, and he was so caught up in it that he actually jumped when Layne tapped him on the shoulder and said, "Where are the kids?"

Mick had been so absorbed he hadn't noticed the alarming quiet. He glanced around and saw no children. Their magazines were spread out in the aisle, but the kids were nowhere in sight.

Layne panicked. She bolted screaming to the end of the aisle, skidded to a stop, and tried to run in two directions at once. Mick caught up with her and took her by the shoulders to calm her down.

"Sometimes they play hide-and-seek," he said smugly. "It's all right. Watch."

He threw his head back, cupped his hands around his mouth and boomed out, "FROG LESS A PIN CORE!"

From two aisles over, among the housewares, came the shrill cry, "I'M OUT OF AMMO!"

Somewhere in the candy section a high voice piped,

"KILL ME!" and another yelled, "THEY'RE EVERY-WHERE!"

The lady with the two little girls in her cart laughed so hard she almost dropped a porcelain lamp, but Layne was not amused. She didn't say much until after they were home and the kids had gone off to their baths. Mick turned on the TV to catch the baseball game and she turned it back off.

"We have to talk," she said. She sat facing him with her elbows on her knees, her fingers tented against each other. She was calm, the way a space shuttle is calm during the countdown.

"Okay, I'm listening," he said.

"I don't want the kids playing those shooting games anymore. There's evidence games like that played an important part in all these school shootings."

"There's also evidence that the alleged shooters wore athletic shoes at one time or another but I don't see anybody banning sneakers."

She paused and took a deep breath, but she pressed on. "Those first-person games put a weapon in your hand and make you the shooter. They normalize violence and justify it as a means of conflict resolution."

"Okay. I can understand that, for girls, but boys are born thinking of violence as a way to resolve things, and speaking as a man, I'm not sure that's a bad thing. Games like that didn't exist when I was a kid, so me and my brothers went out in the yard and shot each other with toy guns—every day. When we didn't have guns we shot each other with sticks. It's genetic. We must have killed each other ten thousand times, but we still managed to grow up knowing the difference between real and pretend."

Her eyes flashed. "But your brother always got back up, didn't he. Shoot somebody in one of those games and you get to watch him splatter."

Normally he would have given up at that point, but he'd seen this argument coming and he'd had time to think about it.

"The point is," Mick held forth, "we need to calm down and look for the real cause and effect. It's not about game control, or even gun control. The truth is, these kids who end up on the six-and-eleven are being raised by cell phone, and I personally think that when our kids are sitting on my lap playing a game on the computer the lap time outweighs any negative impact the game might have." He was getting pretty good at lawyer talk himself.

"You don't know that," she said flatly. "And what's the price if you're wrong?"

With lawyer-like precision, she had punctured Patrick Henry and let all the air out of his carefully constructed argument. In the end he had to admit she was right—he didn't know. And some things just weren't worth the risk.

"All right," he said. "If you feel that strongly about it, no more shooting games. I think I can probably find more constructive ways for the kids to spend their time. We'll find something else. Something that involves fresh air and sunshine. Okay?"

He didn't tell her what he had in mind. He wanted it to be a surprise.

39

The zip line.

IF HE'D heard it once, he'd heard it a thousand times that summer.

"I'm bored."

Boredom was one thing that hadn't changed a lick since the old days. Back in Mick's day they had sticks and rocks, maybe a bike and a ball glove, and they got bored in the summer. A generation later, his own kids had a dog, a goat, a hamster, a parakeet, a yard full of chickens, a swimming pool, bicycles, board games, a million toys, a hundred and twenty-nine channels, video games, computers—and they *still* got bored in the summer.

In the middle of a Georgia summer the hot, humid, white days pressed down so hard he could feel it in his knees, and not a breath of wind. A kind of lethargy worked its way into everything and everybody. It made Mick want to take a nap, but the kids, since they were entitled to a nap and probably needed one, wouldn't have anything to do with it. They'd just plop down next to him, prop a chin on a palm and say, "I'm bored."

They'd been doing that to him for the last two weeks, all three of them, but they would not be bored *this* day.

That morning, as soon as the kids were all up and fed, they all went straight over to Hap's shop. When he told Hap what he had in mind, Hap got so excited about the idea he stopped right in the middle of fixing Mrs. Hardeman's washing machine and started right away digging in his junk pile. It took him less than an hour to find all the parts, cut a couple triangles out of eighth-inch sheet steel, sandwich two ball-bearing pulleys between them and thread a pipe handle through the bottom. Mick found a spool of stainless-steel cable out behind the shed and some industrial-strength clamps in the tool bin of Hap's tow truck.

He didn't tell the kids what they were doing, and they didn't pay much attention until he and Hap started cutting the roof off the back of the tree house. Then all three kids got up under them and bombarded them with questions. The tree house got a little crowded, what with Ben, Toad, Andy, Mick and Hap all up there at the same time, but it didn't shake. Like most of the things Mick built, it was earthquake-proof.

"Whatcha doin'?" Dylan said. Only then did Mick notice that Dylan, who had just turned five and had always been terrified of heights, was up in the tree house with everybody else. He hadn't been up there since the day it was built. The goat bleated at him from the ground.

"We're buildin' you a zip line," Hap said, holding the

little platform in place against the tree so Mick could fasten it to the tree.

"What's a zip line?" Toad asked, staring at the spool of cable by her feet.

Ben answered her. "It's one of those things where you slide down a wire. You know, like they did on *Fear Factor* last week."

Toad's face lit up in recognition. "Cool! Where's it gonna go?"

"To that pool yonder," Hap said, grinning, propping the ladder in place against the platform. Hap was having more fun than Mick. He was pumped.

Ben and Toad still didn't quite see the whole picture until Mick fed the end of the cable through a piece of water hose and started clamping it around the tree above the platform. Their eyes traced an imaginary line from the tree, down across an expanse of grass, over the deck and down the length of the pool to the diving board.

"We're gonna unbolt the diving board and take it off. That's where the other end goes," Hap explained.

They saw it then. Their eyes went wide and both of them slid down the fireman's pole to go put on their bathing suits.

Mick fed the cable through Hap's heavy-duty home-made trolley, then took the other end to the pedestal, tightened it up with a come-along, and clamped it off. They had the job done by lunchtime.

Toad went first, wide-eyed and screaming all the way down, skidding feet first into the deep end, like a duck coming in for a landing. Hap almost broke through the deck falling on his backside laughing at her. It zipped a litle faster than Mick expected, but other than that it worked perfectly. Toad came up whooping and shaking a fist in the air.

Ben was leery of it at first. He overanalyzed everything, and he was fairly sure there was a long list of things that could go wrong and kill him.

Hap looked at Ben, and pointed over his shoulder at Toad, who was already running, barefoot and dripping wet, through the backyard to climb up and go around again.

"Boy, you gonna let a *girl* show you up?" he asked.

That was all it took. Ben took off after her, yelling that it was his turn next.

Dylan watched them with uncommon interest, though he didn't say anything and didn't volunteer to try it out. Mick didn't push him. He and Dylan stayed in the pool while Ben and Toad swooped over their heads screaming like hawks. Hap fixed a tag line of quarter-inch rope onto the trolley so they could walk it back up to the tree house, and the loose rope flipped and danced like a snake when they zipped down the cable. Mick learned to duck after the first time the tail whipped across his open eye while he was standing in the shallow end. Hap tied a knot in the end of the tag line to make it easier to hold on to with wet hands when they pulled the trolley back up. That knot nearly destroyed Mick's marriage.

They worked out a kind of synchronized plan. To keep things moving, Mick stayed in the pool, grabbed the pull rope and towed the trolley back up to the shallow end where he would hand the rope off to Hap, who would walk out to the end of the deck and sling the trolley the rest of the way up to the tree house. By the time one of the kids climbed out and ran the full length of the pool, down the steps beside the deck, across the backyard, and climbed up onto the platform, the other one had already zipped screaming into the pool and the trolley was on its way back. Mick and Hap stayed busy all afternoon crewing for Ben and Toad. Dylan hung out in the deep end and watched. He was very quiet.

It got late. Mick hadn't been paying attention to the time. The afternoon slipped away while Ben and Toad rode the zip line, and they were having so much fun he forgot the time. He didn't hear Layne's Explorer pull into the garage. He didn't even know she was home until he heard Dylan yell, "MOM! WATCH ME!"

There was Layne, standing at the sliding glass door in her suit, all wide-eyed and open-mouthed, taking in the scene. And there was Dylan, standing up there shivering on the high platform, holding onto the trolley with his skinny little hands. Mick hadn't seen him get out of the pool, cross the yard, or climb up there, and until he spotted his mother Dylan hadn't said a word. There was terror in his eyes, and even from the pool Mick could see his little chin quiver, but he could also see something else in Dylan's face.

Determination.

Dylan had learned a thing or two about facing his fears, and he had decided all on his own to face this one. He shouted for his mother to watch, but his eyes were on his dad when he launched himself off that platform.

He looked so tiny, like a toy, like a doll flouncing off a platform fifteen feet up on the side of a tree, dancing high above the backyard, flashing toward the pool.

Naturally, that was when the tag line chose to groove

itself in between two boards on the edge of the tree house. Mick wasn't sure whether Layne started screaming before or after the knot in the rope snagged between the boards.

The tag line snapped tight and the trolley stopped with a jerk.

Dylan kept going.

His feet flew up and his hands tore loose from the grips. Arms and legs flailing, he did an awkward, screaming, spread-eagle full gainer high over the backyard, and sailed clear over the deck railing.

Hap, for a big man, could move quickly when he had to. He jumped into the path of the boy, and Dylan hit him feet first, square in the chest. Hap crashed backwards into a picnic table, but not before grabbing Dylan's legs and making sure the boy landed on top of him.

"Awesome!" Ben yelled. He was jumping up and down, pumping a fist. "Did you see that, Mom?! Dylan dropkicked Hap!"

Hap gashed his arm on the corner of the table, but Dylan didn't get a scratch. As soon as he realized he wasn't hurt he started giggling.

Layne ran screaming onto the deck, snatched her baby up and clutched him to her chest before she collapsed to her knees, crying.

———

"I thought he was going to die," she said later. "I thought I was watching my son die. That's what it felt like." She had put in a movie for the kids in the den, then cornered Mick in the living room and sat him down on the couch.

"I'm sorry," he said. "The pull rope just got caught between the boards. I can fix it so that won't happen again. All we have to do is—"

She interrupted him, leaning toward him and enunciating every syllable. "You can tear that contraption *down*, is what you can do."

He had known her demand was coming. It didn't surprise him, and yet he still thought maybe he could save the zip line if only he could make her understand why it happened.

"Layne, it was an *accident*. There's really no need to get all worked up over it. It's not gonna happen again."

"You're right—it's not going to happen again," she said, then sat back and took a couple deep breaths. Her left eye was twitching, just a little.

"You just don't get it, Mick. You can't *tell* me not to get worked up. I'm still a mother, *no matter what*. I am totally attuned to my children, and that doesn't change, *ever*, even when I'm at work. I worry about my children constantly," she said, averting her eyes. "And now I have to sit at my desk wondering what kind of Rube Goldberg suicide machine my husband is building today. I can't help worrying, Mick. I'm a mother."

"And I'm not," he said. "I told you from the beginning I'm no housewife, and I'm never going to see things the same way a woman would see them. Maybe I haven't done things the same way you would have, but you've got to admit it hasn't been all bad, having me here. How many housewives can build new steps onto the deck, build a playhouse or a chicken coop, or lay ceramic tile?" It had been her idea to put down imported ceramic tile on the kitchen floor, and it had strained the budget.

"But, Mick, none of that makes up for nearly killing my baby with that infernal zip line. And anyway, we wouldn't have *had* to replace the kitchen floor if it hadn't been for the fire!"

He knew it was a mistake to bring up the tile. Anything you say can and will be used. "That, too, was an accident, Layne. A grease fire can happen to anybody."

"Once, maybe, but that's not the whole story. I can put up with the occasional kitchen fire, or having my clothes washed pink, or even the haircuts you've inflicted on the kids, but I don't want my babies turned into insensitive, scratching, spitting, hard-cussing, gun-toting rednecks. At least not while they're in grammar school."

"I still think you're overreacting," Mick said. "I can't turn the kids into something I'm not, and I am *not* insensitive. Besides, our kids are perfectly normal. They're not any wilder than other people's kids."

"Really? What about Dylan's little peeing exhibition at the church picnic, or the 'pretend cigars' at the funeral home? You don't think that was—"

"They'd just been through a two-hour car ride and they were bored. They didn't know what those things were. And Dylan never did that again after I explained it to him."

"Speaking of Dylan, is he ready to start school? Has he made any progress at all?"

"I don't know," Mick said. He put his head in his hands, rubbing his face and muttering through his fingers. "I think so. He can swim now."

"That's nice, but he won't be doing a lot of swimming in the classroom," she said.

"Well, his coordination is better, whether you can see it or not," Mick said. "I'm around him all day and I see things you don't. He runs a little better. He can hit a nail, too. Sometimes. Anyway, he seems happier to me—he never throws fits like he used to, and he hasn't licked anybody's ankles lately, either." Dylan *was* still fond of his fuzzy pink earmuffs, but Mick had a suspicion he just liked the way they looked.

"I guess I just don't see it," she said, then sat back and crossed her arms.

It was a standoff, neither of them knowing where to go from there. He could see her jaw flexing. The tense cease-fire was disturbed only by the faint galumphing of the clothes dryer out in the laundry room.

Dylan wandered through, fresh from his bath, smelling of shampoo and fabric softener, wearing clean pajamas and a towel tucked around his neck like a cape, hand-flying a plastic Batman and muttering a strange phrase over and over in a steady monotone as he passed between them.

". . . goats-in-their-pajamas, goats-in-their-pajamas, goats-in-their-pajamas . . ."

They stared at each other, mouthing the words while Dylan went out the other end of the room and down the hall without looking up. Layne scooted forward, bracing a palm on the arm of the sofa, her mouth open.

"Did he say *goats*?" She was almost whispering.

He hadn't even noticed, but he could still hear it in his head.

"Yeah, he did. He definitely said *goats*." It was the first time either of them had ever heard him nail a hard G.

They both sat frozen in silence for a minute, and then

Layne noticed something else. As she turned and gazed toward the laundry room the anger went out of her and a faint sad smile softened her face. The syncopated thumping of the dryer came across the silence, and finally Mick heard it, too.

The tumbling clothes repeated the same galumphing rhythm over and over again, and once he heard it Dylan's words were unmistakable. The dryer was saying, ". . . *goats-in-their-pajamas, goats-in-their-pajamas, goats-in-their-pajamas* . . ."

When Layne turned back to him her eyes were a little misty, and it dawned on him that sometimes a woman could hear things a man couldn't. Among the normal working sounds of engines and sailboats and children and other dynamic things, if a person only knew how to listen, there was always a "sweet spot," a certain pitch that said to a practiced ear, *"This is good. Keep it here."*

She sighed and said, "Everything's going to be all right. In my calmer moments I know things happen for a reason, and in the end I have faith that everything will turn out okay." She put her arms around his neck and said, very softly, "I love you, Mick, and I trust you. I have never believed there was any better place for my children than right here with their redneck dad. None of that stuff really matters—I just worry, that's all. I can't help it."

He closed his eyes and held her, felt her hair against his face, and remembered. In that moment she was twenty again, with heavy brown hair that rippled like liquid silk in the sunlight, and deep green eyes that could still make his knees buckle.

40

Final exam.

THE JURY was still out on Dylan. Mick had to admit he had been a little slack when it came to his therapy and exercises. He tried to remember them every day but there was a lot going on. He and Dylan had all the animals to take care of, and they were always busy doing projects around the house—building things, fixing things, laying tile, planting flowers, moving shrubs. Sometimes they forgot the therapy sessions. Because Mick was there with Dylan all the time every day, he just couldn't really say if he'd shown any serious improvement, except of course for his swimming and the sudden ability to say the word *goat*. Mick really wanted to know, for his own sake, whether Dylan had actually improved. He didn't have long to wait, because they took him in for testing the next week.

His final exam.

The regular therapist wouldn't do the testing; she sent

them up to Standridge Center in Atlanta to see a Dr. Zubek, who according to the regular therapist had literally written the book on sensory integration dysfunction. Mick was expecting an old, wise, grandfatherly type, but when they finally got into the office he discovered that Dr. Zubek was a mole-faced little girl who looked fresh out of high school. She didn't even have a white coat, just jeans and tennis shoes.

He and Layne sat across from Dr. Zubek at her desk and talked for a half hour or so while Dylan played with cars in the floor. It was a big office, but the only things that made it an office were the desk and a handful of framed diplomas on the wall. It looked more like a toy store. There were train sets and car tracks in the floor, a giant dollhouse, a Nerf basketball hoop on one wall, and action figures everywhere. There were shelves full of board games, coloring books, crayons, blocks, children's books, dolls, trucks and cars—anything a kid could want. Looking around, Mick figured if he could pick that room up and shake it a couple times it would look just like Dylan's bedroom.

Dr. Zubek talked mostly to Layne, even though they told her early on that Mick was the one who'd been home with him. She and Layne were both very professional, and Layne had studied. She knew what all those words meant. Mick mostly listened in; he didn't speak the language.

The doctor made a few notes in a folder while they talked. When she was satisfied, she closed the folder, rubbed her hands together and said, "Well, I know about the parents now. It's time to get to know the child. The two of you can remain here if you wish"—she said this in a way that somehow made it clear they were to stay out of the way—"or you may want to go back out to the waiting room where we have coffee and pastries."

And then she got down in the floor and played. It was as if she became a little girl, the way she acted with Dylan. He was rubbing a truck on the carpet and making engine noises. When she went over and plopped down cross-legged in the floor with him he ignored her at first, so she finally stuck a hand out and said, "Hi, I'm Ruth. Wanta play?"

He looked up at her, hesitated for a second, and then shook her hand. She had him talking in no time, like they were old friends. She asked him all sorts of weird questions in a quiet, conversational tone, while Dylan's hands and eyes were busy with toys.

"Do you want to get married one day?"

"Maybe. Sure."

"Why? Why would a person get married?"

He walked a GI Joe in a circle before he answered. She waited patiently.

"Share the work," he said.

"Do you ever feel happy?"

"Uh-huh."

"When?"

"The goat puts her head right here and I rub around her horns. Sometimes I hold the chickens. And *swimming!*" He glanced up at Mick when he said this, and grinned.

She went and got a couple of action figures off the shelf and played with him. Mick figured there had to be a reason for what she was doing, something she was watching for or judging, but he couldn't make sense of it. They were just playing, like kids. He kept looking over at Layne for a clue, but as far as he could tell she didn't know what was going on, either.

After maybe twenty minutes of getting to know each other Dr. Zubek said to Dylan, "You wanta see our playground? We have swings."

He nodded, and she led them all out, down a corridor and through a pair of swinging doors into a cavernous place that looked more like a gymnasium than anything else. It was brightly lit, with walls painted in Doctor Seuss colors, and it was a wonderland. There were big tire swings hanging from the bar joists high above, thick rubber mats on the floors, monkey bars, a climbing wall, a merry-go-round, seesaws, bicycles, tricycles, and every kind of ball known to man, most of them lying loose around the gym.

There must have been eight or ten other kids in there playing already, whooping and hollering and being kids.

"There are a number of other therapists using the facility," Dr. Zubek explained, and Mick noticed that every kid was paired with an adult. Most of the therapists were young like Dr. Zubek, and dressed the same. There was a line of chairs at one end, half of them occupied by parents.

"If you'll just take a seat over there, Dylan and I will go play now," she said.

So they sat and waited some more.

They watched while Dylan swung, then tumbled on the mats, showing off how he could roll. She put him on a Sit'n Spin, and he loved that. He wouldn't have anything to do with the climbing wall or the monkey bars, but she actually had him jumping rope at one point and taking turns with the other two kids holding the rope. Layne and Mick both cringed when he tripped up several times, but he just laughed it off. Dr. Zubek got him in a game of Twister with a couple other kids, and he tied himself in knots, fell all over himself. They spent a lot of time throwing a medicine ball back and forth, he made a complete fool of himself with a Hula-Hoop, and then the therapists got all the kids together and played dodge ball.

When it became clear that they were going to spend the better part of the day in the gym, Layne and Mick finally went back out to the waiting room for coffee.

"So, what do you think?" he asked, blowing on his cup.

Layne shook her head. "I don't know. I'm worried about him."

"Why?"

"I don't know. I'm just worried. He seems so awkward to me, still."

Guilt. He could see it in her eyes. She felt guilty about going back to work and leaving her son with his father when what he needed was a mother.

"Look. Layne. We'll get through this. Okay, I've lost some time with him, but there's lots of time left. He's just turned five years old. Over the next year we'll do whatever it takes. I'll go back to work. I'll take on a second job if I have to, and we can hire a professional to work with him full time, or maybe you can take a leave of absence and stay home with him yourself. I'll do whatever you want me to do to help Dylan get better." He meant it; he would have done anything. He was carrying more than a little guilt of his own.

"Well," she said, sipping her coffee, dropping the little red stirring stick in the trash, "let's wait and see. Maybe it's not so bad."

———

When Dr. Zubek called them back into her office for the final consult they braced themselves. When she sat down behind her desk and opened the folder she turned into a professional again. She looked stern.

"So, Mr. Brannigan, am I to understand that you were the primary caregiver for this child over the last"—she glanced at the folder—"year?"

"Uh, yeah. I, uh, quit my job and stayed with him pretty much all the time."

"And did you follow the prescribed therapy routine?" Her face was dead serious, and her tone was almost accusatory.

"Well, mostly, yeah. Not exactly. I may have been a little slack now and then, but things can get, you know . . . hectic, at our house."

"Well, I'd like to know what you did. What Dylan did all day. What sort of activities was he involved in routinely?"

He had to think about it pretty hard. It felt like an IRS audit—*Mr. Brannigan, can you justify yourself?*

"Well, he spent a lot of time helping me. You know, projects. Work. Mostly carpenter work, but a little of everything. He was just sort of my sidekick, you know? You have to watch Dylan pretty close, and the easiest way was to keep him up under me, doing whatever I was doing." He was starting to sweat. He glanced at Layne, but her face was completely blank.

"I see," Dr. Zubek said, and turned a page in the folder, studying it. "Well, the reason I'm asking is that, comparing his initial test results to what I've seen here today, he's shown startling improvement in nearly every category."

Mick looked up at her in stunned disbelief. He thought maybe he'd misunderstood, but Dr. Zubek was smiling. Slowly, he turned to Layne. She turned to him in the same instant, with the same shocked expression. She reached out and squeezed his hand, and there were tears in her eyes.

"He's *better?*" Mick asked, shock still apparent on his face.

"Oh yes, considerably. You've done a remarkable job with him. Frankly, I was wondering if the initial assessment was in error." She lifted a chart from his file and stared at it. "According to this file he had speech difficulties, he was reclusive, excessively impulsive and sometimes combative. He had problems with gross motor skills, tactile problems . . . Does he still hate to wear clothes?"

Layne cleared her throat and found her voice. "Well, he does take longer than the other children to get dressed, and he still hates socks—he says they itch him—but he doesn't strip in public anymore, no."

Dr. Zubek made a note on the chart. "So he still has some minor tactile issues, and I noticed he's still easily distractible, owing I think to his auditory acuity. But everything else—his gross motor skills, his interaction with adults and other children, his strength and agility, perception . . . Frankly, Mrs. Brannigan, this kid knocked my socks off."

Layne opened her mouth and drew a breath, but she couldn't talk. She was choking up. Her eyes pooled. Not Mick. He was tough.

"So, is it okay for him to go to kindergarten?" Mick

asked, as soon as he was sure he could control his voice. Starting school had, after all, been the whole point.

"He'll do great," Dr. Zubek said, smiling for the first time, closing the folder. "And I have to tell you, Mr. Brannigan, after seeing your results, I'm thinking of putting a carpenter's corner in the gym."

41

Ghost crabs.

LAYNE took off from work the last week of the summer so she could spend time with her children before they went back to school. They made plans to borrow a pop-up camper from a friend and take the kids to the beach, so Layne spent all day Saturday washing and packing while Mick put a hitch on the Explorer and went to pick up the camper. The kids were psyched about going to the beach. They all were. After the things the therapist said about Dylan, Mick and Layne felt like celebrating. A great weight had been lifted from them.

They couldn't leave until after church on Sunday because Layne's backup couldn't make it and she had to teach the four-year-old Sunday school class. By Saturday night everything they needed for the trip was packed and ready to go. Layne snuggled up to Mick on the couch while the kids piled in the floor to watch a video.

"I wish you'd go to church with us tomorrow," she said casually. It caught him a little off guard. Normally they played this game on Sunday morning. "You're not going downtown in the morning, and it's important for the kids to see their parents together in church once in a while, don't you think?"

He was thinking about it when Ben interrupted, asking if he could split an apple with Toad. He came back a minute later with an apple and a paring knife, and plopped down next to his sister. There had been a time, not that long ago, when Ben and Toad couldn't split an apple without an argument because one of them always got the smaller half, but Mick had taught them a simple principle he'd learned from his own brother when he was a kid.

"I'll cut, you pick," Ben said, slicing.

Toad just nodded, hesitated for a second and took the half she judged to be slightly bigger. Mick had to smile. Childish simplicity was usually foolproof.

"I tell you what," he told Layne. "I'll go to your church if you'll go to mine."

She raised her head off his shoulder and stared at him.

"Your *church*? What are you talking about?"

He hadn't said much about the Beal Street Mission, mostly because he wanted to make up his own mind about things without feeling like he was being pushed.

"Well, it's kind of hard to explain, but I haven't just been taking pictures downtown on Sunday mornings. I mean, I *have* been taking pictures, but . . . there's this mission."

So he told her all about it. He talked quietly, and for a long time, about Beal Street Mission, about what he did there and how it made him feel needed. She listened, fascinated, and then sat for a long time thinking about what he'd said.

Finally, she said, "That's wonderful, Mick. I'm so glad you found that place, and I'm thrilled you feel the way you do about it. But . . . your children need you, too. They need their father with them on Sunday morning."

He nodded, watching Ben and Toad finish off their apple. "I know," he said. "You're absolutely right. We belong together, and I'll be happy to go with you on one condition—once a month I want all of us to go to my church. You can pick which Sunday."

———————

They'd been to Huntington Beach once before, on the Atlantic coast just south of Myrtle Beach. It was a beautiful, quiet place, and there were all sorts of things to do. The campground was separated from a two-mile stretch of deserted beach by a strip of mangroves a hundred yards deep. On the inland side of the campground a shallow bay curled around and formed a huge salt marsh, thick stands of saw grass cut into little islands by narrow wandering passes of dark, brackish water. At low tide, islands of black mud rose up all slimy and slick and covered with crowds of oyster shells like jagged little cities. The salt marsh, where the edge of the ocean pulsed in and out twice a day, was a natural hatchery for fish and shrimp and alligators and birds.

The park service had built boardwalks out into the marsh, and at low tide Mick and Layne would take the kids cast-netting for shrimp off the end of the boardwalk.

Herons and egrets stalked the shallows around the edges of the saw-grass islands feeding on minnows, and once or twice a bald eagle cruised right over their heads, hunting. Mick got some great pictures.

Ben and Toad got the hang of cast-netting right away, spinning a weighted four-foot nylon net through the air so it opened like an umbrella on the way down. They caught a few shrimp with nearly every cast. They tried boiling them but they were kind of small and a lot of trouble, so they mostly used them for bait.

On one end of the beach, next to the channel where the tide pushed in and out of the salt marsh, a long rock jetty jutted out a couple hundred yards into the ocean. Sometimes in the early morning Mick would get the kids up and take them down there to fish for spots and bluefish while Layne slept in. They caught a lot of baby sand sharks, but the kids didn't really care what they caught so long as they caught something. Around nine o'clock, they'd all troop back to the camper, where Layne would already have a big breakfast cooking.

Twice a day, morning and afternoon, Layne and Mick would follow the kids down a sandy path through the mangroves and over the dunes to the beach, where they would tear into the surf and get wild and happy. They rode boogie boards down the waves and came out spitting saltwater, hiking up bathing suits and grinning like they'd won something. Even Layne managed to relax on the beach for once, now that Dylan could swim. The last time they were there she had made Dylan wear a life jacket and stood knee-deep in the surf with her hands on her hips yelling at him to stay in the edge of the water where the undertow couldn't drag him away. Now that he'd proven himself to be a strong swimmer she relaxed and let him go a little.

When he wasn't boogie-boarding, Dylan liked to comb the beach for sharks' teeth, little jet-black things shaped like rose thorns. Most of them were so small Mick's eyes couldn't find them, but Dylan could spot them every time. He had eyes like an eagle. By the time they left he had filled up a medicine bottle with those things.

They took a tour of an old Spanish fort one evening and the kids sat hugging their knees for an hour, spellbound while Ranger Bob told ghost stories in the moonlit stone ruins. Afterward, they all went for a walk on the beach. Layne loved the beach at night. The kids were horsing around, chasing each other, playing tag, being kids. The sea was calm and a low moon silvered the tops of lazy little waves that crawled over their feet while Layne and Mick walked barefoot together in the edge of the ocean. They came upon a whole group of children, eight or nine at least, accompanied by two fathers. The kids all had flashlights and were running pell-mell up and down the beach with plastic buckets. Ben, Toad and Dylan fell in with them, running, laughing, waving flashlights around.

After a while Toad came running up with a boy in tow. He was a head taller than her, and Mick didn't like the way he was looking at her.

"Look what I got!" she said, holding out a plastic bucket. The boy leaned close and shined his flashlight into the bucket so they could see. In the bucket was a pale white crab about the size and shape of a chicken egg. His claws were tucked in against his sides and his little stemmed eyes stared up at them.

"It's a ghost crab," she said. "They're all over the place, and they're a *blast* to catch!"

"Come on, Clarissa," the boy said, tugging at her arm. "Let's go catch another one."

Mick watched them run off and merge with the gaggle of wild kids; then he turned to Layne.

"Did he just call her *Clarissa?*" he asked.

Layne nodded, smiling. "Uh-huh."

"She never lets anybody call her that, except you. Who told him her name was Clarissa?"

Layne took his arm, chuckling, looking at him like she always did when she knew something he didn't. "She did, I'm sure."

"Oh. Oh, no." It was always like that. Just when he thought he had a handle on this child-rearing thing, the next monster reared its head.

The kids were having a ball. They'd spot a ghost crab skittering sideways across the sand and give chase like a pack of hounds, flashlights whipping this way and that. Those crabs were quick. They'd change direction in an instant and zip through the crowd of bare feet while the kids hopped and danced out of the way, screaming. Finally, three or four of the lights would focus on the bewildered crab all at once and he'd freeze. Then one of the kids would rush in and scoop him up in an ice cream bucket.

There was something completely pointless and absolutely wonderful about it. It was one of those random pearly nights when a bunch of kids ran around burning energy because they could, because they had a limitless supply of it, because they were children and every moment was worth celebrating for its own sake. They had their priorities straight.

Right in the middle of the great ghost crab hunt, Layne's cell phone rang. It surprised Mick. He had forgotten he was carrying it in his pocket. Layne's mother was not well, and Layne had been trying to call her, leaving messages. Mick turned away from the pack of screaming kids and walked a few yards up the beach to answer it, thinking it was his mother-in-law calling back.

But it wasn't her. He stood apart from the crowd for a few minutes, ankle deep in the surf, listening. Right when he hung up the phone and slipped it into his pocket he felt a hand on the back of his neck, and Layne was there.

"Was that Mom?" she asked.

"Aubrey," he said, watching the twinkling lights of an oil tanker out on the horizon.

"Is something wrong?"

"No," he said quietly. "Something is definitely not wrong. He called to tell me he heard from Ecklund."

"Who?" She wrapped her arms around his neck, pressed herself against him. She was cold.

"A.J. Ecklund. The guy from the High Museum. The one we sent the portfolio to."

"Really? What did he say?" She said this cautiously, staring at him in the moonlight.

He still couldn't believe what he'd heard, but Mick repeated it anyway as best he could.

"He said they're putting together an exhibition in the spring. Something about the 'New South.' Six or seven photographers on exhibit for two months. He wants *me* in it."

Her eyes went wide and she grabbed him by the shoulders. "Are you serious? *The High Museum?*" She was starting to bounce.

He nodded, numb. "Yeah, ain't that a kick? Ecklund said they still needed representation from street level, whatever that means, and that my pictures were 'gut-wrenchingly real, starkly beautiful.' That's what Aubrey told me, anyway."

Layne started squealing and jumped on him. She almost knocked him down in the surf, but he fought to keep his feet because he knew what saltwater would do to her cell phone.

"It's all just tentative so far," Mick said, pausing, still unable to get his mind around it. "Ecklund said he has to get it past the committee, but he's pretty sure it'll happen. He's the chairman of the committee."

They stood there together for a long time, quiet, their arms wrapped around each other, enjoying the moment. Sometimes the best communication came without words. Mick could see several ships now, pale lights twinkling out on the sea. The moon glinted off the wave tops and the stars shined like new. Children screamed with laughter, and flashlights danced on the beach. He swiped his bare foot across the wet sand, and in its wake, even there, bits of phosphorescence sparked for an instant. Everywhere, there was light.

When they grew tired of the game the children stopped running and set all the ghost crabs free. Later, after the other kids had gone on up the beach and it was just the five of them again, the Brannigans shared the stars. They lay on their backs on the beach pointing out constellations, letting the sea breeze wash over them and listening to the waves rumble ashore. Mick only knew a handful of constellations, and when he ran out of those the kids started making up their own.

Toad found the outline of a sailfrog among the stars.

Before Dylan fell asleep on Mick's chest he pointed out a dog constellation, complete with tail. He named it Andy.

Ben put his fingertips together to form a square the size of a pencil eraser, at arms length. "Did you know there are a thousand galaxies in this square?" he said, peering one-eyed through the hole between his fingertips. Mick had no doubt he was right.

Layne, warm against him with her head on his shoulder, whispered, "Don't go back to work, Mick. Stay home. Take pictures. Raise kids."

In that moment something welled up inside of him again, like it had that morning up in the steel, and busted out like a surprised bird. There still weren't any words, but this time he knew it wasn't a question, it was a thank you—simple, and yet too complicated for words. The thought gathered itself and flew out precisely aimed, not at the stars or the horizon, but at God, whose smile he had learned to see, sometimes, in the eyes of children and other bits of light.

ACKNOWLEDGMENTS

First, last, and always, I thank God.

I would also like to thank:

My wife and sons, who provided the opportunity for this story to be written (not to mention some of the fodder).

Larry McDonald, Bill Dodd, and Peter Beering, who shared their photographic insights and expertise. The blunders are entirely mine.

My sister-in-law, Becky Baker, who gave me reams of indispensable background information on sensory integration dysfunction. Any resemblance to Dr. Lethal is entirely coincidental.

Bobby Johnston, for his insights on the homeless community and an illuminating tour of the monastery.

Paul Leslie, for one of the finer insights in the book.

Carol Pitts, Mike and Deeanna Marshall, Andrea Dodd, Bobby Winkelman, Patty Ivers, Lori Patrick, Jim and Sue Martin, Susan Holloway, Cindy Schade, and any others I may have failed to mention here who suffered through an early draft of this work and offered constructive criticism and encouragement.

Terry Hadaway, who always helps me see the big picture.

Janet Kobobel Grant, my agent and friend.

W. DALE CRAMER, author of the Christy Award winners *Bad Ground* and *Levi's Will* and the critically acclaimed *Sutter's Cross*, lives in Georgia with his wife, Pam, and their two sons.

For more information visit *www.dalecramer.com*, or readers may write to Dale at P.O. Box 25, Hampton, GA 30228.